Staggerford

Staggerford

JON HASSLER

Atheneum

NEW YORK

1977

LIBRARY OF CONGRESS CATALOGING IN PUBLICATION DATA

Hassler, Jon.
  Staggerford.

  I. Title.
PZ4.H3557St   [PS3558.A726]   813'.5'4   76-57757
ISBN 0-689-10793-5

A portion of this novel first appeared
in the *South Dakota Review* and *McCall's*.

For my mother and father
God love them

Oh, why is it that life is for some an exquisite privilege and others must pay for their seats at the play with a ransom of cholers, infections and nightmares?

JOHN CHEEVER

FRIDAY

October 30

FIRST HOUR, Miles yawned.

It seemed to Miles that while the faces changed from year to year, the personality of a first-hour class never varied. It was a tractable class. Most of the thirty students hadn't been out of bed for more than half an hour and they weren't yet sharp or restless. Like Miles, they were sleepy. Moreover, they were slow-witted. The Staggerford High School band rehearsed during first hour, and the better students for some reason were inevitably drawn to band. Each morning as the band marched across the street to the football field, high-stepping and tooting in preparation for its halftime formations, these thirty students were left in the classroom to puzzle over the formations of the compound sentence or the working parts of the business letter. Love poems by Rod McKuen were beyond them. To say that all nonmusicians were dull would have been unwarranted, and Miles would not have said it. What he would have said, however, was that *Staggerford's* nonmusicians were dull But it was an agreeable, easygoing sort of dullness that would never lead to trouble; and since Miles himself was no ball of fire at eight in the morning, he and these thirty seniors moved comfortably through the weeks together, rubbing the sleep from their eyes.

Miles thought of Lee Fremling, who sat facing him in the front row, as the emblem of first hour. Lee Fremling was heavy, good-natured, and lethargic. He was the son of Albert Fremling, editor of the *Staggerford Weekly* and the wildest father a boy could possibly have. But none of this wildness seemed to have been handed down to Lee. Albert Fremling was an alcoholic with a passion for driving on Friday nights as fast as he could go. One Friday last spring Albert Fremling had swerved to miss a tree and smashed, doing eighty-five, into a small house at the edge of town. At the time, fortunately, the widow who lived in the house was in the hospital with a broken hip (she had fallen from the bottom rung of a stepladder while taking off storm windows) and so was spared being run over in bed, but the editor was left with a permanently crippled left arm and a scarred forehead. Mrs. Fremling could recall the names of at least seventy-five people who had tried over the years to cure her husband of his drinking and his suicidal driving—the names of highway patrolmen, psychiatrists, businessmen, neighbors, jailers, and the pastors of three Lutheran churches—all to no avail. By nightfall on Fridays the *Staggerford Weekly* was out on the street, and that was when its editor drank himself cockeyed and got into his red Pontiac and flew off down the highway to Berrington or crisscrossed the prairie south of the river, his headlights sailing over the dirt roads and lighting up, when he doubled back, the clouds of his own dust. People sitting in their houses with their windows open could hear the squeal of the editor's tires as he left town, and sometimes they could hear, shouted from his car, his pledge never to return; but he never traveled beyond the limits of Berrington County and he always came home before morning, sometimes on bail, often sick, and always profoundly depressed.

4

How then (Miles wondered) could there have come from Albert Fremling's house such a son as Lee—slow and congenial and even-tempered? Lee must have been what his mother and grandmother had made him. Mrs. Fremling was a small, cool woman, and Mrs. Fremling's mother, who lived with them, was just like her. These two women—neat and efficient, smart and silent—kept the house and yard and newspaper office and Lee (all except the editor himself) orderly. But in sheltering Lee from the grossness of his father, it seemed to Miles that these two women had prolonged in him the illusions of childhood, and had delayed the coming on of worldly wisdom. Lee's eyes were full of innocence. On the football field, despite his size, he was pushed around a good deal. He was large like his father, but this largeness was not, like his father's, the bulk of self-indulgence. It was baby fat.

Second hour, Miles was off balance.

The issue hadn't been settled yet, but he suspected that second-hour English was out of his control. It was a rowdy class—a mixture of athletes, flirts, musicians, and show-offs. The band was back indoors now, full of fresh air and smart remarks, and the sun was up over the administrative wing across the courtyard, filling Miles's classroom with intense light and shadow. Unable to channel all this nine-o'clock pep where he wanted it to go, Miles had to spend most of second hour patrolling the aisles and twirling about on his toes to see the antics going on behind his back.

Among the students who never sat still were Roxie Booth and Jeff Norquist. In the faculty lunchroom it was said that if something wasn't done about Roxie Booth, she would be the death this year of old Ray Smith, who kept trying to teach history long past his time. At the end of the day Ray Smith's suits were covered with chalk dust where Roxie had clapped erasers on him. Roxie was fat and slung with gold and silver chains from the dimestore. She wore rings on eight of her fingers. She could barely read, but she remembered in detail all the classic stories of world literature that had been made into movies. She was a predator, smiling, batting her eyes, and continually testing Miles's tolerance for suggestive remarks. She exposed more of her skin than was modest. Her father, a career man in the army, had moved his children through seventeen schools in fifteen states, and there was nothing about school curriculum, army lore, or the dark side of human nature that Roxie did not know. She was also nervous and she sometimes broke out in a talking jag. The stories she told were mostly those gathered up in camps where her father had been stationed, and she dumped them now, like garbage, in the middle of Berrington County—five hundred square miles of farmland in the center of Minnesota, where people were unaccustomed to hearing about such things as the corporal who stood at a bar and ate, on a bet, a beer bottle.

"The bartender said it couldn't be done and he gave the corporal a hammer and the corporal pounded the beer bottle to dust on the bar," said Roxie Booth, in relation to nothing that had gone before in English class. "He ate only a handful of it because ground glass is even harder to eat than sand, and he got terrible pains all over his guts and everything, and they took him to the base hospital, where he lived through the night bleeding from just about every opening it's possible to bleed from on the human body, and then he died in the morning. It was about nine thirty in the morning that he died, the same time it is now, and that's why I mention it." Roxie was the youngest student in the senior class, having recently turned sixteen, but on mornings after dates her face looked puffy and forty.

Jeff Norquist was the faculty's worst affliction this year. Yesterday during second hour, Jeff had carried his literature text to the front of the room, torn it in two, and dropped it into the wastebasket. Miles, stifling his anger, had said, "That will be four dollars and eighty cents." Jeff laid a five spot on Miles's desk and told him to keep the change. Today Jeff's girl friend Annie Bird knocked on the door and said that Jeff was wanted in the office for an emergency phone call. It was a ruse, and Miles knew it, but he let him go. It was a better class—though only slightly better—without him.

Third hour, Miles toiled.

His third-hour seniors were unresponsive, almost secretive, and when he was not speaking, the room was filled with a kind of strained silence. It was not the lazy silence of first hour; it was the intense, alert silence of students who absorb everything and express nothing. They read their assignments; they kept their notebooks up to date. They never nodded or shook their heads. Their eyes told Miles nothing. He knew that he would never lose his way in this class. His students wouldn't allow it. He would never digress into that humorous banter which, like a dose of oxygen, could often stir a silent class to life. He would be all business. He would stick to the subject at all times. He would toil. In order to discover what these students knew, he would have to devise businesslike essay tests (the sort of thing first hour could never handle) and he would no doubt discover that they knew quite a lot.

William Mulholland was in this class. In the Staggerford Public Library every book having to do with physics, chemistry, statistics, or any other sort of cold-blooded calculation contained on its check-out card the name William Mulholland, written in letters sharp and slanted, like a sketch of leaning spears. He was the largest student in high school—a husky six-feet-four—but to the dismay of Coach Gibbon, athletics did not interest him. What did interest him was computation. Today, finishing his assignment before the bell rang, he drew from his pocket a small computer and set to work calculating the cubic footage of the classroom. Only once had he spoken in this class. On the opening day of school Miles, taking roll, had said, "Bill Mulholland."

"My name is William," he replied.

Fourth hour, Miles came up for air.

Fourth hour was his free hour, and although it was not strictly free it allowed him the leisure to stretch. The Faculty Handbook forbade the teacher to step off school property during his free hour, lest the townspeople, seeing him loose, imagine him to be shirking his duty. The teachers of Staggerford took a constant, unhealthy interest in their public image, fancying general opinion to be more various and complicated than it really was. Actually, general opinion of teachers was simple and constant. The women of Staggerford tended to overestimate teachers' intelligence while the men of Staggerford tended to underestimate their ambition.

Miles took his briefcase across the street to the football field, climbed to the top row of the empty bleachers, and sat down. Behind him on the riverbank a breeze shook leaves out of the oak trees. Before him on the field a physical-education class cavorted in the end zone, waiting for their teacher. They wore red shorts and white T-shirts. The sun was warm. A plane droned overhead, its shadow crossing the field and just missing the goalposts. Presently Coach Gibbon appeared and blew his whistle and directed his students through their isometric exercises, for which, like beginners at ballet, they struck a series of laughable poses. Beyond the football field leaves and dust were raised off the highway by a grain truck speeding through town on its way to the port of Duluth. Across the highway a woman stood at her front door shaking out a mop. A few elderly men and women wearing suits and hats walked along the sidewalk from the direction of St. Isidore's Church. Sunday clothes on a weekday was the sign of a funeral.

Miles grew sleepy in the sun. He lay down on the top plank of the bleachers, resting his head on his briefcase and folding his hands on his chest. He held himself at the edge of sleep, conscious enough to keep from falling off his perch, yet unconscious of where the hour went.

When the bell rang at noon, it was the custom of students and faculty to cascade into the basement lunchroom and devour whatever hot dish the cooks had stirred together—macaroni-hamburger-tomato, tomato-rice-hamburger, hamburger-tomato-celery, celery-barley-hamburger. A hamburger was never served as a hamburger, nor was a tomato served as a tomato. Each component was mixed with at least two other components, and there was always as much as one wanted, which in Miles's case was not very much. Not that he had a poor appetite. Indeed, at the age of thirty-five he was growing fat from eating more than was good for him, but he did most of his eating between four o'clock and midnight. Because he had grown up in Staggerford and attended Staggerford High School and was now in his twelfth year as Staggerford's senior-English teacher, nearly half the lunches of his lifetime had been eaten in the basement of this school, and they had lost, for him, their appeal.

Today he skipped lunch altogether, so pleasant was the autumn sunshine and so compelling was the call of a crow from across the river. Coach Gibbon, running off the field behind his hungry students, called to him, but Miles did not move from the bleachers. He sat up. He regarded his briefcase. It was full of student papers—114 essays entitled "What I Wish." He had been putting off reading them for over a week. He opened the briefcase, then paused, reluctant to look inside. How many student papers had he read in these twelve years? How many strokes of his red pen had he made? How many times had he underlined *it's* and written *its*. Was there ever a student who didn't make a mischievous younger brother the subject of an essay? Was there ever a student who didn't make four syllables out of "mischievous"? This was the twelfth in a series of senior classes that Miles was trying to raise to an acceptable level of English usage, and like the previous eleven, this class would graduate in the spring to make room for another class in the fall, and he would read the same errors over again. This annual renewal of ignorance, together with the sad fact that most of his students had been drilled in what he taught since they were in the fifth grade, left him with a vague sense of futility that made it hard for him to read student writing. But while he had lost his urge to read student papers, he had not lost his guilt about *not* reading them, so he carried around with him, like a conscience, this bulging briefcase which his landlady, Miss McGee, had given him for Christmas during his first year of teaching. It was the last of the soft-sided briefcases. All his colleagues had switched to flat cases of chrome and plastic like the one his brother, Dale, had sent him from California and which now stood in Miles's bedroom closet holding the three hundred or so typewritten pages that comprised his journal. For work, Miles preferred this briefcase because it was leather, not plastic, and it contributed to the hidebound appearance that for some perverse reason he enjoyed cultivating. Every few days he would dip into this briefcase and read a paper at random, but despite his resolution to read promptly and carefully, he left most of the papers for the last frantic days before grades were due.

He put his hand into the briefcase and drew out Roxie Booth's paper. He shook his head. Before he met Roxie Booth, Miles had come to believe that there was no scribble he could not read and no tangle of clauses he could not untie, but Roxie Booth this year was challenging his reading skill as it had never been challenged before. Her writing was a riddle, which, when he solved it, said this:

What I Wish

Living free with nature in my mind of how it is like dad says no mother always agrees. But if my mind is the one I know no matter whatever rules or whatever. Then why not. Or I'll lose my mind. Isn't it me to say just to get away from this hassle in a cabin? Before I lose my mind.

Losing. That was the melancholy strain running through dozens of papers every year. Parents lost in death and divorce, fingers lost in corn pickers, innocence lost behind barns and in back seats, brothers and uncles lost in Vietnam, friends lost in drug-induced hallucinations, and football games lost to Owl Brook and Berrington.

He turned Roxie's paper over and spent twenty minutes writing in understandable English what he believed she was trying to say. Then he climbed down from the bleachers, and he walked down the sloping bank to the Badbattle River. He crossed the river on stones without getting his shoes wet, for the Badbattle wasn't much more than a trickle in late October, and he walked along the far bank, under oak and birch. He saw four ducks and a flock of red-winged blackbirds. He saw a garter snake, a goldfinch, and a crow. He saw a bittersweet vine strangling a small maple tree. When the bell rang, calling him back to the classroom, he was ditching a channel in the mud and freeing a swarm of minnows that the receding water had left in a landlocked pool.

Fifth hour, Miles rejoiced.

In terms of quick minds and motivation, this was the best class he had ever had. It had been created by the haphazard process of computer scheduling, and he expected that another twelve years would pass before he was assigned another one like it. In this class if Miles paused midsentence in search of a word, one of the students, probably Nadine Oppegaard, was sure to supply the word, and if he wasn't quick she would finish the sentence for him as well. Nadine Oppegaard had a wide, dark face with the patient, heavy-lidded look of Buddha, and her speech was deliberate, wise, and sometimes cutting. She was the genius child of the dentist, Doc Oppegaard, who seemed not at all surprised at having fathered a genius, and of Mrs. Oppegaard, who was astonished. Since the eighth grade Nadine and her violin had appeared in the all-state orchestra, which performed at the annual teachers' convention in St. Paul. One year she was concertmistress and had her hand kissed, onstage, by the governor. At the convention this year she was to be featured in the slow movement of a Mozart concerto. Nadine's science-club project last spring was an exhibit of two dozen gigantic oil paintings of cancer of the mouth. She had painted them from a series of photos in her father's journal of dentistry. The exhibit hung for most of the summer in the public library, where it took up all the room between the ceiling and the top row of books. The day after the exhibit went on display, Miles had gone to the library to browse through the magazines. As he sat at a table reading *Harper's,* he caught himself unconsciously hunching his shoulders against the purple, pink, and ochre blossoms that appeared to be growing malignantly out from the walls. The air seemed contaminated. He began breathing shallow. Such was Nadine's impasto technique that he was unable to think of the paintings as abstractions, or as flowers in the style of Georgia O'Keeffe. He could only think of them as cancer, and although he had always been among Nadine's well-wishers he stayed out of the public library until they were gone.

Beverly Bingham, too, was in this class. It was a wonder to Miles how a girl as pretty and quick and clear-eyed as Beverly could have emerged from the Bingham farm in the gulch—a hopeless, rocky farm on the river-bank west of town where little grew but weeds and chickens because the topsoil had long ago been washed into the river, and because Mr. Bingham had been sent to prison, and because Mrs. Bingham (it was said) was crazy. Mrs. Bingham was better known as the Bone-woman, the ghostly figure that came to town in the evening and carried a gunnysack from door to door asking for bones—chicken bones, beef bones, pig bones—

which (it was said) she ground into meal for her chickens. Mrs. Bingham raised chickens for sale, and if she sold you a fryer or a roasting hen for Sunday dinner she would call at your house on Monday (it was said) to retrieve the skeleton and feed it to the chicken she would sell you next week.

Nearly every day, Beverly Bingham stayed after class to talk to Miles. Until today, the talk had been about schoolwork, particularly *Gone With the Wind*. Miles had recommended it to her, having discovered that girls with wistful blue eyes like Beverly's always fell in love with *Gone With the Wind*. But today Beverly lingered after class to weep. During the three minutes between classes Miles was expected to stand outside his classroom door on hall duty, and it was there in the crowded corridor that Beverly broke down. At first Miles wished she had waited until after school, when he would have had more time to console her, but in retrospect he was glad she hadn't. He was at his worst when confronted with other people's grief, and Beverly's sorrow seemed to spill out far beyond the borders of consolation. Her helplessness rendered him helpless. No, it was better that she spoke to him when she did, thus restricting her tears and his mumbling to the three minutes between bells. She said, "Almost six years ago my sister married a bum named Harlan Prentiss, and nobody knows where Harlan Prentiss disappeared to, but he ran away from my sister right away after they were married and my sister has been living in Minneapolis ever since and she never comes home. She only sends a card at Christmastime and the card has no return address." Up to this point Beverly had been speaking in a matter-of-fact voice, but now Miles saw her anguish suddenly take charge and twist her face into an expression of despair. Tears brimmed in her eyes.

"Goddamn it," she said. "I told myself I wasn't going to cry today." She stepped back into the classroom and put her books on Miles's desk and sobbed silently into the short sleeve of her soiled blouse.

Miles couldn't think of anything to say. His words of solace were blurted out in choppy phrases that he himself did not entirely understand, but which—the wonder of it!—Beverly seemed to find valuable. She wiped her face and smiled at him through her tears. Miles mumbled something more. Sixth-hour bell rang. She picked up her books and went to the door, then turned and said, "I'm sorry, but you're the one I had to tell because you always seem to have your shit together."

As Miles closed the windows of his classroom he saw Superintendent Stevenson looking at him from his office across the courtyard. Miles waved at him. Stevenson carefully nodded, or rather wobbled, his head. Miles turned out the lights and locked the door and climbed the stairs to last-hour study hall.

Last hour, Miles wilted.

Last-hour study hall was large and dismal and entrusted only to veterans. There were five teachers on the Staggerford staff who took charge of it, a year at a time, and this was Miles's year. He entered the long, ill-lighted room containing a hundred stationary desks that had been carved on by three generations of students. Some of the names on the desks matched the names on the World War Two memorial in front of the public library. The study-hall teacher's duty was simply to see that everybody kept his mouth shut. Miles took his place on the platform at the front of the room, scowled at a couple of potential whisperers, and tried to ignore the age-old smells of study hall, which were three in number.

Sweat, at low intensity, smelled much like a salty bowl of chicken soup. Is anyone's nose so well trained (Miles wondered) that he can differentiate between the smell in a gym that tells you where the locker room is and the smell in a dimestore that tells you the lunch counter is in the next aisle?

The second study-hall smell arose from the mixture of manure and Berrington County topsoil, which by this time in the afternoon had dried and was flaking off the boots of the farm boys. The smell, to Miles, was not entirely bad, for it brought to his mind, when he tried for them, images of red barns and rolling pastures. Corn fields and windmills. Lowing herds at sundown.

It was the third smell that bothered him most, for it was without a redeeming feature. It was the inevitable midafternoon smell of hot lunch being converted into air.

This hour, between two and three, Miles wilted. Because he had been stern from the beginning, study hall gave him no sass, but it gave him the blues. The lighting, as mentioned, was dim, and the afternoon sun, when it shone, did not shine on this side of the building. The students' minds were not fresh. They made a weak attempt at homework, then pushed it aside, tomorrow's classes being too distant to imagine. They watched the clock. They dreamed daydreams so dull that they fell asleep. Miles sat on his platform wondering if he would be able to rise from his chair when the bell rang, wondering if he would have the strength to walk home, wondering if life was worth living.

There was a moment today, at 2:25, when study hall came suddenly to life. Heads were lifted and cocked as the siren in the belfry of the city hall announced trouble, probably a fire, somewhere in Staggerford. Students stood up at their desks and strained to see outside. Miles found this sign of vitality so reassuring that he allowed everyone to go to the windows and watch the volunteer firemen run into the fire hall across the street and come out wearing yellow rubber coats and clinging to the handholds of two shiny ladder trucks. When the trucks were out of sight there was a little chatter, which Miles quickly scotched, and then everyone returned to his desk and to his dim and vapid daydreams.

At the final bell of the day, Miles dismissed study hall and went downstairs to take up his hall-duty post outside his classroom. He said goodnight twenty-five or thirty times. When the halls emptied, he put in the required quarter hour at his desk, then he picked up his briefcase, put his coat over his arm, and stepped outside into the perfume of dying leaves.

He crossed the street and walked past the fire station. The firemen, sweating in their yellow rubber coats, had returned from the fire and were backing the trucks into their stalls. He passed the city hall and he passed the spacious lawn of the Staggerford Public Library. At the corner of Main Street he turned and walked past the *Weekly* office, where Albert Fremling was licking address labels and Mrs. Fremling was talking on the phone and Lee Fremling was cleaning the drum of the press with a rag dipped in denatured alcohol and Grandma Fremling was sweeping the floor. He walked past the Hub Cafe, the Morgan Hotel, the hardware store, the bakery, and the bank. He turned right at the next corner and walked down River Street past the houses of Oppegaard the dentist, Hoover the retired farmer, Druppers the mayor, Handyside the baker, and Kelly the auto mechanic. The last house at the end of the second block was Miss McGee's. He climbed the three

17

steps to the wide front porch. The front door with its thick pane of oval glass stood ajar. He went inside and hung his coat in the closet at the foot of the stairs.

"How was your day?" Miss McGeee called from the kitchen.

"A good enough day. It seemed long though. How was yours?"

"The Dark Ages are beginning all over again, Miles."

"What makes you say that?" She often told him this, but her reason for saying it differed from day to day. He walked through the living room (deep soft chairs with worn upholstery, dark woodwork, a bookcase with glass doors) and through the dining room (a round oak table, six chairs, a mirror over the sideboard, linen curtains) and stood in the kitchen doorway.

Miss McGee was gathering together bottles and vegetables from the refrigerator—the makings of a salad—and listening to news on the radio. Miss McGee was a spinster. This was her forty-first year teaching sixth grade at St. Isidore's Catholic Elementary, and this was the house she had been born in.

"How is the world going wrong, Agatha?"

"Oh, I don't know. One thing and another."

It was not like her to be vague, and Miles waited for her to tell him what had happened, but she said no more. She stood at the counter, chopping celery stalks to pieces. She was wearing one of the neck-to-knee aprons that she tied on herself every afternoon when she got home from school.

Miles loosened his tie and said, "I wonder where the fire was."

Miss McGee shot him a quick glance, then went out the back door to her garden, where she lopped a head of cabbage off its stalk.

Miles went upstairs to the room he had been living in

for twelve years, the first room on the right at the head of the stairs.

Few could remember a time when Miss McGee— slight and splay-footed and quick as a bird—was not teaching at St. Isidore's. This was her forty-first year in the same classroom, her forty-first year of flitting and hovering up and down the aisles in the morning when she felt fresh, and perching behind her walnut desk in the afternoon when fatigue set in. In the minds of her former students, many of whom were now grandparents, she occupied a place somewhere between Moses and Emily Post, and when they met her on the street they guarded not only their speech but also their thoughts.

They knew of course—for she had been telling the story for over half a century—that when she was a girl she had met Joyce Kilmer, but who would have guessed the connection between that meeting many years ago and the fire alarm this afternoon? Standing in the garden among her cabbages, she decided that she would never tell a soul—not even Miles—about the cause of the fire alarm. She could not lie, but she could keep a secret.

Agatha McGee met Joyce Kilmer when she was six. She was a first grader at St. Isidore's. The year was 1916 and her teacher, Sister Rose of Lima, primed the first grade for months, leading them in a recitation of "Trees" every morning between the Apostles' Creed and the Pledge of Allegiance; and then on the last day of school before Christmas break, Joyce Kilmer stepped through the classroom door at the appointed hour, casting Sister Rose of Lima into a state of stuttering foolishness and her students into ecstasy. Miss McGee remembered it like yesterday. Mr. Kilmer was handsome, cheery, and a bit plump. He wore a black suit and

a red tie. With a playful sparkle in his eye he bowed to
Sister Rose of Lima, saying he was delighted to meet
her, and then he walked among her students, asking
their names. The children's voices were suddenly unde-
pendable, and they told their names in tense whispers
and unexpected shouts. Jesse Farnham momentarily forgot who he was, and the silence was thick while he
thought. When he finally said, "Jesse," Mr. Kilmer told
him that he had known a girl by that name, and the first
grade exploded with more laughter than Sister Rose of
Lima permitted on ordinary days. (Priests and poets
melted her severity.) The laughter, ending as suddenly
as it began, was followed by a comfortable chat, the poet
telling stories, some without lessons. Before Mr. Kilmer
left, his admirers recited "Trees" for him. For Agatha
McGee his visit was, like Christmas in those years, a joy
undiminished by anticipation.

But that was long ago. Nowadays poetry, among other
things, wasn't what it used to be. Yesterday at St. Isidore's as Miss McGee sat at the faculty lunch table she
overheard Sister Rosie tell Sister Judy in an excited
whisper that Herschel Mancrief was coming to town. He
was touring the Midwest on a federal grant, and would
arrive at St. Isidore's at ten the next morning. The two
sisters were huddled low over the Spanish rice, trying to
keep the news from Miss McGee. She wasn't surprised.
She was well aware that the new nuns, although
pranked out in permanents and skirts up to their knees,
were still a clandestine sorority. How like them to plan
an interruption in the schoolday and not let her know.

"About whom are you speaking?" she asked.

"Oh, Miss McGee," said Sister Rosie, the lighthearted
(and in Miss McGee's opinion, light-headed) principal
of St. Isidore's. "We were discussing Herschel Mancrief,
and we were not at all sure you would be interested."

Sister Rosie was twenty-six and she had pierced earlobes.

"I will be the judge of my interests, if you please. Who is Herschel Mancrief?"

"He's a poet the younger generation is reading," said Sister Judy, blushing behind her acne. "We studied him in the novitiate."

"His credentials are super," said Sister Rosie.

"And he's coming to St. Isidore's? I might have been told. Will he visit classes or speak to an assembly?"

"He will visit classes. But of course no one is obliged to have him in. I know what a nuisance interruptions can be."

"Poets are important to children. I was visited by Mr. Joyce Kilmer when I was a girl, and I treasure the memory. Please show Mr. What's-his-name to my classroom when the time comes. What's his name?"

"Herschel Mancrief. He can give you twenty minutes at quarter to twelve."

So this morning Miss McGee announced to her sixth graders that they were about to meet Herschel Mancrief. They looked up from their reading assignment, a page headed "Goths and Visigoths," and as a sign of their undivided attention they closed their books. Divided attention was among the things Miss McGee did not permit. Slang and eye shadow were others.

"Meeting a poet is a memorable experience," she said. "When I was a girl, my class was visited by Mr. Joyce Kilmer, who wrote 'Trees,' the poem every child carries in his heart from the primary grades, and to this day I can recall what Mr. Kilmer said to us. He came to Staggerford a mere two years before giving his life for his country in World War One." She tilted her head back, in order to read her twenty-four sixth graders through her bifocals—difficult reading these days, for they lurked, boys and girls alike, behind veils of hair.

"The poet, you understand, is a man with a message. His mission is to remind us of the beauty God has made. He writes of the good and lasting things of life. His business is beauty. Are there any questions?"

There was one, and several students raised their hands to ask it: "How does 'Trees' go?"

"Heavens, surely you remember."

But it was discovered that no one in the class had heard it. As Miss McGee began reciting, " 'I think that I shall never see,' " a frightening sensation crept up her spine and gripped her heart—an invisible tremor like the one she had felt in 1918 when her third-grade teacher said that Joyce Kilmer was dead in France. An imperceptible shudder that moved out along her nervous system and left her nauseous. Her name for it was the Dark Age dyspepsia, because it struck whenever she came upon a new piece of alarming evidence that pointed to the return of the Dark Ages.

Dark Age evidence had been accumulating. Last month at Parents' Night, Barbara Betka's father and mother told Miss McGee they would see her fired if she did not lift her prohibition against the wearing of nylons by sixth-grade girls. They were standing in the assembly room where coffee was to be served. Mr. Betka, fidgeting and averting his eyes, did most of the talking while Mrs. Betka, having called the tune, stood at his side and fingered his arm like a musical instrument. "Fired indeed!" said Miss McGee, turning on her heel and snatching up her purse in a single motion of amazing agility, like a move in hopscotch, and she flew from the assembly room before coffee was served. She was followed home by the Dark Age dyspepsia and scarcely slept that night, haunted by the specter of a man in his fifties sent out by his wife to do battle for nylons. "The craven ninny," she said to herself at dawn, rising to prepare the day's lessons.

And that was the day Dr. Murphy from the State Department of Education came to town to address a joint meeting of public and parochial school faculties. Both Miles and Miss McGee attended his lecture. "Never," Dr. Murphy said at the end of a tedious address on language arts, "never burden a child with a book written earlier than the child's date of birth. That way you can be confident that you and your students are in tune with each other, that you are moving with them on a contemporary plane." This harebrained proposal proved to Miss McGee that not even the State Department of Education was immune from the spreading plague of dark and crippling ignorance.

Nor were the sisters immune. More than once, for their spring picnic, Sister Judy had taken her fourth graders to a hippie farm. When Miss McGee first heard about that, she went to the pastor, Father Finn, and warned him about the return of the Dark Ages. Father Finn, ordinarily a man of understanding, did not understand Miss McGee's anxiety. If the Dark Ages were coming back, he had not yet caught sight of them. He told Miss McGee that she was an alarmist.

This morning as she concluded with the line, "But only God can make a tree," the door opened and Herschel Mancrief appeared. He was led into the classroom by Sister Rosie. He was untidy. That was Miss McGee's first impression of him. Under his wrinkled suitcoat he wore a T-shirt and under his nose a thicket of hair that curled around the corners of his mouth and ended in a stringy gray beard.

Miss McGee said, "I am pleased to meet you," and she gracefully offered her hand.

"Groovy," said the poet, tapping her palm with the

tip of one finger. Up close she saw that his neck and his T-shirt were unmistakably unwashed. His asymmetrical sideburns held lint. She hopped silently backward and slipped into an empty desk halfway down an aisle, and Sister Rosie introduced the visitor, training a spit curl as she spoke.

"Mr. Mancrief has already been to three rooms and he has another one to visit after yours, class, and he has to leave by twelve thirty, so when his time is up please don't bug him to stay." On her way out the door, Sister Rosie added, "Room 102 is next, Herschel. It's just across the hall."

The sixth grade regarded the poet.

"I am here to make you childlike," he began, blinking as he spoke, as though his words gave off too much light. "I am here to save you from growing up." His voice was deep and wheezy, and his frown was fixed. "You see, grownups aren't sensitive. They get covered over with a kind of crust. They don't *feel*. It is only through constant effort that I am able to maintain the wonder, the joy, the capacity for feeling that I had as a child." He quit blinking and inserted a hand under his suitcoat to give his ribs a general and thoughtful scratching. "Do you understand what I am saying?"

The class looked at Miss McGee. She nodded and so did they.

"Good. Now here's a poem of mine called 'What I Envied.' It's an example of what I'm saying." He closed his eyes and spoke in an altered voice, a chant:

> "I envied as a child
> the clean manikins in store windows
> because their underwear fit
> their toes were buried in thick carpet
> their happy smiles immutable,

until my father driving us home
past midnight after a day in the country
passed a window full of manikins
and then I knew
the trouble it must be
to smile all night!"

After a silent moment the poet opened his eyes signaling the end of the poem.

Miss McGee had heard worse. Except for the reference to underwear, it came as close to poetry as most of the verse she had read lately, and she set the class to nodding its approval.

Herschel Mancrief shed his suitcoat and revealed that his pants were held up by a knotted rope. It was not the white, carefully braided rope of the Franciscans, who were Miss McGee's teachers in college, but a dirty length of frazzled twine.

"Good," said the poet, laying his suitcoat across Miss McGee's walnut desk. "You remember how heroic those manikins used to seem when you were small and they were larger than life. You would see one in a store window and it was enough to make you salute. The pity is that you gradually lose your sense of wonder for things like that. Take toilets, for example. My poem 'So Tall' is about a toilet."

He recited with his eyes shut. Miss McGee shut hers as well.

"How tall I seem to be these days
and how much I am missing,
things at ground level escape my notice
wall plugs wastebaskets heat registers,
what do I care for them now I am so tall?
I was once acquainted with a toilet
when it and I were eye to eye,

it would roar and swallow and scare me half to death.
What do I care for that toilet now,
now I am so tall?"

There was the sound of a giggle, stifled.

"You are surprised I got a toilet into a poem?" He
was asking Miss McGee, who had not giggled. "But
poetry takes all of life for her domain. The beautiful
and the unbeautiful. Roses and toilets. Today's poet
seeks to represent the proportions of life. You don't very
often pick a rose, but you go to the bathroom several
times a day."

Certain now that he had taken the measure of Miss
McGee's tolerance for the unbeautiful (color was rising
in her face) the poet announced his third selection, "In
My End of Town."

> "In my end of town
> like a cathedral against the sky
> stands the city sewage plant,
> the direction of the wind
> is important to us,
> in my end of town
> man disposes."

He opened his eyes to study Miss McGee's reaction,
but the desk she had been sitting in was empty. She was
at his side, facing the class.

"Students, you will thank Mr. Mancrief."

"Thank you, Mr. Mancrief." They spoke the way
they prayed, in unison and without enthusiasm.

She handed the poet his coat and, not wishing to
touch his hairy arms, she steered him to the door as if by
remote control. "There"—she pointed—"is Room 102."

Nothing in his government-sponsored travels had prepared Herschel Mancrief for the brush-off. "Actually,"

26

he said, blinking as he backed into the corridor, "I hadn't finished."

"I regret we can spare you no more time. We recite the Angelus at twelve."

Looking more surprised than offended, he raised a hand as though to speak, but then thought better of it and stepped across the corridor and knocked on the door of 102. It opened instantly and Sister Judy put her head out.

Miss McGee, afraid now that her treatment of the man had been too delicate, said, "Another thing, Mr. Mancrief. Your poetry is . . ." She searched for the word. The poet and Sister Judy listened for it.

"Your poetry is undistinguished."

Sister Judy rolled her eyes and the poet chuckled into his hand. Miss McGee turned back to her class, pulling the door shut behind her. "Entirely undistinguished, class. You will rise now for the Angelus."

Later, entering the lunchroom. Miss McGee saw at the far end of the faculty table Herschel Mancrief and Sister Judy ignoring their beans and tuna and laughing like ninnies.

"I thought he was to have been on his way by this time."

"We asked him to stay for lunch," said Sister Rosie. "He has agreed to stay a while longer. Isn't he super?"

"He's horribly dated. He said 'groovy.' I haven't heard anyone say 'groovy' for at least three years."

"Oh, Miss McGee, he's super. Admit it."

"Pass the relish, if you please."

Two hours later, after putting her class to work on equilateral triangles, Miss McGee opened her door for a change of air. From behind the closed door of 102 she heard raucous laughter alternating with the excited voice of Herschel Mancrief. The man evidently could not bring himself to leave St. Isidore's. She stepped closer and listened through the door.

"Acquainted with a toilet," said the poet.

The fourth grade laughed.

"It would roar and swallow and scare me half to death."

More laughter.

"There, now you've caught the spirit of the poem. Now repeat it after me."

They did so, briskly, line by line.

"Now let's try another one—a poem I wrote just the other day called 'Be Careful Where You Grab Me.' "

Fierce laughter.

Miss McGee hurried to the nearest fire alarm and with a trembling hand she broke the seal and set off an ear-splitting jangle of horns and bells that emptied the building in forty-five seconds. Two ladder trucks pulled up to the front door and while the fire chief, a former student of Miss McGee's, gave the building a thorough inspection, Herschel Mancrief drove off in his rented car, the fourth grade throwing him kisses from the curb.

"A false alarm," declared the fire chief, emerging from the front door of the school in his yellow rubber coat.

"Someone set off the alarm near your room," he said to Miss McGee as she led her sixth grade up the steps and back into the building. "Did you notice anything suspicious, Miss McGee?"

"Goths and Visigoths," she said.

Miss McGee prepared cole slaw and celery soup for supper. She had never, in her memory, tasted meat on Friday, and she was determined, despite recent revisions in canon law, that she never would. She thought of every Friday as a renewal of Good Friday, and the uniform blandness of all her Friday meals was emblematic to her of the barrenness of a world bereft of its Savior. Six days a week she had the appetite of a farmhand, eating nearly as much as Miles and never gaining an ounce (if anything she diminished slightly by the year) , but her Friday suppers were invariably meager.

"I see we are being holier than Rome again tonight," said Miles as he took his place at the kitchen table. He bowed his head while Miss McGee said grace.

Like his landlady and former teacher, Miles had been reared by Catholic parents and educated by sisters and monks, but ten years ago, at the age of twenty-five, he had lost his faith in the Father, the Son, the Holy Spirit, the Holy Catholic Church, the Day of Judgment, and Life Everlasting. He had lost the whole works. His faith had not been crushed by a disillusioning experience; it had not been argued away by a glib heretic, it had simply evaporated. He was not particularly pleased to have lost it, nor did he long to have it back. His faith was gone, and that was that. He lost it during his second year of teaching, his second year in Miss McGee's house, and he was sorry to discover that the pain of lost faith was never suffered as intensely by the one who lost it as by ones friends who had *not* lost it. On the first Sunday that Miles stayed home from mass, Miss McGee came close to weeping, and for ten years now she had been praying daily that the precious gift he had lost would be given him again. With time, fortunately, the problem had ceased to be a debilitating drain on her nervous system; it became instead a purely intellectual matter on which she spent an earnest but unemotional Hail Mary each morning.

As for Miles's playful remarks about her own faith— usually brought on by his first glance at Friday supper— she had learned easily to turn them aside.

"Being holier than Rome is no fun since they made it so easy," she said. "You eat more than you should anyway, Miles. A man in his middle thirties runs the risk of becoming portly."

"Are you saying that I'm becoming portly?" Miles was tall, heavy, square-jawed, and red-haired.

"Yes," said Miss McGee.

Miles spread his napkin on his lap and considered his stomach. He was wearing a heavy woolen shirt of brown and gold checks, the shirt he wore to football games, and it was much tighter now than when he bought it.

"I think it is written in the stars that I shall be on the heavy side. Both my grandfathers and one of my grandmothers were very large."

"Your father is not large," said Miss McGee.

"Well, that's because of his sclerosis. I think if he were healthy he would be large. He has the frame for carrying a lot of weight. He's over six feet, you know, but it's hard to think of him as that tall because he's so seldom on his feet. He's always in his wheelchair."

"Your father was never heavy, Miles. Your father and I were just three years apart in age, so we have known each other all our lives, and he was never heavy. He was tall and handsome. His job in the creamery started when he was sixteen, and I remember how proud he was when he first started wearing his white trousers and white shirt and white apron. He wore them to school—at least the white trousers and white shirt—not the apron—and I thought he was the handsomest boy in school. And to this day, Miles, you can still see his handsomeness in his eyes."

Miss McGee had accompanied Miles on a recent visit to the rest home in Duluth where his father was being cared for, and she had been struck by the man's eyes. Multiple sclerosis had crippled him and two strokes had confused him, but under his bushy eyebrows his piercing dark eyes belied the disarray that lay behind them.

"They are steady, untroubled eyes," she said.

"Yes, they are." Miles tasted his soup.

"You have the same steady eyes, Miles—the same untroubled look."

"It's a false front, Agatha. I'm a troubled man. I have this landlady that troubles me about my portliness."

"Shush."

"Even though it's written in the stars that I shall be of great size."

"Oh shush, no one's size is in the stars. It's in his diet, especially his diet between meals. At the game tonight you will eat hot dogs and popcorn. You never pass up food."

"One feels a certain obligation toward the senior class. They run the food stand."

"You could give them a dollar and abstain from the food. I'm sure they would accept a donation."

There was a pounding on the back door that set off a drumming echo in the glassed-in back porch. Miles opened the kitchen door and crossed the porch and opened the outer door. It was dark now and he squinted, trying to make out the shadowy form standing below him on the bottom step.

"Yes?" he said.

"Bones?"

It was the Bonewoman. Miles moved aside so that the kitchen light would fall upon her, but she too moved aside, avoiding the light, and he saw only her gunnysack and the hand that held it.

"Bones?" she said again. Her voice was thin.

Miles turned to the kitchen and told Miss McGee who it was.

"Nothing tonight," said Miss McGee.

"Sorry, nothing tonight," he told the Bonewoman.

The gunnysack moved away from the steps and across the soft earth of the garden, which was harvested now, except for cabbages and squash. Miles could hear the Bonewoman's steps on the gravel as she crossed the alley. He stood at the open door, leaning out into the night, and heard her knock on the back door of Lillian Kite's house. In the darkness, the fragrance of Miss McGee's old garden, turned up and tired, seemed to be rising in faint whiffs from the Bonewoman's deep footprints—the tuberous smell of roots freshly exposed and the sour smell of tomatoes spoiled by frost and left with a few blighted potatoes to blacken and nourish the spent, gray soil. He heard her knock again. He closed the door and returned to the table.

"Some people refuse to give her bones, even if they have some," said Miss McGee. "Did you know that?"

"So I've heard."

"And others save bones for her the way they save papers for a paper drive. I myself would never do that because goodness knows when she'll turn up next. It might be next week and it might be next summer, and I don't want dirty old bones sitting in my kitchen attracting flies. If I have bones she gets them, and if I don't she doesn't. I never see her, though, that I don't feel sorry for that daughter of hers."

"Beverly."

"Yes, Beverly. She's so pretty and yet she's so crude. I see her working at the Hub Cafe. What kind of home life must she have with her mother out scrounging bones?"

"Did you know her father?"

"Of course. Clarence Bingham. He was part Indian, and he was much older than the Bonewoman. He was in prison for a time, and after that he was in a hospital somewhere, and that's where he died."

"They say he killed a man."

"That's why he was in prison. Surely you remember."

"Just vaguely. I was away at summer school when it happened."

"Beverly's a senior, I believe."

"Yes, and a good student. She's likely to be second highest in her class by the time she graduates in the spring. Nadine Oppegaard has the top spot sewed up."

"My heart goes out to Beverly. She's so crude. She talks so crudely. Her clothes are not clean."

"Is there more soup?"

"No. We have apple pie for dessert." Miss McGee brought the pie in from the back porch and cut it into seven pieces; Miles ate three of them.

At the football game Miles sat with Imogene Kite, librarian. She was director of the Staggerford Public Library. Miles had been sitting with Imogene Kite at football games, lectures, cantatas, and funerals for years He considered her too tall and bloodless to be attractive He noticed that as she edged into her thirties she was developing the features of a turkey, a tom. He found her company only slightly more exciting than solitude, but at present in Staggerford there was no one else.

Other single girls had come to town in Miles's time— most of them better looking than Imogene—but all of them were in a hurry to find a husband and when they uncovered none within the two-year limit they had set for themselves they moved away. Miles had fallen in love with one of these girls. Her name was Anna Thea Hayworth and she came from St. Paul. She taught home economics. For no good reason except that he didn't catch her name when he was introduced to her, he insisted upon calling her Thanatopsis Hayworth, which always made her laugh. Her hair was dark with a tinge of sable in it. She sewed, skied, cooked, giggled, read books, visited the sick, loved her students, and was obviously going to make somebody a nifty wife. After dating her several times, Miles began to think about marriage; but Miles's thoughts were generally long thoughts, and before he came to a decision Thanatopsis Hayworth married Wayne Workman, who came to town as the new high-school principal. So now she was Anna Thea Workman, though Miles still called her Thanatopsis; and to this day she taught home ec across the hall from Miles's classroom, and Miles was still in love with her.

There was little to love about Imogene Kite. She was all warts and adenoids. Judging by how little she worked to make herself attractive, she seemed to be in no hurry to find a husband. She sewed not. Neither did she ski. She never laughed or cooked or visited the sick. She lived with her mother in the house across the alley from Miss McGee's. What she did, incessantly, was look up information in the card catalog. Miles had never known anyone with such a respect for pure knowledge as Imogene Kite. At one time or another in their steady but distant relationship, Imogene had explained to Miles the difference between deciduous and coniferous trees, and she had told him how Egyptians made bricks, and she had cleared up his ignorance concerning the Kaiser's problems in the Baltic states.

One evening when Miles was browsing in the public library he overheard a brief, whispered conversation between Imogene, who sat behind the check-out desk, and Doc Oppegaard's wife, who suffered from an inferiority complex because her daughter Nadine was a genius.

34

"It makes me so discouraged to know so little," Mrs. Oppegaard whispered to Imogene. "I mean facts. I don't know anything I can tell people and be certain I'm right." She hung her head like a winded horse, and her expensive fur piece dangled down her front like a tether.

"I know what you mean," whispered Imogene. 'Atomic energy, and should we have nationalized medicine."

"That's it exactly." Mrs. Oppegaard shook her head unworthily.

"Atomic energy, and should we have nationalized medicine," said Imogene aloud. "Those are a couple of big scenes I know nothing about. But I know one thing. Before I'm through, I'm going to get to the bottom of the atomic energy scene."

Tonight, sitting high in the bleachers, Imogene Kite was getting to the bottom of the lending scene. "It's a well-known fact, Pruitt"—she never called Miles by his first name—"that there are too many people in this country borrowing and spending beyond their means, and that's the main reason our big cities are going into debt. A big city can't expect to violate principles of sound fiscal policy and not suffer the consequences."

Below them on the field the Staggerford Stags kicked off to the Owl Brook Owls. On the second play from scrimmage Owl Brook scored on a seventy-five-yard pass play.

"A big city has to keep tabs on its treasury the same way a private citizen like you or me has to keep tabs on his purse strings."

The Owls missed their extra-point kick.

"Now one of the most harmful practices in city management is the accrued-income, cash-outgo system."

After falling behind by six points, the Staggerford

team began playing what Coach Gibbon liked to call inspired football. The Stags' defensive line obviously enjoyed tackling and the defensive secondary on passes ranged across the field like leaping gazelles.

"Under the accrued-income, cash-outgo system, you compute your income on an accrual basis. That is to say, you count all your accounts receivable as hard and fast income, even when you know that a certain percentage of your accounts receivable, such as property taxes in the case of a city government, will never be paid; and you compute your outgo on a cash-only basis. That is to say, you pretend the debts you owe are not liabilities. And you know what you end up with, Pruitt? Insolvency."

Imogene lectured until the band struck up "El Capitan" at halftime and Miles went to the food stand for hot dogs and popcorn. Roxie Booth waited on him. She said that the corporal who ate the beer bottle was from Spokane. Because of the frost in the air, Roxie was exposing very little of her skin, but she had compensated for this rare modesty by garishly painting her face. To Miles, her black eyelashes and crimson cheeks suggested a clown with high blood pressure. He gave her a dollar and said, "Keep the change for the class treasury."

Roxie moved her hips and shoulders and gave him half a smile and said, "Don't be funny, Mr. Pruitt. It's a dollar forty."

He took back the one and gave her a five.

"Can I still keep the change?" She winked.

"Don't be funny," said Miles.

In the third quarter, when Imogene Kite finished her hot dog and her box of popcorn, she said that the accrued-income, cash-outgo system of bookkeeping was illegal.

"I shouldn't wonder," said Miles.

36

"But you can seldom discover and prosecute violators until the damage has been done. To discover the violators you would have to audit the books of every business and municipality on a continuing basis."

Miles was watching Albert Fremling on the sidelines. The editor of the *Weekly* had interrupted his whirlwind Friday-night driving to attend this game in which his son was playing. He was sprawled at the edge of the field with his high-speed Graphlex, waiting for an exciting picture to present itself; but Miles could tell, even at this distance, that Fremling was drunk, and when a dramatic play did now and then cross his viewfinder his reactions were too slow to catch it.

"Have you any idea what it would cost to maintain a continuing audit of all the bookkeeping in the United States?" said Imogene.

"I guess it would be a lot."

"My God, Pruitt, you have no idea."

Late in the fourth quarter the Stags scored a touchdown, and Miles saw Coach Gibbon turn his back on the field. It was up to Coach's son Peter to kick the extra point, and Coach could not bear to watch. The Staggerford line didn't hold. It was Lee Fremling, son of the editor, who gave way. Playing center, Lee was at once the largest and the weakest Stag. He was pushed so far backwards that he blocked Peter's kick with his rump. The groan of the crowd told Coach Gibbon the bad news.

"There's a rash of insolvency across the nation," said Imogene. "Insolvency, bankruptcy, and default."

The game ended in a tie. Miles helped Imogene down from the bleachers.

As they walked to the gate, Superintendent Stevenson's wife came up behind them and linked her arms in theirs. "Will you two come home with me for a cup of

coffee and a rubber of bridge?" she said. "Ansel would
be so pleased."

"Of course," said Imogene. "I love beating Pruitt
at bridge."

Mrs. Stevenson was a formidable, triple-chinned
woman, trussed and stayed and never caught slouching;
although it seemed to Miles that she had been altogether more human since the last faculty Christmas dinner, when a loud belch took her by surprise. It had been
a remarkably resonant sound, rising from deep in her
pipes, and it came early in the meal when conversation
was yet relatively subdued. The belch tested everyone's
sense of decorum. Mrs. Stevenson, for her part, behaved
like a perfect lady; that is to say, she behaved as though
no belch had rung through the room; and except for
two or three clods who looked up suddenly from their
soup, so did everyone else.

The Stevensons lived in a small house in the middle
of a large wooded lot. The lot was surrounded by a high
iron fence. Miles and Imogene stood on the front step
and waited while Mrs. Stevenson found a ring of keys in
her purse and unlocked the storm door and then unlocked the inner door. This let them into a small entry
way, where they waited for her to unlock the door to the
living room. In the living room Superintendent Steven
son sat before the fire.

"Ah, Imogene. Ah, Miles," he said, half rising from
his chair. "Come in, come in, come in."

Superintendent Stevenson was a man who had put his
affairs in order about five years early, or so it appeared
to Miles. There was once a time when the superintendent led the Community Fund Drive every spring and
revised the Faculty Handbook every fall and visited
classrooms every day. But now, at sixty, he was rumored

to have a heart condition, and he spent his days in almost perfect isolation. He passed his evenings and weekends in this living room, looking into his fireplace, where the flames always burned high and hot, and he passed his working days looking out his office window, which faced Miles's classroom across the courtyard. Parents coming to school had learned to bypass his office, for he refused to see them. The faculty had despaired of going to him for inspiration or advice. Delia Fritz, his secretary, did all his work. The school board was afraid that if they fired him he would die.

It was said by some that Superintendent Stevenson was not ill, that he used the rumor of heart trouble as a ploy to hold his job while shirking his duty, but Miles was not of that opinion. No man feigning illness could look as ill as Stevenson. When he stood, he brought his shoulders forward as if he were trying to make them meet under his chin. He was a tall man, and he walked hunched over in an attempt to curl himself around his faulty heart and ward off the blows of daily life, like a man cupping a match in the wind. He had come to an absolute standstill, devoting his days to gazing out the window and his nights to gazing into the fire.

"Sit here, Imogene, make yourself comfortable. Sit here, Miles. They say we're in for a hard frost tonight."

Whenever Miles stepped into the Stevensons' living room and sank into one of the sturdy antique chairs upholstered in green brocade he felt that life could never do him any harm. The carpet was thick and it deadened all sound. The pendulum of the walnut clock swung slow, slow. The birch logs never burned with unseemly speed. Here it seemed to Miles that the river of time had receded and left him high and dry like the minnows he had found this noon in a landlocked pool.

Imogene and Miles had spent many evenings here,

and the routine was this: first a chat by the fire, then bridge, then raspberry sundaes, then a tour of the dining room for a look at Mrs. Stevenson's china and silver, then farewell.

Tonight's chat was a reminiscence.

"The Indians," said Stevenson. "You young people probably never knew this, but it was my reputation as a friend of the Indians that brought me to Staggerford. Twenty years ago the Staggerford School Board drove up to North Siding, where I had been superintendent for six years, and said that if I came to Staggerford I could name my own salary. Do you remember, Viola?"

"Like yesterday," said Mrs. Stevenson, settling heavily into the couch.

"Yes, like yesterday. But it was twenty years ago. There was so much absenteeism here in Staggerford, Miles, that their state-aid money was way down and the school district was going broke. You must remember. You were in high school here at the time."

"I guess I wasn't aware of it."

"So anyhow, the school board came up to North Siding—six men in one car—and that's over two hundred miles, mind you—and they said to me, 'Stevenson, we understand you get along with Indians.' "

A long pause. The fire was warm and the clock was slow.

"It was news to me. I had never thought of myself as especially good with Indians. All I knew was I had been in North Siding six years and everything was going smoothly. To tell the truth, Indians weren't even on my mind very much in those days. We had maybe eight percent of our students coming from a nearby reservation—the Pinelake Reservation, the smallest reservation in the state—and those Pinelake Indians came to school in North Siding as regularly as anyone else, except in

September when they were harvesting wild rice. You might say that the Pinelake tribe was a tribe of Indians that you never thought of as Indians. Wouldn't you say that, Viola?"

"That's quite true," said Mrs. Stevenson. "You were hardly conscious of their existence. They came to town and went home again the same way farmers do. No fuss."

"Exactly. So when the Staggerford School Board said, 'Stevenson, we understand you get along with Indians,' I said, 'Who told you that?'

" 'We went to St. Paul,' they said, 'and we talked to the commissioner of education. The commissioner says so. The commissioner says North Siding has the best record of Indian attendance in the state of Minnesota.'

"Well, Miles, you can imagine how I felt when I heard that. I swelled with pride. I suddenly found myself with a reputation as an Indian expert. Blazes, I was proud. You see, I suddenly believed I was an Indian expert. It shows you the danger of jumping to conclusions. There's a lesson in it, Imogene, Miles, and don't you forget it. When someone tells you something about yourself that you like the sound of, it's not necessarily true. You're tempted to believe it, of course, but don't let it color your honest opinion of yourself. After all, you know yourself better than other people know you. Hang on to your own opinion of yourself, in spite of what people say. They told me I was an Indian expert, and I knew better, but all six of them said it, and I swallowed it. And I came down here to Staggerford and fell flat on my face."

"Now, Ansel." Mrs. Stevenson gently laid her hand on his arm.

"No, it's a fact, Viola. I came down here to Staggerford and fell flat on my face."

Miles was sleepy. Stevenson's talk was a soothing drone, unhurried and soft. Miles wanted to close his eyes. He wanted to take off his shoes and sink deeper into his chair and sleep while Stevenson went on all night with his life story. Stevenson's life was a lullaby.

"Such gifts," Mrs. Stevenson said, turning to Imogene. "You cannot imagine the generosity of the people of North Siding. The gifts we received when we moved away. Why, you cannot imagine."

Stevenson said, "You see, what happened was that the Staggerford School Board had gone to St. Paul to consult the commissioner and the commissioner simply showed them where North Siding was maintaining student attendance at such-and-such a level, and the six men jumped to a false conclusion. They thought I was responsible for the high level of attendance. And when they showed up in North Siding and told me about it, I jumped to the same conclusion. I thought of myself as an Indian expert. I remember following them out to their car after we had lunch and had talked about salary and everything. I remember what I thought as I watched them drive off in the mud. It was spring and the streets were muddy. To this day I don't think the streets of North Siding are paved. Main Street, yes, but side streets, Viola? I don't think so. Anyhow, as I watched them drive off I thought my name must be pretty prominent in education. I imagined my name on every tongue in the commissioner's office. Perhaps at that very moment I was being praised in the legislature. I knew that the commissioner was an old man. Maybe the governor would appoint me the next commissioner. I had met the governor once at a conference in Minneapolis. We had lunch at the same table. He spilled a drop of coffee on my shoe."

Stevenson uncrossed his legs and held out his foot,

42

and he and his wife and Imogene and Miles looked at his shoe.

"Well, of course it was all nonsense. I came down here to Staggerford and fell flat on my face."

"I never dreamed of owning sterling for sixteen," said Mrs. Stevenson. "But the pieces kept pouring in. When the North Siding faculty wives heard we were leaving, they said, 'Please tell us the name of your silver pattern, Mrs. Stevenson, we think it's so lovely.' I told them the name—Moonscape, it's called—and wouldn't you know, everybody's going-away gift to us was a piece of Moonscape sterling." She turned and cast a look into the dining room, where glass and china glinted in the shadows.

"You have such nice things," said Imogene.

"Before we left North Siding, I could only serve twelve."

A small flame in the cinders sputtered and turned green. The clock growled and struck. Miles couldn't keep his eyes open.

"It's no mystery why I failed," said Stevenson. "It turned out that these Indians around Staggerford are a different breed from the Indians we had up there at North Siding. An altogether different breed. Ask George Butler. He took my place up there. He'll tell you that to this day those Pinelake Indians are going to school like whites. They're a more ambitious breed than these Sandhill Indians. Less clannish. Maybe they've got more French blood in them. Or less French blood, who knows? All I know is that I came down here and fell flat on my face."

There was a pause. Miles opened his eyes and told Stevenson that he was underrating himself. Mrs. Stevenson said so too. So did Imogene. But Miles knew (did Imogene know? did Mrs. Stevenson know?) that Steven-

43

son couldn't possibly underrate himself. As a superintendent he was a dud. When you considered what he had contributed to the Staggerford school system in twenty years—a mediocre teaching staff, a Faculty Handbook full of platitudes, an average of three Indian graduates per year, compared to perhaps two when he came to town—then you knew the man was a failure. But Miles loved to hear him talk. His voice was a low hum. His life was a lullaby.

Next, the rubber of bridge. Imogene and Stevenson enjoyed bridge and they enjoyed each other as partners When Stevenson chuckled, Imogene chuckled. When Imogene chuckled, Stevenson chuckled. Nowhere else but at the card table, and then only as partners, was either of them known to chuckle. Tonight they won, which was no more than right; Mrs. Stevenson and Miles were stupid at cards, and Miles was bored besides.

After cards Mrs. Stevenson served raspberry sundaes and butter cookies (the ice cream brought a keen pain to the left side of Miles's jaw) and after that she took Imogene into the next room for a tour of her china closet. Stevenson and Miles returned to the fire.

"My contract called for me to be in Staggerford on the first of August," said Stevenson. "That's twenty years ago last August. Viola and I were scheduled for coffee at Bartholomew Druppers' house that afternoon. Bartholomew Druppers was chairman of the school board then. He's still on the board, you know, and he's mayor now besides. Quite a public servant, Bartholomew Druppers. The coffee party was going to be an exclusive affair with the school board and their wives and some of the older faculty and *their* wives and a few selected old-time businessmen and *their* wives. It was set to start at three o'clock at the Drupperses' house.

"So on the first of August Viola and I arrived in town

at ten in the morning. The moving van was to follow the next day. I went straight to Bartholomew Druppers' law office and I said, 'Mr. Druppers, I don't know how this is going to set with your wife, but my wife and I will have to take a raincheck on that coffee party this afternoon. This is a working day and I have to be about my business. School begins in one month and it's none too soon for me to set off on my reservation visits, and my wife has elected to come along with me.'

"Blazes, what a hot-shot I must have been, Miles. I remember the look on Bartholomew's face.

" 'Come with me,' he said, and he led me across the street to Sy Larson's grocery store. Sy Larson was also on the board in those days. Bartholomew told Sy that the coffee party was off because I wanted to get started with my work. I remember Sy was behind the meat counter tying a package with a string when he heard the news. He stared at me for a moment, then he went to the phone and got in touch with two more board members and they rushed right over to the store and stood with Bartholomew and Sy in front of the meat counter. I stood a little apart from them as they held a conference. Miles, do you know how I interpreted the serious expressions on their faces? It shows you how innocent I was at the age of forty. I thought their expressions were the expressions of four men who had found themselves a determined leader who would see them through whatever troubles lay ahead—four men who were at last coming to grips with their old, old attendance problem. I imagined the expressions I saw in Larson's Grocery that day were the same ones you might have seen at the Continental Congress when Jefferson walked in and said, 'All right, boys, I've got a little document here I'd like you to sign; we'll call it the Declaration of Independence.' But, Miles. my friend, I have since figured out

45

what those expressions really meant. They were not the expressions of courage and determination. Hell, those were the expressions of men who were afraid to tell their wives the coffee party was off. But what did I know? I spoke up and said once more that I had to be about my business, and I left the store and drove with Viola out to the Sandhill Reservation. It was our first look at Sandhill."

Stevenson shook his head. Miles searched with his tongue for the source of pain on the left side of his jaw.

"Bleak. Blazes, Miles, it's bleak out there. You know what I mean. You've been out there."

Miles nodded.

"We drove to the village of Sandhill and stopped at the Sandhill General Store. Viola and I went inside and introduced ourselves to Bennie Bird, who's been running the store since the year one. It was dark in there, and Bennie was sitting behind the bar at the back of the store where he serves beer. That was twenty years ago last August, and to this day, I'm told, he's still sitting there. I told Bennie I was Staggerford's new superinten dent of schools and I was learning my way around the Sandhill Reservation because the school was there to serve all youngsters in the district, never mind race or creed. I told him I was eager to get acquainted with all the Indian families, and his store looked like the logical place to start. This seemed to puzzle Bennie. He looked over his shoulder, and I was surprised to see a woman sitting behind him in the shadows. She was sitting on a stool smoking a cigarette. I assumed it was Mrs. Bird I leaned over the bar and introduced Viola to her, but she didn't respond. She just smoked and stared at us. There was a long silence, which I found very awkward. I re peated to Bennie that I was exploring the reservation.

He said nothing. He looked over his shoulder again at the woman. We decided to leave.

"Miles, on the inside of the door there was a sign saying, 'Did you forget shoelaces?' I can see it yet. As we were going out the door, we heard Bennie Bird and the woman making a noise. It sounded like they were laughing. We got into the car and drove another mile or so deeper into the reservation. I could see that Viola's eyes were wet. You know, Miles, how dismal the Sandhill Reservation looks to a white man. Nothing but brush and jackpines, and here and there a yard full of stumps and weeds. Narrow driveways winding between the trees. Never a straight driveway. All of them narrow and crooked. I don't know of a more depressing landscape. Dusty roads. No-good land. Brush. Blazes, it's bleak. I looked at Viola. She did her best to smile, but her eyes were wet. Her instincts were telling her that we had no business on the reservation, and we had no business missing the coffee party. And my instincts were telling me I was no Indian expert, and we had no business leaving North Siding in the first place.

"I turned the car around and we headed back to Staggerford. We drove several miles in silence. Finally I said, 'Viola, did you forget shoelaces?' I was trying to be funny. I thought it would cheer her up, you know. But when I said it, she burst into tears and cried like a baby all the way back to Staggerford."

Imogene and Mrs. Stevenson returned from the dining room and sat down, and Miles tried to imagine Mrs. Stevenson crying like a baby.

The superintendent said, "We should have stayed in North Siding."

A faint reverberation touched Miles's ears. It coincided with another twinge of pain in his jaw, and he assumed that it was a rush of blood to his head; but when he heard it again he called it to the attention of the Stevensons.

"Someone at the door, do you suppose?" said Mrs. Stevenson, rising from her chair. "At this hour?"

"The wind," said the superintendent.

"No, I think it was a knock at the door," said Imogene.

Mrs. Stevenson went first to the front door, where she found no one, and then noiselessly through the carpeted rooms to the kitchen, where Miles heard her unlock doors, speak, and lock them again. She returned to the fire and sat down.

"The Bonewoman," she said.

"The Bonewoman!" said the superintendent with surprising emotion, picking his feet off the floor, then letting them down again. "The Bonewoman? At this hour? I tell you, something should be done about that woman. Coming around at night. It's a scandal. Viola, don't open the door to that woman again."

Mrs. Stevenson patted his arm. "I gave her a bone, Ansel. The beef bone, from supper. What harm could there possibly be in that?"

"Never again, Viola! She comes like a scavenger. A thief in the night. She's a crow, picking over carrion. Never again open the door to that woman, Viola."

Miles saw fear in the superintendent's eyes. He understood its cause. A few hours before, Miles himself had leaned out the back door of Miss McGee's house and sensed that the Bonewoman had somehow brought to the neighborhood the shadows and frost of the end of October—that by walking through the garden she was somehow hastening its decay, its freezing, its cover of snow. And now for Superintendent Stevenson, whose passionate clinging to life had fixed his attention squarely on death, the Bonewoman called up the same emotions, but more strongly—a sense of the end of things. Shadows and frost and the end of things.

"What possible harm?" his wife was saying gently. "The roast we had for supper. A good roast." She turned to Imogene. "It was a delicious roast—tender, and the bone was not large. A very small bone, actually, for so large a roast. What possible harm?"

Imogene stood up and said it was time to go home. Miles agreed, but he was reluctant to follow. For one thing, he was carrying on an experiment in his mouth, finding that if he ran his tongue a certain way along the inside of his lower left wisdom tooth, the pain subsided; and for another thing Stevenson showed signs of dropping back to his normal, relaxed state and appeared ready to begin another installment of his soothing, meaningless biography.

Imogene said, "Come on, Pruitt."

They put on their coats and the Stevensons let them out the front door into a flood of moonlight. The late-rising moon was blossoming over the bare trees, four times its normal size.

"Gracious, look at the moon," said Mrs. Stevenson. "It's a real harvest moon."

"The moon!" said the superintendent, and he retreated to the fire.

"That's where you're wrong," said Imogene. "The harvest moon was last month. This one's called the hunter's moon."

On the way home, Imogene told Miles that the superintendent's problem was definitely heart trouble. Mrs Stevenson had confided in her. It was a bad valve.

"In a case like that," said Imogene, "he can submit to surgery and the chances are sixty-five percent that it will be successful, or he can learn to live with it and maybe survive another twenty-five years, or maybe expire tomorrow. He has decided to learn to live with it. For a younger man the chances of a successful operation would be eighty percent, but he's sixty this year—did you know that?—and he's not particularly robust, so the odds drop to sixty-five percent. I don't know. It would be a hard decision to make. Bad-valve people who are faced with that decision are split almost down the middle. Fifty percent submit to surgery and fifty percent learn to live with it. Now of the fifty percent who learn to live with it, fifty-eight percent live to the age of sixty-five and forty-two percent don't, although those percentages vary if you break it down into the various ages the people are when they are faced with the decision. I mean *obviously*, Pruitt, one hundred percent of those who are sixty-five when they are faced with the decision are going to live to be sixty-five because they already *are* sixty-five."

The moon was the color of a peach.

"Pruitt, what *is* your problem? You keep moving your jaw all the time."

"I'm afraid it's my wisdom tooth going bad."

"Your wisdom tooth! My God, Pruitt, you're thirty-five. What are you doing with a wisdom tooth? I had my first two wisdom teeth extracted when I was nineteen and the other two when I was twenty-one. People seldom carry their wisdom teeth into their thirties. I think you'll find the average age for getting rid of your last wisdom tooth is twenty-three."

They came to the house that Imogene shared with her mother. The peach moon stood at the edge of the sloping roof and seemed about to roll off.

"The wisdom tooth is an unnecessary tooth," said Imogene. "It's a carry-over from our more primitive ancestors in the evolutionary chain."

Miles grasped Imogene roughly by the shoulders and

kissed her hard on the mouth and left her standing at her door. Her surprise was great, but not so great as to leave her speechless. She said to Miles as he walked away, "Goodness, Pruitt, what *are* you thinking of?"

What he was thinking of as he crossed the alley in the moonlight was Thanatopsis Hayworth from St. Paul, whose hair was dark with a tinge of sable, and how he had waited, alas, too long.

When he got home, Miss McGee called to him from her downstairs bedroom: "Is that you, Miles?" She knew that it was, but whenever he came in late she said, "Is that you, Miles?" to indicate that she was awake to receive whatever he might care to tell her about his evening. Tonight he stood at her bedroom door and looked into the darkness and told her that he had kissed Imogene Kite. He told her this because he had never known a woman, whatever her age, who was not delighted by news of a stolen kiss. But he underestimated Miss McGee's delight. She broke into an uncontrollable laugh. "How dreadful," she said when she caught her breath. He could still hear her laughing as he climbed the stairs and shut his door.

SATURDAY

October 31

IN THE BACKYARD near the garden stood a basswood tree that held on to its leaves until late autumn and then released them all between the dusk and the dawn of one frosty night. During the night Miss McGee—her bedroom window open an inch—was awakened by the shower of large, leathery leaves and by the wind that sprang up and shuffled them like parchment.

In the morning Miles raked the basswood leaves into a pile as Miss McGee hung the week's wash on the clothesline. It was another sunny day, unseasonably warm. They heard geese calling and they looked up to see a flock of three dozen Canadas in the western sky. The geese flew over town and disappeared in the east, then returned much higher, heading west. In a few minutes they appeared a third time, flying undecidedly south in a wavering V. They were joined by a dozen more Canadas flying slightly below them and keeping to a V of their own, as if they wished not to merge and lose their identity. The call of the geese was a high-pitched bark, and for some time after they were out of sight Miles heard them on the southeast wind, yapping like a pack of airborne terriers.

When Miss McGee finished hanging out the wash, she

held open a large plastic bag and Miles filled it with basswood leaves. She said it was going to rain.

Miles looked at the sky. A flock of blackbirds was now crossing overhead.

"It's a clear day, Agatha. Not a cloud."

"But the wind is swinging to the east, and that means moisture. Goodness, Miles, look at the perspiration on your face. You really must try to get more exercise and reduce your weight. Are you between six two and six three? I would judge six three. Our health text says that a man of six three should weigh two hundred and five pounds. I daresay you're much heavier than that, Miles. Wayne Workman is your height, and I'm sure he's at least twenty pounds lighter than you."

"Wayne Workman is light of brain."

"Oh shush. You never have a good word to say about Wayne Workman. The Workmans are fine people."

"I like Thanatopsis."

Miss McGee giggled. "You and your nicknames. Do you call her Thanatopsis to her face?"

"I've called her nothing but Thanatopsis since she moved to town. The first few times I met her I kept forgetting what her real name was, and all I could remember was that it had a lot of vowels and *t-h*'s in it, and the word Thanatopsis always came to mind."

"Her name is Anna Thea."

"I know that now. But I like Thanatopsis better. It fits her."

"It does not fit her. Thanatopsis is Greek for 'view of death.' "

"I know what it's Greek for."

"Well, there's nothing fitting about it. Anna Thea Workman is young, and she has a lot of vitality. It's a dreadful name to call anyone. Sometimes I think, Miles, that you are careless where other people's feelings are concerned."

Lillian Kite came across the alley, carrying in one hand her bag of yarn and in the other a man's suit on a hanger. Lillian Kite, Imogene's mother, was a tall woman in her late sixties. She had a red face and white hair. She was the widow of Lyle Kite, who had been a ranger in the National Park Service, and the suit she carried was one of Lyle's uniforms. She handed it to Miles, who had asked to borrow it for tonight's Halloween party at the Workmans'.

"Isn't there a hat that goes with it?" he asked.

"Yes, there's a hat, but I had my hands full. You can pick up the hat tonight when you come to pick up Imogene."

"She goes with the uniform?"

"Well, aren't you planning to pick her up for the party? She has an invitation, too, you know. Don't tell me you're going with somebody else—not after what happened last night. She told me what happened, what you did. You romanced her. Agatha, did you know that Miles romanced Imogene last night?"

"Yes, I did. Here, sit down. I'm going in and put on the coffeepot."

Lillian Kite pulled a lawn chair out from the shade of the house and sat in the sunshine. Miles pulled another chair into the sun for Miss McGee and the chaise longue for himself. It was a flimsy chaise longue and it squeaked and teetered as he carefully lowered his weight onto it.

Lillian Kite began to knit. She was a constant knitter. She never sat down without taking up her needles. She had begun knitting seriously when her husband died—not after the funeral when time hung heavy on her hands, but immediately upon finding him dead. She had gotten up to make breakfast that morning several years ago and when she went back to the bedroom she found her husband tangled up in the bedclothes with a horrible expression on his face—his lower lip protruding and his eyes open. She called the doctor and the minister and the undertaker, and she picked up her needles and a ball of yarn and she went to work at high speed. When one by one the doctor and the minister and the undertaker came to the front door, she did not rise from her chair but said merely, "He's in there," pointing at the bedroom with her right-hand needle. She had been knitting ever since.

"Such weather, Miles, for this late in the year."

"Yes. Very nice. Agatha says it's going to rain."

"Is that so? Then it's going to rain. I don't know how she can tell, but she's always right about rain. She's very rain-conscious."

"She can tell by the wind."

"Miles, have you ever watched 'The Turning of Our Lives'?"

"No, I'm in school when it's on."

"Well, if you ever get a chance to see it, don't miss it. I tell you it's life to a T."

"Is that so?"

"I mean it's a story you'll never forget. It's so lifelike it makes you want to cry. And laugh too, of course, but mostly cry. This week in one installment—Wednesday, I think it was—they had a pregnant virgin and a recovery from epilepsy."

"Our coffee will be ready in a minute," said Miss McGee, coming out from the kitchen. She had put on a fresh apron and tied, against the breeze, a gauzy scarf under her chin.

"Agatha, I was telling Miles about 'The Turning of

Our Lives.' On Wednesday they had a pregnant virgin and a recovery from epilepsy."

"Oh shush, Lillian. That's a program for idiots. The only thing on TV I ever cared for, besides the news, was Perry Como. Miles, who will be at the Workmans' party tonight?"

"The same old faces. The Stevensons, the Gibbons—mostly faculty."

Lillian Kite said, "Superintendent Stevenson is knocking on death's door. Imogene says it's a bad valve in his heart. She told me the percentage of people who die of it. I forget, but it's a great many."

"Poor man," said Miss McGee.

"And the Gibbons! You know what they're saying about Stella Gibbon, don't you? Well, I guess it's more than rumor. Imogene says it's out and out infidelity. Doc Oppegaard is the one. Stella Gibbon is Doc Oppegaard's assistant, you know, and they say it's so *open*. What does Mr. Gibbon think, I wonder."

"Poor man," said Miss McGee.

A party of robins on their way south descended into the back yard and hopped about for a minute, then flew away.

With coffee, Miss McGee served cake and chokecherry jelly. It was noon before Lillian Kite went home and Miles carried the ranger uniform upstairs to his room.

Saturday afternoons Miles went walking. He called it hiking but it was not hiking. For one thing the figure he cut was not that of a hiker. He was an awkward man, pale and tall and tending to corpulence, and he owned no boots. For another thing, he walked not for the sake of getting somewhere but because walking helped him think. Long ago he had discovered that the gears of his memory and imagination were set in motion by putting one foot in front of the other, and the gears were slowed by sitting down or standing still. This explained why in the classroom he was more often on his feet than behind his desk, and it explained why he was so often seen strolling, strutting, trudging, stalking, or skimming the streets of Staggerford—the shape of his thoughts dictating the shape of his walk. Miles owned a car, an old Plymouth with a cracked windshield, but he never used it unless traveling out of town. During the past five summers he had driven the Plymouth to the Grand Canyon, to the Ozarks, to New York City, to Banff, and to graduate school in Colorado, but during the school year it was seldom out of Miss McGee's garage.

Today as he walked, his thoughts were on school, and because he could visualize his lesson plans as far ahead as Christmas, his walk was a glide. A week of book reports, two weeks of *Othello*, a week of Robert Frost, two weeks of composition, then Christmas. In his old tweed jacket with the leather elbow patches he glided down Main Street and into the Hub Cafe, where he sat on a stool and told Beverly Bingham he wanted a cup of coffee with cream and a piece of blueberry pie.

Beverly said, "God, Mr. Pruitt, I was just thinking about you. I've got something to tell you."

Until his conversation with Miss McGee last night, Miles had not realized that Beverly was part Indian; but now in the Hub he studied her for vestiges of the Chippewa nation and he found them in her hair, her complexion, her voice, and in the shape of her face. But in Beverly each Indian trait seemed to have been softened, modified, improved upon. Her long hair was almost black and almost straight, but not quite. It came together under her chin and framed her oval face. The rose tinge in her cheeks, which Miles had assumed was a perpetual blush, was actually a hint of the copper complexion so common in Sandhill. Miles had long been fascinated by Indians' voices, which despite their high and even pitch seemed to be emanating from someplace farther back in the throat and deeper in the soul than other people's voices. Why, when an Indian spoke, did he sound farther away than he actually was? Beverly's voice, too, had that high-pitched, distant quality, but it carried more expression than the typical monotone of the reservation.

Beverly wore the Hub uniform, the orange slacks and the orange zippered top with the vertical blue stripe over the left breast. She was the only one on duty during this quiet hour of the afternoon, and after she served Miles she came around the counter and sat next to him on a stool.

"You know who's home, Mr. Pruitt? Greg Olson. He's home from the air force for two weeks, and he was in here last night after the game and he asked if he could take me home."

"Yes, I saw him at the game."

"God, is he good-looking. He's gotten better looking since he went into the air force."

"It's the uniform."

"He asked if he could take me home, and I was so surprised I said no. But how could I say yes? For one thing I had driven the pickup to work and I had to take that home, and for another thing I don't want any boy to see where I live." She lit a cigarette. "Mr. Pruitt, can you imagine what it's like to be ashamed of where you live? You've never seen our place in the gulch, have you?"

Miles admired Beverly's profile as she blew smoke across the counter. Was that an Indian nose? "No, I've seen your mailbox on the highway, but I've never seen your farm."

"Very few people have, thank God. It's between the highway and the river, and it can't be seen from the highway because it's in the gulch and it can't be seen from the river because of the woods. There are a few people from town who drive out and come into the yard to buy chickens, and whenever they do I'm so ashamed I don't want to go to the door. In the summer we have that produce stand on the highway, you know, and that's different. I like selling tomatoes and squash and onions. But to have people coming right into the yard— God, I can't stand that." Beverly, a beginning smoker, was handling her cigarette like a stick of lead. "All our buildings are leaning over like they were about to collapse into the river. I don't know what's holding them up. And the house. The house is a two-story place that hasn't been kept up, and we've shut off the upstairs because all the windows are broken up there and birds fly in and out. And the yard, God, you should see the yard. Except I wouldn't want you to. It's a dump. It's full of rusty cars that my dad used to bring home, and do you know what's living in the upholstery of the cars?"

Miles shook his head.

"Rats."

Miles frowned into his coffee.

"We shoot rats with a twenty-two rifle, my mother and I. Rats kill chickens."

A long silence, then: "I'd like to marry Greg Olson "

"Don't be stupid."

"What's stupid about that? I'm old enough. I've been old enough to quit school for two years. I don't know what I'm doing in school anyway."

"It's stupid to tie yourself down to a husband at eighteen. Your life is just beginning. What you have to do is get yourself enrolled in a college next fall and get out and see what the world is all about."

"Who says?"

"I do."

"Mr. Pruitt, your trouble is you never married and now it's too late and you don't want anybody else to have any fun either."

"I'll have some more coffee."

"What's the matter? Am I getting too personal? Does the truth hurt?"

"Beverly, the truth is that I am by nature a cautious man, and if I marry, which is still a possibility despite my extreme age, I will not marry someone I met the night before the wedding, as you seem to be threatening to do with Greg Olson—whom I remember as the numskull of last year's senior class."

"I didn't just meet him. I've known him for years."

"How well?"

Beverly got up and poured Miles more coffee. "Don't talk to me about college," she said, hoping he would.

"You've got the second-highest grade average in the senior class. If you don't go to college you'll be sorry all your life."

Beverly sat down again. "For college you need more than grades. You need to have all your shit together. You need to be from someplace better than I'm from."

Coach Gibbon came into the Hub. He was wearing a red jacket that said "Coach" on the front and "Staggerford" on the back. Beverly stood up and Coach took her stool. He ordered coffee.

"Nice game last night," said Miles.

"Aw, that goddamn Fremling. I never should have had him in there at center. If it wasn't for him we'd've won. But who else did I have?"

"What's so bad about a tie with Owl Brook? They haven't been beaten for a year and a half. If I were coach, I'd be proud of a six-six tie with Owl Brook."

Coach Gibbon had a long face with dark brows and a long, pointed nose. He turned to Miles and studied him closely from two or three angles, the way a woodpecker examines bark for bugs. "Are you crazy? You'd be proud of a tie? A tie proves absolutely nothing!" He turned away in disgust. "I'd rather lose than tie!"

"Let's talk about something else," said Miles. "We've never been able to agree on the subject of athletics."

"No, I'd like to hear you explain what's good about a six-six tie. A tie proves absolutely nothing, except that Lee Fremling is a fat-ass weakling."

"Look, Owl Brook has been the best team in this conference since I was in high school, and if I were the coach of a team that played the Owls to a tie, I would take it as a sign that my team was equal to the Owls. And I would be very proud of my players. And I would tell them so."

"That's why you aren't made of the stuff coaches are made of."

Beverly served Coach Gibbon his coffee, rang up his money, then took the stool on the other side of Miles. She lit another cigarette.

"Let's talk about wrestling," said Miles. "What does your wrestling team look like for this winter?"

"Looks good. I've got Lawrence Winters at a hundred ninety pounds, and Willy Samuels at a hundred eighty, and Clyde Albertson at one seventy, and Bill Clifford at one sixty, and John Innes at one fifty, and Jack Worley at one forty, and Charlie Zeney at one thirty, and Doug Smith at one twenty, and some little pipsqueak of a freshman at one ten. Now, what I'd like to do is take ten pounds off Lawrence Winters and wrestle him at a hundred eighty, and take ten off Willy Samuels and wrestle him at one seventy, and take ten off Clyde Albertson

and wrestle him at one sixty, and take ten off Bill Clif
ford and wrestle him at one fifty, and take ten off John
Innes and wrestle him at one forty, and take ten off Jack
Worley and wrestle him at one thirty, and take ten off
Charlie Zeney and wrestle him at one twenty, and take
ten off Doug Smith and wrestle him at one ten, and take
ten off that little pipsqueak of a freshman and wrestle
him at a hundred."

"You're always trying to take weight off your wrestlers. I can't understand that."

"It's the name of the game. If you take off ten pounds
you can wrestle in a lower weight division."

"But what's the advantage of wrestling in a division
below your normal weight?"

"Use your head. The advantage is that when you lose
ten pounds you don't normally lose any muscle. All you
lose is fluid and fat, and in the lower division you might
be wrestling an opponent who *is* wrestling at his normal
weight and who hasn't lost fluid and fat and—zingo!—
he's pinned. Fluid and fat never win. Muscles win."

"Then how come we don't win more wrestling
matches?"

"Because all the other coaches take ten pounds off
their wrestlers too. Balls, if I didn't know any more
about sports than you do, I'd be ashamed to open my
mouth."

"That's why we're now going to move on to a different subject. Are you and Stella going to the Workmans'
party tonight?"

"I'll bet you were never much of an athlete, Miles.
I'll bet your fluid and fat go back to your high school
days." (Conversations with Coach Gibbon seldom took
an unexpected turn. They proceeded and backed up
along the single track that had been running through
his mind since he began coaching.)

"As a matter of fact," said Miles, "I played on the Staggerford football team for two years."

"You're kidding."

"You can look it up in the Stag yearbooks from the fifties. I won two letters."

"You're kidding. What did you play?"

"Guard. I was right guard for two years, but I wasn't very aggressive. I was sort of the Lee Fremling type. I think if I had ever played a whole game I might have been pretty good, but it took me half the game to get indignant at my opponent and by that time the coach always replaced me. What I really liked much better was basketball."

"You played basketball?"

"No, I never made the team, but I tried out every year. I think I could have been pretty good at basketball. I had the size and the endurance. I wasn't quick, but my wind was good."

Coach Gibbon obviously didn't believe any of this. He shook his head and sipped his coffee.

Two women entered the Hub and sat at the table in the front window, where they could watch shoppers pass on the street. Beverly served them coffee.

"Are you and Stella going to Workmans' tonight?" Miles asked once more.

Coach nodded. "You?"

"Yes, unless my toothache gets worse. I've had a toothache off and on since last night. I was eating a raspberry sundae—"

"A raspberry sundae—you were at Stevensons'."

"That's right."

"How can you stand going to Stevensons'?"

"They're very hospitable."

"They're spooks. She's a prude and he's no more superintendent than my dog. He's an absolute zero. Did you know the school board cut my athletic budget by twenty percent and he never went to bat for me?"

"He's not well."

"Then what's he doing in that job? I tell you, talking to that man is just like playing to a six-six tie. You don't win, you don't lose, you don't settle a damn thing. He doesn't say yes, no, or kiss my ass. He just looks out his window and says, 'See my secretary about it.' Now, what right has that old battle-ax of a secretary got making the superintendent's decisions? She's got all the power of a superintendent and what is she?—a former shoe-store clerk. Did you know that, Miles—she was a shoe-store clerk before she was hired at school?"

"Of course. I've known her all my life."

Coach Gibbon crumpled his paper napkin and threw it at the wall. He was full of the smoldering anger that always burned hot and clouded his vision for several days after a lost game. Beyond that, he was said to be losing his wife. "If I was the school board I would fire Stevenson so fast it would make your head swim, and I would put Wayne Workman in his place, and we'd all be better off."

"Wayne Workman?"

"Yes, Wayne Workman."

"I don't think I could work for Wayne Workman."

"What do you mean? You already work for him."

"Well, I don't think of myself as working for the principal. It's the superintendent who hires and fires and signs checks."

"That may be, but when old Stevenson steps down Wayne Workman is going to step up."

"What makes you think Wayne Workman wants to be superintendent?"

"Balls, where have you been? Everybody knows Wayne Workman is just biding his time until he can take over old Stevenson's job. What do you think keeps him in a dump like Staggerford? With his talent, he could be running a lot bigger high school than ours."

"I don't think I could work for Wayne Workman."

"The day is coming when you damn well better work for Wayne Workman, or pack your bags! He's our next superintendent or my name isn't Coach Gibbon!"

Coach Gibbon, whose name was Herbert, finished his coffee and stood up. "I hate ending the season with a tie! It's a hell of a nagging feeling to end a season with a tie!"

He left, rattling the glass in the door as he slammed it.

Beverly, at Miles's side, said, "Do you know what I like about Greg?"

"About who?"

"About Greg Olson."

"No, what do you like?"

"He's in the air force."

"Why is it that girls think so much of a uniform? Why does a uniform make a man seem anything but uniform?"

"It isn't the uniform. It's the travel. A guy in the air force is probably going to travel all over, right? I mean, if there's anything in this world I could use, it's a little travel."

"Me too." Miles stood up and buttoned his tweed jacket. "I'm going hiking."

"Where?"

"Out along the river."

"How far?"

"I don't know. Out past the cemetery."

"As far as my place?"

"I doubt it."

"I get off work at three. We could meet out there in

the gulch and we could talk."

"What about?"

"About my future. Plus whatever you want to talk about. But especially about my future."

"I don't know, Beverly. I've got to get back to town and get ready for a costume party. We'll talk in school on Monday."

Miles left the Hub. Beverly stood at the door and watched him until he was out of sight. She was certain that she could not wait until Monday.

The Badbattle River flowed west from Staggerford, past the cemetery (one mile from town), past the gulch in which the Bingham farm was hidden (two miles), past Pike Park (three miles), and across the boundary of the Sandhill Indian Reservation (four miles).

Along the south bank of the river was a footpath already old when Zebulon Pike walked it in 1806 and described it in his diary. So many and bloody were the skirmishes along this path in the nineteenth century—the Sioux trying and failing to defend it first against the white man and next against the Chippewas—that the Minnesota Historical Society could not be certain which battle the river had been named for. Now, of course, all was peaceful. The traffic had moved from the path to U.S. Highway 4—two lanes of concrete running parallel to the river and leading west to Fargo and east to Duluth—leaving the path to birdwatchers and families on picnics and strollers like Miles.

Miles went home for his binoculars, then followed the river path out of town. As he walked he thought about Coach Gibbon and Wayne Workman. Coach and Wayne were close friends of each other and of no one else. Coach's time on the Staggerford staff went back seven years. Wayne's time went back a little more than

one year. Wayne had come to town and swept Thanatopsis off her feet (Miss McGee's term for it) and
married her. As principal of Staggerford High, he main-
tained a high profile (Wayne's term for it) and, according to Coach, dreamed of being superintendent. He was
both efficient and officious. He got things done, and in
doing them he got into people's hair. Strange, thought
Miles, that I didn't realize Wayne had designs on the
superintendency—but no more strange than my not
realizing a year ago that he had designs on Thanatopsis.

Coach Gibbon was officious too, but without being
efficient. His won-lost record was such that he wouldn't
have lasted very long in a sports-minded community like
Owl Brook or Berrington. Lucky for Coach Gibbon and
his kind, thought Miles, that there were towns like Staggerford to harbor unsuccessful coaches. Staggerford was
used to losing.

How did coaches in Owl Brook, Berrington and
Gopher Prairie handle the problem of fluid and fat?
Miles knew of at least three methods employed by
Coach Gibbon to rid his wrestlers of fluid and fat. For
several hours before a wrestling meet, Coach had his
athletes run, he had them wear long underwear and
overcoats to class, and he had them spit into tin cans
Coach Gibbon had read in a coaching journal that a boy
jogging steadily for an hour could lose as much as five
pounds, that a boy sweating in class all day could lose a
pound and a half, and a boy spitting until he was dried
out lost whatever the spit in the can weighed.

Only once had Miles seen Coach impose all three
methods on one wrestler at one time, producing a sight
so remarkable that Miles never forgot it. This had occurred several years ago, and the wrestler's name was
Flaskerude. Young Flaskerude came to school one morning and found Coach Gibbon waiting for him at his

locker. Coach had just learned that the Gopher Prairie team, whom they were to wrestle that afternoon, was going to forfeit the 170-pound match for lack of a wrestler in that division. All that was needed for Staggerford to win that particular match was to have a 170-pounder step into the ring and step out again. But Staggerford's 170-pounder was home with the flu. Coach Gibbon had two boys at 160 and two boys at 180. First he considered putting ten pounds on one of his 160-pounders by feeding him bananas (his coaching journal said that five bananas, eaten fast, put on one pound) but neither boy could be talked into eating fifty bananas. So it was up to Flaskerude, the weaker wrestler of the two heavier boys, to come down from 180. Coach Gibbon decided that instead of running laps in the gym, Flaskerude would run through the corridors of the school, where he would have to climb steps with each lap. And so all morning poor Flaskerude, clad in long underwear, a sweatsuit, and an overcoat, loped and jogged and walked and finally stumbled through the corridors of Staggerford High, spitting into a can clutched to his heaving breast. And it didn't work. When the Gopher Prairie team arrived, Flaskerude had lost only eight pounds, though it was agreed that even if he had lost ten he wouldn't have had the strength to step into the ring and step out again. The next day while Flaskerude was home in bed with acute exhaustion, his eight lost pounds, in the form of perspiration odor, lingered in the stairwells of the school.

Since graduating, Flaskerude had gone, at his normal weight of 180, into insurance.

Evergreen Cemetery was on high ground. It offered long vistas in all directions. It was surrounded by a new fence erected to keep out snowmobilers, and Miles, climbing up from the riverbank, had to go around to the gate facing the highway. He passed under the wrought-iron arch and left the gate open out of superstition. He followed a row of tall cedars to his mother's grave.

PRUITT, said the polished gray stone at the center of the four-grave plot. AMY, said the small stone at the foot of the only grave occupied. To Miles, Amy Pruitt was the definition of the word "helpmeet." For most of her married life—besides leaving the impression that homemaking was a joy—Amy Pruitt had been her husband's bookkeeper in the Staggerford Creamery; and after her husband was stricken with sclerosis and confined to the house, she ran the business herself until she found a buyer who suited her—a buttermaker with a large downpayment and an honest reputation and a respect for dairy farmers. She had always been the decision maker in the family. She had directed the choir at St. Isidore's. She had suffered a fatal blood clot in her brain while Miles was away at college. After her death, the Pruitt sons, Miles and Dale, transferred their father, who was failing fast, to a Benedictine nursing home in Duluth, and they sold the house.

The Pruitt plot was the highest point in the cemetery. Miles looked south across the highway to the flat farmland. Miss McGee had been right about the weather. Strands of cloud were advancing across the sky, and under them strands of shadow moved across the prairie. The stubble fields were gold where the sun shone and gray where it didn't.

He looked back east, the way he had come. Showing above the distant trees were the grain elevator, the water tower (STAGGER, it said from this angle), the belfry atop the city hall, and the spire of St. Isidore's.

He looked north across the river: woods and more

farms and on the horizon a smudge of smoke from the power plant in Berrington.

He looked west. The land dropped away from the cemetery and into the gulch, then rose again beyond the gulch and climbed to the forested hills of the Sandhill Reservation.

Miles moved along the path from his mother's grave to Fred Vandergar's, and found it still unmarked. Fred Vandergar had been one of his colleagues at the high school, a teacher of bookkeeping and typing. Last December, at the age of fifty-eight, Fred had lost a lung. In January he had lost part of his lower bowel. From that time until his death in June, Miles had seen him only twice.

The first time was in February, when Fred had come home from his bowel operation and Miles, at the request of Superintendent Stevenson, took him a sick-leave form that required his signature. The superintendent was afraid to go, and his secretary, Delia Fritz, didn't have time. It was a dark winter afternoon. The sky was dark, the deep snow was dark, the Vandergar house was dark.

"Fred's not feeling well," said Mrs. Vandergar, answering Miles's knock at the door. She was the only faculty wife whose first name Miles had never learned. The Vandergars were very private people—childless and friendless—and Miles had never been in their house before.

"If I could just get Fred's signature on this form, Mrs. Vandergar."

"All right, come in. You may put your overshoes on this paper."

She showed Miles into the living room, where one small lamp burned. Then she went to the bedroom to rouse Fred.

Presently Fred appeared, hobbling carefully and wearing a bathrobe and doing his best to smile. His medicine had caused most of his hair to fall out, and what remained was standing on end. He seemed to have lost height as well as weight, and his handshake was feeble.

"The superintendent has asked me to give you his best wishes," said Miles.

"Do you take cream in your coffee?" asked Mrs. Vandergar.

"Yes, please."

She went to the kitchen, and Miles and Fred sat down together near the one small lamp. After a few words about basketball and faculty meetings, Fred put his hand over his remaining lung and said, "We're not sure it's cleared up in here. They want me to go to cobalt." Then he put his hand on his belly and said, "I'm waiting for word on my liver, too. If it's in my liver, then it will be no use going to cobalt . . . It's a terrible thing, this waiting to hear . . ."

Miles was speechless. The English language seemed to contain not a single word for him to utter at this moment.

Mrs. Vandergar brought Miles a cup of lukewarm coffee and a dry cookie. "Fred tires easily," she said.

Taking this as a cue, Miles drank the coffee in three quick swallows and stood up to leave. Fred tottered after him to the front door. His wife followed.

"Thank the superintendent for his good wishes. One can always hope." Fred's voice was hollow and hopeless.

"Be careful on the step," said Mrs. Vandergar. "It's icy."

Miles nodded, and as he opened the door he felt Fred's hand on his shoulder.

"It's a terrible thing, this waiting to hear about my

liver, Miles." His eyes were dry and there was no emotion in his face, but he did not remove his hand from Miles's shoulder until he was satisfied that Miles understood his terror.

Miles took the man in his arms and embraced him tightly. This act surprised Miles as much as Fred, but it was the only way to express what he felt. Then he embraced Mrs. Vandergar—awkwardly, for she was very short and standing behind her husband. Then he hurried away, and when he got home he found in his pocket the sick-leave form he had forgotten to ask Fred to sign.

The following week, the doctor told Fred that instead of going to cobalt he should trust in the natural ability of his body to throw off the disease. Fred took this to mean that he was a goner. He was right. He lost more hair and more weight and never left the house but once before he died. His only venture into society was to attend his retirement party on the last day of May.

It was a difficult party to plan for. If the social committee, chaired by Thanatopsis Workman, scheduled the party for late May (the customary time for honoring retirees) the guest of honor might be dead. On the other hand, if they held it earlier they would be calling attention to the precariousness of Fred's condition: No one could pretend in March, say, that Fred was not dying, and Thanatopsis had hosted enough social functions to know that any party lacking pretense and make-believe might as well be called off. She set the date for the last of May.

The party was to be held in the private dining room of the Hub Cafe, and Miles dreaded it. The night before the party this is what he wrote in his journal:

Tomorrow I will take each of my classes to the river bank for a year-end picnic (or, in lesson-plan jargon, a field trip). My students are eighteen and they outgrew picnics in the sixth grade, but like all graduating seniors a kind of year-end lunacy has made them silly and twelve again. Each student will bring along a short poem to read and I will supply the pop. We will have a good time because the weatherman promises sunshine and the riverbank is abloom with crocuses and we will all be full of the vacation spirit. We will do a lot of laughing and inevitably someone will be pushed into the river.

Then after school I will go to the dim back room of the Hub for Fred Vandergar's "party." I fear it will be a wake for a live corpse, too solemn to be comfortable; or it will be a staged attempt at jollity, too phony to be happy.

Life. The light and the dark. Those 18-year-olds sitting on the riverbank in the sun. That dying man in the back room of the Hub. And me standing (in more ways than age) exactly between them. Me, without my students' optimism and without Fred's despair. Without their fidgets and without his courage. Without their youth and without his cancer. Tomorrow, halfway between the light and the dark, I will end my eleventh year of teaching.

The next day it was Miles himself who was pushed into the river, but keeping his balance, along with his temper, he got wet only up to his knees. It happened last hour and he was able to go straight home and change. Then he went to the Hub.

Fred and his wife were escorted to the party by Thanatopsis Workman, and word of Fred's approach spread through the Hub like the news in Poe's story of the approaching Red Death. When Fred walked through the door of the dining room, the faculty was horrified. Though he still breathed, the process of corruption seemed to have begun. His eyes had sunk deep in their sockets and the cords stood out in his neck. He tried to be sociable and he succeeded, but at some obviously terrible cost to his stamina, for in his advance to the head table he had to sit three times on three different chairs.

Some of the faculty gingerly sidestepped Fred entirely, preferring to study him from a distance while pretending to be in conversation with someone else. Some shook his hand, backing away even as they did so. Some went to the rest room until dinner was served, and only when Fred was occupied with his food did they come out of hiding.

Superintendent Stevenson strove valiantly against his dread of death. Supported by his wife on the right and by his secretary Delia Fritz on the left, he approached Fred, gave him the most timorous of smiles, and said, "It's great seeing you again, Fred."

"You too." Fred at this point was halfway to the head table and being helped up from a chair by Miles and Thanatopsis. There was a long silence, during which the superintendent cleared his throat and tried to think of more to say. Miles in a clumsy attempt to help him said, "Mr. Stevenson, I don't believe Fred has heard the name of the smallest fish in Hawaii."

"Humuhumunukunukuapuaa," blurted the superintendent, relieved that Miles had thought of it. During Christmas vacation the Stevensons had flown to Hawaii and brought back this memorized word, which they uttered whenever anyone asked about their trip.

"Humuhumunukunukuapuaa," echoed Mrs. Stevenson.

"That's the name of the smallest fish in Hawaii,' Miles explained to Fred.

"Where?" said Fred.

"Hawaii," said Miles. "You see, the name is longer than the fish. That's the funny part of it."

Stevenson held his thumb and forefinger about three inches apart to indicate the length of the fish. Or the word.

"Hawaii?" said a waitress pushing into the room a cart of salad bowls. "Who's been to Hawaii?"

"I have!" said Stevenson, and he made his getaway with the waitress, walking beside her to the head table and teaching her to say humuhumunukunukuapuaa

After dinner, Superintendent Stevenson took his place at the lectern and from notes supplied him by Delia Fritz he reviewed Fred's career: four years in college, four years in the army, four years in the office-machine business, twenty-seven years in the classroom

Then Thanatopsis, representing the faculty, gave Fred a watch.

It was Fred's turn to speak. He remained seated at his place and delivered a short, surprisingly sensible speech, concluding thus:

"I was a teacher at the best possible time. Public-school teaching wasn't much of a profession, at least for a man, before my time, and it doesn't look like it's going to be much of a profession after my time. But *during* my time it was good. Before my time, the majority of teachers were women, most of them underpaid, over worked, and undertrained. And now as my time comes to an end, the majority of students are falling into a mood of sullen defiance. The majority of students, though they graduate all right, have no interest in learning, except learning the things they suspect their elders might not approve of. And the majority of teachers are shifting their attention from teaching to collective bargaining. But my time was a good time. During most of my teaching years, teaching was a good profession. Most of my colleagues were conscientious, and so were most of my students. I saw my students go out and become stenographers and office managers, and some of them worked themselves into a business of their own. I saw new respect for education among the legislators in St. Paul. I saw federal money come in and buy electric typewriters for my classroom. I did my best. I have no regrets. Thanks for the watch."

At that moment, as though a class bell were calling them away, the faculty vanished from the dining room, leaving Thanatopsis and Miles to help the Vandergars home.

The next day Fred was hospitalized. The next week he was dead.

Today the outline of his grave was still visible where the sod had been disturbed.

Before leaving the cemetery, Miles again studied the sky. Now a heavy cloudbank was moving over the prairie like a sheet of slate. When its forward edge put out the sun, the wind doubled its force, blowing a flock of blackbirds out of a cedar tree and causing Miles to shiver in his tweed jacket.

He left the cemetery and descended the hill to the path along the river. He had intended to return to town, but here at the bottom of the riverbank the wind was not so strong. He felt warmer. He stepped out onto a large rock in the river and looked upstream. He looked downstream. He looked at his watch. Ten to three. He followed the path downstream.

The gulch was a mile beyond the cemetery. It was a steep-walled ravine that ran perpendicular to the Badbattle and emptied into it two nameless creeks, one from the north and one from the south. When Miles reached the creek flowing in from the south he sat on a rock and studied, with his binoculars, a flock of grosbeaks in a bare tree across the river. The tree was a birch, standing at the point where the creek from the north joined the river. The grosbeaks were impervious to the gusts of wind ruffling their feathers. Grosbeaks liked being chilly. This flock of nine, perched one above the other on nine different branches and facing into the wind, had just arrived from their summer in the Arctic. They were waiting in this birch to see if it was going to rain (a sign they had flown too far south) or snow (in which case they would settle down until spring). One of the birds turned and looked directly into Miles's line of vision. It was a male, with bright yellow chevrons on his wings and bright yellow eyebrows.

"I knew you'd come." The voice startled Miles and he turned suddenly about. He saw Beverly coming toward him along the creek, pushing aside the low-hanging branches of the bare aspen trees. Over her Hub uniform she was wearing an old checkered jacket, a man's wool jacket, probably her father's. It had buttonholes but no buttons. It had been worn so long that the checks (red and white? black and red?) had become gray and off-gray.

"What were you looking at?" she asked. She sat near him on the trunk of a fallen elm. Since their visit in the Hub, she had applied something chartreuse and oily to her eyelids. He wanted to tell her to leave her eyes alone. They were large and blue and couldn't be improved upon. Keeping her hair from falling in front of them was the only attention they needed.

"I was looking at grosbeaks in that birch over there They're gone now."

She did not look at the birch but kept her eyes on Miles. "I never notice birds," she said.

"This is a good place for birdwatching. I've even seen eagles out here circling over the gulch."

"Yeah? So what do you do when you see them?—just see them? That's why I've never understood birdwatching. All it amounts to is watching birds."

"They're interesting."

"The only birds I ever notice are chickens. Our place is overrun with chickens. Listen."

Miles heard, over the wind, the distant hum of traffic on Highway 4.

"I thought maybe we could hear our chickens from here, but I guess not. They're always clucking like crazy. Our place isn't very far back there along the creek." She reached into the pocket of her orange uniform and pulled out a flip-top box of Marlboros. She put one in her mouth and offered one to Miles. He declined.

"I haven't been smoking very long." She lit up. "I started when I got my job at the Hub. That's two weeks ago. I work Friday nights and Saturdays and Sundays. Everybody that comes in lights up, especially the kids, so I thought what the hell."

Miles drew up his binoculars and watched a crow land on the opposite bank and poke his beak into the sand.

"I don't ever come down here to the river anymore, the brush has grown up so thick between here and the house. When my sister was home we used to come down here and fish, but I really don't care for fishing."

"I don't either," said Miles, "but I like to watch water move."

They watched the surface of the Badbattle sliding west toward Pike Park, toward the reservation, toward its confluence with the Red River of the North. Mingling with the Red, this water would then flow through

Fargo and up to Winnipeg and from there it would angle northeast and divide itself into dozens of channels across Ontario and come together once more before emptying itself into Hudson Bay.

"Why?" said Beverly.

"Why what?"

"Why do you like to watch water move?"

Miles shrugged, his eyes on a ripple of water gurgling below a midstream rock.

"I can't figure out guys like you. There must be girls you could be out with right now instead of sitting here watching water move."

"Is that what you wanted to talk to me about, my relationship with women?"

"Why not?"

"It would be dull talk, I'm afraid."

Beverly picked a strip of bark off the elm and set it adrift toward Hudson Bay. "I just want to talk. You know, there aren't too many teachers a girl can talk to. I mean about things other than school."

"How about Mrs. Workman?"

"No, I hardly know her. I never took home ec. Anyway, she's a woman. Don't you know a girl, if she's got a choice, would rather talk to a man?"

"Is that so?"

"Oh, come on now. Don't play dumb."

A cold gust of wind shivered the water. Beverly threw her cigarette into the river and pulled her jacket together at the throat.

"Mr. Pruitt, could I really make it in college?"

"Of course."

"I don't mean the academic part of it. I know I could handle that. I've known real stupes who went to college and made it. I'm talking about the social part of it."

"That's the easiest part."

"But I can't imagine myself on a college campus."

"Why?"

She took a deep breath. "I don't know. I just can't. There are reasons why I don't fit into places other girls fit into."

"What reasons?"

"And then there's the whole money part of it. What do I do for money? All I get at the Hub is minimum wage, and it seems like everything we make on the farm goes to feed the chickens."

"There's money these days for anybody who wants to go to college—grants, loans, scholarships, work-study. Start out at the junior college in Berrington. You'll get by cheap. In fact, you might get by free. Your father was Chippewa, wasn't he?"

"Half."

"Then there's federal money for you. All you need. Tuition, books, room and board. Maybe even spending money. We'll look into it and see."

There was a noise behind them in the brush. "Oh God!" said Beverly, and she jumped up and darted down the path toward the cemetery. Miles stood, ready to run, as soon as he saw what he was running from. Something was snapping sticks and kicking through the fallen leaves along the creek. He expected to see a bear. Hunters told of seeing bears in the gulch.

It was the Bonewoman. She was striding forward like a bear, heedless of the spongy wetness of the creek that covered her shoes, heedless of the saplings and vines that hung in her way.

And she was heedless of Miles. She passed him and stopped at the fallen elm and looked down the path where Beverly had run.

Miles said, "Hello, Mrs. Bingham."

The Bonewoman made no reply except a noise of

83

disgust like a snort, which she directed toward the river. She turned and re-entered the heavy brush, and Miles stood listening to the splash and crackling of her disappearance.

This was his first look at the woman in daylight. He was struck by her relatively youthful face. He had imagined that anyone as legendary as the Bonewoman had to be old, but this woman was not old. Her face was not lined by age. The only mark of having lived a lifetime in the gulch was a hint of desperation in her eyes. And twigs in her hair.

Miles set off down the path toward the cemetery, expecting to find Beverly waiting for him, but she had disappeared somewhere in the thick undergrowth of the riverbank. He was amazed by the acuteness of his disappointment. He lingered for a time at the bend of the river where he last saw her, then he continued along the path toward town. He heard the mournful call of geese, but light was dying in the sky and he could not see them. He hoped they were not the same confused flock he and Miss McGee had seen that morning.

Miles put on Lyle Kite's green ranger uniform—the percale shirt stiff as canvas, the gabardine pants with hanger creases at the knees, the short jacket not coming together over Miles's stomach—and he walked across the alley and called for Imogene.

Lillian Kite, clutching her knitting and trailing a ball of yarn, opened the door and said, "Imogene will be ready in a minute. My, if you don't look nice in Lyle's uniform. But I see it's a bit snug on you."

"What's Imogene wearing?" Miles asked, sucking in his belly.

"I'm not allowed to say. She wants to surprise you Come and sit down."

He sat on the arm of the couch, the tight pants allowing him to bend no further.

Lillian took her place in the swivel chair before the TV set and spoke over the sound of a commercial for contraceptive cat food. "It's a shame that uniform doesn't get more use. I really should contact some of the younger rangers and see if they might not like to buy it from me. Lyle wore it only once, and it's in such handsome condition. I can remember the argument we had when it came to buying that uniform." Her eyes were neither on Miles nor on the TV but on her speedy needles. "It was shortly before Lyle retired and he could have gotten along with the uniforms he had, though they were beginning to look a little threadbare, and he said, 'Lil'—he always called me Lil—'Lil,' he said, 'I've got half a notion to splurge and buy myself a new uniform for my last six months of work.' I said, 'No, we can make do with what you have,' and it was true, we could have got along very nicely with what he had in his closet. I think he had three uniforms at the time and although two of them had patches on the seat where he carried his billfold, he could have made do very nicely. But he said, 'Lil, what about the retirement party?' and of course I could see his point. All the rangers from this region and their wives were going to give this retirement party for him and two other retirees at the Sheraton Ritz in St. Paul, and it was customary for the retirees to wear their uniforms to the party. So I said, 'I guess you're right, Lyle, I guess we'll go and invest in another uniform.' And we did, and it was a mistake. I mean not that we could tell ahead of time, but it turned out to be a mistake in the long run because those last six months he never wore that new uniform to work lest he have an accident with it of some kind—tear it or get ink on it, you know—and it wasn't until the day of the retirement party that he put it on for the first time. He put it on and we set out for St. Paul in a snowstorm and we got stranded. It was the twentieth day of March and there was a blizzard, and we had to stay overnight in St. Cloud. We got a motel room there in St. Cloud and Lyle called the Sheraton Ritz in St. Paul and told them he was stranded. Well, the director of rangers was there from the Department of the Interior, and he read his speech to Lyle over the phone. It was a handsome tribute to all the men who were retiring but especially to Lyle because he had been with the Park Service longer than the others. It was *such* a handsome tribute, although I've always said that it wasn't undeserved. Lyle never took a day of sick leave in his life. I was sitting beside him on the bed in that motel room, and Lyle held the phone so I could hear the speech too. Later the director sent him the speech in the mail. I've got it here in my knitting bag. Would you like to read it, Miles?"

"Yes, I would."

"I read it again last Sunday afternoon. On Sundays I get to thinking about Lyle, and that's when I usually read it. Agatha's read it, and some of the folks at the Senior Citizens' Club have read it, and they all say it's a handsome tribute to Lyle." She took a sheaf of papers from her bag and handed them to Miles.

"It's long," he said.

"Yes, that's the only fault I find with it. I wish it weren't quite so long. The next day when we paid for our motel room, the phone bill was five dollars and a half."

Imogene stepped into the room. She was dressed in a cap and gown. Perfect, thought Miles. What could be more fitting for Imogene, the walking encyclopedia?

"Isn't she handsome?" said her mother.

"Yes," said Miles. Handsome was the word for her.

She was too sexless to be pretty, but the black cap and gown accentuated the bone-white pallor of her angular face and made her as handsome as young Abraham Lincoln. He would have to be careful tonight not to call her Abe.

Imogene said, "Pruitt, must you always be so early?"

"I like to be on time." He looked at his watch. "The party starts at eight, and it's five to."

"Anything up to half an hour late is considered on time, Pruitt. Don't you know anything about etiquette?"

"Very little, I'm afraid."

"Well, anything up to half an hour late is considered on time, but anything *before* the appointed time—even a single minute—is downright gouchy."

"Downright what?"

"Downright gouchy."

"Downright what?" said her mother, pausing in her knitting.

"Gouchy," said Imogene, clearly irritated.

"You mean gauche," said Miles. "It's pronounced *gosh,* with a long *O.*"

"I mean gouchy, Pruitt. It means crude."

"My, my, you ack-comedians," said her mother.

"What did you call us?" said Imogene.

"Ack-comedians. It means scholars."

"You're pronouncing it wrong," said Imogene. "You mean academicians."

"Academicians? I always thought it was ack-comedians. Who's right, Miles?"

"I love ack-comedians," said Miles. "If it means scholars it's perfect."

"Pruitt, you're impossible. Let's get going."

Mrs. Kite handed Miles her husband's ranger hat. It had a round, flat brim wide as a pizza platter.

Outside, in the wind, Imogene discovered that Miles had not brought his car.

"But we always walk," he told her. "It's only three blocks."

"Pruitt, are you out of your mind? I'm wearing a cap and gown."

"So what? It's dark." He took her hand and pulled her along the street.

Here and there they met clusters of small children wearing masks and carrying bags for candy. Two such youngsters followed close behind them at a trot, and one said to the other, "What's he got on?"

"He's a cop," said the other.

"No, I mean the other one."

"That's a woman. She's got a witch robe on."

They came abreast of Miles and one of them said, "Are you really a cop?"

"Yes, I am."

"Where are you taking that woman?"

"To jail. She's under arrest."

"Pruitt, you're impossible," said Imogene.

"Why is she under arrest?"

"She's been acting very gouchy."

They walked some distance together, the four of them, before one of the children said, "Do you mean grouchy?"

"No, gouchy. It means crude."

The children lost interest and veered off toward a house where they knocked on the front door.

"Pruitt, you're impossible. And don't walk so fast, I'm wearing heels."

"Sorry."

"And I wish you wouldn't try quite so hard to be funny."

"I can't help it. I'm an ack-comedian."

* * *

Wayne and Thanatopsis Workman lived in a modern apartment at the back of a large old house belonging to a man who had become rich selling tractors. It was a commonly held opinion in Staggerford that the high school principal ought to be living in a house of his own and thus paying his share of property taxes, but Miles could understand the Workmans' reluctance to leave this apartment. The retired tractor dealer doted on them. Like most people, he loved Thanatopsis, and he had remodeled the apartment to suit her taste—lots of orange carpet and figured wallpaper and fancy light fixtures to warm up the large, high-ceilinged rooms. He bought them new appliances for the kitchen and he built a new garage in the back yard. Best of all, he spent all but three months of the year out of sight, sunning his sinuses in Long Beach.

Imogene and Miles were the first to arrive. When Thanatopsis greeted them at the door and shrieked at their costumes, Miles felt his heart leap. He had never known anyone like Thanatopsis, whose enjoyment of life was so headlong, and whose habit it was to call up this surge of gladness in everybody's heart. Miss McGee called her a treasure. The only person who seemed not to love Thanatopsis was her husband, and Miles wondered what ailed him. Didn't Wayne understand what a treasure he had in this girl? Miles also wondered why he (Miles) always thought of her as a girl. She was as close to thirty as Imogene, but whereas he thought of Imogene as a woman (if not as a turkey) he thought of Thanatopsis as a girl. It must have been her smallness, her freshness, her habit of wrinkling her nose when she laughed.

Thanatopsis kissed Imogene and she kissed Miles and she led them by the hand into the living room. She wore a tight oriental gown as richly designed as a Persian rug. It glittered with sequins.

"I hope we're not too early," said Imogene. "You know Pruitt." Her black tassel hung over one eye.

"We've been waiting for you," said Thanatopsis. "I've been so excited about this party I've had everything ready since ten o'clock this morning. I simply couldn't wait. I got up at five and cleaned house and made the snacks and by ten I was ready. You should have come at ten and spent the day. Don't you just love these fall days? I was outside in the yard most of the afternoon. I just couldn't seem to get enough of the kind of day it was. I raked leaves and I turned over the soil in the flower beds and then you know what I did?" She laughed. "I lay down flat on my back. On the ground. The wind was coming up by that time and I lay there and watched the leaves coming down out of the cottonwood. We've got this cottonwood tree in the back yard that must be the tallest tree in town, and when you lie on your back and look up, the top branches seem to be miles away, and when the leaves are swirling around and falling on you it makes you dizzy. Oh, I just *love* a day like this."

"Pruitt made me walk over here in this outfit. You know how tight Pruitt is. He never starts his car from one year to the next."

"Let's *all* go outside in our costumes," said Thanatopsis. "What a fantastic idea. When everybody gets here we'll all go out for tricks and treats."

"Where's Wayne?" asked Miles.

"He's still getting ready. He's been dawdling all day— just having a good lazy time, dawdling and watching football on TV. Wayne loves his Saturdays, and I know how important they are to him. Poor Wayne gets so tense at his job that he needs Saturdays to relax. I just love to see him spend Saturdays dawdling and relaxing and coming down to earth again after a week at school. You know, Wayne is so *serious* about everything. That's what makes him a good principal of course, but I'm trying to make him a little less serious. Right now I'm working on his Saturdays—making them worry-proof. I've decided it's the one day each week he's not to think of school. Tonight I put him in charge of the drinks. He's out in the kitchen, Miles, looking over his liquor supply. Why don't you go out there and help him get organized?"

As Miles left the room Imogene was saying, "And the worst of it was he wanted to run all the way. And me in heels. If he wanted to get here so fast why didn't he take his car out of the garage for once?"

Wayne Workman was sitting on a kitchen stool, reading the label on a bottle of rum. He wore a suit and tie. A cigarette stuck out from under his shaggy mustache and the smoke was getting in his eyes.

"Hello, Pruitt, what will you have?" Miles was called Miles by everyone except Wayne Workman and Imogene Kite.

"A screwdriver."

"Make it yourself. The ice is in that bucket." He went back to his reading.

When Wayne Workman first came to town, people remarked that he resembled Miles. Both men were tall and square-jawed and although Wayne's hair was not red, it could be mistaken for red at first glance. So Miles, who from the beginning felt a latent antipathy toward this man, grew a mustache; but that was about the time mustaches became fashionable and Wayne grew one of his own, so Miles shaved his off. Now the resemblance, with or without mustaches, was disappearing as Miles gained weight and Wayne stayed lean.

91

Miles mixed two screwdrivers, one of them for Imogene. "What about Thanatopsis?" he asked. "Shall I mix her one?"

"Pruitt, will you please stop calling my wife that crazy name?"

"Sorry. It's a habit I somehow—"

"Her name is Anna Thea. It's a perfectly good name and anybody with average intelligence should be able to say it."

"Sorry."

"Pruitt, how do you make a daiquiri? The last time Mrs. Stevenson was here she asked for a daiquiri and I didn't have what I needed. What do I need?"

"Lime juice."

"I don't think I have any lime juice."

"Wayne, why aren't you wearing a costume?"

"Well, I'm glad you noticed. But I'm not sure I should tell you."

Miles shrugged and mixed a screwdriver for Thanatopsis.

"Where did you get that ranger outfit?"

"From Imogene. It belonged to her father."

"It's kind of tight on you."

Miles sucked in his belly.

"Pruitt, would you really like to know why I'm not wearing a costume?"

"Yes."

"It's a test." He put out his cigarette and lit another. "I decided to wear one of my everyday suits and see if people notice that I'm not in costume. This is one of the suits I wear as principal, and it's possible that some people will subconsciously assume that I'm in costume. I want to see who those people are."

"I don't follow you."

"Well, if they think this suit is a costume then deep down inside they probably don't think of me as a real principal. They think of me as an impostor."

"Are you serious?"

"I'd like to know where I stand with certain people."

"Like who?"

"Like Doc Oppegaard. He's chairman of the school board this year, and I've never been sure exactly where I stood with him. I'm on the good side of quite a few prominent people, Pruitt. I get along well with Mayor Druppers. But when the time comes, the chairman of the school board is the kingpin."

"When the time comes for what?"

"Well, let's face it, Ansel Stevenson isn't going to last forever. I mean one way or another he's going to be replaced before too long. How do you like the sound of Superintendent Workman?"

"Superintendent Workman?"

"How do you like the sound of it?"

"Swell." Miles downed his screwdriver.

"I played golf last Sunday with Mayor Druppers. He's not such a bad golfer for his age."

"That so?"

"He shot an eighty-nine."

"Mmmmm."

"Myself, I shot an eighty-three."

"Nine holes, or eighteen?" Miles regretted this remark, but he couldn't seem to help it. Wayne Workman for some reason always brought out the worst in him.

The Gibbons arrived, and Coach Gibbon came out to the kitchen dressed in a Staggerford High School wrestling uniform. The red tank-top shirt revealed the pimples on his broad shoulders and the tights revealed a great pouch of genitalia. He nodded at Miles and

Wayne without looking them in the eye. His mind was on the tie with Owl Brook, and he seemed to be studying, with a scowl, the point of his long nose.

"Nice game last night," said Wayne, whose rare pleasantries were reserved for Coach Gibbon and for members of the school board.

"Aw, that goddamn Fremling. Did you see what happened on our try for point? Finally this year I get a team with some size and I figure we'll beat Owl Brook for once, and what happens? That goddamn Fremling turns out to be a fat-assed weakling. Give me scotch and water."

"Help yourself. The ice is in that bucket."

As Coach helped himself he asked, "How come you aren't wearing a costume?"

"I'm glad you noticed. Did it ever occur to you that some people might think I *am* wearing a costume?"

"I don't getcha."

"I mean they might look upon me as an impostor in my job."

insecurity

"Let's go into the living room," said Miles.

"I mean subconsciously they might think that."

"I expect we'll do all right in wrestling, though," said Coach. "We've got Lawrence Winters at one ninety, and Willy Samuels at one eighty, and Clyde Albertson at one seventy, and Bill Clifford at one sixty, and John Innes at one fifty, and Jack Worley at one forty, and Charlie Zeney at one thirty, and Doug Smith at one twenty, and some little pipsqueak of a freshman at one ten."

"Let's go into the living room," said Miles.

"How do you mix a daiquiri?" asked Wayne.

"I told you. You need lime juice."

"I'm not asking you. I'm asking Coach."

"You need lime juice," said Coach.

94

"That's what I thought," said Wayne.

Miles downed his second screwdriver and mixed a third.

"Now what I'd like to do is take ten pounds off Lawrence Winters and wrestle him at one eighty, take ten pounds off Willy Samuels and wrestle him at one seventy, take ten pounds off Clyde Albertson and wrestle him at one sixty, take ten pounds off Bill Clifford and wrestle him at one fifty, take ten pounds off John Innes and wrestle him at one forty, take ten pounds off Jack Worley and wrestle him at one thirty, take ten pounds off Charlie Zeney and wrestle him at one twenty, take ten pounds off Doug Smith and wrestle him at one ten, and take ten pounds off the little pipsqueak and wrestle him at a hundred."

Miles went into the other room, where Thanatopsis was laughing and explaining to Imogene and to Stella Gibbon, "Tonight we're really having two parties. It's always two parties when you invite the Stevensons. The first party, which is always very proper, ends at ten thirty when the Stevensons go home, and the second party, which is sometimes very *im*proper, ends whenever we please."

Miles handed Thanatopsis and Imogene their drinks, and he asked Stella Gibbon what she would have. Stella was dressed as a Staggerford cheerleader (short red skirt, anklets, tennis shoes, a red *S* on a white wool sweater) and this outfit, together with her new front teeth, made her very attractive. Since going to work part-time as Doc Oppegaard's dental assistant, Stella had acquired a mouthful of new bridgework, which (it was said) hadn't cost her a penny.

"Fix me something strong, Miles, and sweet. I'm dying for something strong and sweet. I tell you that husband of mine has been nothing but a sourpuss ever since that game last night, and then at the office today it was nothing but rush, rush, rush. We had an impacted wisdom tooth and a broken incisor and neither one of them was scheduled ahead of time. I'm supposed to be done at noon on Saturdays, but I was still there at quarter to two. I mean, I couldn't leave Pappa Doc alone with those patients on his hands, could I?"

"How about a Tom Collins?"

"That sounds wonderful, Miles honey."

In the kitchen Wayne Workman had finished reading his rum bottle. "Pruitt, I was just saying to Coach that I have come up with a new plan to encourage Indian attendance. I don't see how it can miss. I'm going to spring it on the faculty Monday afternoon, but I don't suppose it will do any harm if you learn about it beforehand. I'm going to tell Superintendent Stevenson and Doc Oppegaard about it tonight, and you can listen if you want to."

"Swell." Miles finished his screwdriver and made himself another. The alcohol relieved his toothache.

Next to arrive were the Stevensons. The superintendent came stooping into the kitchen nodding benevolently at Miles and Coach and Wayne. He wore a flannel shirt and a pair of large overalls. "I'm here as a farmer," he said. "I grew up on a farm and I know the kind of healthy life a farmer leads. My one regret is that we sold the family farm. If I had spent my life as a farmer instead of a schoolman, there's no doubt I would be enjoying robust health to this day." His overalls were the right length but much too big around. The straps over his shoulders seemed to be the only parts touching his body.

"What do you want to drink?" asked Wayne.

"Water, if you don't mind."

"There's the sink." He handed the superintendent a glass.

Stevenson filled the glass and said, "Why aren't you wearing a costume?"

"Oh, it's a long story. You might say I am testing people's reactions."

"Reactions?" He lowered himself carefully into the breakfast nook.

"Yes, reactions."

"Reactions to what?"

"Reactions to my not being in costume."

"Oh . . . Well, what kind of reactions have you been getting?"

"I've been getting about what I expected."

"And what did you expect, if I may ask?"

"I expected people to ask me why I wasn't in costume."

The superintendent considered this for a moment, then went back to farming. "My father homesteaded eighty acres, and when he homesteaded it, all but five acres were woods. It was seventy-five acres of oak and willow and a little bit of pine, and five acres of open land. And, you know, he spent his whole life clearing that land. All the while we boys were growing up we cut off the timber and grubbed out stumps. Now that's hard work, let me tell you, grubbing out stumps. Have any of you ever grubbed out stumps?"

"Never," said Miles, full of screwdrivers. "I've never grubbed out stumps."

"It was my dad's ambition to have the whole seventy-five acres cleared off by the time he quit farming and turned the place over to his sons, but the woods were so thick we never cleared more than two or three acres a year, and by the time he quit farming there were sixty arable acres and twenty wooded acres, and that was a disappointment to him. People didn't value woods in those days the way they do now. To a farmer, a stand of woods is a hindrance to farming and the sooner you log it off the better."

"What would your wife like to drink?" asked Wayne.

"A daiquiri."

Wayne bit his mustache—always his first sign of nerves.

Miles said, for fun, "Mr. Stevenson, didn't you think we did well to tie Owl Brook last night?"

"Oh, yes, by the way, Coach, congratulations. The Stags played a fine game, from what I hear."

"Aw, that goddamn Fremling. Did you hear what happened on our extra point?"

"No."

"Lee Fremling backed into the ball just as Peter was kicking it. In all my years of coaching I never saw such a fat-assed weakling as Lee Fremling." Coach folded his arms and looked out the kitchen window at the black night.

"And another disappointment to my father was the fact that none of us boys wanted to be farmers. We were determined to get off the farm. I think it was the result of grubbing out all those stumps. And when each boy in turn went into a profession other than farming, my father was disappointed. Nowadays, of course, a man doesn't expect his boys to follow in his footsteps so much as he did in those days." He looked about him. "I bet none of you are the sons of teachers, for example. Miles, you're not the son of a teacher. You're the son of a buttermaker. Wayne, what did your father do for a living?"

"My father was a teacher. Excuse me, but I don't seem to have any lime juice."

"And what about you, Coach? What did your father do?"

"My father was a coach," said Coach.

Wayne put on his coat and went out into the night for lime juice.

The Oppegaards arrived. Doc Oppegaard joined the men in the kitchen. The dentist, father of the genius child, was a shriveled wisp of a man with an enormous nose and a lecherous reputation. Certainly his succession of pretty assistants—Stella Gibbon included—did more for him than sterilize his tools and send out his staggering monthly statements. Miles did not understand what women saw in this wasted man. Except for his large nose, there was nothing to him. His skin was the color of oatmeal. Tonight he was wearing a loud sport shirt open at the neck and a cowboy hat.

The superintendent said, "Doc and I grew up in the days when sons followed in the footsteps of their fathers, didn't we, Doc? Tell me, Doc, was your father a dentist?"

"My father was a bum. Hello, Miles, nice to see you. How is Nadine doing in English?"

"If she does any better she'll be teaching it."

"That's fine. Just so you keep her working up to her potential."

"Don't worry. By the way, Doc, what did you think of the game last night?"

"A good game. Congratulations, Coach."

"Aw, that goddamn Fremling."

"Anyhow, Doc, I was telling the fellows here that my father was a farmer." Stevenson was still speaking from the breakfast nook. "Farming is hard work, I'll admit that, but there are many joys connected with farming that you don't find in a lot of other lines of work. A sense of accomplishment, for one. I cannot truthfully say that I feel, after twenty-six years as superintendent of schools, a sense of accomplishment. I know you don't believe it, Doc and Coach and Miles, but I have to say it. I've given my life to school work and what has school work given me? I wish I had stayed on the farm and cleared those acres my father left in woods. Out there I would be filling my lungs with God's fresh air. We had a John Deere tractor and I can still see myself sitting up there on that tractor cultivating corn and breathing in God's fresh air. Farming makes a man robust. Farming is an honest, robust life, and I shouldn't be surprised to see more and more people turn back to it as time goes on and our cities become uninhabitable." He took a sip of his water. "I wonder if you men have noticed how it's become the fashion among our young people to wear overalls with straps like this. Don't you think it's their way of expressing their belief in a simpler way of life? A more honest, robust way of life? That's the way I see it, and I wonder if any of you men see it that way? Young people's overalls, I'm talking about."

Doc asked Miles where he got the ranger uniform.

"It belonged to Lyle Kite."

"Oh, yes. I remember Lyle. He didn't live long after he retired from the Park Service."

"Miles!" said the superintendent. He struggled out of the breakfast nook. "You're wearing the clothes of a dead man!" He backed out of the kitchen.

Doc shook his head. "Poor jerk."

Stella Gibbon came into the kitchen and said, "Miles, honey, have you forgotten about me?"

He had. He mixed her a strong sweet drink as Doc Oppegaard patted her fanny. Coach was still at the window staring at the night. Or was he watching his wife and Doc reflected in the glass?

"Where is the host?" said Doc. "He said he wanted to talk to me about Indian attendance."

"He went out for lime juice," said Miles.

Stella said, "Why are you men hiding out here in the kitchen anyway? Come into the living room." She took her husband by the arm. "Come into the living room, honey, and show the girls your wrestling tights." She led him away.

From the kitchen Miles saw Imogene Kite impulsively cover her eyes when Coach walked, crotch first, into the living room.

"I like Stella's new teeth," said Miles.

"Yes, I've done wonders for her," said Doc. "You know, as long as I've known Stella her old teeth were the only flaw in her appearance, though they never caused her to keep her mouth shut, and I was hoping that some day I could go to work on her. Now with that new bridge across the front, she looks like a million dollars."

"And what do you think of Coach's wrestling tights?"

"He's an exhibitionist. He and his wife are both exhibitionists, but with her it's okay, you know what I mean. She looks like a million dollars."

"And what do you think of Thanatopsis Workman? I mean as a woman isn't she a treasure?"

"Miles, are you drunk?"

"All I want to know is what you really think of Thanatopsis Workman."

"You mean Anna Thea?"

"Yes, but Anna Thea is her nickname; her real name is Thanatopsis, and it makes her husband angry when everybody calls her Anna Thea."

"Her real name is Thanatopsis?"

"Yes, isn't she a treasure?"

"Thanatopsis means 'view of death,' Miles. What the hell kind of a name is that?"

"And what do you think of Imogene Kite? Doesn't she remind you of young Abraham Lincoln?"

"Miles, you're drunk."

"She's a rail splitter if I ever saw one."

"Let's go into the other room."

In the other room everyone was at the front door saying good-by to the Stevensons. Miles looked at his watch to see if it was already ten thirty. It was eight forty-five. The Stevensons were hurrying to their car.

"He gets so agitated," said Imogene Kite.

"What a shame," said Stella Gibbon. "Did you catch what he was saying?"

"Something about the clothes of a dead man," said Thanatopsis. "Somebody in this house is wearing the clothes of a dead man."

"Poor old jerk," said Doc Oppegaard. "He has that terrible phobia."

"He's a goddamn zero," shouted Coach Gibbon. "You guys on the board cut my athletic budget twenty percent and he never went to bat for me."

"Shut your mouth," said his wife. "You've been nothing but wicked ever since that game last night. If you can't learn to be civil . . ."

"I think we all need a fresh drink," said Thanatopsis. "Where is Wayne?"

"Out for lime juice."

"Well then, Miles, you help me freshen everybody's drink."

Doc said, "Brandy for me, Thanatopsis," as he sat down on Stella Gibbon's lap.

In the kitchen Miles, spilling and misjudging proportions, helped her with the drinks. He mixed himself a double screwdriver.

"I'm the one wearing the clothes of a dead man," he said.

"So what. Go see what Mrs. Oppegaard is drinking."

"Mrs. Oppegaard? I didn't know she was here."

"She's easy to overlook. She's on the couch with Imogene."

Miles found the dentist's wife under Imogene's wing. She was wearing a dunce cap. Imogene was listing for her the names of the men who developed the atomic bomb. "And there was Enrico Fermi, who died in 1954. He was an Italian."

"I know absolutely nothing about the atomic bomb," Mrs. Oppegaard despaired.

"Fermi was an Italian. I'm researching atomic energy, and today I read about Fermi. He was Italian."

"I know nothing about Italians. Italy."

"Mrs. Oppegaard, can I fix you a drink?"

She looked up at Miles, then she looked to her husband for help, but Doc was tracing with his finger the scarlet *S* on Stella's breast and saying, "Shouldn't this be an *A?*"

"Maybe just a teeny little bit of wine, do you suppose?" said Mrs. Oppegaard.

"Fermi was born in 1901," said Imogene, averting her eyes from Coach Gibbon, who was parading his bulging sex organs back and forth through the room. "I've got Lawrence Winters at one ninety," he was telling himself.

In the kitchen Wayne Workman was standing with his coat on, chewing his mustache and holding a bottle of lime juice. "So the Stevensons went home, did they! That's a fine how-do-you-do. Just pick up and leave before I get a chance to talk about my new attendance plan."

Thanatopsis said, "He was very agitated, Wayne. You know how careful we have to be about his becoming agitated. I think it was best that they went home."

"And, Pruitt, you're the cause of it. You're the one wearing a dead man's clothes. Did you do that on purpose? Just to make a shambles of my party?"

"What will Mrs. Oppegaard have, Miles?"

"A gin fizz," said Miles, who had no idea.

The rest of the party was not clear in his mind, and the next day his memory provided him only the briefest of glimpses. He remembered going out for tricks and treats with Thanatopsis in her oriental gown and coming back with a candy bar, a cigar, and a water glass full of whiskey.

He remembered going to the Workmans' bathroom and sitting on the lid of the toilet in the dark and running his tongue over his wisdom tooth.

He remembered Thanatopsis, by popular demand, fetching from the bedroom her blind poodle named Ducky—a small white dog who, on a diet of tuna and digitalis, had lived to an unheard-of age for poodles, thirteen or thirty or some such age; and he remembered the women vying for the right to hold Ducky to their bosoms.

He remembered how the voices of the women rang like a steady peal of little brass bells while Wayne Workman and Doc Oppegaard and Coach Gibbon met in solemn conclave in a distant corner of the apartment, discussing no doubt Wayne's plan for the Indians.

He remembered people repeating themselves. He heard certain utterances dozens of times: "He's been nothing but wicked since last night's game." "I'm such an underachiever, I know so little, I know absolutely nothing about Italy." "What's the matter with Miles, and why is he calling everybody an ack-comedian?"

He remembered asking Coach Gibbon to tell him once more how much the pipsqueak weighed.

He remembered (or did he imagine it?) Thanatopsis coming away from the telephone with tears in her eyes. He must have imagined it.

He remembered seeing Stella Gibbon and Doc Oppegaard leave together.

He remembered sitting on the couch between Imogene Kite and Mrs. Oppegaard and telling them about the corporal who ate a beer bottle, and then subsiding into a smiling trance until Mrs. Oppegaard, having finished her gin fizz, vomited across his lap.

SUNDAY

November 1

At 7 A.M. Miss McGee walked to church in the dark, tilting her umbrella into the small, cold rain. On Sundays she was the first to arrive at St. Isidore's so that she might pray without distraction.

She switched on the light in the vestibule, shook out her umbrella, opened the swinging doors, and walked down the middle aisle toward the small red flame burning in the sanctuary. At the altar of the Blessed Virgin she felt for a book of matches and lit three candles. She dropped thirty cents into the metal box and she said a Hail Mary for the restoration of Miles's faith.

By the light of the candles she found her accustomed pew and sat down to unpack her purse. She took out her rosary, her 1272-page missal, a leaflet containing the archbishop's new prayer for religious vocations, and a Kleenex in case she sneezed. Then with her eyes on the red flame over the high altar, she went to her knees.

At seven thirty when Father Finn entered the church and turned on all the lights, Miss McGee picked up her thick missal and opened it to Prayers for the Dead, which with the passing of time had had to serve for more and more departed souls. She prayed for her parents, who at the time of their deaths were considerably younger than Miss McGee was today; for her brother, taken by the flu of '19; and for assorted relatives, teachers, schoolmates, colleagues, friends, and students who had passed from this life. "May they rest in peace," she murmured. "May the souls of all the faithful departed rest in peace." She had a pretty good idea who was in Heaven and who was in Purgatory, but she prayed with equal fervor for all of them. She hoped (though she knew better, particularly in the case of certain students) that no one was in Hell.

She turned then to Prayers for Good Health, for Peace, for a Happy Death, and for Seasonable Weather. By the time she finished these, the church was filling with people—their coats smelling of rain—and she went back to her rosary, an instrument that measured the advance of her prayers even when her mind wandered.

Three widows dressed alike in slacks and imitation-leather coats—the Pelletier sisters—took their places in the pew ahead of Miss McGee. She gave each of them a nod and half a smile. Bartholomew Druppers, mayor of Staggerford, scurried up the side aisle toward the sacristy; she noticed the bald spot on the back of his head. A little girl with a dime left her parents' pew and lit a candle at the altar of St. Joseph; she stood for a moment looking up at the grandfatherly plaster face, then hitched up her leotards and returned to her place. Two high-spirited servers, forgetting to genuflect, readied the altar for mass and began a fencing duel with their candle lighters before they had quite disappeared into the sacristy. Then they came out again, followed by Mayor Druppers, who wore the same black suit he wore to meetings of the school board and the city council, and by Father Finn, who wore dazzling white robes for All Saints' Day.

And Miles slipped into the pew beside Miss McGee. She thought for a moment that she would topple over. She steadied herself by gripping his arm. "Your faith has been restored," she said aloud, causing the Pelletier sisters to turn around.

He smiled at her and shrugged.

Father Finn, beginning the mass, said, "Let us call to mind our sins."

Miles thought of his subconscious as a large and careless cleaning woman, a clumsy Amazon with calluses on her hands and tennis shoes on her feet who could not be held back from rearranging, as he slept, the furniture in his head. She was forever airing out the closets of his memory and failing to put all the heirlooms and junk back where they belonged. How else could he explain his disjointed dreams, his disorientation upon waking? Last night had been such a night. He had gone to sleep, dizzily, thinking about Enrico Fermi and the atomic bomb, he had dreamed for what seemed like hours about his high-school sweetheart, Carla Carpenter, and he had awakened this morning to the knowledge that it was All Saints' Day.

Holy Days of Obligation were seldom on his mind anymore, and he had not been to mass on All Saints' Day for at least ten years; yet today he sat up on both elbows in bed in order to get a better look at what the Amazon had left hanging from a hook in his memory: the liturgical calendar that his parents had kept, year after year, on a nail by the kitchen door. "The Feast of All Saints," it said, in the first square of November.

It was much earlier than his normal time for Sunday rising. He felt a dull screwdriver ache in the left front quadrant of his brain. But trying to assimilate Enrico Fermi and Carla Carpenter and All Saints' Day had brought him fully awake, and he got up. He dressed and shaved and picked Lyle Kite's pants out of the bathtub, where he had left them to soak. Mrs. Oppegaard's vomit was gone, but it had left patches of discoloration across the front of both legs. The seam in the seat was split. He dropped the pants back into the water and went to church.

"Glory to God in the highest," said Father Finn and the congregation—all except Miss McGee and Miles. Miss McGee said, "Gloria in Excelsis Deo."

Mayor Druppers climbed into the pulpit and made Paul's letter to the Colossians sound like a city ordinance. "We send thanks to the Father, who has made us worthy to share the lot of the saints in light," he concluded. Miles looked up at the saints that the dawn was bringing to life in the stained-glass windows: Michael swooping like a falcon toward the earth; Peter flinging out a net; Marus pulling Placidus out of a pond; Isidore, patron of farmers, patron of this parish, resting in his labor, leaning on his plow. Isidore looked bilious. All the saints, for that matter, were sallow this morning, for the dawn was gray and rainy.

After the Gospel (the Beatitudes) and the sermon (the coming expense of winter fuel), everybody but Miles and Miss McGee said, "We believe in one God." Miss McGee said, "Credo in unum Deum."

"This is my body," said Father Finn at the consecration, "this is my blood," and for an unguarded moment Miles was his former self, believing that what the priest held in his hands had ceased to be bread and wine.

Then it was handshaking time, the silliest innovation of all, in Miss McGee's opinion. The Pelletier sisters turned around. All three of them had underslung jaws and their coats of imitation leather crackled as they extended their hands. "Peace be with you," they said.

"Peace be with you," said Miles.

Miss McGee said, "Pax."

Communion. While Miss McGee went up to the altar rail, Miles flipped through the pages of her missal. Half of its mass prayers were obsolete, but he knew she would rather be wrong half the time than give up these 1272 double-column pages of litanies, vigils, introits, and collects, with the Latin and English printed side by side— the frozen Latin looking as archaic and attractive on the page as it used to sound on the lips of the priest when he would turn his back on the congregation and raise his hands and his voice and implore the bronze figure over the high altar to come down again from the cross. Priests didn't do that anymore. Now they faced the congregation and celebrated mass on what Miss McGee called the high picnic table.

On the way out of church Miles suggested breakfast at the Hub.

"But it's so expensive," said Miss McGee. "We can have eggs and sausage at home."

"It's the Feast of All Saints."

"But it's raining."

"I brought my car."

The Hub was busy. They sat at the table in the window. Miss McGee, polishing her silverware with a paper napkin, said, "Now tell me, Miles. Are you getting the faith back?"

"I wish you didn't take such an interest in my spiritual life, Agatha. It's really not all that interesting."

"You went to mass. Your faith is being restored."

"It's not faith. I simply woke up with the desire to start the day at St. Isidore's. When I was in grade school, the sisters—and you—marched us to mass every morning and told us that's what gave meaning to the day. And it did."

"And it does."

"No. It did. But it doesn't."

"It does for me."

"Of course. I'm not denying that. But it doesn't for me. Not anymore. Although for a minute this morning I almost believed the bread was flesh."

Their waitress was Beverly Bingham. She wore yesterday's uniform, soiled. Her long hair, unwashed, hung in strings. She gave Miles a quick smile, but she was intimidated by the presence of Miss McGee and her visits to the table were brief, almost furtive.

Miss McGee said, "If you don't believe, what were you doing in church?"

"It was a whim. I always liked the idea of a feast of all the saints. A great annual dinner party in the sky. A fiesta for everybody who died good."

Beverly brought pancakes.

"Who is your patron saint?" asked Miss McGee. "I don't believe I know a St. Miles."

"There is no St. Miles, but how I wished, in the first grade, that there were. My name was no end of trouble to my first-grade teacher."

"Sister Odilia."

"Yes, Sister Odilia. When she discovered no Miles in the roster of saints, she tried to assign me to St. Leonard because Leonard is my middle name; but while there were three Leonards to choose from, and my friends were enthusiastic about the one whose eyes were gouged out by heathens, I was ashamed of my middle name in those days, and I flatly refused patronage from anybody named Leonard. 'Very well,' said Sister Odilia, 'it will have to be a saint with at least the first three letters of your first name,' and she offered me St. Miltiades, a Negro pope of the fourth century. I said I didn't want a black man. 'Very well,' she said, 'then it will be St. Mildred.' Mildred! I had a tantrum and was sent to the cloakroom. Eventually she found me a patron I could live with—St. Mylor, who was famous for his piety and beheaded by his uncle."

"St. Mylor," said Miss McGee. "I don't know him." She took her missal from her purse and studied the calendar of saints.

"He's probably been stricken from the rolls," said Miles. "Everybody obscure was purged a few years ago."

"Here he is. October first. That's St. Remigius's Day. Mylor has been overshadowed by Remigius."

"Who's Remigius?"

"In the fourth century St. Remigius converted the king of the Franks."

"Your calendar is pre-Vatican Two, Agatha, like everything else in that missal of yours. How can you call yourself a Catholic when you haven't retooled?"

"I was given this missal by the sixth grade of 1938."

"You haven't retooled, Agatha. Do you realize that with your litanies and novenas and Prayers at the Foot of the Altar you are no closer to being a Catholic today than I am? We're both out of step with the church."

"Anybody who believes that the bread turns to flesh is in step."

"It was only for a moment I believed it. An unguarded moment."

"Your faith is coming back."

As Miles followed Miss McGee out of the restaurant, Beverly rushed up to him and said, "Are you going for a walk again this afternoon?"

He said he wasn't.

"Oh, please. I have to talk to you."

"It's raining."

"Well, how about driving out to Pike Park. I could meet you there. I'm off at three."

"I'm afraid by then I'll be asleep. I was up late."

"Please, Mr. Pruitt. I have to see you."

"It's urgent?"

"Yes. Please."

"All right. Three o'clock."

By three o'clock the rain had become a splattering downpour. Miles got into his car and followed Highway 4 west to Pike Park, a clearing on the south bank of the Badbattle carpeted with pine needles and cluttered with picnic tables.

Pike Park was the smallest piece of ground in the National Park System, so small that since Lyle Kite's death no ranger had been assigned to replace him. The park had been named after the explorer Zebulon Pike, who in 1806 met on this spot with the Sioux Chief Onji and conveyed to him President Jefferson's warmest greetings. Pike and Onji met to discuss two nuisances, British trappers and drunken Indians. It was a cordial meeting. Pike promised Chief Onji that all British trappers (who couldn't seem to get it through their heads that England had lost the war) would be driven from the territory. Chief Onji promised Pike that his people would lay off the firewater. Pike went next to Colorado, where he discovered a peak, leaving Onji to deal with greater nuisances to come: American trappers and Chippewa hunters.

Pike Park by day was a wayside rest for weary travelers and by night a refuge for teen-age lovers. Besides picnic tables it contained several stone fireplaces and a pump. At the entrance to the park there had once been a large rock in which was embedded a bronze plaque commemorating the Pike-Onji meeting, but several years ago somebody rolled the rock down the steep bank and into the river. Near the pump a path led down to a thick stand of willows along the water's edge—a good spot in the spring for fishing walleyes, and in the fall when the water was low for reading the bronze plaque.

It was ten after three when Miles drove into the park. He saw the Binghams' black GMC pickup standing next to the pump. He pulled up beside it and almost before he came to a stop Beverly opened the door and got into the front seat with him. He thought at first that she had been crying, but what he took to be tears on her cheeks were raindrops. She kicked off her wet shoes and sat on her feet. She was dressed in yesterday's clothes—the orange uniform, the worn wool jacket.

"I began to worry that you weren't coming." She hooked her wet hair behind her ears, then laid her left arm along the back of the seat and rested a finger on Miles's right shoulder. "I don't think I could bear sitting here in the rain waiting for you and then have you not show up. I think I'd die. I've gotten so dependent on seeing you every day that if you didn't show up I don't know what I'd do. God, you've got it hot in here."

Miles turned off the ignition and, with it, the heater fan. He squirmed uncomfortably. Beverly's finger weighed heavily on his shoulder.

"Why am I so dependent on seeing you every day? I never used to be like this. I mean I used to just go along living my life, but now if I can't talk things over with you every day I feel all screwed up."

"It's a phase."

"Well, I hope it's a phase, and I hope it isn't a phase. I mean I hope I get over feeling so screwed up all the time, but I would hate to quit seeing you because . . I don't know."

"Because I have all my shit together."

"Right. And I haven't. And somebody who hasn't feels a strong attachment to somebody who has. You must attract a lot of people like me. Mixed-up people."

"Not so many. Now and then somebody wants to talk. But not really all that often."

"What do you tell them?"

"I tell them to get their shit together."

"No, seriously."

"That's what I say. Or words to that effect."

"Well, that isn't much to go on."

"It's the best I can offer."

"Why don't you tell them *how* to get it together?"

"Everybody knows how. You simply go out and start gathering it up and putting it in one place, and before you know it, you've got it all together."

"Where do I start gathering?"

"Start with the College Entrance Exam. Then after that, you write to the junior college in Berrington and you ask them for application forms and scholarship forms and student-loan forms—the whole package. Be sure to tell them you're a quarter Chippewa. They'll fix it with the Bureau of Indian Affairs so you get a free ride."

"You told me all that before."

"Then why do you ask?"

On the highway a car slowed down at the entrance to the park. How stupid, Miles told himself, to be lured out here to lovers' lane in broad daylight. To his relief, the car did not turn into the park but made a U-turn on the highway and headed back toward town. It looked, through the rain, like Doc Oppegaard's Lincoln. Doc and Stella searching for a place to park? Absurd. Nadine and a boyfriend? Nadine had no boyfriends.

Beverly took off her jacket, folded her arms, and spoke to the windshield, which was steaming up. "The thing that's got me off balance is my mother. If I go away to college, what's going to happen to my mother? I don't think she could make it by herself. She's getting worse every day. Yesterday I found her out in a field by the highway, and she was turning left and turning right and lying down and acting just crazy. I asked her what she was doing and she said she was obeying God's command. She said it was in the Bible that she was supposed to leave the house and walk so many paces east and then turn left and walk so many paces north, and then lie down on the ground, and then get up, and on and on like that. Her shoes were all wet from walking in the creek and her dress was torn and her stockings were torn and her legs were bleeding from thorns. There wasn't a thing I could do about it. She kept it up until she got tired and she couldn't go on anymore, and when she came to the fence along the highway she sat down on the ground and looked at the sky for a long time. I sat down beside her and waited till she was ready to get up and go back to the house, and finally she did. But can you imagine what it was like sitting there in the weeds with cars going by and people looking at us? What else could I do? I was afraid she might try to climb the fence and wander out onto the highway. But when she stood up she went straight back to the house and changed her clothes and fed the chickens."

"Was that after we saw her down by the river?"

Beverly nodded. "She was doing the same thing down there when we saw her, only I didn't realize it. She was pacing off some distances that the Bible told her to. I ran away because it embarrassed me to have you see her."

"That was the first time I've ever had a good look at your mother. She's younger than I thought."

Beverly nodded. "I can't trust her to be alone anymore. Not for any length of time."

"There are people who handle problems like that. There are doctors who can help her. If she needs care, there are places she can go."

"Like where?"

"A home of some kind. A mental hospital if necessary. If she's going out of her mind, you can't be expected to care for her single-handedly."

"Then what would happen to me? I wouldn't have a home."

"You'll be going away to college. You'll be starting your own life."

"But I wouldn't have a home. College isn't home. Where would I go during vacations? I wouldn't have any home to go to in the summertime."

"Summers you could get a job in Berrington. You could rent yourself a room."

"But what kind of a home would that be? I wouldn't have any ties. I just can't stand not having any ties. My sister has broken all her ties and she's just sort of out there somewhere. And nobody knows where. And she was the only person I was ever able to confide in."

"You'll make friends in college."

'But I wouldn't have a home. How can a person get along without a home? I mean what I've got now isn't much, but it's the place where I grew up and it's got the river and the woods and the garden and the produce stand. And Mother isn't all that bad . . . when she isn't crazy. I mean if she'd just be content to gather bones, I could put up with that. If she could stay halfway sane I could come home weekends and be with her. And summers. There's no nicer place to be summers. Our garden is big and we have that produce stand by the highway and that's fun. That month or so at the end of summer when we open that stand is the best part of the year for me. I wouldn't want to give that up. But, God, if she's going to be like this, wandering around the fields because she's hearing voices . . ."

"Have her see a doctor. Have her go to the Stagger-ford Clinic."

"She'll never see a doctor."

"Have her see Dr. Maitland at the clinic."

"She'll never do that."

"Then *you* see him."

"I can't."

"Why?"

"I can't tell you why. It's too complicated. Seeing a doctor isn't going to help anything. It would only make things worse."

"Why?"

"Just take my word for it."

"You've got a secret."

"God, have I got a secret."

"You want *me* to see Dr. Maitland?"

"No!"

"All right, that's my best offer."

Beverly said nothing. She lit a cigarette and blew the smoke into her lap. Miles wiped the steam from his side window. A car sped past on the highway, trailing a cloud of spray. The trees, black with rain, stirred in the wind. It was getting cold in the car. He started the engine and turned on the heater fan.

Beverly said, "Are you in a hurry to get home?"

"I've got a stack of papers to read. I'd like to hand them back tomorrow."

" 'What I Wish' papers?"

"Yes."

"Did you read mine?"

"Not yet."

After another long pause Beverly threw her cigarette out the window and said, "Do you know what I really wish?"

"What?"

"I wish you and I could be in love with each other."

Miles squirmed. He looked at his watch. "You're breaking Greg's heart."

"Whose?"

"Greg Olson's, the airman you're going to marry."

"Oh, that! Did you believe that? I made that up."

Miles turned on his windshield wipers and told Beverly that he had to get home.

Beverly put on her shoes but she didn't get out. She sat with her arms folded, looking at the windshield, watching the steam disappear over the defroster vent. She looked angry. She said, "How do you like living with that crabby old bitch?"

For a moment Miles was stunned. "If you mean Agatha McGee, I like it just fine. She's really quite human, you know."

"That isn't what the Catholic kids say. They say they never thought they'd live through the sixth grade. She was even stricter than the nuns. Because of her, some Catholic kids leave St. Isidore's after the fifth grade and come over to the public school, did you know that?"

"I've heard that, but there can't be many. Maybe one every year or so."

"Anyway, I'm glad I'm not Catholic. I got by pretty easy in sixth grade. Mrs. Torkelson."

"Miss McGee would have been good for you. The age of twelve is about the right time to be put through the mill. And I think most people would agree with me, judging by the respect her former students have for her."

"Not her former students *I* know. Only her *old*

former students whose memories are failing." This was anger, called up by the thought of the other woman in Miles's life.

"No, the younger ones respect her too. But respect for Miss McGee is not something you admit till you're at least twenty."

"Well, I can't believe fear is a good way to motivate students."

"There's no fear involved. That's a mystique her students enjoy keeping alive because it makes heroes out of them."

"Mr. Pruitt, is there any chance you'll fall in love with me?" She opened her door as she said this, and before she stepped out into the rain she leaned over and kissed him quickly on the cheek.

Miss McGee sat in the wing chair near the lamp in the front window. The lamp had a ruffled shade. On the arms of the chair were squares of embroidered linen that her mother had made. Her mother had always placed them on the arms of the chair before the arrival of eminent guests and laundered them after the guests left. Miss McGee's father had been a state senator, and the McGees were often visited by Governor Rice. They once had Archbishop Burke to dinner. Since then, these linen squares had been lying in the cedar chest, waiting forty years for the next guest of distinction. Yesterday as Miss McGee was taking stock of her linens, she decided to put them to use once more. What was she preserving them for? Who, when she died, would want embroidered linen antimacassars?

This afternoon in the wing chair Miss McGee was mending a slip and listening to the rain. She was also working up the courage to read the Sunday paper. Because of the predictable awfulness of its news, she thought of the Sunday paper as an adversary, and she put off reading it until her curiosity got the best of her—for the only thing worse than reading bad news was being unaware of it.

Finishing her mending, she picked a section of the paper off the coffee table. It was indeed a day for bad news. She took it all to heart. Engaging the enemy, she gave voice, like any valiant soldier, to the exertions of battle. She groaned to read of the American families being evacuated from the Middle East. Her reaction to the photograph of the Secretary of State being spat upon in Central America was a loud snort of disgust, a more fitting response (she thought as she studied the photograph) than the sappily smiling Secretary had permitted himself. How can you smile, she wondered, with spit on your glasses? She clucked her tongue and shook her head at news of the secret agent who revealed to the press that he had been assigned to kill Fidel Castro with an exploding cigar.

When she came across the priest in Seattle, she was struck dumb. She put down the paper and went to the kitchen for a cup of coffee. This priest in Seattle, it said, had announced from the pulpit that he was the father of his housekeeper's eight-year-old boy. While the coffee was heating, Miss McGee went back to her chair and peeked at the next paragraph. "I hope," said the priest, "that this will not in any way alter my relationship with my dear parishioners. I wish to be a father to Toby and a father to my flock at the same time."

"Where's the man's bishop?" cried Miss McGee, hurrying back to the kitchen.

On her third try, with a steaming cup of weak coffee in hand, she finished the article. The bishop, when asked his opinion of the matter, said he would have to think it over. Miss McGee threw the paper on the floor

I isn't this the most interesting book.

and turned off the lamp. She watched the cold rain. It spattered the street and sidewalk and it agitated the broad brown leaves of the dying ferns in the flower bed.

Rain's only value, for Miss McGee, was that it reminded her how precious was good weather. She despised rain. But she knew that to the earth, rain was as necessary as sunshine. Could it be, she wondered, that the vice and barbarism abroad in the world served, like the rain, some purpose? Did the abominations in the Sunday paper mingle somehow with the goodness in the world and together, like the rain and sun feeding the ferns, did they nourish some kind of life she was unaware of?

Miles, returning from Pike Park, entered the house through the back door, turning on lights as he came.

"What are you doing in the dark, Agatha?"

"I was having a thought."

"Yes? Tell me." He took off his coat and rubbers and went to the closet at the foot of the stairs.

"Don't put your coat in there until it's dry, Miles. Hang it over the banister."

He did so.

He sat in the other chair by the lamp, a Victorian chair with a back shaped like a bass fiddle. "Tell me your thought, Agatha."

"Well, it's this, Miles. You see the rain. It's uncomfortable to the touch and depressing to the mind and just generally bad from every human point of view."

"I never think of rain that way."

"Well, I do. I've never cared for rain. But look at those ferns in the flower bed."

He looked. They were bowing and turning under the weight of the rain.

"They're still alive, Miles. It's November and everything else in the flower bed is dead, but those ferns are still alive and beautiful."

"Yes, but they're dying. See how brown they're getting at the edges."

"Of course they're dying. They've been dying since the day they sprouted if you want to be that way about it. But the fact remains it's November and there is still a bit of life in them. And do you know why?"

"Why?"

"Because of yesterday's sun and today's rain. They've been thriving since the middle of April on sunshine, which I think is lovely, and on rain, which I think is dreadful, and now at the end of a long season of sunshine and rain they're their most beautiful."

Miles agreed. Each frond was gold-green at the center and rust-brown at the lacy edge. The colors, despite the darkness of the afternoon (or perhaps because of it), were luminous.

"So what I was thinking, Miles, was that maybe there is a similar process going on in human affairs. If you let sunshine stand for the goodness in the world and you let rain stand for evil, do goodness and evil mingle like sun and rain to produce something? To bring something to maturity, like those ferns? Does God permit sin because it's an ingredient in something he's concocting and we human beings aren't aware of what it is? Is there sprouting up somewhere a beautiful fern, as it were, composed of goodness and sin?"

"It's an arresting thought."

"After all, sin must be in this world for some purpose. Nothing is without purpose, Miles, and I was pondering the possibility of sin having a purpose."

"Why must sin be on your mind so much, Agatha? It's a lazy Sunday afternoon, and while most people are watching TV or taking naps or having a late dinner, you're sitting here in the dark, pondering sin." He switched on the lamp. "I'm not sure I believe much in sin anymore."

"It's as real as rain, Miles."

"Which probably means you've been sitting here reading the Sunday paper." He picked up the section from the floor.

"It's as real as rain and I was trying to understand why God permits it. You asked me why I was sitting here in the dark, Miles, and now you know."

"Well, it's an arresting thought, a fern of goodness and sin," he said absently. He was reading about the Secretary of State.

"But it's nonsense, of course."

"It is?" He turned the page.

"It has to be. How could evil produce anything useful or beautiful?"

"Mmmm. And here I thought you had settled the matter."

"No, it was an idea that came to nothing."

"Mmmm." He was reading about the priest in Seattle.

"Evil cannot produce anything good."

The phone rang in the dining room and Miss McGee answered it.

"It's for you, Miles. It's that girl."

Miles was on the phone for several minutes, speaking in what Miss McGee took to be a secretive manner. For one thing, he stretched the cord from the dining room around into the kitchen. For another, he mumbled.

"What *is* going on between you two?" she asked when he returned to his chair.

"I don't know. I really don't know." He sorted through the remaining sections of the paper.

"Don't say you don't know, Miles, when I ask a civil question."

127

He looked up at her. "I really don't know what's going on *between* us, as you say. Beverly Bingham seems to be going through some kind of emotional spasm. And it's to me, for some reason, that she's turning for help. Every day in school she asks me for advice. I'm not able to give her much, but that seems to make no difference. It's as though she can't get from one day to the next without checking things out with me. At first, five days a week seemed to do the trick, but now it's weekends as well."

"Is she unbalanced? Her father, you know, was unbalanced."

"No, she's not crazy. She's scared."

"Of what?"

"Of the future. She's coming to the end of her high-school days and she's got brains and a certain amount of ambition, but she doesn't know what to do next. And she comes from such an abnormal home life that she's not sure she can make it in the normal world, and her mother is making life very difficult, and all in all she's just plain scared."

"Yes, she's had a wretched upbringing. Why is there so much wretchedness in the world? But, Miles, it's dangerous for a young man to get too close to a girl student, you know."

"I tell her she must go to college, and she says, 'How can I go to college and have people ask me about my family?' That's what she asked me on the phone just now. 'What will I tell people about my family?'"

"I need not go into detail, Miles. I simply say it's dangerous for a young man to get too close to a girl student. You're smart enough to understand that. Now I'm going out to the kitchen and make us some supper."

"I am not a young man," he called after her with some heat, "and I feel nothing toward Beverly Bingham."

This last was not true. He thought it was true when he said it, but when he went upstairs and pulled Beverly's paper out of his briefcase, her handwriting conveyed, like a photograph, the blush of her cheeks, the blue of her eyes, and he felt his heart do the same trick Thanatopsis Workman always made it do. It leaped a little. He was dismayed and delighted—mostly dismayed. Don't tell me I'm falling in love with Beverly Bingham, he said to himself, don't tell me that.

What I Wish

Binghams' on the Badbattle. If that phrase reminds you of Browning's "Bingen on the Rhine" and all the romance that goes with it, forget it. Binghams' on the Badbattle is where I live, and it's a dump. Our buildings are falling down. Rust from our dozen old cars has been seeping into the ground for so many years our drinking water tastes like metal. The cars are there from the days when my dad was around. My dad was fascinated by cars. By anything that worked mechanically. He made a study of machinery without ever learning anything. Anything in working order he studied by the hour, and when he could get away with it he went at it with his screwdrivers and wrenches and tried to find out what made it work. Maybe it was the lack of order in his own life that made car engines such a mystery to him. I mean, there should have been a sign at the end of our driveway warning people that the whole place was out of order. My mother was deranged (and she's getting worse) and my sister was a hellraiser, and all you can grow on the land we own is chickens, plus a garden from the chicken manure—so that's the kind of place it's always been. Nothing ever seemed to work out for my dad. So

the way I see it, he consoled himself by tinkering
with cars. The twelve junk cars in our yard were
not junk when he bought them. Each one he drove
home under its own power, then after a few days of
tinkering it never ran again. He pulled out wires
and unclamped hoses and took apart switches and
he never got any of it back the way it was. He
unscrewed all the plugs and bolts from the engine
block and then couldn't remember where they belonged. When he got done with a car there was
nothing left to do but sell the five tires. Anyhow,
he's gone now and so is my sister. It's a worse place
now than when they were around. It's weird. My
mother has spells which I won't go into at this time.
I will only say this: How would you like to have a
mother on your hands who's a little more deranged
every day? How would you like to be known as the
Bonewoman's daughter? How would you like to
live in a dump? So there's a lot of things I wish.
I wish my dad had had a normal sort of life and
I wish my mother was normal and I wish I knew
where my sister was and I wish I lived in a house
where the birds didn't fly around upstairs and I
wish I knew what was going to happen to me in the
future. Please help me, Mr. Pruitt.

These last words, this blunt plea, were like a quick
kiss on the cheek. Miles sat at his desk for several minutes, pondering what he should write on her paper with
his red pen. Should he put down the phone number of
Dr. Maitland? Should he outline the steps necessary for
enrolling at Berrington Junior College? Should he set
up an appointment for another talk with her (not in
lovers' lane) and urge her to spill out the secret she
hinted at? No, Miss McGee was right. He must guard

against becoming anything more than her English teacher. At the top of her paper he wrote, "This should be more than one paragraph."

He took from his briefcase the other 113 "What I Wish" papers and stacked them in four piles on his bed. He lay down beside them. He often corrected papers in this manner and he was aware of its significance: lacking a wife, he was married to his work. He turned on his bedside lamp and picked up the first-hour pile, intending to read through all of it before supper. After supper he would finish the other three piles. He would write cogent advice on every paper. "Beware the comma splice." "Organize." "Buy a new pen."

But he could not read. He could not focus his eyes on the papers he held. He was seeing the angle at which Beverly sometimes held her head when she was listening intently in class, her dark hair falling forward about her face.

He flung the papers across the bed and stood up. He lifted his old L. C. Smith off the floor and set it on his desk. He sat down and cranked a sheet of paper into it and began to type.

Nov. 1

Don't tell me I'm falling in love with the Bone-woman's daughter. Don't tell me that. It's too absurd. A wily, middle-aged fart like me becoming infatuated with a messed-up girl half my age? It's unnatural.

There have been only two other girls in my life who made me feel this way. Thanatopsis Workman and Carla Carpenter. It seems so natural to be in love with Thanatopsis. Was there ever in history a woman better suited for marriage and motherhood than Thanatopsis? I should have asked her to marry me on our first date. She had a hope chest and a wealthy father and a huge collection of recipe books and a way of looking at small children that convinced you she wanted and deserved a dozen of her own. And what has Wayne given her? Nothing. Thanatopsis and I have always hit it off. We agree on what is funny and what is dumb (does she agree with me about Wayne?) and our classrooms face each other across the hall.

And it seemed, years ago, so natural to be in love with Carla Carpenter. We were both in high school. We were the same age. We were planning similar futures (in music, of all things) and we both had all the confidence that ignorance bestows on eighteen-year-olds. I did ask Carla to marry me.

But this. A man of thirty-five falling for a high school girl. I don't believe it's possible. What I am feeling for Beverly must be pity. It couldn't be the same kind of thing I felt for Carla when she was eighteen. What did I feel for Carla? Love. Positively and without reservation, love.

Miss McGee called Miles to supper. Meatloaf and sweet potatoes. Cake. After supper Miles wiped the dishes, then returned to his room and sat at his typewriter and pondered what he had written. "Positively and without reservation, love." He sat for a long while with his arms folded on his L. C. Smith, gathering in his mind the details of his love affair with Carla Carpenter. Then he went to his closet and brought out the chrome and plastic briefcase his brother Dale had sent him from California and which contained the hundreds of loose, typewritten pages of his journal. He opened it and set it on the floor beside his desk. He typed another page, then another. He typed all evening, dropping the pages one by one into the briefcase.

Carla was beautiful (Miles wrote). *Carla's, like Beverly's, was a dark beauty. During my high school days, Carla was the standard by which I judged new girls in town. When we were juniors and the braces came off her teeth I asked her for a date.*

"Let's go see House of Wax," *I said. "They give you 3-D glasses at the door."*

"No," Carla said, "I've heard it's not good for the eyes. And besides, I have a vocation."

That's what a girl said in those days when she planned to become a nun. It didn't surprise me because that was the year Carla was acting so distant. Everything she did seemed halfhearted. She never missed a choir concert, but neither did she open her mouth very wide when she sang. As a cheerleader she did the splits and punched at the air and spelled V-I-C-T-O-R-Y and T-E-A-M, but she didn't look committed. Her beauty, in my opinion, was reason enough for her to be standing out there facing the bleachers. But Carla's was the kind of demure appeal best admired in silence—and if it hadn't been for the other two cheerleaders I'm afraid the fans would have lost heart, because Staggerford High School won only three games that year and you cannot shout the spelling of V-I-C-T-O-R-Y and T-E-A-M for very long in a losing cause if your leader looks demure and skeptical both. In English class one day (Mrs. Cochran's class) Carla said, after reading Poe, that she never believed her dreams, not even while dreaming them. She let her hair grow and by spring it was falling around her face like a mask. She was on my mind all the time. I remember that when her hair was at its longest I asked Dale at the dinner table one Sunday if he thought Carla was a mystic.

Dale came home every weekend from St. Andrew's College.

He was a freshman and learning from the monks what seemed to me an astonishing lot about women. "Women are moody and very seldom mystical," Dale said. "They rather enjoy a good languish now and then." Dale always pointed his chin at everyone he spoke to, as though aiming his smugness down his nose.

Mother said, "Like mother, like daughter. Mrs. Carpenter has always been . . . distant."

Father said, "Not always. In her younger years Mrs. Carpenter was a great—friend, shall we say?—of salesmen and railroaders."

"I believe we have discussed this quite enough," said Mother.

As soon as our junior year ended Carla went to live in a convent somewhere, and I got a summer job as assistant caretaker at St. Isidore's, and spent most of my time cutting grass with a power mower that belched out clouds of gray exhaust. To ease the monotony of following the machine back and forth, I got into the habit of singing songs. I must have walked a thousand miles in the fumes of that Briggs and Stratton, trying to sound like the Four Freshmen. I sang "The Day Isn't Long Enough" and imagined Carla walking dreamily through a convent garden at sundown, surrounded by butterflies and black-eyed susans. I sang "Slow Boat to China," and sought the details of an exotic tale of love and peril that began when Carla, to her delight, discovered me at the rail of the ocean liner she was taking to the mission fields. I tried singing "The Little White Cloud That Cried" from beginning to end with my eyes closed because somebody had told me Johnny Ray was blind (untrue), and I ran into a rock. During the two days it took to have the reel of the mower straightened and sharpened, I was put to work caulking the huge rose window above the front steps of St. Isidore's Church.

*Sixty feet above the sidewalk I stood on a plank sus-
pended from pulleys, and when I wasn't nearly fainting
from fright I was imagining how Carla would receive
the news of my death. She would doubtless take her final
vows years early. She would keep to her cell and become
a legend of purity. On her deathbed she would have a
vision, and at her canonization her secret diary would
reveal that I, in my untimely death, was the major instrument in her progress toward sainthood.*

*Carla did not return to Staggerford for the beginning
of our senor year. I asked the other two cheerleaders
about her, but they didn't know much. They said she
was allowed to write only two letters a month and she
wrote them to her pastor and her parents. I asked the
pastor of St. Isidore's—in those days old Father Trask—
and he told me only that Carla would be St. Isidore's
twentieth vocation in its hundred-year history.*

*I hated to ask her parents. Mrs. Carpenter always
looked so grim, and Mr. Carpenter always looked so
surprised that she looked so grim. In stores and on the
street and at parish dinners you would see the two of
them and you knew it was a miserable marriage. Mrs.
Carpenter was tall and fat and she had a crook in her
nose like a knuckle. Mr. Carpenter was a barber without
a hair on his head. He was always doing things to please
her but never doing them right. He carried her purse
while she shopped. She gave him hell in public. At
check-out counters and wedding receptions she would
study him until she found something amiss and then she
let him have it. Filing slowly out of church one Sunday,
my brother and I heard her say, "I did not, you idiot!"
each word twice as loud as the one before, "idiot" echo-
ing off the vaulted ceiling. On the way home my brother
made a pronouncement. "Mrs. Carpenter is food for
thought," he said. "I will not be quoted as saying that*

women are shallow, but they are often marked by an
absence of emotional reserve. And as for poor Mr. Carpenter, what can you expect when a man marries someone twice his size?"

One day in October, meeting the Carpenters in the
grocery store, I introduced myself and asked them what
they heard from Carla. Mrs. Carpenter immediately
turned to face the wall. She moved her jaw, grinding her
teeth. Mr. Carpenter gave me his amazed look and said
softly, "I don't understand her." He said nothing else.
He probably meant Carla. He might have meant his
wife.

Then in November, the vocations from St. Isidore's
slipped back to nineteen and the high school had, once
again, three cheerleaders; for Carla turned up in Staggerford, convent life behind her. Her first day in school
she was slow to speak and she moved from class to class
as though deep in prayer. Her hair was short, but she
did not look pale and ascetic. She looked well fed. She
was, in fact, voluptuous, and I asked her to the movies.
She said, "Yes, yes!" and squeezed my hand.

I walked to her house to pick her up. In the Carpenters' front yard a half-dozen empty birdhouses were
perched on long poles and several homemade lawn
ornaments stuck out of a thin layer of snow. Carla was
standing on the porch ready to go. Her eyes were large
and lovely and she seemed to have grown accustomed to
smiling. Gone was the brooding beauty of grade eleven.
We went to High Noon but we saw only part of it,
because after whispering through the newsreel and car-
toon we discovered we had a hundred things to tell each
other and midway through the feature the manager
asked us to be quiet or leave. It was impossible to be
quiet. I hadn't yet told her about caulking the rose
window and she had only begun her convent stories. We

left. We ate a hamburger at the Hub. Everybody crowded around our booth and told jokes and vied for our attention. We were the main attraction.

As I walked her home the moon shone on the snow the way it does in movies. She said she was glad she had gone to the convent and glad to be back and she'd never go again. On her front walk I kissed her. I used the Howard Keel method. You bend the girl over backwards and swoop down on her lips, a method Howard Keel probably never used on an icy sidewalk. We tipped over in the snow and laughed so loud her mother turned on the porch light and sent her father out to see what was the matter. "Shush them down," I heard Mrs. Carpenter say from behind the door. I got up and shook Mr. Carpenter's hand. I said it was a nice evening. Without his wife at his side, he looked like a man you could talk to. Carla got up and began brushing herself off. I flicked some snow off her shoulder and let it go at that. It is hard for a young man to determine exactly where to stop in brushing snow off a girl.

"Yes," said Mr. Carpenter, looking around at his empty birdhouses, "it's two below zero but you'd never know it."

"No," I said. "It's so still."

"Yes," he said. "No wind."

Carla gave her father a little hug and I saw, in the light from the porch, something like happiness rise up in his big astonished eyes. "Will you come in, Pruitt?" he asked, apparently losing his good judgment, for I had never known anyone to be invited into the Carpenter house.

"Oh, Daddy," said Carla, "you should see how much homework I have. Let's ask Miles over sometime when he can spend the evening. We'll serve him dinner."

"What a nice idea," Mr. Carpenter said.

"*Thank you for the good time,*" *said Carla.*

They both shook my hand. As they crossed the porch the front door opened for them.

The following weekend my brother called me into his room. He had his name, DALE PRUITT, *lettered on his door. He was born toward the end of an era in Staggerford when half the families named one of their sons Dale. Today you won't find a Dale in Berrington County under the age of thirty. I went in and sat on his bed. He closed the door and settled in behind his desk and lit his pipe. At the age of nineteen Dale saw only the studious tranquillity of bachelorhood ahead. His room was neatly packed with everything he wanted in life: a wall of books, a transoceanic radio, a typewriter, a cannister of his own mixture of tobacco. Pinned on the wall, between pictures of Pius XII in ermine and Alec Guinness in* The Lavender Hill Mob, *were rejection slips from journals like the* American Benedictine Review, *to which he sent scholarly articles I never understood about people I never heard of.*

"*Mother tells me you had a date with the Carpenter girl.*"

"*She's back from the convent,*" *I said.* "*She's really looking good.*" *I went on to say that Carla was the girl for me. I tried to describe for him the buoyant feeling she gave me whenever I looked at her, whenever I thought about her, and I became buoyant in my brother's room, bouncing on his bed.* "*I want to make her mine,*" *I said.*

When my brother finally spoke it was to say, "*As for the way she looks, it's only skin deep, you know.*"

"*That's okay with me,*" *I said.*

"*Don't be impertinent. What I wanted to tell you is this. Carla's mother has three strikes against her.*"

"*So?*"

"One, she is unattractive. Two, as a young woman she was not known for her virtue, and three, she's unbalanced."

"I know all that," I said.

"If you know all that, you might consider restructuring your love life."

"I'm not in love with Carla's mother."

By this time my brother's pipe was red hot. He spoke from a cloud. "All girls turn out to be like their mothers. And that's what I called you in here to say. Now, my duty done, I can get back to Chesterton." He turned to his typewriter.

I told him he was crazy.

"If you want to know what a girl will be like in twenty years," Dale said to his typewriter, "if you want to know how her voice will sound, or how her knees will look or what she'll be doing to amuse herself, look at her mother."

"Bullshit," I said.

During December I kissed Carla twelve times. I took her to two movies and I took her Christmas shopping and when I was given the family car I took her skiing. In the Christmas issue of the school paper, it said CC and MP, ain't love grand? I showed it to Dale.

"Beware of woman's beauty," he said, "for passion burns like fire."

On New Year's Eve Carla and I and Harvey Polk and his girl friend went to Minneapolis in Harvey's car and saw Burt Lancaster in The Crimson Pirate. *Three of us thought it was a rotten movie but Carla insisted it was a spoof of pirate pictures. She said it was a masterpiece. After hamburgers and malts, Harvey took from his trunk a quart of gin and a half gallon of sweet wine which we mixed in paper cups and drank on the way home. We hadn't gone far when Harvey got too dizzy to drive and I changed places with him. "I'm fine except for my head and my body," he kept saying in his sleep. After making four wrong turns and parking next to somebody's barn, I too passed out and when I woke up it was nearly noon and I was lying on the rug inside our back door. Mother was preparing duck for dinner, and when she saw me begin to stir on the floor she turned her back until I made my way out of the kitchen. I showered and vomited and put on a tie and took four aspirins and came out to dinner expecting to catch hell, and there sat Carla. Mother had invited her to dinner. She looked fine.*

"Hey," I said. My brain was all gummed up and "hey" was the only word I could think of. I wanted to tell her how I liked seeing her at our table and if she would just be patient my blinding headache would pass and we could become engaged and marry and have as many children as possible and bring them here to Grandmother's every New Year's. So much seemed possible in the world. Except speech, of course. "Hey," I said again, and sat down.

Carla's appetite was ferocious, unsurpassed. Only by limiting myself to celery and water and keeping my eyes off the duck was I able to remain at the table. Carla told the story of The Crimson Pirate, *and when she said it seemed to her like satire my brother stopped chewing and gave her a close look.*

"Fabulous insight for a high school girl," he said. "Of course you were with the sisters for a while. St. Raymond's, was it? Yes, I thought so. Did you read the reviews? No? You saw the satire on your own? One reviewer I read missed it altogether but five others agreed it was a parody. I wrote a little review of my own entitled 'The Pirate's Thrust.' You see the pun? I've been mailing it here and there. Not a bad review but

too late, I think. I have a copy in my room if you would care to read it after dinner. Yes, a good movie, a good parody. Didn't you think so, Miles?"

"Hey," I said, affirming and denying everything. I wanted to ask him to be best man at our wedding and godfather to our first child. Perhaps he would like to come and stay at our house for a few days when his writing wasn't going well and he needed a change of scene. I wanted to suggest he dedicate his first collection of essays to Carla. "Hey," I said.

We finished dinner with no mention of my drunkenness. My father and I left the table to lie down, he in the living room with Harry Wismer speaking to him from the Rose Bowl, and I in my bedroom with the shakes. Carla and my brother helped with the dishes, and when they were done I got up and suggested to Carla that we go for a walk. This was my first hangover and I was beginning to wonder how much of the damage was permanent. I wanted to try out my legs.

"Yes, we could do with a walk," said Dale. "But first I want to show Carla my review. Come into my room, Carla." Behind his back Carla smiled at me, assuring me that she realized Dale was stuffy. She went into his room and read his review.

Finally when we stepped outside, away from the smell of duck, and I took a deep breath of the cold air all my faculties returned with a rush. I felt like running. Carla and I ran ahead of my brother and when we got to the corner we hid behind a garage. He reached the corner and turned in a circle, looking for us, the steam of his breath going this way and that. Then he hunched his coat up to his ears and walked home alone.

At Carla's house her father was waiting for us. He stepped out on the porch and said, "Pruitt, we've set the date for your visit. Saturday, the first of April. Please *come to dinner and plan to spend the evening."*

He shook my hand and went into the house. Carla kissed me and followed him. The sky was purple where the sun was going down.

In January I kissed Carla fourteen times. In February I could have hit thirty because she was taking a passionate turn. But we both got the flu. She recovered before I did and one night when I was still sick my brother took her to a choir concert in Minneapolis. It was my idea. I had two tickets to a sell-out, and with my temperature hovering around 101° I asked him to take my place. Choral music was one of the few interests Dale had in common with Carla and me. In spite of his stuffiness he wasn't bad looking, and I knew Carla could put up with him for an evening in order to hear the final movement of Beethoven's Ninth, *which was on the program. It was Carla's ambition to be a teacher of choral music. It was mine to be a composer. When Dale got home he woke me to say it had been a fabulous concert—two hundred voices and a full orchestra. Besides Beethoven, they performed Carla's favorite section of Handel's* Israel in Egypt *and something from Grieg. "Fabulous," he said, and he began writing a review in his head, aloud, standing over my bed. Fabulous was his favorite word in those days.*

In March I kissed Carla twenty times. Was she as happy with me as she had been in January? I was almost sure of it. With my income-tax refund I bought a sixty-dollar suit—a green wool double-breasted—and on April first I wore it for the first time. It filled me with a strong sense of my masculinity. On the way to Carla's house I swaggered. It was a warm evening full of puddles and robins and the squeak of tricycles, and it occurred to me that it was time to advance beyond the kissing stage of our courtship. I would see tonight what lay beyond.

The Carpenters kept their house so hot it dried out your nostrils the minute you stepped inside the front door. Carla gave me a peck on the cheek, sidestepped my hug, and led me into a long, austere living room where her father stood in a stained apron. He gripped my hand like a drowning man and said Minnesota could expect little change in temperature. Mrs. Carpenter entered the room from the other end and the three of us held our breath as she approached me with the kind of smile that makes your face tired if you hold it very long. She had been gaining weight steadily all winter and seemed to fill the room. She, too, wore an apron, but hers was freshly starched. "I feel I know you better than I do," she told me, and I could sense Carla and her father breathe easier. The three of us spoke to her at once, wishing, I suppose, to congratulate her on her fine statement, and we created with the sudden noise of our voices the illusion of conviviality. But then we sat down in chairs too far apart to be convivial and fell silent. Mrs. Carpenter's smile faded into an expression of absolute woe.

"Little change in the weather," said Mr. Carpenter, "except the possibility of showers in the southwestern part of the state. And that doesn't include us."

"No," I said. "And a good thing, too. The river is high."

"Yes," he said. "The river is high."

Mrs. Carpenter cleared her throat. She said that as a girl she knew an old man who had a saying for every kind of weather imaginable. She paused, trying to imagine a kind of weather. "A saying for rain," she said, and paused again. "A saying for . . ."

Mr. Carpenter was gentle with her. "A saying, Margaret? What do you mean, a saying?"

We waited, listening to the tick of a clock and the

faint whir of the furnace fan. Finally she gave her hands a quick toss in the air to indicate it was no use. She turned to the wall and moved her jaw, grinding her teeth. Carla said it was time to eat.

She and her mother brought to the table a huge capon on two platters. From one platter Mr. Carpenter served Carla and me and himself. The other platter contained a monstrous drumstick and thigh, and Mrs. Carpenter set it down in front of herself, made the sign of the cross, and dug in. She began by cracking the joint apart with her hands and then she shredded the meat from the bones with an oversized fork, twisting and snapping the tendons like rubber bands. She ate nothing else and never glanced up, her attention entirely absorbed in the meat. She didn't close her mouth when she chewed and Mr. Carpenter, to cover her smacking, spoke at length about the weather. Flash floods and sunspots. Blizzards. Fog along creek bottoms. Frost in May.

After dinner we took our coffee into the living room where Carla and I talked about school. The conversation sounded rehearsed, but it pleased Mr. Carpenter, who said yes and no whenever it seemed appropriate. Then Mrs. Carpenter made a sudden violent movement. She slammed her cup and saucer down on a table and cleared her throat and said I made her ass tired. She said I was nothing but a goddamn idiot and if I didn't know what I was talking about why didn't I keep my mouth shut. Carla and her father rushed me out the front door. "Thank you for coming," he said, closing the door on my heels. Carla stood with me on the porch. She said her mother couldn't help it, that her mother was ill. I was full of capon and imperturbable. In my green wool suit I was invincible. I said her mother was a great woman. I said I loved her mother and I loved her father and most of all I loved Carla and we would marry and have a houseful of children and feed them capon. We would surmount all difficulties. We would make the rough places plain.

The sky still held a warm rosy light, though the robins were asleep, and we stepped off the porch and went for a walk. In front of the Hub we talked to friends who sat on the curb and wanted to know what I was doing in a suit. We went inside and the friends followed us and we talked for hours about the State Basketball Tournament. It was to be played in Minneapolis the following week and our team and coaches and cheerleaders, though not participating, had tickets. I was not on the team, though I had yearned all my life to play and did my best every year at tryouts. Carla, to my disappointment, was planning to go. I thought she might stay home because we were in love.

It was after eleven when I walked her home. There was a light in the garage and Carla said her father spent a lot of time out there in the evenings. I looked in the window and saw for the first time his woodworking shop. Along the far wall were his power tools—a jigsaw, a bandsaw, a turning lathe—and piles of lumber. Near the door, under a reading lamp, Carla's father was paging through a magazine. In a corner next to a pot-bellied stove was a sagging old couch where Carla said her father sometimes slept. We backed away and sat in a pile of old leaves and straw that had been raked off the rose bushes now that spring was here. We lay back and did some heavy breathing and rolling around, but try as I might we didn't get much further than the kissing stage. I felt ground moisture soaking through my new suit and I remembered Sister Odilia's warning in the first grade against sitting on the ground in any month whose name contained an r. This was only the first of

145

April, but the nun of course had never been in love. Then Mr. Carpenter turned off the light in the garage and we lay still.

There was no moon and the yard was dark. He stepped outside, pulling the door shut, and walked to the alley, where we heard him urinate on the sand. Then he went into the house. I suggested we go into the garage. Carla said all right but only for a minute. We went in and left the light off and once I got my bearings I moved her toward the couch. I told her my suitcoat was wet, and I took it off and laid it on the bandsaw. I said my trousers were wet and she asked me what in the world I was doing and I said I was taking them off to dry. "For God's sake, Miles, don't be an idiot!" she said. I laid my trousers on the bandsaw and pulled her toward the couch but she held back. I said I wanted to make her mine and she said that was fine but not now. I said if she was going to Minneapolis for three days of basketball I needed something to remember her by. She broke away and switched on the light. I've never been much to look at in my shorts—especially with my shoes on, for some reason—and I leaped at the switch and turned it off. I knew she was doing the right thing and I loved her for it, but I also loved her for other things, and I took her roughly by the arm and twisted it up behind her back to show her I meant business.

I'm not sure my desire was the entire reason for this. I may have been experimenting with her virtue, putting it to a sterner test. It was a stupid thing to do because she reached out with her free hand and turned on the bandsaw which jumped alive with a deafening scream. Then it began to choke on my suit tangled around the blade, and the noise subsided to a chugging growl as the electric motor shot out sparks and blew a fuse. Then silence. I struggled to free my suit, tugging at it and asking Carla to turn on the light. She responded with something like a sob. Or was it a laugh? I heard her father come out of the house and I crouched behind the saw. He opened the garage door and tried the light switch but it didn't work. "Who is it?" he said into the dark. I heard Carla sob again. "Carla?" He came in and pulled open a drawer and turned on a flashlight.

I could tell by the way the light jumped that I startled him.

"I was trying to get my suit out of the saw," I said.

He pointed the light at my legs and my face. I tried to raise the saw blade but I couldn't budge it. He took a wrench off the wall and while I held the light he dismantled the saw. My trousers came free first. The crotch was split open. To free my suitcoat he cut it to pieces with a tin snips. He cut off one sleeve at the shoulder and he cut off a lapel and he cut a square hole in the back.

It seemed to me he cut more than he had to, but I didn't say anything. I handed him the flashlight, and while I dressed he flashed it around the garage. Carla was gone. He went over to the couch and examined it closely.

"Well," I said buttoning my one-armed suitcoat, "I guess I'll be going." He aimed the light at the open door.

Outside I turned and looked back into the beam and said, "I took my suit off to dry."

He turned off the light and I groped my way out to the alley and headed home, holding up my trousers because my belt was cut in two.

With Mother and Father in bed and Dale busy typing, I was able to slip into my room unnoticed. Standing in front of the mirror, I lost all hope of having the suit mended. It hung on me in shreds. I put it in the box it *came in and stashed it away in the closet. Later, when Mother asked me why I never wore it, I told her I had taken it back for a refund. I said there was an imperfection in the weave.*

In school on Monday Carla didn't speak to me. She looked like the Carla of grade eleven, thoughtful, unapproachable.

That night my brother called from college to say his review of The Crimson Pirate *had been accepted by the* American Quarterly Screen Review. *I called Carla. It was the kind of news I needed to break the ice.*

"Dale already called to tell me," she said. "Isn't it fabulous?"

Tuesday and Wednesday we spoke, but only about schoolwork.

Thursday morning the basketball team and coaches and cheerleaders packed themselves into four cars in front of the school as Harvey Polk and I watched from a lavatory window. A cold mist was falling out of a low sky.

"They say the city is wide open at tournament time," said Harvey.

"That's what I hear," I said.

"They say at the Astoria Theater you can see five strippers, one right after the other, for sixty cents."

"That's what I hear," I said. Carla was getting into a DeSoto with four players and a coach.

"They say the hotels are so crowded there's guys and girls in the same bed and nobody cares. My cousin was down there last year and he stayed three nights in three different hotels and never paid a cent. He just followed the crowd. He says you do things you'd never think of doing at home. He met girls from all over the state. Rochester girls are the best looking and Duluth girls will show you the best time, but you have to tell them

you're from Minneapolis before they'll look at you. He says up to that time in his life he was nothing but a babe in the woods. He says if he ever has a daughter he'll never let her go to the state tournament. He says everybody's drunk."

I had heard all that, and more. I had heard every man and boy in Minneapolis roamed the streets at tournament time, picking and choosing among the high school girls coming into the city—maidens from Middle River, from International Falls, from Hermantown. I had heard if you didn't have a strong hold on your girl you could lose her in the blink of an eye. My hold had never been weaker. The cars pulled away from the curb as the first-hour bell rang.

"Come on," said Harvey, "we're late for class."

I said, "Harvey, let's you and me go to the state tournament. We'll go in your car. I'll buy the gas. We'll go home and we'll pack and we'll tell our folks we've been excused from school to go with the team. We'll say Staggerford High got two extra tickets, and you and I got first chance to buy them because we tried out for the team four years in a row and the coach was impressed with how we never gave up. Always in there, giving it all we had. Always good sports."

We sneaked out the boiler-room door and got to Minneapolis at noon. The downtown streets were jammed with traffic and Harvey inched his way around looking for a place to put his car. Flocks of boys moved along the sidewalks, each boy in the plumage of his letter jacket. At Seventh and Hennepin, as Harvey began a left turn, a cop came running toward us blowing his whistle and waving a revolver. People crowded to the curb and stood in the rain to watch. Harvey rolled down his window and the cop pointed the revolver at him and said he was turning into a one-way street the wrong way. The cop was obviously a man out of control, driven mad by traffic and teen-agers and dreary weather. He asked Harvey if he could read signs. In a shaky voice Harvey said he could, and he slouched down in the seat, trying to move his head away from the muzzle of the gun.

"It will be like this three days and three nights," said the cop. "You hayseed sons of bitches bring us nothing but trouble. The best thing for you hayseed sons of bitches to do is to stay home and take care of the live-stock." He was interrupted by the honking of drivers backed up in four directions. "Don't let me catch you in Minneapolis again as long as you live." He put his revolver into its holster and waved us away.

We drove off under a cloud of gloom. The cop's out-burst reminded me of Mrs. Carpenter's in her living room, but this time I couldn't seem to lift my spirits above it. I wasn't full of capon. I wasn't with Carla. My hands, like Harvey's, shook. The seat springs in Har-vey's car were shot and we sat very low, with our eyes barely up to window level. We seemed to be viewing the city from the gutter. Harvey said if he didn't find a parking place in two minutes he was going home. He didn't find one, and he headed out of the city, muttering. In a suburb I got out of the car with my bag and took a bus back downtown. I couldn't stand leaving the city Carla was in.

I went to the hotel where the team was staying and asked the desk clerk where I could find the Staggerford cheerleaders. The clerk said the cheerleaders were in Room 746 but only registered guests were allowed above the first floor.

"I'm with the Staggerford team," I told him.

"Sorry, the team checked in an hour ago. All twelve

of them." He showed me a card with the names of the players. "Your name isn't one of these, is it?"

I hesitated.

"What's your name?"

"Pruitt."

"Pruitt. Well, why didn't you say so? Let's see. Yes, here we are. Dale Pruitt, Room 420, a single. Sign here please. Here's your key. I'll have to ask you to carry your own bag. We're short-handed this afternoon."

Dale Pruitt, *he said. I signed my brother's name.*

"Sorry for the mix-up. We get so many freeloaders at tournament time. There's the elevator. Up you go."

I got off on the fourth floor and let myself into 420, a small room with a rusty radiator, a double bed, and a picture of Hong Kong over the desk. The closet had been converted into a half bath. What was my brother doing with a hotel room in Minneapolis in the middle of the week? He was no basketball fan. He was a scholar. I couldn't figure it out, but whatever the reason, it was a stroke of luck. I would make 420 my headquarters and split the cost with him. I unpacked my bag and changed my shirt, preparing to go up to the seventh floor and announce myself to Carla. As I waxed my butch, someone knocked on the door and a voice called, "Dale, are you in there?" A girl's voice. Carla's voice.

I didn't go to the door. It was wise of me not to, of course, but I doubt if I knew that at the time. I was simply paralyzed by shock. "Dale," she called once more, and then she went away. It was a while before my power of locomotion returned and I began to pack my bag.

Sad to say, a certain other power never did return. I'm talking about the ability to see life as simple and cohesive. Up to that moment in my life, everything had been running according to plan. Even my humiliation in Carla's garage had been predictable, for in the garage Carla had acted according to my expectations—exceeded them, in fact. But her knocking on my brother's door fit absolutely no plan I knew. Like the ravings of her mother and the traffic cop, it was nonsense. That was when I began to see that everything in life was subject to change—without notice.

I called the lobby and told the desk clerk I was not Dale Pruitt after all; I was really somebody else and I had registered as Dale Pruitt only to get upstairs and now that I was up on the seventh floor where all the action was I wouldn't be needing Room 420. The real Dale Pruitt could have it. The clerk said that if I wasn't out on the street in two minutes he was coming to look for me and he would bring the house detective along. I hung up.

I stepped into the corridor and locked the door and put the key on the elevator and sent it down to the lobby. I walked to the end of the corridor where some chairs were arranged around a low table. I slipped my bag under the table and picked up a newspaper and settled into a chair, and whenever the elevator opened I peeked over the paper to see who it was. Sometime later Carla stepped out of the elevator in a dress I had never seen before, not the kind a girl wears to a game. She knocked on 420, waited a moment, and left.

About three o'clock my brother arrived with a suitcase and a bag of groceries. He let himself into 420 and in less than a minute Carla showed up again, this time with a suitcase and a heavy garment bag. She stood outside the room and called my brother's name. The door opened. She went in. The door closed.

What is truer than a platitude? "Beware of woman's beauty," my brother had said, "for passion burns like

fire." I hitchhiked home from Minneapolis that afternoon and my eyes burned with tears. My brother, too,
got burned when Carla, about graduation time, discovered herself pregnant. They were married in June,
with me as best man (I was tempted to wear my
shredded suit; my resentment was that strong) and they
left immediately for California, where Dale got a job
driving a tour bus around Hollywood and wrote verses
for a greeting-card company on the side. In a few years
they had a second baby, another daughter, and my
brother went to work for the greeting-card company full
time.

"Girls turn out to be just like their mothers," was
another thing my brother used to say. When he and
Carla walked into our ten-year class reunion, I couldn't
believe my eyes. (This was their first trip back to Minnesota together. Dale had come alone when Mother
died, and some years later Carla had come alone when
her mother died.) At the reunion Harvey Polk said
Carla would go 200 pounds if she'd go an ounce. I
doubted that. Maybe 180. She was wearing a long fur
coat over a scarlet pants suit. She said that Minnesota
in her memory was always cold and, August or not, she
wasn't leaving California without her fur coat. There
was a large rip in the fur under one sleeve, and with
the red showing through when she raised her arm she
looked like a kodiak with a fresh wound. The skin of
her face was coarse. All evening we had to keep calling
her back to the conversation from wherever her mind
was slipping off to. If my brother was aware of how
Carla had gone to hell, he didn't show it. He talked
only about his work.

He cornered Harvey and me at the bar and described
his house in Los Angeles—how he had converted his
garage into a den, and that was where he spent his

evenings writing verse. He had a bed out there and sometimes he spent the night. In the daytime he was an editor for this greeting-card company. He edited anniversary cards, birthday cards, sympathy cards, and a new card he said was coming on strong—the love card.

"It's a nonoccasional card," he said, pointing his chin at Harvey and me. "It's catching on like wildfire because love knows no season and lovers need no reason. That's the line we use on our displays: 'Love knows no season and lovers need no reason.' I wrote it."

Was this the same man who once wrote scholarly articles and lectured to me about love? Everything the monks told him about love he was now turning into money. He said young people in love thought nothing of spending a dollar for a love card that cost eight cents to manufacture. They sold like wildfire. Was it for this the monks instructed him in the fiery nature of passion?

And Carla. Was this the same girl I once loved? When the reunion banquet was served, my brother and I and Carla shared a table. Chicken was brought in on large platters, and, as we ate, the emcee came around and asked each of us to describe one experience from our high school days. I told the story of how my suit was cut to pieces in Carla's garage. I had had several screwdrivers and I got carried away. I stood up and moved to an open area to reconstruct the layout of the garage. I brought in every detail I could remember, and I demonstrated how to dismantle a bandsaw. Carla didn't laugh. That surprised me. Everybody else laughed, at least a little—even my brother, who was never much of a laugher. When I returned to my place at the table, I told my brother how I had once considered wearing the shredded suit to his wedding. The thought tickled him.

"And believe it or not, I still have the suit," I said. "I've kept it all these years. At first it was a matter of never getting around to throwing it out, and then after Mother died and we sold the house and I moved into Miss McGee's I kept it. I thought it might come in handy some day as a joke."

"What kind of joke?" asked Carla, glaring at me.

"I don't know, but it just seemed to want another wearing."

"I'd love to see you in that suit," said my brother. "If we come over to Miss McGee's tomorrow, will you put it on for us?"

"You Pruitt brothers make my ass tired!" said Carla. She was wrenching apart a chicken joint and glaring at us across the table. She was loud enough to be heard all over the room, and most of the talk and laughter died away. "Every time you Pruitt brothers get together you make my ass tired!" It was our first time together in years. You could hear the clink of silverware for the rest of the meal. Others took their turns at the microphone, but nothing was funny. When Carla finished her chicken and my brother told her it was time to leave, she followed him out the door, wiping her greasy hands on her fur coat and scowling back at me.

They did not come to Miss McGee's house the next day. If they had, I might have put on the suit at their request. But today I wouldn't do it. I've had the suit around since the days that used to follow one another in simple and perfect order, and if some day I bring it out of the closet and take it out of the box, it will not be as a joke.

MONDAY

November 2

ON HALL DUTY outside his classroom door, Miles was expected to discourage scuffling, running, necking, and eating in the halls. It was his policy, when standing at his post, to look stern. He had learned long ago that a teacher's success in his profession depended largely upon his facial expressions and that a look of sternness was nowhere more valuable than in the corridors between classes. This morning, however, try as he might to look stern, he looked merely sullen. He had stayed up too late typing his recollection of Carla Carpenter, and when he had finally gone to bed his toothache kept him awake. Now it was nine thirty of a rainy Monday morning and his first-hour class, particularly groggy on Mondays, had done nothing to clear his head.

Thanatopsis Workman came out of her home-ec room across the hall and said that her husband refused to grant her a day off for the funeral of the mother of her best friend.

Miles said he didn't believe it. He also said, "Slow down there," and "Stop chewing gum," but these orders went unheard in the racket of the passing students.

"I couldn't believe it either," said Thanatopsis. "I got the call Saturday night during the party. Joanie Cooper and I were like sisters. Her mother was a second mother to me. The funeral is tomorrow in St. Paul and I assumed Wayne knew I was planning to attend, and this morning on the way to school I told him I wanted him to get Mrs. Peterson as my substitute tomorrow rather than Mrs. Carlson, who never cleans up properly, and Wayne said I could have anybody I wanted as long as I paid them out of my own pocket. Out of my own pocket, Miles! My God, I haven't missed a day of school in over a year for fear people would think I was taking advantage of being the principal's wife. I haven't taken one day of sick leave or one day of professional-growth leave. And now, just once, I ask for a substitute so I can go to my best friend's mother's funeral and Wayne says I have to pay her out of my own pocket. He says the Faculty Handbook doesn't allow for a funeral like that. He says it allows for the funerals of relatives and that's all. Joanie Cooper was my friend from the time we were little. We roomed together in college. We slept at each other's houses. I'll go to her mother's funeral no matter what, Miles, don't think I won't, but it's so unfair of Wayne. He's so stern about these things. He wouldn't think of going against the Faculty Handbook. Where did that Faculty Handbook come from anyway?"

"Stevenson wrote it years ago when he first came to town, but I don't think even he believes in it much anymore. Until Wayne resurrected it, there were several years when it was completely forgotten."

"Well, it's the most arbitrary, legalistic document ever written, and wouldn't you know it's because it's so arbitrary and legalistic that Wayne loves it so much. He reads it sometimes in the evening. It's his Bible. He wouldn't think of making special allowances for emergencies that the Faculty Handbook doesn't provide for.

He has to be firm, he says. I can see that. He's trying to establish a reputation for firmness. But I'm afraid all it will get him in the long run is a reputation for bull-headedness."

"Why don't you see Stevenson? He'll give you a day with pay. He's really mellowed a lot since he wrote that book."

"Wayne would kill me if I went over his head."

The bell rang for second hour as the halls emptied.

"But pay or no pay, I'm going to St. Paul tomorrow," said Thanatopsis, returning to her classroom, her small hips lifting smartly under her tight red skirt.

"I'll talk to Wayne," said Miles gallantly. "I'm on the Grievance Committee."

Miles turned and entered his classroom just as Jeff Norquist jumped out the window. Jeff had come into the room, put his books on his desk, and vaulted through the open window. It was a drop of only a few feet to the courtyard where his girl friend Annie Bird was waiting for him in the rain. The rest of second hour popped out of their desks and watched Jeff and Annie hurry across the street toward the pool hall, trying to light a wet cigarette between them on the way. Miles saw Superintendent Stevenson watching from his office window across the courtyard.

Second hour couldn't get over Jeff's heroic, defiant act. Second hour, which overreacted to every stimulus—a joke or a sentimental story, a threat or a burp—was crazy all hour. Lawrence Winters dropped his books on the floor. May McClure dropped her compact. Gordie Albertson's eyes crossed. Charlie Zeney had an attack of asthma. Roxie Booth bled at the nose. At wit's end, Miles gave them a surprise test, composing it as he went along and finishing it off with an essay question designed to keep them quiet for twenty minutes. The slowest student answered it in five.

Because his toothache grew worse and it hurt him to talk, Miles gave the same test to third hour. As he expected, third hour regarded it with great seriousness. Bernadine Temple changed her glasses to see the questions on the board. Bill Clifford sharpened four pencils. John Innes read each question with a grimace, as if he were lifting weights. William Mulholland, the scientist, studied the test from beginning to end, considered its value in the larger picture of his whole education, seemed satisfied, wrote his name at the top of a sheet of paper, cracked six of his knuckles, and went to work.

During his free hour, Miles went to see Wayne Workman. In the outer office, where Wayne's secretary had her desk, two sheets of paper lay on the floor, and standing on the paper, one foot on each sheet, was Hank Bird. Little Hank Bird was a sophomore and the youngest of the Sandhill Reservation family of Birds. He was the son of Bennie Bird, proprietor of the Sandhill General Store, where Superintendent Stevenson began, and ended, his tour of the reservation twenty years ago. He was the brother of Annie Bird, Jeff Norquist's girl friend.

Wayne's office was open and empty. Miles went in and sat down. It was a small office: two chairs for visitors, one window with a dusty venetian blind, no carpet. To the right of Wayne's desk was a bookcase stuffed with lost-and-found items—mittens, notebooks, padlocks —and to the left of the desk was a closet door. Wayne kept a clean desk, covered by a sheet of glass. Under the glass was a snapshot of Thanatopsis and a printed card. From where he sat, Miles read, upside down, the title on the card: "The Secret of Success." He read the secret: "Plan your work, and work your plan."

"Hello, Pruitt, what can I do for you?" said Wayne, stepping out of his closet.

"What were you doing in there?" asked Miles.

"Never mind. What can I do for you?"

"I came to ask you to grant Thanatopsis a day's leave with pay."

"Pruitt, if you don't stop calling my wife that crazy name, I'll have to take measures. Her name is Anna Thea."

"Sorry. I came to ask you to give her a day off."

"Out of the question." Wayne sat down and with the sleeve of his suitcoat he polished the glass on his desk.

"I'm on the Grievance Committee, Wayne. It's a reasonable request."

"It goes against policy." Wayne opened the top drawer of his desk and pulled out the Faculty Handbook, a black loose-leaf notebook. "Read this."

"I know what it says."

"Read it anyway." He found the page and handed the notebook to Miles.

Miles read a line or two, then, hoping to impress Wayne with how ridiculous it was, he backed up and started over, aloud:

" 'Absence from Duty: Illness and Death.

" 'Leave shall be granted by the principal, subject to the authority of the superintendent, for absences made necessary by reason of serious illness or injury to the faculty member, or by reason of death in the faculty member's family. The faculty member's family shall be defined to include his spouse, his children, and the spouses and children of his children; his brothers and sisters and the spouses and children of his brothers and sisters and the spouses and children of his wards; his parents or guardians and his grandparents and his uncles and aunts; as well as the parents or guardians, grandparents, brothers and sisters and spouses and children of the brothers and sisters of the spouse of the faculty member. The uncles and aunts of the spouse too.' "

Wayne Workman was impressed. He nodded with satisfaction.

"Do you believe this Handbook covers every exigency in life, Wayne?"

Wayne lifted his hands and shrugged. He couldn't help policy.

"Does this mean a teacher can't go to the funeral of a friend without losing a day's pay?"

"We play funerals by ear, Pruitt. We can usually work something out if the funeral is close by. Funerals take an hour, and we can usually find somebody to cover a class for an hour. But my wife is asking for a whole day."

"St. Paul is a hundred miles from here, Wayne."

"I know where St. Paul is."

"This woman was like a mother to Thanatopsis."

"Goddamn you, Pruitt, for the last time, will you stop using that ridiculous word when you're talking about my wife? And will you please let me interpret the Faculty Handbook according to my own lights? And as for Joanie Cooper's mother, I daresay you never once met the woman. Admit it."

"What's that got to do with it?"

"I have known Joanie Cooper's mother as long as I have known Anna Thea, and you don't have to come in here and tell me how close a friend she was of Anna Thea's. I know all that. I also know that it's part of my job to interpret the Faculty Handbook according to my own lights, Grievance Committee or no Grievance Committee."

"These days no enlightened employer docks an employee's wages for going to a funeral."

"Pruitt, what have you got against policy? You're always defying policy."

Miles stood up. "Let's go see the man who made this policy."

"You go see him. I'm busy."

"All right, I will." He turned to go. "And another thing, Wayne, why is little Hank Bird standing in your outer office?"

"He skipped school Friday."

"Is that supposed to answer my question?"

"I've tried every punishment in the book on little Hank Bird and he still skips, so now I'm trying one that isn't in the book. He's got to stand with his two feet on those two sheets of paper for forty minutes. Maybe that will make him think twice next time he gets the urge to skip. Forty minutes is a long time when you're standing on two sheets of paper, Pruitt. Have you ever tried it?"

"No."

"I tried it for five minutes yesterday. Five minutes seems like an hour when you're standing on two sheets of paper."

Miles knew little Hank from study hall. Like so many of his fellow Indians from Sandhill, he was a good-natured stoic. On his way out of the office, Miles laid his hand on little Hank's black thatch of hair and said, "How much time do you have left?"

Great line

Little Hank smiled broadly and said, "Till I'm sixteen."

Miles crossed the hall to Stevenson's outer office, where Delia Fritz, counting lunch money, told him that the superintendent was occupied. Miles said he would wait. Delia pointed to a chair and went on counting her pile of coins, four at a time, pulling them off her desk with four fingers and dropping them into a metal box on her lap.

Delia Fritz, former shoe-store clerk, and now, since Stevenson's abdication, the true administrator of the Staggerford school system, was a whiz. She was chubby and quick. Today she was wearing three pencils in her wig. Her phone rang, and she rested the receiver between her shoulder and ear and went on counting. The caller was a parent requesting conferences with five teachers, including Miles. From memory Delia told the parent when each of the five had a free hour and added, "If you're coming in tomorrow, you may not find Mrs. Workman. She will be away attending the funeral of a friend. If you wish to talk to Mr. Pruitt right now I think I could find him for you." Delia winked at Miles. "Yes, that's the one. He teaches English. Yes, senior English. Yes, a bachelor, a good catch for somebody. But he gives the young ladies very little encouragement. He's all wrapped up in his teaching, you know. Yes, you know the type. He's forever running off worksheets and quizzes and things like that on the Xerox. Yes, he seems to have a comfortable rapport with his students. The only criticism I've heard about his teaching is that his lesson plans are sketchy. I have another call on line two, Mrs. Holt. Yes, it was nice talking to you. Good-by."

Line two was a salesman calling long distance. "Don't bother," said Delia. "We're up to here in office furniture. We overbought when we built this wing. No, even if you make the trip, the superintendent will not want to talk to you. Send me your card and if the day ever comes to open bids on office furniture we'll let you know. No, all our carpeting is like new. You're welcome." She hung up.

"Since when did it become your job to read lesson plans?" said Miles.

"Don't get testy, Miles, I'm only repeating what Mr. Workman said to Mr. Stevenson about your lesson plans. 'Sketchy' was his word for them."

"And about my rapport with students? Were you quoting Mr. Workman about that too?"

"No, that was what Mr. Stevenson said to Mr. Workman. He said you have a comfortable rapport with students. You're Mr. Stevenson's fair-haired boy, you know. That's why he was so shocked this morning to see Jeff Norquist jump out your window."

"What did he say?"

"He came out here to my desk, where he never comes anymore, and he said, 'Delia, you will never believe what I just saw. I saw the Norquist boy jump out Miles Pruitt's window. Please make an appointment for me with Dr. Maitland.' He thought his heart was stopping."

Miles heard the toilet flush in the superintendent's private lavatory. Delia nodded toward the inner office.

Miles entered and saw Superintendent Stevenson making his way slowly across the deep carpet of his office, his long, angular body contracted around his heart. He cocked his head at Miles and motioned for him to sit down.

Miles shut the door behind him, but he did not sit. "Mr. Stevenson, I've come to ask you to waive a regulation in the Faculty Handbook. Mrs. Workman would like to take a day of emergency leave tomorrow. She wants to attend a funeral."

It was some time before the superintendent spoke. He was settling into the position Miles saw him in from eight till three every day. He turned his swivel chair to face the window beside his desk, then tilting the chair back, he rested his feet on the pulled-out bottom drawer. He looked out across the courtyard at the windows of Miles's empty classroom.

"Please sit down, Miles."

He sat.

"Now, Miles, I am not a man who is easily alarmed. As a rule I take things in my stride and I don't fuss about them." The superintendent brushed dandruff off his left shoulder and lapel. "But I was alarmed this morning when I saw the Norquist boy jump out your window. It gave me a start, Miles. I thought for a moment I was dreaming." He found a speck of dandruff on his sleeve. "That classroom of yours is usually the picture of good order, Miles. I see you carrying on in there day after day. I see classes coming in and classes going out. I see students raising their hands. I see students writing at the blackboard. I see their heads bending over their work. I see good order. I see education."

"Thank you, sir."

"Then suddenly this morning I see the Norquist boy jump out the window."

"I'm sorry, sir."

"It was that window there on the right." Stevenson pointed to the window with a long, unsteady finger.

"Jeff Norquist is hard to handle."

"I understand that, but he should be kept from jumping out the window."

"Yes, I agree."

"And I'll tell you why."

"I'm sure I understand why, sir. It gives the towns-people a mistaken impression of what goes on in school."

"Oh, *that*. Never mind *that*." He swept the air with his hand, as though brushing away a fly. "That's not what I'm getting at. What does public opinion matter? Poof! It's nothing. There was a time when public opin-ion was foremost in my thinking, but not anymore. What I'm getting at is *my* opinion, *my* reaction. When I saw Norquist jump, I thought my heart was going to stop."

There was a long pause while Stevenson slipped his hand under his necktie and felt his breastbone. The clock on the wall was approaching lunch hour.

"Now of course there was nothing dangerous about the jump," he continued. "The window is only four feet above the ground. It wasn't the acrobatics of the jump that startled me. It was what the jump symbolized. This is a school with a long history of attendance problems, Miles. For twenty years it has been my job to get stu-dents into this school who don't want to be here, and once they're here, to keep them here. And when I saw the Norquist boy jump out the window, I recognized the curse I've been fighting for twenty years—the desire of a certain percentage of our students to run away from school, to stay away, to reject what we offer them. I call it the Staggerford Curse. It's inevitable, year after year, like sun and darkness. And to tell the truth, I'm not much concerned about it anymore." He brushed dan-druff from his right lapel, his right shoulder, his right sleeve. "No, I'm not much concerned about absenteeism anymore, not consciously at least. It's a curse peculiar to Staggerford, and I tried to overcome it, to change it, and I couldn't, and I've taught myself to face it with equanimity. I don't wear myself down with worry. I can keep it out of my consciousness."

He turned to look Miles in the eye.

"But I can't control my subconscious, Miles. My *emotional* reaction to absenteeism. These twenty years have left me with a conditioned reflex, a strong involuntary emotion concerning the Staggerford Curse. When I saw the Norquist boy jump out the window I could reason with myself and say in my mind, 'So what,' but I couldn't control my heart, Miles. I thought my heart was going to stop."

The lunch-hour bell rang. The halls filled. Here in this office, where the superintendent had insulated himself from his school, the voices and the noise of slamming lockers sounded far away.

"Do you understand what I'm saying, Miles?"

"Yes," Miles said, although he wasn't sure. Stevenson's voice always made him sleepy.

"We can't control our involuntary reactions to things, can we?"

"No, I guess we can't."

Delia Fritz poked her head in the door and said she was going to lunch. "When you leave," she told Miles, "shut the outer door. It will lock after you."

The halls grew quiet. Everyone was down in the lunchroom, standing in line for butter sandwiches and hamburger-macaroni-tomato hot dish.

"I'm sorry it happened," Miles said.

"Think nothing of it," said Stevenson. "I only mention it because you know about my little secret." He lowered his voice. "Viola, I believe, told Imogene Kite all about the valve in my heart when you were over for bridge, and I assume Imogene told you. Any shock, you know . . ."

"I won't let it happen again."

The superintendent nodded. "I'm sure you won't. And even if it did happen again, I doubt if my heart would stop. It's only the first time that one is startled by something like that. But even so . . ."

"It won't happen again."

"Of course not."

"Now, what I came to ask is this. Mrs. Workman would like a day of emergency leave for the funeral of her best friend's mother. I think she should have it."

"What did she die of? Was it her heart?"

"I'm not sure."

"I'll bet it was her heart."

"It may have been. I'm not at all sure."

"How old was she?"

Miles didn't know. "Eighty-nine," he said.

"Eighty-nine. Think of it."

"Yes."

"Eighty-nine. That's a good long life."

"Yes. And she was very close to Mrs. Workman. I really think she should be granted a full day with pay."

"Of course she should."

"But there is no provision for it in the Handbook."

"The what?"

"The Faculty Handbook."

"Oh, *that.*" Stevenson swept the air again with his hand, indicating that the Handbook, like public opinion, amounted to no more than a pesky fly. "Never mind *that.*"

He took his feet off the pulled-out drawer and set them carefully on the carpet. He turned in his swivel chair and for no reason Miles could think of, except perhaps that his insulated office had made him lonesome, he warmly shook his hand.

"Tell Anna Thea Workman she shall have her day with pay. Excuse me for not getting up."

"Thank you, Mr. Stevenson."

"Be sure you hear the snap of the lock when you close the outer door."

Leaving the office, Miles glanced back and saw the superintendent facing the windows again, but bending forward now in his swivel chair with his elbows on his knees. He was brushing the dandruff from his eyebrows and watching it settle on the carpet.

Miles pulled the outer door shut and heard the snap of the lock.

Miles used his noon hour to visit Doc Oppegaard's office on Main Street. He found Stella Gibbon and the dentist sitting together in the waiting room, lunching on wine and cheese.

"Wine at noon?" said Miles, not finding fault, merely surprised.

Stella and the dentist looked at each other and giggled.

Miles told them he had a toothache.

"Help yourself," said Doc Oppegaard, pointing to the wine bottle, obviously not ready to go to work.

Miles thanked him, and as he looked about the waiting room for a third wine glass, Stella went into another room and brought him a paper cup meant for mouthwash.

The dentist poured. "Here's to Stella," he said. They touched wine glasses, and when Miles held forward his soft paper cup, the dentist and Stella collapsed from laughter. Stella sank into a chair, shaking until her eyes watered and her thighs were exposed under the creeping skirt of her scanty white uniform.

"You must have started early," said Miles, pouring himself more wine, for his cup held but a swallow.

Doc took off his glasses and wiped his eyes and blew his large nose. "We did for a fact," he said. "We had a cancellation at eleven."

After Stella quit laughing and pulled down her skirt, she and the dentist led Miles into the examination room, where they fitted him out in a lead vest and trained the X-ray machine on him and set it to buzzing for what seemed like a dangerously long time. The picture must have been alarming, for Doc grew sober as he studied it, then he peered into Miles's mouth, causing Miles to gag on his cheesy breath.

"Do you want to see something?" Doc asked Stella. She crowded in for a look. "It's the wisdom tooth on the lower left. It has come in sideways and the root is curled around his jawbone."

"Oh, it's so *ugly*," said Stella.

"Go ahead and pull it," Miles said. "I have forty minutes left of my lunch hour."

"No, no," said the dentist. "I wouldn't touch it with a ten-foot pole. That's a job for Karstenburg in Duluth."

Stella said, "Yes, Dr. Karstenburg is your answer."

Looking up at Stella as she spoke, Miles saw the bright new lines of gold outlining her eyeteeth and anchoring the handsome new bridge that didn't cost her a penny. Her smile was splendid.

"Yes, Karstenburg is your man," said Doc. "He specializes in wisdom teeth. He's been known to pull forty-eight teeth in one day. And I'm not talking about baby teeth. I'm talking about impossible cases. Teeth with roots like fishhooks. Teeth like yours."

"Call him," said Miles.

Stella went to the phone and called Duluth and got

Miles an appointment with Dr. Karstenburg for the next day.

"So soon?" said Miles. "If he's so busy, how is that possible?"

"He works fast," said Doc.

On the way out of the examination room, Miles glanced at Doc Oppegaard's appointment book and saw (confirming his suspicions) nothing scheduled any day of the week between eleven and one.

Like the host and hostess at a party, Doc and Stella saw him to the door, and on the front step the dentist asked him how old he was.

"Thirty-five," said Miles.

"I was rid of all my wisdom teeth by the time I was twenty-three," said Doc.

Stella giggled.

The rain was all but over. The brisk west wind was tearing the clouds to shreds.

After fifth hour Beverly Bingham approached Miles as he stood at his door, but she was shouldered out of position by Wayne Workman, who said angrily, "Pruitt, I understand you went over my head."

"I told you I was going to see Stevenson. You said, 'Go ahead.'"

"Pruitt, what do I smell on your breath?"

"Oh . . . Well . . ."

"For godsakes, Pruitt, don't tell me you nip at lunch."

"You'd be the last man I'd tell."

"Pruitt, if we ever get to the point of dissension in this school, it's going to be your fault. You and your Grievance Committee. Now that Stevenson has over-ruled his own Faculty Handbook none of us know where we're at. Is that a policy handbook or is it not? We were all led to believe that it was, and now we find the policy broken by the man who made the policy. Where does that leave us, Pruitt, in regard to policy?"

"If you'll pardon me for a second, Wayne, I have this student here who wants a word with me."

"Tell her to come back some other time. I'm not finished."

"I'm sorry," Miles told Beverly. "See me some other time."

"I just wanted you to look at this letter I've written to Berrington Junior College." She gave Miles and Wayne a lovely smile.

"You and your committee fancy yourselves such a progressive bunch of schoolpeople," said Wayne, "but you're not in the least progressive after all, and I'll tell you why. You ignore the rules. Ignoring the rules is anarchy, and anarchy is not progress. Someone ought to explain to your committee how progress is really made. First the rules are formulated and then abided by and then, and only then, is progress possible."

"It's only a page," said Beverly. "Maybe I could just leave it with you and pick it up after school."

"When all is said and done, I'm more progressive than you are, Pruitt. That may strike you as ironic, but it's true. Every day that Staggerford High School operates smoothly is a day of progress, and every day that somebody like you comes along and throws a wrench in the ointment is a day of backsliding. I'm perfectly willing to listen to any suggestions anybody might have concerning the betterment of Staggerford High School, but I keep in mind all the while that any changes have to be made within the framework of policy."

Beverly said, "What I wanted to ask you about was the first paragraph. I must have written the letter ten times, and the first paragraph is still awkward."

"So actually what it amounts to is that you are an

obstacle in the road to progress. Anyone who disregards the Handbook—"

"I'm not optimistic about the future of the Handbook, Wayne."

"What's that supposed to mean?"

"I'm just not optimistic about it, that's all."

"And do I start the letter by saying 'Dear Sirs,' or 'Gentlemen,' or what?"

Miles took the letter from Beverly.

"You're never optimistic about anything, Pruitt. That's your trouble. You're an obstacle in the road to progress around here."

The bell rang. Beverly hurried away. Miles locked his classroom and started up the stairway. "I'm late for study hall, Wayne."

"You're an obstacle in the road to progress," Wayne called after him.

At the landing, Miles turned and saw Wayne standing at the bottom of the steps in his most earnest pose, his hands outstretched, palms up, like a beggar. He was painful to look at.

After school Miles went into the basement lunchroom and burned his tongue on a quick cup of the coffee that had been simmering on the stove all day. It tasted like tinfoil. Then he went to the faculty meeting in Ray Smith's history classroom.

As Miles entered, Wayne Workman was at the lectern saying, "I would like your input on how we should handle Parents' Night, and on this new-style report card I am passing around for your inspection. And I would like your input on what can be done about the smoking and the writing on the walls in the rest rooms. The meeting is now open."

The faculty offered this input:

"What's wrong with the report card we've got?"

"When is Parents' Night?"

"*Why* is Parents' Night?"

"I thought we should have beat Owl Brook by two touchdowns. We were that much better."

"Aw, that goddamn Fremling."

"I'm wondering if there's anyone besides myself who would like to see the Faculty Handbook burned."

"Huzzah."

"This report card would be a lot more work to fill out. Look, it asks for an attitude rating and a behavior rating."

"Behavior *is* attitude."

"Does it ask for a grade?"

"I say let them smoke. What's the harm?"

"It's only the parents of good students who show up on Parents' Night anyhow. We never see the parents of the problem students."

"What would you say to them if they *did* come?"

"If you were the parent of a problem student, would *you* come?"

"They could be doing worse things in there than smoking and writing on the walls."

"Have you ever considered throwing out the traditional grading system and going to something else?"

"If only we could have scored in the third quarter when we were on their twenty-five."

"Aw, that goddamn Fremling."

"We had a hundred and five kids at the door for tricks and treats. My wife counts them."

"Somebody dumped garbage on my steps."

"The front of my house is covered with eggs and tomatoes."

"I got off easy this year—a few soaped windows."

"You know what I read in the boys' can downstairs? It's over the sink. I'll tell you after the meeting."

"I'd like to see two grades—pass and fail—instead of five."

"I must confess that when I'm figuring grades, I always give the benefit of the doubt to the kids of the parents who show up at Parents' Night. I wish I wouldn't do that."

"Do we get to vote on which report card we want?"

"Do you realize how long it would take to make out each card—to mark each student on attitude *and* behavior? Besides times absent and times tardy and the scholastic grade and signing our names?"

"Behavior *is* attitude."

"Last year we had more. We had a hundred and thirty and we ran out of candy."

"Well, I for one am going to see the Faculty Handbook abolished."

"Miles, what's the matter with you today? You don't look so hot."

"I've got a bad tooth."

"Let's vote. I make a motion that behavior is attitude."

When Wayne Workman had all the input he wanted, he said, "Next Monday night is Parents' Night. The Public Relations Committee will handle the arrangements. We'll need publicity and ushers and coffee and cookies. Who is chairman of Public Relations?"

"Right here," said Coach Gibbon.

"We want a good turnout of parents, Coach."

"Right. Now can I go? I've got my wrestlers waiting for me in the gym."

"Well, we've got the report card and the rest room

walls yet. And I want to tell you about my new Indian attendance plan."

"But this is the first night of practice. I've got to get down there and get things organized."

"All right, Coach."

"Now wait a minute," said Thanatopsis. "The Faculty Handbook is very specific about who is excused from faculty meetings and who isn't."

Coach Gibbon stole out of the room.

"Next I would like to appoint a committee to oversee the smoking and writing on the walls in the rest rooms," said Wayne.

His wife said, "I'm not through, if you don't mind. On page six of the Faculty Handbook it says, 'Absences from faculty meetings will only be allowed persons who have sought and obtained, at least two hours prior to the meeting, the principal's or superintendent's permission to be absent.'"

"Please, Anna Thea. We'll take that up in good time."

She continued, "And I want to point out that this morning you denied a certain member of this faculty the right to attend a funeral because according to the Handbook it was the wrong kind of funeral, and now, in defiance of the Handbook, you allow another member of this faculty to leave so that he can show his wrestlers how to put on their jockstraps."

Wayne was cornered. He chewed his mustache and frowned. His eyes seemed to be crossing. His tie seemed to be unstraightening itself.

Thanatopsis said, "Now it isn't your inconsistency that I wish to point out, although I guess I already *have* pointed it out. What I wish to point out is that this Faculty Handbook is stupid, and any enlightened fac-

179

ulty should be able to get along with fewer rules and more common sense."

"We don't have the power to abolish the Handbook," said Wayne. "It's been handed down to us by the superintendent and the board."

"The superintendent and the board are all reasonable men. I'm sure they will listen to our analysis of its shortcomings."

"*Our* analysis?"

"A committee's analysis. Appoint a committee, Wayne. I volunteer to chair it."

"Very well, I will appoint a Handbook Committee."

"When?"

"Before our next meeting."

"Very well," said Thanatopsis.

On the matter of report cards, opinion was equally divided between the new card and the old. Wayne appointed a Report Card Committee.

No one knew what to do about misbehavior in the rest rooms, so he appointed a Rest Room Committee, or what Coach Gibbon (when he discovered himself a member) chose to call the Can Committee.

Now it was time for Wayne to unveil his new idea for Indians. He stepped out into the hall for a drink of water and re-entered the room wiping his mustache with the back of his hand.

"May I have your attention. I would like to tell you about my new plan to improve Indian attendance."

Miles wondered how many times these futile words had been spoken in Staggerford. There arose from the faculty a barely audible sound—not a groan, not a hiss, but a kind of suppressed sigh.

"I call my plan 'Befriend an Indian.'" Wayne held up a sheet of paper with a list of names down the left-hand side and the words BEFRIEND AN INDIAN printed in red across the top. "An Indian, like everybody else in Minnesota, can legally quit school when he is sixteen. And most of them do. Every dropout at sixteen decreases our state-aid monies. I have prepared this list of all the Indian students in Staggerford High School who will turn sixteen between now and the end of the current school year. You will see that here at the top I have printed, 'Befriend an Indian.' That's exactly what I'm asking you to do, befriend an Indian. I will pass this paper among you and you will please write your name next to a name on the list. And then proceed to befriend the Indian with that name."

The paper went from hand to hand.

"To give you an idea of how serious our problem is, I give you these statistics. In grades nine and ten the proportion of Indians to whites is approximately eighteen percent. In grades eleven and twelve the proportion is three percent. That's because as soon as Indians turn sixteen they drop out. Last year we graduated only two Indians, both of them girls, and I don't think it's any secret that both of those girls stayed in school till they graduated because they were befriended by my wife. If it hadn't been for Anna Thea, those two girls wouldn't have graduated. Now I grant you that my wife has an inside track where girls are concerned, because the home-ec department is a place where a lot of girls naturally feel at home. But there is no reason that you, Mr. Jennings for example, could not seek out an Indian student with a talent for science and bring him along to the point of graduation, is there?"

Ross Jennings, biologist, shrugged.

"And you, Mr. Pruitt. Is there any reason why you couldn't discover an Indian boy or girl with a talent for English—poetry or adverbs or some such thing—and bring him along to the point of graduation?"

"No reason whatever," said Miles.

"Do your utmost to find the right Indian then, and encourage that Indian to make good. Encourage him to keep his nose to the ground and earn his diploma. Tell him to be like everybody else. Tell him about Nancy Bigmeadow. The last I heard Nancy Bigmeadow was still in Washington."

"Who is Nancy Bigmeadow?" asked Ross Jennings, new on the staff.

"Nancy Bigmeadow is a girl from the reservation who graduated a few years back and now she is in Washington."

"Washington, D.C.?"

"Yes."

"What's she doing in Washington, D.C.?"

"I can't tell you exactly what her job at this time might be, but I know that when she went to Washington it was on some kind of program that trained Indians for jobs in some aspect or other of the federal government, and Nancy Bigmeadow was the only Indian chosen from Minnesota. It was quite a feather in our cap."

Ross Jennings said, "But if we don't know what Nancy Bigmeadow is doing in Washington, how can we use her as an example? Are we supposed to say to Indians, 'Look here, before you quit school consider Nancy Bigmeadow—she went to Washington, D.C.'? Mr. Workman, let's be realistic. That isn't much to go on. Where I taught last year I had a student who quit school and went to Wyoming, but it was to take a job servicing prophylactic dispensers in rest rooms. How do we know Nancy Bigmeadow is doing any better than that?"

The faculty laughed.

Wayne was wounded. "If you can ask a question like

that, Mr. Jennings, then you don't know Nancy Big-meadow."

"That's precisely my point. She is unknown to me. This is my first year in Staggerford."

By the time the Befriend an Indian list was handed to Miles, all the Indians were befriended but one—a boy he didn't know named Sam LaGrange. Miles wrote his name next to Sam's.

"Nancy Bigmeadow is maybe not my best example," said Wayne. "But all of us who have been here a while can point to others."

Ray Smith, historian, said he knew an Indian who went to North Dakota to hoe sugar beets.

The faculty laughed.

"No, seriously—" said Wayne.

Everett Tillington, mathematician, said he once knew an Indian who went to Iowa to work in a banjo factory.

The faculty laughed. The meeting was falling apart.

"Before we adjourn," called Wayne, trying to look stern through his misery, "I would like to call on my wife to tell us how she befriends Indian girls in her field of home economics."

At the word "adjourn" half the teachers stood up to leave.

"To befriend an Indian," said Thanatopsis, "feed him pie."

Over the laughter Wayne asked if there was a motion to adjourn. There wasn't. The faculty was rushing, like sophomores, to the door.

Miles went to his classroom for his briefcase and his coat and the sack containing Lyle Kite's ranger pants. He crossed the hall to the home-ec room and asked Thanatopsis what could be done about the pants.

"You must have got acid on them," she said. "Look what it's done to the fabric. What kind of acid was it?"

"It was Mrs. Oppegaard's vomit."

Thanatopsis shrieked. "Take them to the dry cleaners," she said, laughing. "But I doubt if they'll ever be the same again."

He took them to Bud's Cleaners, where Bud said, "It looks like you got acid on them. I can try to clean them but I can't promise what they'll look like. What kind of acid was it?"

"Stomach acid."

On the way home, Miles stopped at the Kite house to tell Lillian he was having the uniform cleaned and would return it in a few days. He also mentioned, in Imogene's presence, that he was going to the dentist in Duluth the next day.

"Oh, super," said Imogene. "Tomorrow's my day off. I can go along and look for a new winter coat."

"I thought I'd leave before seven," he said, hoping to discourage her. "I thought I'd visit my father on the way into the city."

"I'll be ready. Just honk in the alley."

TUESDAY

November 3

WHEN MILES HONKED his horn at sunrise, Imogene was ready. Smelling of perfume and shoe polish, she settled herself into the front seat of the Plymouth and said, "This is going to be fun. We will go to dinner and take in a movie. They've brought back *Virginia Woolf* at the Strand. I love Burton and Taylor together."

Duluth was two hours away—a hundred miles through forests of jackpine and leafless aspen. Miles was so distracted by the beauty of the morning that twice he nearly left the road. Every twig on every tree was hung with a silver drop of melting frost. Three deer stood in a clearing near the highway, a buck, a doe, and a fawn. Formations of ducks and geese crossed the sky. Imogene slept all the way.

In Duluth's West End, the old End, Miles parked on a narrow street and pointed to a four-story building of sooty brick.

"That's where my father lives. I'll just be a minute."

"I'll tag along," said Imogene. "I'd like to see the old boy."

Inside the front door a decrepit nun behind a desk asked them what they wanted.

"I'm Leonard Pruitt's son."

"Oh, dear old Mr. Pruitt," said the nun. "His feet are so big. You'll find him on the third floor."

They took the elevator to the third floor, where all the old folks who could move under their own power had come out into the hall for a stroll and those who couldn't had come out for a ride. Miles spotted his father in a tangle of wheelchairs. Since Miles had last seen him, Leonard Pruitt's teeth had come out and his face had fallen in. As always, the old man wore the white shirt and pants of a buttermaker.

"Hello, Dad, it's me, Miles."

Seeing Miles and Imogene, all the walkers and riders came to a stop.

"It's me, Miles. And this is Imogene Kite."

Leonard Pruitt put his hand to his ear. Webbed in the spokes of his wheelchair was a gummy mixture of dust and gravy.

"Your son!" Miles shouted, scattering most of the onlookers.

Leonard Pruitt nodded. "Do you want to see my room? I have a picture of my boys in my room." It was what he always said to visitors, anybody's visitors.

Miles pushed the wheelchair into Room 30, and Imogene followed. Leonard Pruitt showed them a photograph of his sons, Dale and Miles, at the ages of thirteen and twelve. It had been taken by a sidewalk photographer on Seventh Street in Minneapolis, and in the background Miles saw the old Century Theater and a streetcar. The Century had been torn down and replaced by a nightclub about the time streetcars were replaced by buses.

"They're grown up now," said Leonard Pruitt. "One's in California and one's a schoolteacher. One of them is married and has two daughters. I don't know which one. We had ice cream last night." He was wearing sandals, his feet and ankles swollen too large for shoes.

An old man wearing suspenders over his pajama tops wandered into the room, lay down on Leonard Pruitt's bed, and snapped his eyes shut, pretending to sleep. Leonard Pruitt maneuvered his chair over to the bed and hit the old man on the leg. The old man smiled but did not open his eyes. Leonard Pruitt hailed a nurse, who came in and pulled the old man from the room.

A tiny lady, attracted by the commotion, came into the room and gave Miles a stern look and said she didn't see why he had so much trouble driving through the snow. She had just traveled that road barely an hour before, coming in from teaching country school, and she had no trouble. Her voice was high-pitched, like the whine of a little girl. She said the only snowdrifts were along the open stretches of road near Hartle's Corner, but if you had a Ford coupe with chains on the tires as she had there was no excuse for getting stuck.

"How would you like us to take you out for a spin around the block," Miles shouted at his father.

He nodded and pointed to his jacket, which hung on a hook in the closet.

In the elevator he said they had been promised Mulligan stew for Sunday dinner but got hamburger instead—hamburger mixed with macaroni and tomato sauce. He said it was very good.

Outside in the warm sun he said, "I would like you to see my room. I have a picture of my boys up there."

"Fine," said Miles. "But first let me push you around the block for a breath of fresh air."

"Nonsense, I've had enough fresh air. Come with me to my room."

When the elevator opened on the third floor, Leonard Pruitt said, "Come again," and went spinning reck
lessly down the hall.

"So now you've seen my father," said Miles.

"Quite the old boy," said Imogene.

Miles found Dr. Karstenburg's office in an urban-
renewal neighborhood, where all the trees were seed-
lings and the odd shapes of the new buildings resembled, from a distance, ruins. Imogene slid over behind
the wheel of the Plymouth and said she would return
for Miles in an hour. She drove downtown to shop.

Miles sat alone in Dr. Karstenburg's waiting room, a
funhouse. The walls were carpeted in purple and green,
and tacked to the carpet at crazy angles were posters of
football stars and country-music stars and movie stars. A
pinball machine stood in one corner, blinking. From a
speaker in the ceiling came a number entitled, "I Took
My Broad to the Beach," the lyrics of which consisted
entirely of that statement, repeated forty or fifty times.
It appeared to Miles that he was rather far along in life
to be visiting a wisdom-tooth specialist.

After a long wait, a frail girl in a white uniform led
Miles into a small room with a padded black chair—not
one of the sleek new dental chairs that adjust at a touch
to twelve different positions, but an upright, old-fashioned barber's chair. He sat down and she tied a bib on
him. "I'm Joy," she said. Then she blindfolded him.

"Is that necessary?" Miles asked.

"Yes, it's so the light doesn't bother your eyes."

"Light doesn't bother me," he told her.

"It might," she said. He heard her leave.

Except for the trickle of water, the room was silent for
a long time. Then a man's voice said, "Hi, Karstenburg
here." He lifted one of Miles's hands and squeezed it

The doctor's was a fat hand. "You've got a real doozy in that mouth of yours," he said happily. "Oppegaard phoned me about it."

He gave Miles a shot of Novocain in the hinge of his jaw, then he left the room. In a few seconds he was back to ask if his mouth was numb. Miles said it wasn't. The dentist gave him a second shot and went immediately to work. He clamped his pliers on the wisdom tooth and tried to rock it loose. Miles's head rocked with the tooth.

"Joy," called the dentist, and soon Miles felt a pair of hands press themselves around his head—Joy's hands, surprisingly strong.

Novocain never worked fast with Miles, and the gum around his tooth hurt where Karstenburg was tearing it with his pliers. Miles began to sweat. The dentist rocked the tooth until he was out of breath. Miles felt him take the pliers out of his mouth and heard him pull up a chair or a stool and sit on it, panting. Joy sponged off Miles's forehead.

When the dentist went back to work, it was with a larger tool, something with a handgrip that felt to Miles's upper lip like a pipe wrench. The dentist squeezed and grunted. The tooth crumbled. He dropped the wrench and went in with a pick. Miles fainted.

He awoke with his head on his knee and something cold on the back of his neck. He was still blindfolded. He could not hear the doctor breathing. Was he alone? He straightened up and felt Joy remove the ice pack from his neck.

"He's coming out of it," she called, and the dentist returned.

The Novocain was at last beginning to take effect, and although it required effort, Miles was able to re-main conscious through the rest of the slicing, prying, and picking. When it was over the doctor left the room without a word of farewell. Joy removed the blindfold and bib. Miles didn't feel like standing up.

"You may go now," said Joy.

It was so good having nothing going on in his mouth that he wanted to remain in the chair for a while and savor the peace.

"It's over," she said.

It was all he could do to stand up. He was not steady on his feet. Joy wiped blood from his chin with a Kleenex and turned him toward the waiting room.

He tried to say good-by (it was to be his first word in what seemed like days), but discovered his mouth full of rags.

"Keep the cotton pressed into the hole," said Joy.

He nodded and staggered through the waiting room, where "I Took My Broad to the Beach" was playing again (or yet) with no one to hear it. He went outside into the sunlight where Imogene was supposed to be waiting, but Imogene wasn't there.

He stood on the curb and took out his handkerchief to catch the string of blood that hung from his mouth. It was an elastic string without an end. In retribution to Dr. Karstenburg he took the handkerchief away from his mouth whenever a car passed and let the blood swing from his lower lip and drape itself into the gutter for all the world to see. During the half hour he waited for Imogene, sensations returned to his jaw, nerve by nerve —a series of prickles under the skin like a plucking of strings, building to a crescendo of full, rich pain. In that half hour no one entered Dr. Karstenburg's office. Miles wondered if Karstenburg was a joke in the profession. A butcher your dentist sent you to if he didn't like you? If you called him an ack-comedian?

"Drive me home," Miles mumbled when Imogene

finally appeared. "Karstenburg has done me wrong."

"Oh dear," said Imogene. "That means no movie and no dinner. And no winter coat."

She got onto the highway leading out of the city.

"I'm tall for a woman, Pruitt. You may not believe this but I am taller than eighty percent of the women in the U.S.A., and therefore I have difficulty finding clothes in Staggerford."

She talked all the way home—the size of women, the styles for winter, the origins of dentistry, and the harnessing of atomic energy—changing the subject at ten-mile intervals.

Miles, at ten-mile intervals, ate aspirin.

Arriving home from school at three o'clock, Miss McGee found Miles watching "The Turning of Our Lives." His pain had expanded to regions of his brain and collarbone. She served him broth. When "The Turning of Our Lives" ended with the pregnant virgin finding that she was not pregnant after all, merely flatulent, Miles went upstairs to lie down.

In a few minutes Beverly Bingham drove up to the house in her black pickup. At the front door she rang the bell and crossed her fingers, hoping Mr. Pruitt would answer, not his crabby landlady.

The door with the oval glass opened. Miss McGee said, "Yes?"

"I have to see Mr. Pruitt. He wasn't in school today and there's something I have to see him about."

"I'm sorry, but he's not at all well this afternoon. You will have to see him tomorrow. Or perhaps you wish to leave a message with me."

"He has a letter of mine to the junior college in Berrington. I'm applying for admission. I wanted to get it in the mail today."

"Well, I'm sure it can wait. It's very early to be applying for college."

"But Mr. Pruitt says there's a lot of competition for scholarships. He says it's best to be early."

"I'll tell him."

Beverly did not turn to go. She was peering beyond Miss McGee into the dark living room. Were those books behind glass?

"Would you like to come in?"

Beverly was undecided. She had heard about this fearsome woman all her life. She had not expected her to be civil. She looked back at her truck parked at the curb.

"Come in and we'll have a glass of nectar."

This was her chance to see how Mr. Pruitt lived. She stepped inside and while Miss McGee prepared the drinks she stood before the glass doors of the bookcase and read the titles stamped on the faded spines of the old lady's library. Joyce Kilmer's *Anthology of Catholic Poets.* Belloc's *Path to Rome.* Chesterton's *Orthodoxy.* A set, in black, of Hawthorne.

"If you see anything you wish to read, you may borrow it," said Miss McGee, carrying in a pitcher of something purple and icy.

Merton's *Seven-Storey Mountain.* Bernanos' *Diary of a Country Priest.* Mauriac's *Vipers' Tangle.* "I don't recognize anybody but Hawthorne," said Beverly.

"Well . . ." Miss McGee sighed for what was lacking in a secular education. "Come and have some nectar."

Beverly sat in the wing chair, where Governor Rice and the archbishop had sat in their day. She tasted what Miss McGee handed her in a heavy goblet.

"This is nectar?"

"It is."

"It tastes like Kool-Aid.

"It is."

Beverly studied the old lady. She saw that each of the old lady's shoes had five pairs of shoestring holes. She wore a skirt of some heavy, pale blue material and an open jacket to match, and spilling down her front were the folds and frills of the most ruffled, ornamental blouse Beverly had ever seen. The blouse and shoes didn't go together, and yet they did go together, thought Beverly. The fanciness of the blouse made it as old-fashioned as the high black shoes. The old lady's hair, nearly white, was pulled back in a bun tight enough to withstand a day in the classroom and the walk home in any weather. The old lady's eyes, like her own, were blue.

Miss McGee considered the girl. Her jeans and shirt were dirty. Her fingernails were chewed and her hair was snarled. With cosmetics she had done something ghastly around her eyes. She was sitting on one of her feet without having removed her dirty tennis shoe.

"It's such a lovely day for November," said Miss McGee.

Beverly nodded. Her eyes were on the frills of the blouse at the old lady's throat.

"Poor Mr. Pruitt came home in great pain from his visit to a dentist in Duluth."

Beverly said nothing. There was a long silence.

"This is grape," said Miss McGee. "I think grape is tastiest."

Beverly said nothing.

"Miss Bingham, is your mind on something other than the conversation I am trying to start? If so, I wish you would speak up and tell me about it, rather than sit there speechless." Silence, golden in the classroom, was unrefined over nectar.

"I was wondering how long it takes you to iron that blouse."

195

"This? Oh, I suppose a quarter of an hour."

"A quarter of an hour. God."

"No more than that, certainly. It's of a synthetic fabric and no work at all."

"I don't like anything I have to iron."

This fact was too obvious to pursue, and Miss McGee turned back to the weather. "I don't remember a day this warm this late in the year."

"It's nice all right."

"After two such dreary days it's a godsend. I am not fond of rain."

"Our chickens aren't fond of it either. When it rains hard like it did Sunday, the henhouse floods."

"But you live in the gulch. Surely there's enough slope in the gulch to carry off the rain."

"Not where our henhouse is. It's in sort of a scooped-out place."

"Then you must do some ditching. Take a spade and ditch from the henhouse in the direction of the creek. You can't have a henhouse standing in water."

"Christ, if it was up to me we wouldn't have a henhouse at all. I'm so sick of cleaning and picking and gutting chickens—God."

"Tut. You must pull your weight. You can't expect your mother to run your farm single-handedly."

"Well, my mother . . . I mean you've got that all wrong. My mother doesn't do hardly anything and hasn't for a long time, except grind up bones. I'm doing it all, you might say—well, anyway three-fourths of it, and I've gotten to the point where I despise chickens. It's different with the garden. I work all summer in the garden and I never get tired of that. I could work in a garden year-round and never get tired of it. We have a produce stand on the highway, you know, July and August."

"Yes, I know. I'm told your green beans are superb."

"It's the chicken manure. I like the garden and I like selling the produce. That whole end of things I like. But I'm just plain damn sick of chickens."

"I have my own garden, otherwise you can be sure I would be one of your best customers. My neighbor Lillian Kite says your green beans are superb."

"Is she the one who always wears a floppy hat? There's an old lady drives out in a green car and she's always wearing this floppy hat. She buys a lot of stuff including beans."

"No, you're thinking of Mrs. Murphy, the housekeeper at St. Isidore's. Father Finn's housekeeper. She, too, does a good deal of shopping at your stand. She buys a good many onions, doesn't she."

"When we have them."

"Yes, Father Finn is a great one for onions." Miss McGee shook her head, regretting the odor of onions in the confessional. "Would you like more nectar?"

"Yeah. Can I smoke?"

"Smoke?" Miss McGee went to the dining room and drew from her china closet a cut-glass ash tray. She placed it on the coffee table next to the wing chair.

Beverly asked Miss McGee if she had a cigarette handy.

"Goodness no. Neither Mr. Pruitt nor I have ever smoked. No one in my family ever smoked. My father, who was otherwise quite a man of the world—"

"That's okay. I've got some in the truck." Beverly ran outside and returned with a flip-top box containing, besides three or four cigarettes, a rolled-up dollar bill and a tube of lipstick. She struck a match and brought it up to her cigarette, crossing her eyes to see what she was doing.

"Now that I think about it, my brother would smoke

a pipe now and then," said Miss McGee. "But he died of the flu in nineteen."

"In other words, I'm about the first one to ever light up in this house."

"No, we had a Mrs. Mulloy in our circle one time who smoked constantly, but she moved to Denver. And Father Finn is a great one for cigars. When he stops in for a visit, he always has a cigar." She shook her head, regretting the odor of cigars in the confessional.

"I just started a couple of weeks ago when I got my job at the Hub. It really does a lot for my nerves. It calms me down."

"It looks like a very nervous activity to me. And furthermore, though I mean no offense to you personally, I dislike seeing a woman smoke."

"That's an old attitude."

"It may be old, but I am currently holding it. Old attitudes are not necessarily bad attitudes."

"No, but they're old." Beverly clumsily poked her ashes in the direction of the ash tray. "I mean that attitude is from the days when women were down." She sucked in smoke and coughed it out. "In your day women were down more."

"And now we're up?"

"Well, at least we're on our way. Don't you think so?"

Miss McGee sat back and closed her eyes. She could feel the strength leaving her body. It was the Dark Age dyspepsia. She wished to hear no more about old attitudes as opposed to new. There was no point in telling this girl what was really happening to womanhood, no point in telling her what womanhood had once been. The girl could not hope to understand. There was no point in discussing with her the way the world was going, no point in telling her that doom was about to crack.

"Miss McGee, are you okay?"

She opened her eyes and offered Beverly more nectar.

"No, I've got to go. I thought you looked funny there for a minute."

"Merely a slight tremor of the nerves. A passing thing."

"Will you tell Mr. Pruitt to bring my letter to school tomorrow?" Beverly had been smoking fast, and a great part of her remaining cigarette was a long, bright coal, from which several sparks fell, burning tiny holes in the embroidered linen on the arm of the wing chair.

"I will tell him."

"Thanks." Beverly stubbed out her smoke and picked up her flip-top box and went to the door. "What if he's still sick tomorrow?"

"Then drop by after school for your letter."

"Okay." She crossed the wide porch and went down the steps into the sunshine and turned and said, "Thanks for the nectar."

"You're welcome."

Miss McGee stood at the door and watched Beverly climb into the black truck, start the engine, light a cigarette, lean over and look up at the upstairs windows, shift gears, and drive away. The truck left a disagreeably oily haze in the street.

So that was the Bonewoman's daughter. She would be a pretty girl, thought Miss McGee, if she knew how to care for herself. If she had had a decent upbringing. If she didn't use the name of the Lord in vain. If she kept herself clean. If she didn't smoke. Here obviously was a case of faulty training and wasted potential.

"That is, if training counts for anything anymore,"

she said aloud as she unpinned the linens from the arms of the chair. For Miss McGee was not so innocent as to believe that training, these days, made as great a difference as it used to. She knew today's youth. She saw them walking to high school dressed in the style of Fagin's urchins. She read news items from the Berrington County Juvenile Court. She listened to tales out of school as told by Miles. So woeful was the degeneration of young people after they left the sixth grade that Miss McGee avoided them whenever possible. Indeed she saw their bad behavior as a personal affront. The young of the world seemed to be telling her, "Look, old lady, what your teaching has done for us. It has meant nothing." And so, against everyone between the ages of thirteen and twenty-five, against this whole sector of humanity, Miss McGee had developed—and she knew it—the first intemperate bias of her life.

Last spring this bias, this aversion to the new flawed generation, had actually brought about Miss McGee's retirement. After forty years of teaching (and after Patty Hawk's wedding on the first day of June) she gave Father Finn her letter of resignation. Her retirement lasted fourteen days. By coincidence, it was a wedding that prompted her to retire and it was another wedding that changed her mind.

Now, it would be unfair to say that Patty Hawk's wedding was the cause of Miss McGee's contempt for the modern world. After all, Miss McGee had caught sight of the approaching Dark Ages and had considered retiring long before Patty Hawk got married, or engaged, or even pregnant. It was simply that Patty's wedding settled the matter.

Patty was married in front of her parents' cabin on Birch Lake, and Miss McGee drove out there in Miles's

Plymouth. Patty wore a red pants suit—a maternity pants suit, for she was eight months along. The bridesmaids, too, wore red. Later, the article in the *Weekly* said they wore rust, but Miss McGee saw with her own eyes that they wore red. Besides a pregnant bride, the wedding featured a foul-mouthed bridesmaid, a drunk from Sioux City, and a cold wind off the lake. Furthermore, the father of the bride had a black eye.

Most of the guests were from out of town, and when Miss McGee walked among them on the beach after the ceremony, she found scarcely anyone to talk to. Finally Mrs. Hawk came to her rescue and said, "Oh, Miss McGee, we're so glad you're here. Wendell and I have always said that you were one of the very best teachers Patty ever had, and Patty has always said so too. Isn't that right, Wendell?"

Wendell Hawk was standing at his wife's side in a new suit the color of a banana. Miss McGee shook his hand and tried not to notice his black and purple eye, which was surrounded by a fine network of inflamed arteries.

"Don't mind this shiner, Miss McGee," he said heartily. "Last night I slipped on a rug in the living room and went down like a ton of bricks and hit my head on the magazine rack. I hit my head right here above the eye and I bled like a stuck hog. There isn't a bit of flesh under a person's eyebrows, so you tell me where the blood came from. Feel your own eyebrow, Miss McGee, there's nothing but bone underneath, is there. But let me tell you, bone or no bone, I bled like a stuck hog. And do you know what caused me to slip? My good wife here had waxed the floor. She had the place all waxed for our guests and I came walking through the room last night and the rug we have by the fireplace went right out from under me and down I went like a ton of bricks.

Would you believe there's six stitches under this scab?
My good wife can vouch for that. She took the stitches
with her own needle and thread." He laughed and
slapped his wife on the back, and his wife laughed too,
but not happily. Her laugh was shallow, and the look
she gave him was lacerating.

"Please excuse us," she said to Miss McGee, "we have
to get back to the reception line."

One of the few people Miss McGee recognized was
another former student, Jennifer Molstad. Jennifer was
Patty's maid of honor. She was twenty and had been
away at college. She was standing under a cottonwood
tree by the water's edge, talking to a middle-aged man
with a goatee. Jennifer and the man had one cup of
punch between them and they were both sipping from
it as the wind furled and unfurled Jennifer's red pants
around her long legs. The man with the goatee was so
engrossed in what Jennifer was telling him that Miss
McGee stopped at a respectful distance and waited her
turn to speak. She looked about her at the convivial
crowd of guests, whose chatter was carried first toward
her and then away from her on gusts of wind, and she
was overcome by a feeling of self-consciousness. It was
not, to Miss McGee, a familiar sensation. Ordinarily
when she went out in public she went with a certain
eminence, attracting the nod of the head and the smile
of respect that a small town pays to forty years of virtu-
ous example, and her slightly eccentric habits of dress
(the lace hankie pinned to her lapel, the sturdy black
shoes) were her marks of distinction. But here on the
beach, among strangers, she felt both odd and old. She
wished she had not worn her high, round hat, for the
wind was catching at it, and having to cling to its brim
was making her tired. She wished she had worn a coat,
for the wind was turning chilly. She wished her heels

didn't keep sinking into the sand, making her feel shorter than she really was. She wished, most of all, that she had mailed her gift and stayed home.

Jennifer and the man with the goatee moved to higher ground as the gray-green waves licked at their high heels, his and hers alike, and Miss McGee took this opportunity to break into their conversation.

"How nice to see you, Jennifer," she said. "You look so lovely."

It was true. Jennifer was a stunning girl. Her golden hair was even more lustrous now than it had been in the sixth grade when Jennifer was elected, on Mayday, to crown the statue of Mary Queen of the May.

"Oh, hello, Miss McGee," Jennifer said. She turned again to the man with the goatee and took up her story where it had been interrupted.

"When I think of how I waited for him every Wednesday and Sunday night—Wednesdays and Sundays were his only nights off—sometimes I would wait for him till one, two in the morning."

Miss McGee did not understand that she had been dismissed. She continued to stand, listening, at Jennifer's side.

". . . and do you know what he was doing all that time, till one, two in the morning before he came over to my place? He was out with other chicks. And you know in whose car? In my car."

The man with the goatee shook his head gravely.

". . . he was using my car because his license plates were out of date, and he was out with other chicks in *my car*. And these other chicks would leave their shoes and purses and shit in my car. I mean even their pantyhose. Only he would always put their stuff in the trunk before he came to pick me up, so I never knew. But one day I was out driving—big deal, driving my own car—and I saw my friend Dorie Burkhart standing by the side of the road trying to flag down help and I stopped. Dorie had a flat tire and she didn't have a tire wrench. She asked me if I had one, and I said, 'You tell me, I don't know what a tire wrench looks like,' and I got out and unlocked my trunk for the first time since I bought the car and there were all those shoes and purses and shit belonging to all those other chicks he had been taking out. Well, screw him.''

Jennifer and the man moved off in the direction of the punch table, leaving Miss McGee hanging on to her hat and squinting into the wind. She was stunned. Jennifer, she knew, had been brought up to know better than that. When Jennifer was twelve she had crowned Mary Queen of the May. That was the horror of this new generation: They had all been brought up to know better. But they were reverting, one after another, to the perverse savagery that the human race had been liberated from ages ago. They were going under in a flood of immorality. Nowadays (thought Miss McGee) as soon as children outgrew their childhood innocence, they became foul-mouthed and disobedient. They became robbers and dope addicts. They became murderers, perjurers, prostitutes, and embezzlers. Men became rapists and women aborted their babies. Every morning in the Minneapolis *Tribune* you could read what these people were up to, and every suppertime on TV you could see their pictures. What was the use of teaching Christian standards to twelve-year-olds, if they were going to throw them to the winds by the time they were twenty? What was uglier than the foul language women were using these days? It was uglier, in its way, than Wendell Hawk's purple eye. This new generation was sapped of all the momentum that had carried civilization ahead for a thousand years—and now in the last quarter of the twentieth century the world waited once more on the threshold of the Dark Ages.

Thus, standing under the cottonwood tree at Patty Hawk's wedding, Miss McGee despaired. She decided to go home and call Father Finn and tell him she was resigning her teaching position. She circled the crowd on the beach and walked toward the driveway where she had parked the Plymouth. She passed the gift table and the guest-book table and was almost past the punch table when she was suddenly seized by the wrist. It was a fat man she had never seen before who held her. With his other hand he was stirring the punch.

"Like a snort?" he said.

"No, thank you. I must be on my way." She had tasted the punch and knew that it was heavily spiked with gin. Floating on the surface now was a bottle cap.

"Oh, come on, just a little snort for the road." The fat man tightened his grip on her wrist and continued to stir the punch. He was stirring it with a twig.

"No, thank you," she repeated. She tried to retain her composure by turning her back on the man, and with her free hand she straightened her hat.

"If you're like me, lady, you could probably use a snort. If you're like me, you probably came a hell of a ways to see this wedding, and it turned out to be the damnedest wedding you ever saw. I mean they have everything at this wedding. In the first place they have the wedding outside in a goddamn windstorm, and in the second place they have the wedding party dressed up in red overalls, and in the third place they have a knocked-up bride, and in the fourth place the father of the bride was cold-cocked last night by the mother of the bride. Now I know Wendell Hawk has been going around telling everybody that he hurt his head by slipping on a rug. In fact he even tried to tell *me* that he slipped on a rug, but I'm a cousin of his wife's and I got the story from her this morning before Wendell was out of bed. I drove up here early this morning from Sioux City. What happened was that Wendell went out with the boys last night and he came home drunk and when his wife said he ought to be ashamed of himself he slapped her face. And you know what she did? She's my first cousin. She took a bottle of salad dressing and she cracked him in the eye with it. She cold-cocked him with a bottle of French dressing. So now you know."

Miss McGee said that she believed she would have some punch after all, and when the man let go of her hand in order to pour her a cup, she fled. When she got home she called Father Finn and told him that she was retiring as soon as school was out.

"You're not serious," he said.

"Father, I have just returned from Patty Hawk's wedding and I have seen my teaching come to nothing."

"Why? What did you see?"

"It wasn't only what I saw. It was what I heard as well."

"Why? What did you hear?"

"Unspeakable things. The world is in ruins, and I'll not teach another year. My teaching has come to nothing."

"Agatha, you're an alarmist."

"I know, and with good reason."

Miss McGee called the principal, Sister Rosie, whose only reaction to Miss McGee's announcement was to sigh into the phone, indicating that she thought Miss McGee was bluffing (St. Isidore's pension plan was lousy) and she was waiting for Miss McGee to talk herself out of her decision. But Miss McGee, who had very little time for Sister Rosie, hung up.

The following week when the school year ended,

Father Finn and Sister Rosie began looking for Miss McGee's replacement. There were in the parish three housewives certified by the State of Minnesota to teach sixth grade, but one of them had a new baby and the other two, when they heard that their salary would be four thousand dollars for the entire year, laughed out loud. Sister Rosie called the placement directors at seven colleges and Father Finn advertised in parish bulletins throughout the diocese. Sister Rosie alerted her mother superior in St. Paul, who, out of nuns, alerted the archbishop; but the only unemployed teachers the archbishop uncovered were as amused by the four thousand dollars as the two housewives had been.

At this point Sister Rosie said to Father Finn, "There's only one person who will teach sixth grade for four thousand dollars and do a creditable job of it and that's Agatha McGee. We're out of options. You'll have to talk her into coming back."

"But we had a farewell party for her," said Father Finn, "and her picture was in the paper, and the alumni gave her a watch. How could she go back to work after all of that?"

"She's duty-oriented. Tell her she owes St. Isidore's one more year. Tell her there's been a groundswell of sentiment in the parish to have her back."

"What I think we should do is combine fifth and sixth grades under one teacher."

"What kind of an option is that? Two grades in one room went out with the country school. Where have you been? Call her up and remind her that she quit on short notice and left us in the lurch. She'll give in. She's duty-oriented. Tell her there's a petition going around to have her back."

"I'll tell her no such thing. If I call her I'll tell her the truth. I'll tell her we're desperate."

The next morning when Father Finn called to say he was desperate, Miss McGee was not at home. She was visiting, by invitation, the Senior Citizens' Club. She had received the invitation in the mail from a certain Mr. Lutz and she assumed that the Senior Citizens were holding open house for the community at large, and since it was a sunny, windless morning she put on her high, round hat and walked the four blocks to the Community Center.

Some years earlier Lyndon Johnson's Great Society had come to Staggerford in the form of this Community Center, a three-story hulk of windowless concrete in which there were (besides a Senior Citizens' Room) a Teen Room, a Physical Fitness Room, a Community Planning Room, a Bake Sale Room, and a row of ten offices occupied now and then by ten civil servants with incomprehensible titles. Printed on the door of one such office was the word OUTREACH. On another were the words FORCED AIR CONSULTANT. A third door said EQUALIZATION. This was Miss McGee's first visit to the building and once inside she got lost. Outside, the lines of the building were square, but inside they were crooked. Corridors met each other at oblique angles, and some of them sloped up and down. Miss McGee opened dozens of doors. There were three-sided rooms and five-sided rooms and split-level rooms, all of them empty and all of them plastered with what looked to her like textured mustard. Water pipes and electrical conduits hung from the ceilings, giving her the illusion that she had dropped down a manhole. She passed through the furnace room and an empty kitchen and a room that reeked of soiled gym clothes. She found a room with a large bay window that gave her a view of a room containing a mimeograph machine and a broken piano. After opening all these doors, Miss McGee, who had not voted for Lyndon

Johnson, began to suspect that the Community Center was purposely designed as a maze to throw the intruder off stride, to demoralize her, to conceal—like the passages in a pyramid—the secret that lay at the center of things; and thereafter, with each room she looked into, she half expected to come upon the sarcophagus of a king.

From behind an unlabeled door on the second floor, she heard an excited cackle. She knocked and the cackle stopped. "Yoo hoo," she called, and she heard whispering. She opened the door and looked into an enormous five-sided room that might have been a ballroom. In it were thirteen old people sitting on thirteen folding chairs. They were sitting in two groups and they were all staring at her. One group consisted of four women who had been making tulips out of egg cartons. They sat around a table on which were several jars of tempera paint, a scissors, a stack of egg cartons, and a bottle of Elmer's glue. The other nine people were clustered in the center of the room and had obviously been visiting together before she interrupted them. A humpbacked woman was coiled in her chair like a withered stem, and to look up at Miss McGee she had to point one ear to the floor. A man in a lumberjack shirt had two hearing aids and one eye. The woman next to him wore a fur coat and bedroom slippers. There was a man showing a great distance between his socks and his cuffs and exposing the lengths of dingy underwear that covered his shins. They all sat with their hands in their laps and looked expectantly at Miss McGee, as though she had come to announce doomsday, or lunch.

"Why, it's Agatha McGee," said a voice from the group of nine, and Miss McGee saw that it was Lillian Kite, knitting. She went over and sat down beside Lillian on a folding chair.

"We thought the bride was coming in," said Lillian. "We're having a mock wedding here this morning and we thought you were the bride."

Through the door now came a young man in a checkered suit. He was carrying a small tape recorder, and Miss McGee decided at a glance that he was a simpleton. He pushed aside the egg cartons to make room on the table for the recorder and he pressed a button that caused it to play Mendelssohn's "Wedding March." As it played, he giggled and pulled busily at a hair growing out of a mole on his chin. When the music stopped, he rewound the tape and started it over again just as Vera Collins came through the door.

Miss McGee knew Vera Collins. She was the widow of the blacksmith Varner Collins. She was the mother of eleven children and the grandmother of twenty-eight and the great-grandmother of four. She was wearing her wedding dress.

"What *is* this?" said Miss McGee.

"It's our mock wedding," said Lillian. "Isn't Vera lovely?"

There was nothing lovely about her. The wedding dress had taken on the color and smell of the attic in which it had hung for fifty-five years, and Vera Collins herself was emaciated.

"Stand up everybody," said the Simpleton, switching off the music. "Get over here, Harry. You agreed to be the groom and it's too late now to back out."

The one-eyed lumberjack came forward with Vera Collins, and they stood before the Simpleton, who raised his eyes to the pipes running along the ceiling and said, "Lord, we are gathered here today to unite these two children of yours in Holy Matrimony. If anyone knows of any reason why these two should not be joined together, let him speak now or forever hold his peace."

Having said this, the Simpleton scanned the faces in the room and noticed for the first time Miss McGee.

"I never saw you here before," he said.

"I was invited by a Mr. Lutz. I thought it was open house."

"I'm Lutz. Ozzie Lutz. I send out invitations to everybody in town who retires. I'm the director of this Community Center. Call me Ozzie. And be sure to sign in downstairs before you leave. I have to keep a record of everybody who uses this building. I hope you'll keep coming. We have fun."

Vera Collins and Harry the lumberjack exchanged vows and exchanged rings, and the Simpleton said, "By the power invested in me by the Department of Health, Education and Welfare, I now pronounce you man and wife. I hope you'll be very happy. I have to go now and fix the slot machine in the teen room."

The lumberjack, with a wrinkled pucker, brushed the bride's wrinkled cheek, and Miss McGee was the only witness not transported by the sight. Everyone else was smiling tenderly, and there were tears in the eyes of Lillian Kite. The senior citizens lined up to kiss the bride, and the first woman in line, the one in bedroom slippers, said, "Where are you and Harry going to be living?"

Miss McGee was horrified. She hurried out the door after the Simpleton and said, "Do you realize there are certain people in that room who believe they have just seen a real wedding?"

"I know it, that's half the fun." Ozzie Lutz was behind schedule. He walked very fast along the corridor and spoke over his shoulder to Miss McGee, who fell behind. "That's why the oldsters are more fun than teens. Teens are almost impossible to entertain, but oldsters will believe anything. Last week we had a mock funeral in that room, and one of the oldsters asked me why the newspaper didn't print an obituary. I tell you, once an oldster gets into the swing of this program, nothing can keep him home. Oldsters think the world of this program. They're here in the morning waiting for me to unlock the building. Just give the program a chance and you'll see. We have fun. Right now we're in the middle of a contest to see who can make the most tulips out of egg cartons. On your way out, sign the book. My office is the one by the front door. Tell the girl at the desk that I told you to sign the book." Ozzie Lutz spoke these last words while disappearing up a dark curving stairway.

So this was what awaited one who retired, thought Miss McGee: putting on sham weddings and making tulips out of egg cartons. She recalled Patty Hawk's wedding, which to Miss McGee's way of thinking was as great a hoax as this one, and she felt trapped between the moral wasteland of the younger generation and the stale slough of senior citizenship. Which was worse? She had to face one or the other, and by retiring she had chosen the latter.

She did not sign the Simpleton's book. She went straight home and called Father Finn.

Now Father Finn was a prayerful man. Every day he was conscientious in his reading of the Divine Office—not the new, abbreviated version, but the old edition, tedious and beautiful. He read his Office because he believed in its efficacy before God and because the hour he spent in his favorite vinyl chair was more soothing than milk to his ulcer. In a drawer of his desk, Father Finn kept a list of favors that had been granted him through prayer. Some of them, such as finding a box of lost cigars, he had to admit were small potatoes; but others, such as his sister's recovery from cancer and the fantastic mileage he was getting out of his Montgomery Ward tires, bordered on the miraculous. Such was Father Finn's faith that he wouldn't have been surprised to learn that one of his prayers had moved a mountain. He was astonished, however, at the speed with which today's prayer moved Miss McGee. He had just begun offering up one of the penitential psalms for the intention of her return to the classroom when the phone rang.

"If you have not yet found my replacement, I will come back in the fall and teach," she told him. "I am not ready to become a senior citizen."

"My prayers have been answered," he said. "The Spirit is at work."

"I am not ready o attend mock weddings," she said. "I am not ready to attend mock funerals. I am not ready to spend the rest of my days making tulips out of egg cartons."

"God bless you," said Father Finn.

WEDNESDAY

November 4

AFTER A NIGHT of fitful sleep, Miles looked into the mirror and barely recognized himself. His left cheek was swollen and his left eye appeared higher than his right. He was pale and shaky and his mouth was crooked. He looked like a portrait in chalk, smudged.

He called school and left word with Wayne Workman's secretary that he was taking another day of sick leave.

He called Doc Oppegaard and described his trouble.

"You'll be fine by noon," said Doc. "The inside of the mouth heals fast."

It was another clear, golden morning. Miles dressed and took his coffee and his briefcase out the back door to the lawn chairs under the basswood tree. He opened his briefcase and felt in his pocket for his red pen. He had left it upstairs, luckily. He closed the briefcase and drank his coffee. He said good-by to Miss McGee, who walked down the alley toward St. Isidore's. When he finished his coffee he moved to the flat chaise longue and fell asleep.

In a few minutes the ringing phone drew him out of a dream, and he went into the house to answer it.

"I can't have you missing another day, Pruitt." It was Wayne Workman.

"But I have no choice, Wayne. I'm in bad shape. I had this tooth pulled yesterday and—"

"I don't care what your excuse is. If you are alive you've got to come to school. Mrs. Horky took your classes yesterday and she had a devil of a time with your second hour and with your study hall. She came back again this morning, and she's in your classroom right now with first hour, but she says she will not under any circumstances be in that room when it comes time for second hour, nor will she go upstairs at two o'clock and take over your study hall. She says at two o'clock she's going home."

"Now wait a minute, Wayne. When people sign up to be substitute teachers, don't they agree to take the bad with the good? They're *paid* to take the bad with the good. I'm in no shape to be teaching today."

There was a long pause. Perhaps Wayne was paging through the Faculty Handbook for the solution to this problem. When he spoke it was at a higher pitch. "Pruitt, are you refusing to do what I say?"

"Yes."

Another long pause. Perhaps he was chewing his mustache. "Pruitt, second hour begins in ten minutes. If you can't be here for second hour I will understand. Ten minutes wouldn't be enough time for you to primp for the young ladies in your classes—"

"What do you mean by that?"

". . . but if you aren't here to take your study hall at two o'clock—that's almost five hours' warning I'm giving you—then we shall see what we shall see." Wayne hung up.

Miles understood why Wayne loved to use the telephone. On the telephone it was so easy to have the last word.

Under the leafless basswood, Miles lay so that the sun fell on the swollen side of his face. It felt good. He dozed again. The phone rang again.

"Pruitt, your Indian is missing!" It was Wayne.

"My Indian?"

"He's gone."

"What do you mean, my Indian?"

"Sam LaGrange. Your Indian. At the faculty meeting Monday you signed up to befriend Sam LaGrange, and now this morning he's absent."

"He doesn't want to be friends."

"For godsakes, Pruitt, quit trying to be clever. Today is LaGrange's birthday. He's sixteen and he has quit school. Your job is to bring him back. You could do it right now, before study hall. You could bring him back."

"Do you mean by force, or what?"

"I mean find him and talk to him. Think of the example you would set for the rest of the faculty if you followed one out to the reservation and brought him back."

"Wayne, to tell the truth, I'm not optimistic about your plan for befriending Indians."

"I'm not surprised, Pruitt. When were you ever optimistic about anything? Remember what I told you about being an obstacle in the road to progress? Well, you are. You're keeping the world from advancing."

"Now that's saying quite a lot, Wayne. I don't think—"

"You're an obstacle, Pruitt. You're holding back the advance of the world."

Miles expected him to hang up, but apparently these

were not Wayne's last words. He waited to hear more.

"Pruitt, you still there?"

"Yes."

"Pruitt, do you know what it looks to me is wrong with you?"

"What?"

"It looks to me like you're prejudiced against Indians." He hung up.

This time Miles took a pillow and one of Miss McGee's afghans out to the chaise longue and he went back to sleep.

"My, if we aren't the picture of comfort this morning," said Imogene Kite, striding across the alley. She was on her way to work.

Miles opened and shut his eyes. Imogene stood slightly to one side of the sun and she was blinding to look at. "I'm recuperating from yesterday's ordeal, Imogene."

"You're certainly playing that tooth for all it's worth."

"Imogene, would you care to look in my mouth and see the destruction?"

"Don't be gross, Pruitt. You're making a big case out of a swollen cheek which will be down to its normal size by nightfall. Mark my words. Mucous membrane heals fast."

"That's what Doc Oppegaard said."

"Don't you know that the mild chemical components of mucus act as a soothing balm to mucous membrane?"

"Imogene, before I forget it, I'm sorry for yesterday. But you realize I had no alternative but to come straight home."

"Well, I did want a winter coat, and goodness knows when I'll get back to Duluth again. As I said yesterday,

Pruitt, I am tall for a woman." She turned to go.

"Have a good day in the stacks," said Miles.

Later, Miles put on a tie and walked to Doc Oppe-gaard's office. Stella Gibbon and the dentist had finished their wine and cheese and were reading jokes to each other from two issues of the *Soybean Monthly*.

"My tooth," Miles pleaded. "Karstenburg did me wrong."

In the inner office Doc looked at the damage Karsten-burg had left. "Boyoboy," he said, "what a mess. Look here, Stella, he's developing a dry socket."

Stella peered into Miles's mouth, then reeled back. "How absolutely ugly!" she said.

Doc packed the hole with cotton dipped in something sour. "Hold that in there and come back tomorrow. Boyoboy, Karstenburg really butchered you. I could have done better than that."

"Then why didn't you?" said Miles.

"I don't pull the tough ones. No small-town dentist pulls the tough ones because the tough ones are always painful no matter who pulls them, and a small-town practice depends on a painless reputation. That's why I sent you to Karstenburg. It's better for Karstenburg to take the blame than me. But I swear to God I could have done better than that."

"I have one more wisdom tooth," said Miles, getting out of the chair, "and when that goes bad, I'll let it rot before I'll go back to Karstenburg."

"Go to Hoover in Fargo. He has his office right in downtown Fargo, and he's a crackerjack."

"Oh, Dr. Hoover," said Stella. "He's out of this world."

Once again the two of them saw Miles to the door,

and on the front step Doc said, "How much did Karstenburg soak you?"

"I don't know yet."

"It will be high. You've got to pay a guy plenty to take the blame for a mess like that."

Toward the end of fifth hour when Mrs. Horky saw Miles standing with his briefcase in the hall, she left her class and seemed to be on the verge of falling into his arms. "Miles, thank God! You can't imagine what I've been through. Jeff Norquist is a brutal, incorrigible, hellish criminal. He insulted me and disobeyed me. And Roxie Booth is absolutely irredeemable. She told two stories this morning about incest. How in the world do you get up in the morning when you know second hour is waiting for you? If I had to teach second hour every day, why I simply wouldn't teach. I would take my pension and go clerking at the five-and-dime. This fifth-hour class is a charming class and I got along all right with first and third hour, though there's not a bit of sparkle in either one of them, but I absolutely refuse ever again to take your second hour, Miles, even if it means striking my name from the substitute list. And the same goes for study hall. I told Wayne Workman that never again in my life would I step foot into the same room with Jeff Norquist, and I find that he's not only in your second hour, he's in your study hall as well. That boy needs help, Miles. There's something bad cooking in that boy and I don't want to be around when it boils over. And between classes he hangs all over that little Indian girl, Annie Bird. I mean he's all over her *body* right out here in the hall. I'm going home and dust. I've been here two days and all the while there's been dust settling on my furniture." Mrs. Horky streaked out the front door. The bell rang and students came spilling out of classrooms.

Beverly Bingham had not seen Miles for forty-eight hours. Now, using the crowded hallway as an excuse, she pressed herself against him. She said, "You don't look so hot."

"Hello, Beverly." He tried to back away from the touch of her body, but there was no place to go.

"Do you have my letter?"

"Yes, it's here in my briefcase, but I didn't get a chance to look at it yet."

"Maybe you could read it this hour and I'll pick it up after school."

"Yes, I'll do that. I'll meet you back here in an hour."

She smiled and brushed her attractive front across his arm and was swept away down the hall.

Across the hall Wayne Workman had been standing on tiptoe in order to see over the stream of students. He had been watching Miles and Beverly.

In study hall, little Hank Bird pulled a knife on Jeff Norquist and said, "You better lay off my sister."

Later in thinking it over, Miles couldn't believe that Hank had been serious. Hank had an IQ of 99, which was enough sense to know what was bound to happen if he threatened somebody two years older and considerably larger. Maybe it was Hank's way of showing off the knife he had stolen during the noon hour from Olafson's Hardware. Maybe Hank secretly admired Jeff Norquist (Jeff had once stolen a new LTD from the Ford dealer) and was awkwardly trying to strike up a friendship between thieves.

But Jeff Norquist didn't see it that way. In the time it took Miles to get from his desk at the front of the room to the fight halfway down the middle aisle, Jeff put little Hank out of commission. He closed one of Hank's eyes, knocked out one of his front teeth, and broke one of his fingers.

Miles separated them and picked up the knife, which still had Olafson's price sticker on it. It was a large jackknife with two blades, a bottle opener, and a screwdriver. Three ninety-five, plus tax.

The screaming of the girls in study hall carried all over the school, and as Miles rushed Hank down to the nurse's office, he met Wayne Workman on the stairs.

"What's happening?" asked Wayne.

"I'll tell you later. Watch my study hall for me."

The nurse was not in her office. Miles found a bottle of aspirin and handed it to Hank, whose eyes were filling with tears of pain. Miles put him in a chair and told him not to move. He ran to Delia Fritz's office for the keys to the school car. He returned to the nurse's office and led Hank outdoors and across the street to the shed behind the football bleachers where the school car—a green station wagon—was kept. He drove to the emergency room of the hospital, where Hank was drugged and his finger was put in a splint. Then he put him back in the car and headed west out of town. He passed the road leading to Evergreen Cemetery, he passed the Bingham driveway, and he crossed the Badbattle near the entrance to Pike Park. He came to the weathered wooden sign marking the border of the Sandhill Reservation, and as he approached the village of Sandhill he saw short, crooked trails leading from the highway to clearings in the forest. In each clearing an old car was parked next to the only door of a small house. The Indians had not built their houses in clusters; they were scattered like this throughout the forest of the reservation. Each car had on its roof a wooden structure like a rickety pulpit, a platform from which at night an Indian with a spotlight was allowed to shoot deer along the reservation roads.

Miles turned off the highway and onto the single street running through Sandhill. The street was sand. He parked in the shadow of the Sandhill General Store.

"You belong to Bennie Bird, don't you?" Miles asked the boy, making sure.

Little Hank nodded slowly. He was groggy from the shot he had been given at the hospital.

Miles helped him out of the car and through the doorway of the dark store. Mrs. Bird was inside, alone. She was sitting in the shadows behind the bar at the back of the store, probably on the same stool where Superintendent Stevenson saw her twenty years before. When she saw her son being half-carried, half-pushed toward her, she stood up and came around from behind the bar and took him in her arms. She was tall. Her skin was very dark, and her gray, coarse hair was tied together at the back of her neck by a piece of bright red yarn. Her face was expressionless but she drew herself up so erect that her height became a reprimand, and Miles felt, for no good reason, quite guilty.

Little Hank struggled feebly against his mother's embrace, and Miles began to explain what had happened. "What started the fight was that Hank drew a knife—"

Mrs. Bird spoke to him over Hank's head. "Get away from here before his father sees him."

Leaving the store, Miles saw this sign tacked on the inside of the door: DID YOU FORGET SHOELACES?

He got into the school car and drove ahead, thinking that he would circle the block, but he found that Sandhill was not laid out in blocks. Sandhill was a dozen buildings strung out along this one bumpy street. He drove past the Sandhill Public School, which had been

closed when the Sandhill and Staggerford school dis-
tricts consolidated. The building, according to a small
sign above the door, was now the "Chippewa Folk-Arts-
And-Crafts Center, Open June 1—September 1." He
passed St. Paul's Episcopal Church, a small replica of the
white, wooden churches of New England, but falling
now into ruin. The spire above the empty belfry was
bent; it leaned, like the leaning jackpines all around it,
with the prevailing northwest wind. The white paint
had flaked off the walls and the windows were covered
with boards. He passed the Sandhill Post Office, a square
brick building (the only bricks on the reservation) no
bigger than his classroom. Over the door a brand new
American flag moved limply in the breeze; it was illu-
minated by the late-afternoon sun, and it shone like a
jewel against the gray November landscape. He passed a
gas station with one pump. He came to a narrow, two-
story house and slowed down to read the lettering on
one of the windows:

SANDHILL TRIBAL CENTER

Alexander Bigmeadow, Chief
Ernest LaGrange, Scribe
Bennie Bird, Constable

Miles made a U-turn, then stopped to let a black-
haired girl cross the road. She was carrying a black-
haired baby and she was followed by four black dogs of
four different sizes. Next he was met by the school bus
from Staggerford, which extended its stop signal and let
out ten or twelve students in front of the General Store.
They ranged in age between six and sixteen. Miles had
seen them all at school but he knew only one by name:
Annie Bird. As Annie crossed the street in front of the

school car, she turned and gave Miles a look that startled
him: two angry eyes in a face round as a saucer, an
expression that said, "The trouble has only begun, Mr.
Pruitt—you haven't heard the last of this." Unlike her
mother, Annie was small—smaller than Hank—but like
her mother she had mastered the intimidating expression. Her eyes spoke of storms. She went into the store,
slamming the door behind her.

The bus driver and Miles exchanged a wave and
drove off in opposite directions. On the sandy street
Miles took it slow. The street was full of holes, and the
school car, although only two years old, had been abused
by dozens of different drivers and seemed about to rattle
itself to pieces.

Once on the highway, he sped back to town. He
parked the car in the shed behind the bleachers. Everyone except the secretaries and wrestlers had left school.
When he gave Delia Fritz the car keys, she told him to
call Wayne Workman at home. He used her phone.

"How's the Bird kid?" Wayne asked.

"His eye and his finger will be all right. He lost one
of his front teeth."

"Your study hall kids told me what happened. I suspended Jeff Norquist."

"For how long?"

"Two weeks."

"Did they tell you Hank pulled a knife on him?"

"They did. I'll suspend Hank too. We can't stand for
that kind of thing. Somebody could get hurt."

"They could at that."

"Where's the Bird kid now?"

"I took him home."

A pause. "You've been out to Sandhill and back?"

"Yes."

Another pause. "Did you ask about Sam LaGrange?"

"Who?"

"Your Indian, Sam LaGrange."

"It slipped my mind, Wayne."

"Pruitt, I have to have a talk with you."

"I'm listening."

"Not over the phone. Come over to my place tonight after supper."

"All right."

"You know, it's really a shame you didn't ask about Sam LaGrange as long as you were out there anyway. Think of the example you would have set for the rest of the faculty if you'd have gone out there and brought one back." He hung up.

Delia Fritz said, "It isn't turning out to be a good week for you, is it?"

"If you're referring to the fight in study hall—"

"Monday it was Jeff Norquist jumping out the window and yesterday it was your tooth and today this. I don't need to tell you that the superintendent was plenty upset this afternoon."

"He was?"

"He was sitting in his office with his window open and all of a sudden he heard this screaming. Study hall is right above us, you know, and the screaming carried down here and through our open windows. The sound was terrifying. Mr. Stevenson came out here and asked me what was happening. I said I didn't know. He said, 'Find out, and if it's awfully bad don't tell me.' He put on his hat and went home. He was gone before you came for the keys."

"I suppose I should tell him about it myself."

"I think you should, Miles. Do you want me to call him and tell him you're coming over?"

"Okay. Tell him I'll be over after supper."

* * *

Miles walked home and found Beverly Bingham's truck parked in front of the house.

In the kitchen Miss McGee was showing Beverly what bleach was for. "Being clean is second," she was saying as she added Hi-lex to a basin of water. "Being good is first, and being clean is second."

"What's third?" said Beverly.

Miss McGee shot her a glance to see if the girl was being insolent, and she saw Miles coming through the dining room. "Here he is now. How's your tooth, Miles?"

"Mr. Pruitt, I came for my letter."

"The letter is here in my briefcase. Something came up and I didn't get a chance—"

"You two go sit in the front room and take care of that letter once and for all," said Miss McGee. "I'll be done here in a minute and we'll have a glass of nectar."

Miles saw that Beverly was wearing a blouse of Miss McGee's. It had pearl buttons and the letters AM embroidered on the pocket. When Beverly saw that Miles noticed, she smiled helplessly and shrugged.

He said, "Really, Agatha, this isn't the kind of thing young people are wearing these days."

"It's what Beverly is wearing while we wash her blouse. Tend to your letter."

While Beverly's blouse dried in the automatic dryer, the three of them sat around the coffee table and drank grape Kool-Aid. Again Beverly was sitting on her foot without taking off her shoe, but Miss McGee (a shrewd judge of how much learning a pupil could stand in one session) let it pass. And the girl was smoking again. No more gracefully than yesterday, but at least more carefully. Her sparks and ashes were under control.

Folding her letter, Beverly said, "If applying for college is this much work, what's it going to be like when it comes time to actually *go?*"

To actually go—a split infinitive, thought Miss Mc-Gee. Will Miles correct her, or must I?

To actually go—a split infinitive, thought Miles. And Agatha is waiting for me to correct the girl.

He said, "In college I had to sometimes study all night."

Miss McGee turned away, hiding her annoyance and her amusement.

In the evening, Miss McGee had unexpected company. First, Lillian Kite came across the alley, emptied her bagful of knitting onto the coffee table, and settled down for a chat. Lillian was followed by Imogene, who was hoping to find Miles at home. She had nothing in particular to say to him—she wanted to research him. The Friday-night kiss he gave her had come to be much on her mind, mainly because her mother spoke of it incessantly, and she was beginning to wonder if Miles was falling in love with her. Today, as she manned the check-out desk at the library, she brought her analytical powers to bear on him. For one thing, there was the kiss. For another, there was his uncharacteristically tender apology as he lay under the basswood tree this morning. He had never kissed her before. He had never apologized for anything before. She was building up evidence. Tonight she would look for more clues.

Imogene was followed into Miss McGee's house by Thanatopsis Workman, who had been asked by her husband to clear out for the evening because he had private things to say to Miles.

"And what might those private things be?" asked Miss McGee, serving tea and sugar cookies to the three women.

"Oh, it's all so stupid and unimportant," said Thana-topsis, with the kind of bounce and good looks that made Imogene glad Thanatopsis was married and out of circulation. "You know how a person will run a streak of bad luck for a few days. It's bound to happen. It happens to all of us. Well, poor Miles has had a few days of bad luck—none of it worth mentioning, none of it important, but you know what a serious husband I have. I tell you my husband is so *serious* I can't believe I married him. What was I thinking when I married a man that serious? I know what I was thinking, and I'll tell you. All the while I was growing up my father told me how frivolous I was and how I should be more serious, and I got the idea that if I married someone serious I could go on being just the way I always was and my husband could take care of the serious side of things. So along came Wayne, the most *serious* man I've ever known, and I said that's the man for me, and I married him just like that." She snapped her fingers. "And it has worked out just fine. I *love* Wayne for his seriousness. Not that we don't have our spats, but I mean how could you help loving a man that *serious?* I seem to have this great capacity for loving people—it's just crazy. I love all my students and I love all the faculty and I love the janitors. I go to a basketball game and I love all the players. Show me a person's most obvious trait and that's what I love. For example, every-one pretty well agrees that poor Ansel Stevenson is a dud. That's what Miles calls him, a dud."

"Now, Anna Thea," said Miss McGee. "I'm sure Miles—"

"No, that's what he calls him, a dud, because of course that's what he is. But for a dud, Ansel is such a dear. The poor man is so afraid of a sudden heart attack that he has become absolutely motionless. He reminds me of a little boy sitting in a chair concentrating on behaving himself. And whenever I see him sitting in a chair I want to go up to him and kiss him on top of the head, and I would, too, if I could be sure it wouldn't kill him."

Thanatopsis spoke at such speed that Lillian Kite, knitting to the rhythm of her voice, lost control of her needles.

"Anyhow as I was going to say about Miles—don't you just love Miles? Some say he's distant, but nobody who really knows him—"

"Who says he's distant?" asked Miss McGee.

"Miles has a reputation among some people for being distant."

"Not me," said Imogene Kite. Her mother nodded.

"Nor anybody else who really knows him," said Thanatopsis. "Do you know what Mrs. Vandergar told me? Well, you remember last year when poor Fred Vandergar was home dying of cancer. Miles went over to visit him one afternoon, and Mrs. Vandergar told me that as they stood at the door saying good-by, Miles hugged each one of them very tightly. Mrs. Vandergar said that nothing else in the last months of Fred's life meant so much to him. Now, does hugging the Vandergars sound like the act of a distant man? And what I'd like to know is why more of us didn't have sense enough to go over to the Vandergars' and hug both of them, Fred because he was dying and his wife because she was watching him die. Well, anyway, that's beside the point. What I was going to say was that poor Miles has had a series of unlucky things happen to him, not that all of them taken together would fill a thimble, but last Saturday night at our party Miles frightened Ansel Stevenson, and the Stevensons went home before Wayne had a chance to talk to him about his new plan for keeping Indians in school, and Wayne resented that. Then on Monday Jeff Norquist jumped out the window during Miles's English class and of course that made Miles look bad—"

"Miles never told me that," said Miss McGee. "Did you actually see the boy jump out the window?"

"No, my room faces the other direction."

"It sounds like something I'd be inclined to doubt unless I saw it with my own eyes."

"Oh, it happened all right. Jeff Norquist is a problem to everyone, you know, Agatha, except maybe to Annie Bird his girl friend, who was waiting outside in the courtyard, and when he jumped out the window they went to the pool hall together. So that, as I say, made Miles look bad. And then that very same day—and I'm afraid I am responsible for this—Miles had a run-in with Wayne over a ruling in the Faculty Handbook. He went over Wayne's head and had Ansel Stevenson reverse the ruling, and of course Wayne, being the serious man he is, took that very hard. And then—well, I hate to go on. This is all so insignificant. It's silly. I must be boring you to death."

Thanatopsis tasted her tea, and Lillian Kite picked up the stitches she had dropped.

Miss McGee asked, "What was the ruling that the superintendent reversed?"

"It concerned funerals. According to the Handbook, I could not go to the funeral of my best friend's mother in St. Paul without losing a day's pay, and Miles, being chairman of the Grievance Committee, took it up first with Wayne, then with Ansel."

"I suspect his being chairman of the Committee was not the main reason. With Miles I suspect it was his native sense of justice."

"Of course. But Wayne took it awfully hard." She sipped her tea.

"What else?" Miss McGee passed the cookies.

"Well, there were those two days he was absent."

"Don't tell me Wayne is questioning his honesty about these two days! If there is any question about Miles's indisposition both yesterday and today, I'll talk to your husband myself."

"No, no, Wayne knows Miles was ill, but Miles has a class that's very hard to handle and Wayne has a hard time finding a substitute for him. And then there was the incident this afternoon in study hall. Did he tell you about it?"

"Yes, he told me at supper."

Imogene asked what happened.

"There was a scuffle in study hall. Little Hank Bird pulled a knife on Jeff Norquist, and Jeff Norquist beat him up."

"And Wayne is blaming it on Miles?" asked Miss McGee.

"Of course not. In fact, if Miles hadn't been good enough to come back to school even though he was taking the day off, he wouldn't have even been there to witness it. But the fact remains that it happened in Miles's study hall with Miles present, and you know how that looks to a principal as serious as Wayne. It looks bad."

Miss McGee filled the teacups. "I hope you have come to the end of Miles's tribulations."

Thanatopsis said nothing.

Lillian Kite said, "I wonder what Miles spilled on Lyle's pants."

Miss McGee said, "Anna Thea, is there more to tell?"

"Agatha, this is absolutely preposterous. I wasn't

going to bring it up, but it's so absolutely preposterous that mentioning it couldn't possibly do any harm. One of the things Wayne wants to speak to Miles about is his relationship with Beverly Bingham."

Imogene and her mother stopped chewing their cookies.

Miss McGee spilled her tea.

The air had turned cold after sundown but Miles, as always, was warmly received by the Stevensons. He sat before the fire and described what had happened in study hall.

The superintendent took it like a man. He said, "Bennie Bird of the Sandhill General Store is not an easy man to deal with. They say he can become quite vocal. But it is our good fortune to have Alexander Bigmeadow on our side. There are two kinds of Indians, Miles, happy Indians and unhappy Indians, and Alexander Bigmeadow is one of the happy Indians. He's been a happy Indian ever since we at the school got his daughter Nancy into the Federal Program for Apprentice Indians or whatever it was called. I shouldn't say 'we,' I should say Delia Fritz and Anna Thea Workman. Those two were responsible for that. They got Nancy Bigmeadow to apply for the program and they wrote sterling letters of recommendation for her and had me sign them. Sterling letters. Two of the best letters of their kind that I have ever read. I didn't know Nancy Bigmeadow personally, but Delia and Anna Thea assured me that she was a good Indian, a happy Indian, and of course if you can't take the word of Delia and Anna Thea, who can you take the word of? Delia is so up on things, and Anna Thea is such a dear girl. And Nancy Bigmeadow proved to be everything they said she was. She was taken into the program—the Apprenticeship Program for Federal Indians or whatever it was called—and she was sent to Washington, where if I am not mistaken she still resides, and that's what made her father a happy Indian. That's what put him in our camp."

"And now he's chief," said Miles.

"And now he's chief, and that's more good luck. First thing in the morning would you please ask Delia to phone Alexander Bigmeadow and smooth everything over? I don't suppose you know this, Miles—Delia is too modest to say anything—but she has taken over a good share of my work load. She will take care of this matter. Tomorrow morning you just mention this to her and she will smooth everything over."

The logs in the fireplace shifted.

Miles said, "Do you know what else I saw out there in Sandhill today? I saw the sign about shoelaces in the General Store."

"No."

"Yes. It's still on the inside of the door."

"Think of it." The superintendent turned to his wife, who was carrying a tray into the living room, and said, "Viola, did you forget shoelaces?"

"Please don't say that, Ansel dear. It's too, too vivid in my memory." She handed Miles a spoon, a napkin, and a large raspberry sundae.

To a man with a dry socket, what is more dismaying than a raspberry sundae?

Wayne Workman was too hot under the collar to give Miles a warm welcome. Opening the door, he said, "Come in and explain what you think you're doing with that Bingham girl."

Miles was speechless. He sat down with his coat on.

Wayne stayed on his feet. "For a man to be carrying

on with a female student is dynamite. It's no secret that you and I don't see eye to eye on a lot of things, Pruitt, but by God we'd better understand each other on this. If you don't know, at the age of thirty-five, with twelve years of teaching experience, that carrying on with a female student is out-and-out dynamite, then I'd say you have a lot of growing up to do." He swiveled about and walked the length of the living room, then walked back. "Dynamite!"

Miles got up to go.

"Sit down, Pruitt, and hear me out. I can tell you exactly how many times in the last two weeks I've seen you standing in the hall after fifth hour talking to Beverly Bingham. I've seen you talking to her eight times!"

Miles sat down. He was determined to stay cool, though he was getting very hot in his coat.

"And I wish that's all the evidence I had. But I have more. Last Sunday afternoon, Pruitt, your car was seen in Pike Park next to the Bingham pickup truck. It rained hard Sunday afternoon, and what anybody might be doing with a good-looking girl in Pike Park on a rainy afternoon is not all that difficult to figure out. Nadine Oppegaard and her friends were driving out that way and they saw your car and the Bingham truck—Nadine Oppegaard, daughter of Doc Oppegaard, chairman of the school board, no less. And Coach's son Peter was among those who were with her. And when they got back to town, Nadine Oppegaard told her father and Doc told Stella Gibbon and Stella told Coach and Coach asked Peter if it was true and Peter said, 'Yes, it's true,' and so Coach told me." Wayne stepped back and folded his arms, studying Miles. "Well, do you wish to say something, or shall I go on to the next piece of evidence?"

"Go on to the next piece of evidence."

237

"Very well. That was Sunday. Now the very next day, which was Monday, Beverly Bingham passed you a note in the hall after fifth hour. I saw it with my own eyes. You put it in your briefcase. And then on Tuesday she visited your house after school and stayed for at least thirty minutes, and that too I saw with my own eyes because her truck was sitting in front of your place from three thirty, when I went home from school, until at least four, when I drove uptown for a pack of cigarettes. And now, today, Wednesday, it was the same thing, the truck sitting in front of your house for a goodly length of time, and what I can't figure out is how you think you can get away with anything so scandalous and how you can be so careless with your reputation, to say nothing of the reputation of the Staggerford faculty, and—most puzzling of all—how you can bring that kind of shame upon the house of Miss McGee, who is the most moral person on God's green earth." Wayne sat down, resting his case.

Miles said nothing.

"Now speak up." Wayne clamped his lower teeth on his mustache. Sweat stood out on his brow.

Miles said, "Do you have a toothpick? I have a raspberry seed here between—"

Rage lifted Wayne out of his chair. "I do *not* have a toothpick!"

"That's all right," said Miles, going to the door. "I have some at home."

Outside on the dark street, Miles was convulsed with the anger he had been holding in check. His knees trembled, his scalp burned. He walked home and saw through the front window that Miss McGee had company. He did not go in. He walked down Main Street to the Hub to soothe his emotions with a piece of chocolate cake, and that was where he first heard about the Indian invasion. Someone said that everybody living on the Sandhill Reservation was planning to come to Staggerford at first light in the morning and seek retribution for what had happened to little Hank Bird. Someone else said that the Indians were going to camp on the football field across the street from the school until Jeff Norquist was scalped.

THURSDAY

November 5

THE SUN WAS SCARCELY above the horizon when the first car arrived from Sandhill. It was an old white Buick carrying seven men, including Alexander Bigmeadow and Bennie Bird. It came to a stop near the flagpole across the street from Staggerford High School. The seven men got out, stretched, passed through the open gate by the ticket booth, and walked out onto the football field. They stood under the goalpost, silhouetted against the orange sun, and they watched the arrival of the students.

Next, a red pickup pulled in behind the Buick and three women emerged from the cab and three more climbed down from the box behind. Then two more cars and another pickup, then three more cars and a van.

Wayne Workman's office faced the street. Between eight o'clock and nine, Wayne stood at his window and peeked through the blinds, watching the Indians arrive in a steady stream. At nine he called the governor and said his school was under siege by Indians.

The governor asked why.

"I don't know," said Wayne.

"Well, ask them."

"Yes sir."

"And have you called the county sheriff?"

"No."

"Call the county sheriff."

"Yes sir."

"And when you find out what they want, call me back."

"Yes sir."

"In the meantime, I'll send you a fleet of highway patrolmen."

Wayne called the sheriff in Berrington, but he did not go across the street and ask the Indians what they wanted. He was paralyzed with fear. He continued to stand at his window, peeking through the blinds. He counted the Indians. With the arrival of the final car-load at about ten o'clock he counted 507 men, women, and children of the Chippewa nation. The sun by this time had dried the dew, and most of the Indians were sitting on the grass like clusters of picnickers.

Classrooms were full of tension. Even first-hour English was wakeful—coughing and stretching between yawns. Lee Fremling, manifesting uncharacteristic imagination, said he wished the classroom faced the football field instead of the courtyard, so he could see what was going on.

Second-hour English, with Jeff Norquist conspicuously absent, was on the verge of a nervous breakdown. The only thing all hour that quieted the class was Roxie Booth's story about a black soldier who had raped an Indian girl. The girl's family and friends kidnapped the black soldier and castrated him with the edge of a torn tin can.

Next hour, Miles was summoned by Wayne Workman's secretary. He put William Mulholland, the scientist, in charge of his class and he went to Wayne's office, which he found empty. He stepped to the window and raised the blind. Wayne rushed out of the closet (blowing smoke out of his nose) and grabbed the rope from him and lowered the blind.

"Pruitt, are you crazy? That's the enemy out there. And do you know how many of them there are?"

"How many?"

"Five hundred and seven. Go out and ask them what they want."

"Me? Why me?"

"Because it happened in your study hall. They've come to get even with Jeff Norquist."

"If we know that, then we don't need to ask them what they want, do we?"

"The governor says to ask them. I called the governor and he said to ask."

Suddenly little Hank Bird was standing in the office doorway. Smiling shyly through his bruises, he said, "My dad says for the principal to come outside." He left as quickly as he came.

Between bites of his mustache, Wayne said, "Pruitt, you're coming with me." He waited for Miles to lead the way.

As Miles and Wayne crossed the street, several men who had been sitting on the grass got up and came off the football field through the ticket gate and gathered at the curb under the flagpole. No flag flew this morning because Sorenson the janitor had been afraid to cross the street and raise it.

"Good morning, what do you want?" Wayne said, stepping up on the curb. His voice had a tremor in it.

A lean, dark man with a face full of deep wrinkles came forward and glared first at Wayne, then at Miles. "I'm Bennie Bird. I expect satisfaction for what happened to my boy Hank." His voice was an ominous rumble, like distant thunder. He had the same kind of face as the wise old Indian Miles had seen in countless movies, the Indian who had weathered seventy years of sun and wind on the slopes of the Rockies and who told his great-grandchildren with a faraway look in his small eyes that the plains were once a sea of buffalo. But this wasn't the movies, this was Staggerford, and this Indian was Bennie Bird, whose face was weathered not by sun and wind but by seventy years of smoke and shadow in the Sandhill General Store. These small eyes were not gazing far off across the plains, they were gazing at Miles.

"Glad to know you," Miles said, putting out his hand in case Bennie Bird wanted to shake it. He didn't.

Another man stepped forward. "I'm Alexander Bigmeadow," he said. Under his very large stomach he wore his belt like a sling. This was the chief of Sandhill, and both Wayne and Miles were glad to see him. They had spoken to him at meetings of the Staggerford PTA and they had known him, on occasion, to smile. But he wasn't smiling this morning.

"Well, Mr. Bigmeadow," said Wayne in a very high voice, "what brings all you folks to town this morning?"

"It's not good, Mr. Workman. We have to have satisfaction for little Hank. When the noon-hour bell rings, we expect to see that Norquist boy step out the front door of the schoolhouse, and if he doesn't, we're going inside and search him out."

"You goddamn right," said Bennie Bird. "Satisfaction for what he did to Hank."

Little Hank was edging away from the group of men, hoping his duties were over.

Wayne said, "Jeff Norquist isn't in school today. I've suspended him. You see, he's already being punished for what he did." Wayne's voice was deserting him. Its pitch kept rising.

"That's for you to do if you want to," said Bennie Bird, "but we ain't yet done what's for us to do. We want satisfaction."

"What do you have in mind?" asked Miles.

Bennie Bird said, "Satisfaction for Hank. Eye for an eye."

Bigmeadow said, "We'll decide on the satisfaction when the time comes. When we meet with the Norquist boy we'll decide."

Wayne squeaked, "But he's not in school today. He's home."

"Go get him."

Wayne then said something unintelligible, and one of the men standing behind Bigmeadow was amused by his high, tremulous squeak. This man, a middle-aged Indian wearing the kind of lime-green hat sold at carnivals, laughed out loud. One of his friends snickered. A third man smiled. Bigmeadow scowled at them. So did Wayne. When the carnival-hatted man quit laughing and the other two quit smiling, Wayne turned abruptly and marched across the street, Miles following him.

Wayne called the governor and told him what the Indians wanted. The governor said he was sending twelve highway patrolmen to Staggerford, and Wayne's job was to keep the lid on until they arrived.

Wayne said, "The student they're after is not in school today. Do you think he should be?"

The governor thought he should be.

Wayne put his hand over the phone and said, "Pruitt, get Norquist."

Miles went across the hall to Delia Fritz's desk to call the Norquist house, and picking up the phone he caught the end of Wayne's conversation with the governor.

"By the way," said the governor, "is Ansel Stevenson

still your superintendent in Staggerford?"

"He is, but he's not here this morning. He went home."

"Well, as long as Ansel Stevenson is your superintendent I wouldn't worry if I were you. Old Ansel is a great hand with Indians, you know."

"Yes, sir. Thank you, sir." Wayne hung up.

Mrs. Norquist answered Miles's call. She said Jeff was in bed.

"Did he tell you why he is staying home today, Mrs. Norquist?"

"No, he never tells me anything."

"He's been suspended for fighting. But it's imperative that he come back to school now because we want him to attend a meeting. He has made a lot of Indians mad."

"He's a thorn in my heart," said Mrs. Norquist, and she hung up.

Miles called her again. "Am I to understand that you will send Jeff to school right away, Mrs. Norquist?"

"If you think he'll get out of bed and go to school just on my say-so, you must be a fool, Mr. Pruitt." She hung up.

Miles went back to Wayne's outer office and scanned the morning attendance report. Nearly every Indian student was absent; but Annie Bird, as Miles expected, was in school—no doubt in defiance of her people.

He looked up Annie's class schedule and went to the gym where four teams of girls in red shorts and white shirts were playing volleyball. He called Annie aside and said that he and she must somehow bring Jeff Norquist back to school before twelve o'clock.

Annie said it sounded like a dumb idea. She said the

football field was full of Indians and Jeff was better off at home.

"It's what the governor wants," said Miles.

Annie looked him in the eye, brought an insolent pucker to her lips, and said, "It *still* sounds like a dumb idea." Her eyes flashed the same anger he had seen yesterday when she got off the school bus in Sandhill, the same anger he had just seen across the street in the eyes of her father.

"It's part of the governor's plan to avoid violence, Annie. It's the only way."

"All right, I'll change." She started toward the locker room.

"There's not time to change. The noon-hour bell rings in twenty minutes."

Miles and Annie went out the back door of the school and down an alley and across Main Street. Annie's red shorts, too big for her tiny waist and skinny brown legs, were gathered at the belt like a potato sack. She wore an oversized pair of white tennis shoes that flapped when she walked. The initials *J N* were printed in black on the rubber toes.

The Norquist house had gone to seed. What had once been an attractive bungalow at the crest of a sloping lawn was now hidden in a tangle of vines and overgrown shrubbery. The lawn had been left uncut all summer.

As Miles knocked at the front door, Annie said, "I'll knock on Jeff's bedroom window," and she disappeared around the corner of the house.

Miles knocked three or four times. Finally Mrs. Norquist came to the door. Miles had not seen her for a long time—not since her daughter Maureen graduated—and he was surprised by how much older she looked. She was wearing a worn-out bathrobe and smoking a cigarette.

"I'm sorry, Mrs. Norquist, but it's imperative that Jeff come to school right away."

"If you think you can do anything with him, Mr. Pruitt, be my guest." She stepped aside to let him come in.

At that moment, Annie and Jeff came around the corner of the house, holding hands, and set off toward school.

"God, look at that, would you," said Mrs. Norquist. "What a pair."

"Please excuse me, Mrs. Norquist. I have to get right back."

"I almost wish they'd run away and leave me in peace. It's coming up on eight years since my husband drowned, Mr. Pruitt. My only comfort in life is my daughter Maureen in New Jersey. She's married, you know. She writes every week."

For lack of anything better to say, Miles blurted, "Thank you," and he followed Annie and Jeff across Main Street.

Jeff was short and broad. His back muscles bulged under his tight T-shirt. He lit a cigarette, turning to make sure Miles noticed, and he gave Annie a drag. His curly hair stood out from his head in a massive blond afro.

Twice Jeff asked Annie, "What's going on?" but Annie wouldn't tell him.

Miles followed them down the alley and through the back door of the school. They got to Wayne's office one minute before twelve. The office was empty.

Miles opened the blinds and saw Wayne and two highway patrolmen standing at the base of the flagpole across the street. The patrolmen were dressed in burgundy uniforms with braid at the shoulder and wide, flat-brimmed hats like Lyle Kite's ranger hat. Alexander

Bigmeadow was speaking to them. Bennie Bird had turned his back on them, and with his arms folded he was glaring at the sky. All 507 Indians, preparing to invade the school, were on their feet now, crowding through the ticket gate and gathering at the curb.

"Jeff," said Miles, "you see those people out there? They would like to have a word with you."

Jeff looked out the window, then backed into Wayne's closet.

"Don't worry, Jeff. They just want to have a word with you."

"Don't be afraid of fat bastards like Alexander Bigmeadow," said Annie. "Where's your guts?" She tried to tug Jeff out of the closet. So that (thought Miles) was why she hadn't told Jeff what he was in for. She knew he would turn coward.

If it had been Spanish rice day or hamburger soup day, no one in school would have bothered to eat, but the menu called for everybody's favorite, sloppy joes, and when the bell rang the faculty and students dropped into the basement, then rushed outside, still chewing, to watch what many of them hoped would be bloodshed. The students packed themselves into the street, leaving only a narrow passage between the front steps of the school and the opposite curb.

The Indians began shouting, "Norquist come out!!" and the students took up the chant. It sounded like a football cheer.

"They're calling my name," said Jeff from deeper in the closet.

"Don't worry," said Miles. "Just come outside with me and see what they have to say."

"You think I'm crazy?"

"There's nothing to fear. The state troopers will keep them under control. I see another patrol car coming."

"It would take five of them Indian bastards to knock you down," said Annie, pulling on Jeff's arm.

"NORQUIST COME OUT!"

Jeff shook Annie loose and pulled the closet door shut.

Miles spoke through the door: "Mr. Workman wants you to help him negotiate."

Annie added, "If they want to fight, I'll help you fight, Jeff. I know how to kick them fat bastards where it hurts."

"NORQUIST COME OUT!"

"Are you coming out?" asked Miles.

"Bigmeadow's all flab," shouted Annie.

A state trooper in a burgundy shirt, having come in by a back door, suddenly appeared in the office and introduced himself as the governor's official arbitrator. He was a giant in sunglasses. Miles, for all his size, felt suddenly diminished, for he stood no higher than the trooper's shirt pocket. Except in a sideshow one time, Miles had never seen a man so large. The trooper's shirt front and sleeves were a collage of decoration: a badge, a rope of gold braid, a miniature American flag, a leather holster strap, and several cloth patches with the messages you read on bumper stickers. KEEP MINNESOTA GREEN, said one.

"Are you the principal?"

"No, my name is Miles Pruitt. And this is Annie Bird. And in here"—he tried to open the closet door—"is Jeff Norquist. He's the one they're after."

"What's he doing in there?"

"He's a chicken!" said Annie.

The governor's Giant pulled the closet door open and looked in at Jeff. Jeff looked up, astonished at the man's size

"Stay the hell out of sight," said the Giant, and he shut the closet door.

"But the governor recommended—" Miles began.

"Never mind. The worst thing to do would be to bring the kid into it. We can't bring the kid into it till everybody cools down. I've been through this kind of thing before. You don't just throw a kid to an angry mob. You wait a day or two, till everybody cools down."

"You call that bunch of fat bastards a mob?" shrieked Annie. "They're nothing but flab. I could handle two or three of them myself." In the Giant's presence Annie did not diminish the way Jeff and Miles seemed to.

"NORQUIST COME OUT!"

Miles went to the window. Bennie Bird, dragging little Hank by the arm, was crossing the street. Alexander Bigmeadow and Wayne Workman and the troopers (four of them now) were a step behind, followed by the rest of the Indians.

"They're coming," said Miles.

"Stay the hell out of sight, kid," the Giant said to the closet door. Then to Miles: "See that nobody gets the kid. I'm going to try to break up the mob before they get inside."

"I'll help you," said Annie, clenching her fists. She followed the Giant out of the office, her tennis shoes slapping the floor.

Miles watched from the window. Delia Fritz, one of the few people left in the building, came across the hall to watch with him. She threw open the window to hear what was said.

As Bennie Bird, dragging his son by the arm, approached the school, the governor's Giant stepped out the front door. Everyone, including the students in the street, drew back a step, startled by his size. The Giant

253

slowly descended the steps and put his hand on Bennie Bird's shoulder and swore in the name of God and the governor that Jeff Norquist was nowhere in the building.

Annie stood at the Giant's side and said, "Yeah."

Bennie Bird said, "We want satisfaction for the tooth he knocked out of Hank's mouth. Satisfaction from that goddamn no-good Norquist."

Annie spat at her father. He lunged at her but was restrained by two patrolmen.

"How come you're sober this late in the day?" she screeched, hopping in her excitement from one foot to the other.

Little Hank stepped up to his sister and said, "Blow it out your ass." Annie punched him in his bruised eye, reopening one of yesterday's lacerations. Bennie Bird lunged again at his daughter, but was held back. Little Hank whipped out a knife—this time a paring knife—but before he knew what was happening the Giant lifted him off the ground and handed him to another patrolman, who put him in a patrol car and drove off toward the hospital.

By this time there were six or eight patrolmen on the scene, mingling with the Indians and looking very majestic and unruffled in their burgundy shirts and gold braid. The pair restraining Bennie Bird seemed not to notice that he was struggling helplessly in their grasp.

A silver car with a siren and a flashing red light pulled up, and the Berrington County sheriff stepped out. He was wearing knee-high boots, a riot helmet with goggles, and a bulletproof vest. A number of Indians thought he was funny.

Alexander Bigmeadow turned and looked at his followers and sensed that their determination was leaking away. Most of them were hushed, straining to hear the cursing of the Birds.

"Satisfaction!" shouted Bennie Bird. "Goddamn missing tooth! Goddamn Norquist!"

Annie kicked her father in the crotch.

"Good Lord," said Delia Fritz.

Annie skipped up the steps and into the school.

Her father was bent over in pain. This amused the carnival-hatted Indian who had earlier found Wayne's voice so entertaining. Three or four of his friends joined him in open laughter. At that moment the Staggerford Uprising (as Editor Fremling was to refer to it in the *Weekly*) fell apart. Bigmeadow knew it was over. He put his hands up and waved his people back to the football field. Was it a gesture of disgust or relief? Miles wasn't sure. While most of the Indians moved back to the football field, a few went uptown for picnic supplies.

Two patrolmen picked up Bennie Bird by the armpits and with his knees drawn up to his chest they carried him across the street and set him down at the base of the flagpole.

"Ring the bell," Miles said.

Delia Fritz looked at her watch. "It's ten minutes early."

"Ring it anyway."

She went across the hall and did so. The faculty and students came inside and filled the halls with a great racket and then dispersed into their fifth-hour classrooms, where they discovered too late they had been tricked.

Miles went to his class and took roll, then was summoned once more to Wayne's office—this time to be party to the negotiations. The office was packed. The governor's Giant, still wearing sunglasses, sat behind

Wayne's desk. Wayne shared a bench with Albert Fremling, who held his high-speed Graphlex on his lap. Chairs were brought in for Alexander Bigmeadow, Bennie Bird, the sheriff from Berrington (still in riot helmet and goggles), and Doc Oppegaard, chairman of the school board. Miles stood in the doorway, adding nothing but his presence to the Articles of Arbitration, which the Giant wrote on a sheet of paper:

One. The Chippewa Indians of the Sandhill Reservation demand restitution for the injuries and humiliation suffered by Hank Bird at the hands of Jeff Norquist on Wednesday, November 4, in the study hall of Staggerford High School.

Two. The Staggerford School District agrees to make reasonable restitution for said injuries and humiliation, but determination of said restitution shall be made only at such time when both sides have cooled down and can come together as reasonable men.

Three. Therefore the next step in these negotiations shall be a meeting at noon on Saturday, November 7, at Staggerford High School. It shall be attended by a peaceful delegation of Indians and by a peaceful delegation of whites. Both delegations shall be small.

Four. The Staggerford delegation shall be led by the governor's official arbitrator and it shall include Mr. Workman, Mr. Pruitt, and Jeff Norquist. The Indian delegation shall be led by Chief Bigmeadow and shall include persons yet to be appointed.

Arriving at these terms was the work of half an hour, and when all was settled Doc Oppegaard (who because of prostate trouble interrupted every meeting he attended) stood up and said, "Is this your bathroom,

Wayne?" and opened the door to the coat closet. There on the floor sat Jeff Norquist, terrified.

"There's the son of a bitch!" said Bennie Bird, leaping to his feet. "You said he wasn't in school!" Instead of attacking Jeff Norquist, Bennie took a swing at the Giant across the desk. Alexander Bigmeadow and the sheriff carried Bennie outside and deposited him with a group of patrolmen chatting in the street.

Bigmeadow returned to the office and said that because the Giant had lied about Jeff Norquist, the whites would have to make two concessions. To the Articles, therefore, these points were added:

> Five. Saturday's meeting shall not be held in Staggerford as previously stated, but in Pike Park, a neutral site.
>
> Six. The Staggerford delegation shall include no member of any law-enforcement agency.

Fifth-hour English was eager to hear the terms of the agreement. Miles told them, adding, "Thus the Chippewa nation returns to the reservation without getting what it came for."

"It isn't the first time," said Nadine Oppegaard.

Alexander Bigmeadow, Bennie Bird, and little Hank left school and went across the street to join their friends, who were lunching on peaches, sandwiches, and beer. Doc Oppegaard went back to his office and Stella. The governor's Giant drove Jeff Norquist home.

When everyone had cleared out of his office, Wayne Workman went into his closet, shut the door, and smoked a cigarette in the dark. Then he went to the home-ec room where Thanatopsis gave him a neck rub, a cup of cocoa, a tranquilizer, and a pat on the back. "The crisis is over," she said.

"Till Saturday," said Wayne.

He returned to his office and sat down and looked across the street. The Indians were drifting off the field and climbing into their cars. The flag was run up the pole by Sorenson the janitor, who then unlocked the ticket booth, brought out a waste barrel and a pointed stick, and began to pick up the bread wrappers and six-pack cartons scattered across the field.

Wayne felt good. He believed that Albert Fremling had shot a picture of him as he stood under the flagpole talking to Bigmeadow. And there might have been another picture as he shook hands with the Giant before the meeting broke up in his office. Albert Fremling was sober today, so the pictures would doubtless turn out sharp and appear in tomorrow afternoon's *Weekly*. They would establish Wayne's reputation in Staggerford as an efficient administrator. Wayne imagined a headline: WORKMAN THE PEACEMAKER. These words he found so compelling that he phoned the newspaper office and suggested them to Fremling.

Workman the peacemaker, after calling Fremling, gazed out the window and planned who should receive copies of the *Weekly*. Two or three copies should go to the governor, and at least one to the commissioner of education. Minnesota's congressmen should each have one. And why leave out the President of the United States?

In the distance, Wayne saw a group of children out for a walk. They were led by a woman and they were approaching the far end of the football field from the direction of St. Isidore's. The children followed the woman to the fifty-yard line, where she stopped to talk to Sorenson the janitor. Sorenson doffed his hat and with a sweeping motion of his arm he indicated the difficulty of his chore—the scraps of paper being set in motion now by a chilly breeze rising from the east. The woman turned to her group of children and gave them instructions. They leaped instantly to work, scurrying after paper and bringing it back in handfuls and stuffing it in the janitor's barrel. The woman left them at their work and approached the school. Wayne saw that it was Miss McGee. A few moments later he turned in his chair and saw her standing in his doorway.

"Miss McGee," he said, getting to his feet. "Please sit down."

"I'll stand, thank you." She set her purse on his glass-topped desk. She pulled off her gloves, a finger at a time.

Wayne straightened his tie and buttoned his suit coat. "What can I do for you, Miss McGee?"

She carefully placed her gloves on top of her purse and told Wayne to sit down—which he did immediately. He was genuinely frightened by Miss McGee's expression, which conveyed either ill health or anger. He was afraid it was anger.

"I have taken my class of sixth-graders out on a field trip this afternoon, Mr. Workman. I have told them that the purpose of our field trip is to identify birds, and since leaving the front door of St. Isidore's we have seen four sparrows in the street and a small flock of approximately twenty blue-fronted geese flying very high in a southwesterly direction. This of course is not the time of year to be birdwatching. You know that as well as I do, Mr. Workman. Most of our migratory birds have left by this time. The robins are gone, the woodpeckers are gone, the bluebirds are gone; the thrushes, cedar waxwings, thrashers, and swallows are gone; the martins and finches are gone. I had a pair of finches nesting in my back yard this year, Mr. Workman, and they left in September. Now it's true that the grosbeaks and chickadees are moving into our area for the winter, and it's also true that the cardinals, bluejays, and sparrows are going to remain with us, but it is not, on the whole, a good time of year for birdwatching."

Wayne nodded, tasting his mustache.

"So identifying birds was not my true purpose in bringing my class outside today, but I kept my true purpose to myself, and as we approached your athletic field we found that Mr. Sorenson was having difficulty picking up the paper left by the Indians, and so I have put my pupils to work under his supervision in order that I might come in here and have a word with you. I was on my way over here during my noon hour, but I saw that you were occupied with visitors, and so I have waited until now to say, Mr Workman, that you are a malicious liar, that you are an unscrupulous purveyor of calumny, scandal, and libel, and that if it were to Miles Pruitt's advantage I would encourage him to take you to court for defamation of character. But of course a lawsuit would not be to Miles Pruitt's advantage, for it would only serve to broadcast the unfounded rumor you are spreading concerning Miles and his student, Beverly Bingham. I have it from your own dear wife and from Miles himself that you accused him of having an illicit affair with that poor girl. The fact is that the conditions of Beverly Bingham's home life are extremely sordid and discouraging, Mr. Workman, and in trying to rise above her difficulties and make something of her life, she has turned for counsel to one of her teachers—counsel, I might add, which she evidently did not find available from her principal—and her dependence upon the guidance of Miles Pruitt explains why she has been seen speaking to him between classes eight times in two weeks—am I correct, Mr. Workman, is eight the count?—and it is a tribute to her good sense that she chose to confide in a man as dependable and helpful as Miles.

"Furthermore, you expressed an interest in a paper you saw her give Miles. Actually that was a letter in which she was applying for admission to Berrington Junior College. And you expressed interest in their meetings outside of school, two of which were at my house. I myself was present when Beverly Bingham came to my house to see Miles, and I took advantage of the opportunity to do some counseling of my own. If she continues to visit my house I will continue to offer her my help, and when the day comes that her black truck no longer stops at the curb in front of my house, I hope it is because she has finally grown to a full independence and is able to meet life on its own terms and not because some simpleminded busybody is offended by the sight of that truck at my curb.

"Now I see that my pupils have finished clearing your athletic field of paper, Mr. Workman, and I will be on my way, yet before I go I will mention that I am aware of your ambition to be superintendent of the Staggerford school system—a natural ambition for a high-school principal—but before I would be in favor of your becoming superintendent in a school district where I pay taxes I would want to be sure that you were a steadfast defender of your faculty and a man more interested in justice than in scurrilous rumor, a man of high moral standards with the courage to live up to those standards. We all know that in the foreseeable future the Staggerford School Board will be voting for a new superintendent—and lest you think that the opinion of one old maid doesn't count for much, Mr. Workman, let me remind you that three members of the board are former students of mine with whom I have always seen eye to eye, and a fourth member—Mayor Bartholomew

Druppers—has been a neighbor of mine all my life. That's four votes out of six—a majority. My students and I shall now set off to a grove of trees along the river where I recall seeing a pileated woodpecker."

Wayne Workman sat in a knot with his mustache in his mouth. His forehead hung an inch or so above his desk, so he did not see Miss McGee smile at him (having delivered her message, she looked refreshed) and pick up her gloves and purse. Only when he heard the sound of her heels in the outer office did he look up through his eyebrows at the empty doorway.

When fifth hour ended, Beverly Bingham told Miles that she needed a ride to her pickup, which was standing with a flat tire on the shoulder of the highway. It was out beyond Evergreen Cemetery. Miles said he would meet her at Miss McGee's house after school, and he would drive her out there and change the tire.

She had been hoping he would suggest meeting at Miss McGee's. It would allow her, for the third straight day, a visit to that curious oasis of order and peace on River Street. Before Tuesday, Beverly had never been in a house better than her own (she had been in a few on the reservation that were worse) and she had never felt quite so self-indulgent as Miss McGee's wing chair made her feel. Not that she could imagine herself living in a house like that. The rooms held the dead air of ancient history and reminded her of pictures she had seen of boring museums where people paid money to look at tables and chairs. No, the house was the perfect setting for Miss McGee, who was herself a museum piece, but not for anyone as young as eighteen. Yet it was nice to sit in that chair for a few minutes in the afternoon, before going home, and to be served grape nectar in a heavy goblet, and to see your reflection in the glass doors of the bookcase, and to sense the cleanliness and harmony that dwelt like presences in the dark, elegant rooms.

Today of all days Beverly wanted to sit in the wing chair. It had been a hell of a day.

"I've had just a hell of a day," she told Miss McGee, who served her hot chocolate instead of nectar because the temperature had dropped ten degrees since noon and there was a whistle in the east wind.

"Oh?" Miss McGee decided that today she would broach the subject of Beverly's cursing and swearing. But first she would hear her out. What she heard alarmed her.

"First of all, at breakfast this morning I came that far from being shot through the head by my mother. We were in the kitchen and my mother saw a rat sniffing around the henhouse, and she picked up the twenty-two and went and stood in the doorway and took aim and pulled the trigger and nothing happened. About half the time our twenty-two misfires because it's made for longs and when we buy shells we always buy shorts because they're cheaper, but shorts don't fit in the chamber. So the rat got away and my mother got mad and threw the rifle on the floor, and it fired and the bullet went right past my head. Christ. I was standing by the sink looking out the window at the rat, and I was holding a peanut butter sandwich in one hand and a cup of coffee in the other, and the bullet went right in front of my face a little above the cup and it lodged in the window frame. Christ, I stood there and shook. And then as if that wasn't enough, I had a blowout on the way to school. I got into a whole string of cars that were coming into town from the reservation and one of my back tires blew out. I was still scared from being shot at, and when the tire blew out I went to pieces. I came to a dead stop on the highway and bawled. All the cars behind me had to stop. They were nice about it, though. A whole bunch of Indians got out and pushed the truck off the highway and onto the shoulder, and then they gave me a ride to school. It turned out that's where they were going anyhow. And then"—Beverly picked her cup of hot chocolate off the coffee table, poked the marshmallow down under the surface, licked her finger—"then third hour I got another scare, only this one proved to be a false alarm. In social studies I and everybody else went to the window to look at the Indians on the football field, and at first glance I thought I saw my mother over there with them. I just froze. My mother seldom comes to town except at night after people have had supper and are likely to have bones for her, but once in a while some Indian women— some cousins of my dad's—will stop by the farm and take her to town to buy feed or just for the hell of it. I thought maybe they stopped by this morning and brought her along. God, I just froze. I live in dread of her coming to school because one time when I was a sophomore she did just that. It was the day my dad died in the veterans' hospital and she came to town to tell me about it. She came into school and she found what class I was in and she came right into the classroom, came barging right in without knocking or anything, came walking right across the room in front of the teacher and over to my desk. She was dressed just terrible. She had on her old sweater with the elbows out and the dress she cleans chickens in. God, I wanted to die. And that's what I thought this morning. I thought she was coming in to find me. But it was my imagination. She wasn't out there. God, was I relieved."

Miss McGee sipped her hot chocolate, and when she looked up again Beverly was weeping. In a split second the girl had been jolted by the force of her sorrow. Shaken by sobs, she was spilling her chocolate on her lap and on the arm of the wing chair. Like the time a week ago when she had wept in the corridor of the school, and like this morning in the pickup when the tire blew out, despair overcame her in the wink of an eye. There were never, it seemed, any preliminary stages to Beverly's sorrow—no languid dampening of her spirits, no gradual sinking of her heart. Sorrow came to Beverly like a disfiguring blow to the face. Like a baby, she cried with her chin.

Miss McGee leaned forward and took Beverly's cup, then offered her hand. Beverly took the hand and studied it through her tears. A homely hand—spotted and wrinkled and bumpy. Blunt fingers. She put the hand to her face and wiped her eyes with it.

Beverly, Beverly (Miles wrote in his journal that evening), *what were you on the verge of telling me as I changed the tire on your truck this afternoon? A family secret you call it. You say it is the reason nothing in your life will work out, and the reason you were crying all over Miss McGee when I got home from school.*

Getting you home was an altogether miserable experience: trying to extract you from Miss McGee's living room, then trying in the car to convince you that your future held hope, then trying to loosen the rusted lug nuts on that ancient GMC with the wind blowing so cold across the prairie that it made my hands and ears ache, and trying to make out what you were saying as you stood there with your back to the wind and your hair flying out in front of your face, and trying to keep my own heart from growing heavy as I watched you drive off down the highway and then turn down into the dark woods of that gloomy gulch you live in.

265

Something has to be done about you, Beverly. As soon as this Indian squabble is over, you and I and Agatha will get together and talk things out. I would also like Thanatopsis to be in on it. Thanatopsis will know what's best for you. Throughout high school you have avoided her homemaking courses, and though you haven't admitted it to me, I know why: Coming from the kind of home you do, you are afraid of making a fool of yourself among all those new stoves and sewing machines. But Thanatopsis has more to offer than homemaking courses. She knows what's good for people. She makes people glad.

Thanatopsis, come to think of it, is just the person we need to go to Pike Park on Saturday and meet with the Indians. She would make them all glad. Poor Thanatopsis is going to have her hands full with Wayne for the next two days. As the meeting approaches, he will become edgy and harder than ususal to live with. Today at the base of the flagpole, Wayne lost his voice. How embarrassing it must have been for him to open his mouth and speak to Alexander Bigmeadow in that tiny squeak. I felt sorry for him, yet I was as amused by it as that green-hatted Indian was, and I too wanted to laugh. I was hoping, in fact, that Wayne would make a few more remarks in that ridiculous little voice. The wildest laughter often springs from tension, and—who knows?— if Wayne had kept speaking, the whole tribe might have called off the confrontation and gone home in stitches. But Wayne's chagrin was so great that he, like Bigmeadow, scowled at the men who were snickering, and when the last signs of lightheartedness drained from their faces and they glared again with vengeance, Wayne nodded curtly as if to say, "That's better," and turned and marched back to school. How easily our pride destroys our good sense.

What's it like to go through life astonishing people by your mere existence? I am thinking of the governor's Giant. When the Giant stepped out the front door of the school this noon, it wasn't only Bennie Bird who recoiled in amazement. I saw a thousand people take a step backward, Indians and students alike. The Giant is over seven feet tall, perhaps seven two, and even for all that height he is overweight. He must weigh close to four hundred pounds.

But Annie Bird wasn't impressed. Annie Bird, who could fit with room to spare into one of the Giant's pant legs, accepted him for exactly what he is: a public servant. She used him as her bodyguard. She went out and sized up the invasion and turned it back with a well-calculated kick to her father's crotch. She humiliated her father in the eyes of the tribe (he is the constable of Sandhill) and thereby transformed a mob into groups of picnickers. There was nothing for the Giant to do but to stand rather uselessly at her side. Heaven help Jeff Norquist if he marries Annie Bird.

Since I last saw Jeff Norquist's mother, she has gone into a speedy decline. She looks haggard and slightly dirty. I remember when she was classy. When I had Jeff's sister Maureen in class, Mrs. Norquist was a frequent visitor at school, and she didn't look much older than Maureen. That was five years ago. Now she's old The change is primarily in her wrinkled and milky complexion. It was apparent today that her delay in opening the door was due to a desperate attempt to fix her face. She wore two smears of crimson rouge, and the smear on the right side was not on the cheekbone where it belonged, but back by her ear.

I remember Mr. Norquist—I forget his first name—as the Berrington County Attorney. He divided his time between Staggerford (where he was a law partner with

Bartholomew Druppers) and the courthouse in Ber-
rington. He drowned in the Badbattle. But it couldn't
have been his drowning that caused Mrs. Norquist to lose
heart. He was already dead when I had Maureen as a
student. What caused her decline has been something
more recent. Jeff's vicious behavior? Or did her losing
heart precede, and perhaps cause, his viciousness? Jeff
was not vicious today. He will not be vicious in Pike
Park on Saturday. He will be scared.

I cannot believe that Saturday's meeting will be all
that grim. I cannot believe that vengeance runs very
deep in the Sandhill Indians. I cannot believe that
Alexander Bigmeadow can hold his stern pose for more
than a day at a time. Of the 507 Indians who came to
town today, at least 500 seemed to be having fun.

Miles dropped these thoughts, typewritten, into the
plastic briefcase, closed it, and put it in the closet. He
then opened his old leather briefcase and fished out Jeff
Norquist's paper:

What I Wish

When my father was living we used to go down
to the river on picnics. One Sunday when I was ten
my father tied a long rope to the branch of a tree
that grew out over the water and we put on our
bathing suits and swung out on the rope and fell
into the water. It was great fun until I swung out
too far and fell into a dropoff we didn't know was
there. When my father, who couldn't swim, saw me
go under he panicked and ran out to save me. I
guess he forgot that I knew how to swim and that
he couldn't. He went in over his head and never
came up.

I wish I'd had a father for more than ten years.

My mother is probably doing the best she can, but we don't have anything to say to each other anymore. All she ever talks about is my sister Maureen. A mother isn't a father.

No wonder the briefcase was so heavy, thought Miles. He should have known better than to collect all 114 papers at one time. The wrongs and losses and near misses of 114 people, when packed together in one briefcase, took on the heaviness and solidity of rock. So it wasn't the poor penmanship after all that made reading these papers so difficult. Nor was it the futility of trying to teach English grammar. It was the way these papers teased him off the road of hope into the gulch of despair.

Miles stuffed Jeff's paper into the briefcase and snapped it shut. If Coach Gibbon were to read these papers, he thought, then Coach Gibbon would understand why a tie was as good as a win.

FRIDAY

November 6

I T W A S book report day.

The boys in first hour (about four years after the rest of the senior boys) had discovered John R. Tunis, and Lee Fremling was one of six who reported on *All-America,* though he was one of only two who had actually read the book. For seven weeks Miles had watched Lee reading the book in study hall, forming his heavy lips around each word. Today, after hearing the story from Lee, five other boys stood up in the front of the room and told the plot to the class, but a question or two from Miles revealed that four of them had never read it, and he gave them F's. None of the four contested the F. They all shrugged as if to say, "Well, anyhow I tried," and returned to their desks and yawned.

Love was big with second hour. Miles sat at Jeff Norquist's empty desk and listened to Roxie Booth, who had never read a book in her life, review *Love Story,* which had been last night's late show on TV. She concluded her review by saying, "It would be almost worth it to die young so you could see how hard your boyfriends would take it. Boys make me cry all the time. Just once I'd like to see *them* cry."

Miles asked her if she saw the movie on TV.

"No, I never did."

"You read the book?"

"Yeah, I read the book." She adjusted the ropes and chains and spangles that hung around her neck.

"Then why do you refer to one of the characters as Ali MacGraw?"

"Because that's who took the part in the book."

Miles gave her an F.

Miles expected weighty matters from third hour, but nothing so dull as William Mulholland's review of *The Computer Programmer's Handbook*. His stoical classmates gave all thirty minutes of it their grave attention. Miles covered his eyes and slept.

During his free hour, Miles was the guest of Thanatopsis Workman's home-ec class. Once or twice each year Thanatopsis liked to give her girls a guest to practice on. He sat at a square table with three sophomores and ate a grapefruit, a pile of underdone macaroni, and a tasty apple turnover. The girl on his left, a large blonde named Tina, was in charge of serving; and the girl on his right, a small blonde named Dee Ann, took credit for the cooking. The third girl, a skinny bundle of nerves named Virginia, had been assigned to keep the conversation alive, but as she took her place at the table something struck her funny and she spent the entire meal giggling behind her hand.

"What's so funny, Virginia?" asked Tina with a scowl.

"Stop laughing, Virginia, we have a guest," said Dee Ann.

"You've got an A going in this class, Virginia, now don't blow it on one of your silly spells."

"Virginia, you aren't touching a bit of your food."

"Mrs. Workman, can't you do something about Virginia?"

Virginia, behind her hand, turned purple and began to strangle on her laughter, and Tina, to save her life, carried her away to the nurse's office.

As Miles expected, fifth hour got off to a superb start with Nadine Oppegaard's review of *John Brown's Body*. Nadine was hooked on the Civil War, and she reviewed Benet's book without notes. She was eloquent, and she ran her fingers over her face as she spoke, exploring for pimples. She recited from memory the sad section about Stonewall Jackson's death, concluding with his dying words, " 'Let us cross over the river and rest under the shade of the trees.' " The class was a hushed audience. Miles gave her an A.

Nadine did not return to her desk, but remained at the lectern and said, "Stonewall Jackson died at thirty-nine, Mr. Pruitt. Are you thirty-nine yet?"

"No, why do you ask?"

"I'm trying to picture thirty-nine. Wouldn't it be nice to have your place in life and in history established by the time you were thirty-nine, like Stonewall Jackson?"

"Or like Alexander the Great," said Peter Gibbon, place kicker and reader of ancient history.

"Or like Mozart," said Nadine, violinist.

"Or like Keats," said Peter, who wrote sonnets in secret.

"Or like Toulouse-Lautrec," said Nadine, painter of cancer of the mouth.

"Or like Mr. Pruitt," said Beverly Bingham.

The discussion stalled. The class turned to look at Beverly, who was gazing at her teacher with such bald-faced admiration that Miles blushed. The class saw the blush. They looked back at Beverly and saw in her blue eyes that she loved him. Even those who had not heard the rumor began to wonder what this was all about.

Nadine said, "What I mean is that here was Stonewall Jackson in his thirties with the respect of all his troops and the respect of his commanding general, Robert E. Lee. How many of us will be able to claim that much respect for ourselves by the time we're thirty-nine?"

"Mr. Pruitt has the respect of his troops," said Peter Gibbon. "We're his troops."

Several students nodded and warmed Miles's heart.

"All right, if we're his troops, who is his Lee?" asked Nadine, who was enjoying her position at the lectern.

Somebody said, "Mr. Workman is his Lee," and the class groaned.

Somebody said, "Mr. Stevenson," and the superintendent must have wondered why at that moment the entire class turned to look at him across the courtyard.

Nadine said, "A man's Lee has to be the person he lives for and is ready to die for."

The class thought further, and so did Miles.

"Who are you close to, Mr. Pruitt?" asked a girl from the back row—someone afraid that this investigation into her teacher's private life would die on the vine. Nothing interested a class more than the details of a teacher's private life.

"Don't you have any family?" prompted Nadine. "I mean, we know you're not married, but don't you even have parents?"

"I have a father and a brother."

"Are they your Lees?"

"To be honest, the closeness we once felt doesn't really exist any longer. In the seventeen years since my brother moved to California, we haven't exchanged one letter, and in the five years since my father became senile we haven't exchanged one thought."

"Miss McGee is his Lee," said Beverly Bingham.

"How can that old maid be his Lee?" said Nadine. "They don't have a thing in common."

"They have a great respect for each other," said Beverly, "and that counts for a lot."

Again the class turned to study the message in Beverly's blue eyes.

Miles called on Peter Gibbon, who took Nadine's place at the lectern and reviewed *The Last Days of Pompeii.* He said that now the football season was over he intended to begin *The Decline and Fall of the Roman Empire,* which he claimed (with a grin) was written by his Uncle Edward. In college he would major in ancient history and his ambition was to become a professor at a Big Ten university. Miles wondered what had made Peter the scholar he was. The only reading materials in the Gibbon house were his father's coaching journals and Stella's magazines, featuring the same subjects month after month: diets, movie stars, and breast cancer. He gave Peter an A.

Beverly Bingham, dressed in the blouse Miss McGee had bleached and laundered, reviewed *Gone With the Wind.* She said it was a combination of love and disaster, and it made her weep and hope at the same time.

"I've heard that's a book only a female can love," said Peter Gibbon. "Is that true?"

Beverly said she didn't know. "Ask a man."

"Is it a book only a female can love, Mr. Pruitt?"

"I don't know. I haven't read it."

The class reacted with mock amazement.

Nadine Oppegaard asked Beverly what she thought of the ending.

"The ending is beautiful," said Beverly.

Nadine said, "I think *Gone With the Wind* has the stupidest ending I've ever read."

"Oh, no. It's inspiring. 'Tomorrow is another day,' says Scarlett. That's inspiring."

"I say it's melodramatic. Scarlett's plantation is a ruin and her daughter is dead and her husband has run away, and we're supposed to believe she's hopeful about her future? She must be out of her mind."

"No, she's doing the only thing a person *can* do when everything goes wrong. She's putting her faith in tomorrow and hoping that things will be better."

"It's melodramatic."

"No, it's not, damn it. It's very true to life. It's the only thing a person can do when everything goes wrong. You probably haven't had anything go wrong in your life, Nadine. Well, I have, and that's how I get through it. I say tomorrow's got to be better."

"And *that's* melodramatic—for you to say that. What's so much worse about your life than mine? I think we all have the same degree of troubles. I'm living with something I'd trade for just about any other kind of trouble I can think of, and so is Peter, and I still say the ending of *Gone With the Wind* is stupid." She was clearly referring with her customary frankness to her father's affair with Peter's mother.

"All right, listen, I'll tell you what's gone wrong in my life, because it's been on my mind ever since I was ten and if I don't tell somebody pretty soon I'll go crazy. My father was sent to prison for murder, did you know that?"

Beverly's voice was a desperate screech. Nadine lowered her eyes, wishing she had not probed.

"And did you know it was a murder he was innocent of? He had a trial in Berrington and he was convicted and sent to Stillwater, but he wasn't kept in Stillwater very long. He was taken out of prison and put in a hospital, and that's where he died about three years ago." She was no longer speaking to Nadine but to the whole class. Her copper blush was vanishing, leaving her face the color of ash.

"He was convicted of killing a salesman who sold kitchenware to brides. It happened on our front porch when I was ten, and I know exactly what happened because I was standing on the porch when it happened and so was my sister, who was seventeen at the time and getting ready to marry Harlan Prentiss, who wasn't a very good marriage prospect—even I knew that—but I admired my sister for finding a way to get off the miserable farm we lived on. The miserable farm I still live on. It was the middle of the summer and this salesman showed up at the farm not long after my sister's engagement notice appeared in the *Staggerford Weekly*. He asked for my sister and I went in the house and got her, and he gave her a card with his name on it and said he was selling cutlery and kettles. 'What will you do for pans when you are married?' he asked my sister. 'What will your new husband think if you have no pans or knives in the kitchen when you return from your honeymoon? Will you have the courage to say, "To-night I will cook the first meal of our married lives, but first be a dear and go to the hardware store and buy some pans and knives. Buy a frying pan, a double boiler, and two or three other pans of various sizes"? Will you have the courage to say that? "And get a bread knife while you're at it, a carving knife and a paring knife." Will you have the courage to say that? What will your new husband think if you don't bring knives and pans to your marriage?'

"I was on the porch and my mother and father were

standing in the front room listening through the screen
door, and my mother was getting very impatient. 'Get
out of here,' she said through the screen, but the salesman ignored her. 'Who do you think brings pans and
knives to a marriage if it isn't the bride?' he asked my
sister. 'The husband is not the one to plan what will be
in the kitchen. The bride, by tradition, takes care of
those things, and I have an idea that you are not aware
of that tradition. Let me show you the samples I've got
here in my bag.'

" 'Get out of here and this is my last warning,' my
mother said from the front room. I went and looked
through the screen door to tell her to shut up because I
wanted to see the samples he brought in his suitcase, and
when I looked through the screen into the front room I
saw she had the rat gun in her hand. Our rat gun is a
single-shot twenty-two that we shoot rats with around
the chicken coop. 'Get out of my way,' my mother
shouted at me. I looked back at the salesman to see if he
knew she had a gun, but he wasn't looking through the
screen. He was stooping down getting a sample pan out
of his suitcase. His last words were, 'This frying pan is a
sample of what I can give you.' He no more than said
those words and straightened up to hand my sister the
pan when my mother took aim through the screen and
shot him with the rat gun. My sister screamed and
jumped off the porch and ran off into the woods. I went
into the front room. It didn't occur to me to be afraid of
my mother. I was afraid of the salesman, who was lying
on the steps with his feet on the porch and his head on
the ground. I didn't believe he was dead because none
of us really believe our mothers are capable of killing
anybody, but he scared me all the same and I wanted to
get away from him and inside the house and be safe. But
he was dead all right. My mother handed the rat gun to

my dad and she went to the phone and called the sheriff in Berrington. We had a phone in those days. When the sheriff came she said my dad had done the shooting. I never told this to anybody before."

Beverly hung her head and put her hand in her hair and scratched her scalp. The class drew a deep breath. Miles rose from his chair at the back of the room and said, "Do you realize what you're saying, Beverly?" She ignored him and continued.

"The sheriff took my dad away. He didn't argue. He was never one to argue. My sister ran away with Harlan Prentiss that night. Neither my mother nor I went to the trial in Berrington because my mother said what was done was done and once a man was accused of murder there was nothing anybody could do to get him free. I don't suppose I had any concept of there being a trial. I was ten. I imagined they had taken him away to jail and that was that. Another thing my mother said was that if he was put in jail he would have the treatment he needed for his mental problem. To this day I don't know what his mental problem was, but I don't think it was craziness. I think he was simply retarded. He was next to useless around the farm but he was always agreeable, and I think my mother knew she could accuse him of the murder and he wouldn't know what was going on. She knew she could get away with it because he trusted her. I'm sure he never raised any objection at the trial and neither did anybody else. We were the only ones who knew the truth and we weren't there.

"I suppose, too, that once they got him in prison they realized what they had on their hands—a retarded man who wasn't responsible for his actions. And so they transferred him to a mental hospital and that's where he lived for five more years.

"I was fifteen when he died. They brought his body

up to the Sandhill Reservation for the funeral. He was
part Chippewa and he had lived on the reservation
before he was married. The funeral was in the Episcopal
Church out there. The church was never used except for
emergencies like funerals. The windows were all
boarded up and the pews and everything were covered
with dust. They didn't even have a regular preacher.
They had Alexander Bigmeadow. When the service was
over they put the coffin in the back of a pickup and
drove it along the little road leading to the cemetery,
which is quite a ways back in the woods. The pickup
drove slow and everybody walked behind it in the two
ruts of the road. Some of the graves out there are big
mounds where they used to bury people in a sitting
position, and some have little houses on top of them
where the dead person's spirit can live if it wants to.
Some of the spirit's favorite things are left in the houses
so they'll be handy, like shoes and tobacco. But the last
few years they've been burying people flat, and that's
the way they buried my dad. There wasn't any marker
put on the grave and I've lost track of where he is. The
first thing I did when I got my driver's license was go
out there to visit his grave, but the grave I thought was
his had a birch tree growing out of it. A big birch tree,
ten or twenty years old."

The bell rang, but nobody moved.

"So that gives you some idea why the ending of *Gone
With the Wind* didn't strike me as melodramatic. If
tomorrow isn't a better day than yesterday, then I'd be
better off to kill myself."

Beverly went to her desk and sat down. A few students stood up to leave.

This was not Miles's finest hour. He was confused.
"Wait a minute," he said, hurrying to the front of the
room. The students sat down. "We've just heard some-

thing serious and we'd better decide what we're going to do about it. Beverly, do you realize that in front of thirty people you have just accused your mother of murder?"

Her eyes shifted away from his. She nodded. She took a box of Marlboros out of her purse.

"What we've just heard is serious," he said again, then stammered, then said, "I don't think any of you should leave this room until you've pledged yourselves to secrecy."

Nadine Oppegaard said, "Don't be dumb, Mr. Pruitt. You can't expect thirty people to keep a secret like this."

Peter Gibbon said, "I'm going to be late for physics."

Nadine added, "Why should it be a secret? The sooner the matter is settled the better off certain people are going to be, especially Beverly."

He knew she was right, of course. "Okay, we'll leave it at this: If you can't keep this business to yourselves, at least keep calm, and keep your parents calm. Don't let your parents do anything rash about this. I'll do what has to be done."

When he dismissed the class, Beverly did not linger behind the others. Miles followed her through the crowded corridor and caught up with her near the front door. He put his hand on her arm. She pulled away.

"Now that you've told your secret, Beverly, I'm sure you feel better, but I must say you picked a hell of a place—"

"Please, Mr. Pruitt, I need a smoke." She pushed open the door and stepped outside.

He followed her to the bottom step, where the Giant had lied to Bennie Bird. He said, "Now what we'll have to do is call the police in on this. I'll explain it to the police and they can take it from there. You'll have to talk to them. Where will you be after school? Why don't you go to Miss McGee's and wait there?"

She avoided his eyes. She was trying to strike a match Her hands were shaking.

He took her matches and lit her cigarette. "You hear me, Beverly? Go to Agatha's after school."

She nodded. "You'll be late for sixth hour," she said.

"So will you."

"I'm not going to sixth hour. I need to think. And smoke." She crossed the street to her truck.

"Go to Agatha's and wait for me," he called.

He went to Wayne Workman's office, saw that it was empty, and sat down to use the phone. He called the Staggerford police office. Old John Kern was on duty. Miles told him about the Bonewoman. Old John Kern said it was a shame. Miles told him to go out and arrest her. Old John Kern said she lived outside the city limits and therefore outside his jurisdiction.

"Whose jurisdiction is it?"

"The sheriff's."

"Then I'll call the sheriff." He asked the operator to get him the sheriff in Berrington.

He let the phone ring a dozen times before he hung up and left the office.

When Miles was gone, Wayne came out of his closet.

Upstairs in study hall—in that murky chamber of dismal thoughts—it occurred to Miles that Beverly might have been lying. She might have made up the whole story in order to get rid of her mother once and for all. But no, she couldn't have made it up. But yes, it was a possibility. It might explain why she suddenly became shifty-eyed and ran from him after class. She was ashamed of her lie. Yet before he called on her to give her report she had been gazing at him fondly with her steady blue eyes. That was not the look of someone calculating a lie. No, her story had to be spontaneous and true. It was the story she had been trying to tell him all week. It was what she was trying to say, or trying to keep from saying, yesterday as he was changing the tire on her pickup.

Or was it a lie? What did he really know about the Bonewoman, aside from what Beverly told him? He had seen her dark shape in the alleys of Staggerford, and he had heard her voice when she asked for bones. But only once had he got a good look at her, and that was last Saturday in the gulch when she brushed past him and went splashing along the cold creek and crashing through the undergrowth. That day she definitely looked distracted. But that did not prove her a killer.

From study hall Miles went to the home-ec room and told Thanatopsis about the Binghams, mother and daughter.

Thanatopsis said that whether the story of the murder was true or not, both Beverly and her mother needed help. She put on her coat and drove Miles home in her yellow Mustang. Beverly was not there.

Miss McGee came in from St. Isidore's and they told her about the Bonewoman.

Miss McGee said, "You've got to find that girl and get her back here." She put on her apron and began making hot chocolate, shaving a bar of cocoa into a saucepan. "Why is everything so dreadful nowadays?" she asked of the clock above the stove. It was nearly four.

Miles and Thanatopsis went looking for Beverly. Thanatopsis drove. Miles went into the Hub, but she was not there. The cook said Beverly had not shown up for work. He bought a copy of the *Staggerford Weekly* and went out to the car. He told Thanatopsis to drive the streets, and as she did so he looked for the black pickup.

285

"She must have gone home," he said after they searched every street.

"Shall we go out and see?"

"Let's."

It was five o'clock as Thanatopsis sped out of town. It had been a dark day, and night was falling early. The only light in the sky was a brown glow sinking in the southwest—barely enough light for Miles to scan the *Weekly*.

Across the front page was the headline STAGGERFORD UPRISING. In a photo the governor's Giant stood with one hand on Bennie Bird's shoulder and the other hand pointing to the front door of the school. The picture was taken by Albert Fremling just as the Giant told the big lie about Jeff Norquist. "Confrontation Contained," was the caption.

On page two there appeared the only action photo that Albert Fremling, sprawled on the sidelines, had salvaged from the game against Owl Brook. It showed his son Lee being pushed backward into Peter Gibbon as Peter tried to kick the winning point.

On page three, where the Uprising article was continued, there appeared a photo taken in Wayne Workman's office. Between the Giant and Alexander Bigmeadow, who had their fat backs to the camera, Wayne was scowling with his mouth open and his hands stretched out in beggarly fashion. He was obviously saying something from his heart. The caption said, "Workman the Peacemaker."

Next to the Bingham mailbox stood a soldier. He wore his pants tucked into his boots, a drill jacket, and a long-billed cap. As Thanatopsis slowed down, the soldier brought his rifle up across his chest and kept her from turning into the driveway.

"What's happening?" said Miles, getting out of the car.

"This is off limits, move on." The soldier stood in the headlights and looked very young.

"What's happening? Tell me what's happening."

"It's classified, move on."

"I have to see somebody on this farm. Let me walk in."

"Nobody goes in. Those are my orders. Move on."

Miles got into the car. "Drive back as far as the cemetery," he said.

Thanatopsis made a U-turn on the highway, peeling rubber. "Is he a soldier or a boy scout?" she said.

"Turn in here," said Miles.

She drove up to the cemetery gate and stopped.

"I'm going back to the farm by way of the river path and see what's going on. You better go home. Wayne will be wondering where you are."

"I'll wait," she said.

Miles circled the cemetery and dropped down the bank to the river. The path along the river was not difficult to follow, for although the sky held nothing but darkness a lingering twilight glimmered in the shallow water. Boy and man he had walked the path, and he knew every turn and dip, every rock and root. Leaving the path and making his way along the creek in the gulch was the hard part. Here all was blackness and he made a great noise breaking through the brush.

But a greater noise was coming from the direction of the farm: the noise of shifting gears and slamming doors and shouts. He followed these sounds up from the creek. He stopped at the edge of the woods and saw, under the Bingham's yard light, an armed camp. Parked on the slope of the farmyard were four army trucks and six jeeps. Soldiers with rifles strapped over their shoulders were swarming from shed to garage to barn, looking for a place to bed down. It was obvious from their joking and complaining that they were enjoying themselves. The house was dark. It was a smaller house than Miles had imagined it to be—a story and a half with a door and a single window under the roof of the porch and one window (with no glass) above it. A soldier sat on the porch with a rifle across his knees.

Another, on patrol, passed within a few feet of where Miles was standing. Miles held his breath, and when the soldier was gone he returned to the creek and to the path and to the cemetery and to Thanatopsis waiting in the car.

"What did you find?" she asked.

"The National Guard."

They returned to Staggerford and saw, at the edge of town, several police cars parked in front of the Big Chief Motel. Miles asked Thanatopsis to stop, and he went to the office and asked the manager if a giant had checked into the motel. He had. He was in Room 8.

Miles knocked on Room 8.

The governor's Giant opened the door. "You're early," he said.

"Early for what?"

"I've called a meeting of the Staggerford delegation for seven o'clock. That's you and Workman and the Norquist kid. I want to brief you on tomorrow's plans. I called your house and your landlady said she'd tell you."

Miles said, "I'm not here about that. I'm here to find out why the National Guard is parked in the Bingham barnyard."

The Giant caught his breath. "Who told you?"

"Nobody. I was just out there."

"Come in."

Miles stepped into Room 8, which because it contained the Giant seemed very small. But for all his size, the Giant was less imposing than yesterday, perhaps because he wasn't wearing his hat, which yesterday had concealed his baldness, or perhaps because he had unstrapped his holster and laid it on the bed.

"This is confidential, Pruitt. That's your name, isn't it—Pruitt? No one's supposed to know, so keep it to yourself. The Guard is out there in case there's trouble tomorrow in Pike Park. The Bingham farm is perfect for bivouacking the Guard. They can't be seen from the highway, yet at a signal from me the Guard can be out of that gulch and into the Park inside of two minutes. That's logistics for you. On paper it works out to two minutes. If the Indians cause us any trouble they'll be looking at sixty men armed to the teeth inside of two minutes."

"How much trouble do you expect from three or four Indians?"

"Three or four! Who you trying to kid? If the American Indian Movement has got wind of this meeting tomorrow we're going to see a hell of a lot more than three or four Indians. We're liable to see Indians from all over America. We could have a real hot time of it, Pruitt, and you're going to be damn glad the Guard is on your side and not on theirs. Don't you know what happens when minorities get militant?"

Miles said he did. Then he explained about the Bonewoman.

The Giant scratched his head. "She's a killer, eh?"

"That's what her daughter claims. And I don't think the daughter should be out there overnight with her."

"Are you sure the daughter's out there?"

"No, but I can't find her anywhere else."

"Come with me." He led Miles outside into the red glow of motel neon and he opened the door of his patrol car. He recited a string of numbers into his two-way radio, and the numbers brought a reply from a guardsman.

Miles said, "Ask if there's a black GMC pickup out there in the yard."

The guardsman said there was no pickup. Mrs. Bingham was alone in the house and everything was A-okay.

"No black pickup and everything is A-okay," the Giant told Miles. He shut his car door.

"I'm afraid those soldiers will drive that woman crazy."

"Nothing to worry about. The men have been told they can bed down in the outbuildings, but the house is off limits. Nothing to worry about. I talked to Mrs. Bingham, you know."

"You did?"

"I was out there this afternoon before the Guard arrived. I cleared it with her. She seemed all right."

"What did she say?"

"Well." He scratched his head. "Come to think of it, she didn't say anything. She opened the front door and I told her I was going to station the National Guard on her farm overnight and she gave me a look that seemed to say, 'Suit yourself.' At least that's the way I took it. I don't know. It was kind of a strange look, now I think about it."

Two more patrol cars pulled up to the motel, and the Giant assigned the men to Room 12. Miles went back to the Mustang.

The Giant called, "Say, Pruitt. I was just thinking. You know, if that shooting took place eight years ago, it's a dead issue. Seven years is the longest you can wait before you prosecute anybody in Minnesota. Didn't you know that?"

Miles didn't know that.

Thanatopsis and Miles returned to Miss McGee's. Miss McGee told Miles he was expected at the Big Chief Motel at seven. She served him an omelet and fried potatoes and a pear on a lettuce leaf. She said she had called Bartholomew Druppers to see what could be done about the Bonewoman and he told her about the statute of limitations. Eight years had passed and the Bonewoman was beyond the law.

"What we'll have to do," said Thanatopsis, "is go about this business from a medical angle. We must get Dr. Maitland to recommend that she be committed to a hospital for examination. We'll do it as soon as this Indian business is over. We'll do it Monday." Thanatopsis and Miss McGee drank tea and watched Miles eat. Anxiety had spoiled their appetites. Miss McGee was keeping Beverly's hot chocolate warm on the stove.

"I'm sure Monday will be soon enough," said Thanatopsis. "It's been eight years since she shot the man, and the man who was wrongly punished for it is dead—so Monday will be soon enough."

"It's Beverly I worry about," said Miles. "What if the National Guard drives the Bonewoman loony and she loads up the rat gun and Beverly comes walking in on her?"

Thanatopsis said, "With the kind of life Beverly's had, she's probably good at taking care of herself."

True, Miles nodded, chewing.

"And once her mother's gone, she can move to town," said Thanatopsis. "We have scads of room in our house."

"It's all so dreadful," said Miss McGee.

* * *

Wayne Workman, looking for his wife and his Mustang, walked to Miss McGee's house. He would have phoned, but he was afraid Miss McGee would answer.

He found his Mustang parked at the curb and got into it and waited in the dark for Thanatopsis. When she came out of the house, Wayne gave her hell for taking the car without telling him and for not having supper ready on time. Then he asked her to go back into the house with a message for Miles.

"Go yourself."

"I can't. Miss McGee doesn't like me."

So Thanatopsis went back into the house and told Miles to bring Jeff Norquist with him to the meeting at the motel. Then she went home and fried Wayne a steak.

Miles phoned the Norquist house. Mrs. Norquist said Jeff wasn't home. She hadn't seen him all day. She had no idea where he went.

"Did he pack a bag?" asked Miles. "Did he leave town?"

"There's no telling. And if you want to know the truth, Mr. Pruitt, I'm relieved. I shouldn't say it, but I'm relieved."

"Could he be at a friend's house? Who are his friends?"

"And I shouldn't say this either, Mr. Pruitt, but I'll say it anyway." She took a deep breath. "I hope he's gone for a good long time. I tell you these last two years have been hell on wheels around here. The first few years after George drowned, I had difficulties, sure, but nothing this bad. Jeff was still under my control in those days. He came up through the grades and junior high as easy as pie. Of course Maureen was still at home then, and she had a nice way with him Maureen has a nice way with everybody, Mr. Pruitt, you know that, you had her in twelfth grade. But ever since Maureen got married and moved to New Jersey I tell you it's been hell on wheels around this house. I never know what's next. There was that stolen-car thing, and the broken windows at the school, and who knows what-all else I haven't heard about . . . Well, I've heard some things . . . I've only heard about them, mind you . . . Rumor, you know . . . I mean drugs . . . I don't know . . . And now that little Indian girl, that Annie Bird . . . It's so bad sometimes, you know what I do?"

She paused for Miles to ask what she did, but he said nothing. He didn't want to know what she did.

"Mr. Pruitt?"

"Yes?"

"It's so bad sometimes you know what I do?"

"No."

"I cry."

"I'm sorry, Mrs. Norquist."

"I cry alone."

"I'm sorry."

"It's as though the grief of George's drowning is just now coming to me eight years late . . . I feel so bad . . . A year or so ago I started crying at night, which was bad enough, but now I cry in the morning, too. I get out of bed and sit in the breakfast nook with the coffeepot and a package of cigarettes and I look out the window and cry."

"Have you considered a change of scene, Mrs. Norquist? Moving away and making a fresh start?"

"Have I considered it! Lord, it's all I've been thinking about for the past two years. New Jersey. Near Maureen. But I wanted Jeff to finish school here . . . and now it's anybody's guess whether he'll finish school here or anywhere."

"He can finish. His suspension is only for two weeks. But he's got to attend a meeting with me tonight, and then there's the meeting in Pike Park tomorrow at noon. If you have any idea where he might—"

"I tell you, Mr. Pruitt, I wish I was a drinker. I've never been one to drink, but I know a couple of women in this town who *are* drinkers. They sit home drunk every day and they're a lot happier than I am."

"No, they're not, Mrs. Norquist."

"How do you know?" She hung up.

When Miles left the house, Miss McGee sat in the front window praying the rosary for Beverly's safe return from wherever she had gone.

At the motel, Miles found the governor's Giant and eleven other troopers pressed together in Room 8, drinking whiskey from plastic water glasses.

"Come in," said the Giant. But there was no room.

"Jeff Norquist has disappeared," said Miles.

The eleven patrolmen looked at the Giant.

The Giant said, "Roadblocks."

The men set their glasses down on the Giant's Formica dresser top and filed majestically out the door to spend the night in their cars. The Giant held one man back. This man he sent to Berrington for a judge's warrant to search the Norquist house.

"That won't be necessary," said Miles. "Jeff isn't home. His mother wouldn't lie to me about that."

"You never know," said the Giant. "We've got to find that kid and have him with us in Pike Park tomorrow or this whole thing is liable to blow sky-high. Now, it's obvious to me the kid is hiding someplace right here in Staggerford. He has no car, and he wouldn't risk hitch-hiking because he might get picked up by an Indian. My men will keep the town surrounded all night, and then at first light in the morning they'll move in toward the center of town, searching every house if need be. We'll find the kid by noon, I promise you that."

After the eleven patrol cars had left the motel, Wayne Workman drove up in his Mustang and hurried into Room 8. The Giant served whiskey.

As Miles took his drink from the Giant, it finally dawned on him why the man was less imposing today. It was not because he had taken off his hat and his holster, it was because he had taken off his dark glasses. The Giant had small eyes and drooping eyelids. Without his shades, he looked melancholy.

"Where's Jeff?" asked Wayne.

"My men went to get him. Sit down. I want to go over tomorrow's plans."

Wayne turned to Miles. "You were supposed to bring Jeff," he said.

"Sit down," said the Giant. "Now, tomorrow at ten minutes before noon you two will leave Staggerford with Jeff Norquist and you will drive out to Pike Park, arriving at the stroke of twelve. You will drive your Mustang, Mr. Workman. You will park—"

"My Mustang? Why my Mustang? That's a new car There's not a scratch on it. What's the matter with Pruitt's Plymouth?"

"I have already told my men it will be the yellow Mustang. It will be easy to spot from the air and from the hills across the river. We're going to have two state troopers in a helicopter over the park and another trooper in the hills across the river. They're going to have you in their binoculars at all times, and if they see anything like the slightest little scuffle, or if they see the approach of a mob of Indians like we had in town here yesterday, they will signal the National Guard in the gulch The Guard will be ready to pounce Within two minutes of the signal you will have sixty men at your side, armed to the teeth."

"They'll be carrying guns?" said Wayne.

"They'll be armed to the teeth. Now I will be stationed at the entrance to the park. As you know, I have been restricted from taking part in the meeting, so technically I will not be in the park. But I will be on the shoulder of the highway and I, too, will have you under constant observation at all times. And I will have a number of troopers patrolling the highway, keeping away Chippewas and sightseers. There's always sightseers turning up at times like this."

"I don't think they should carry guns," said Wayne.

"Now, you arrive at the Park in the yellow Mustang at twelve noon, and you drive in and park in the open area next to the pump. You got that? You pull up right next to the pump, and you park so you're facing the river. I will try to allow only one carload of Indians into the park. That's all they're entitled to, one car. But if I'm shot and killed and more cars get in, don't panic. The Guard will be on the way. But if it's one car, and one car only, you go ahead and conduct your negotiations."

Wayne asked, "Did you talk to the governor about the Bird kid's tooth?"

"The governor says money is no object. Promise them we'll pick up the tab on all the kid's medical and dental bills. Promise them we'll tar the street that runs through Sandhill. Promise them sewers and water. Promise them a Community Center. Promise them anything they want, as long as money will buy it and as long as it will keep peace. But promise only one thing at a time. When you negotiate, you don't give everything away at once. You give up one thing at a time. And whatever you do, don't let them get their hands on Norquist. If they want

Norquist to get out of the car so they can give him hell, okay. But if they lay a hand on him, the Guard will come up out of the gulch."

"Where *is* Norquist?" said Wayne.

"Never mind. My men will have him ready to go by noon tomorrow. Now, here's another thing. When you negotiate, you must get out of your car and stand out in the open where you can be seen from all angles. Don't under any circumstances get into an Indian's car. Never, never get into an Indian's car. And don't let an Indian get into yours."

"What if it's raining?" said Wayne. "The forecast says rain."

"Raining, snowing, sleeting, hailing, never get into an Indian's car and never let an Indian into yours."

The meeting ended. Wayne hurried out of the room and sped home in his Mustang. The Giant put on his hat and holster and offered Miles a ride. He was on his way to the Norquist house, where he intended to wait at the curb until his search warrant arrived. Miles got into the patrol car. A short-barreled shotgun stood at his left shoulder. The two-way radio made unintelligible, scratchy noises. The Giant invited Miles to wait with him in the car and help him search the Norquist house, but Miles declined. He pointed the way and the Giant drove him home. As they turned down River Street, it began to rain.

"Man, you people sure live in the sticks up here," said the Giant. "When my radio sounds like that, you know you're really in the sticks."

"Goodnight," said Miles.

In the kitchen he found Thanatopsis buttering bread and Miss McGee slicing a large tube of bologna.

"We're making sandwiches and coffee for you to take to Pike Park tomorrow," said Miss McGee. "Differences are always settled quicker over coffee and sandwiches."

"Any word from Beverly?" asked Miles.

"No, but she'll turn up by morning. I prayed that she would."

"How many sandwiches shall we make?" said Thanatopsis.

Miles said, "I look for three or four Indians, but I don't expect the meeting will last long. I really don't think sandwiches will be necessary."

"Plus you and Wayne and the Norquist boy," said Miss McGee. "That's seven. That's fourteen sandwiches if we make two apiece. We'd better make twenty to be on the safe side." She was slapping slices of bologna onto the bread, snapping her wrist like a blackjack dealer.

"Twenty will be fine," said Miles.

"Isn't this crazy?" Thanatopsis laughed with delight.

SATURDAY

November 7

MILES AWOKE at first light. In his bath robe he went down to the kitchen and set the coffeepot to perking. He looked out the window at the damp, gray dawn. He went up to his room and brought down his briefcase and set it beside the wing chair. He pulled out a paper at random.

What I Wish

I wish I could please Coach Gibbon. I can never seem to do things right. At least not the way he wants me to do them. At football practice he hollers at me in front of all the guys. I wish there were more guys out for football so I wouldn't have to play so much. I wish my dad didn't want me to go out for football in the first place. We've got one game left. It's against Owl Brook. I'm going to do everything right. Just once I want to make Coach Gibbon happy. And my dad.

—Lee Fremling

There was a rumbling knock at the back door. Miles went out through the cold back porch and found one of the Giant's troopers standing on the step. He was making his way up the block, searching houses and garages. His face was gray and weary. His twenty-four-hour whiskers were white. A cold mist was falling on him. The wide brim of his hat was warped. He unfolded a sheet of moist paper which he said was a search warrant.

"But I'm one of the delegation," said Miles, meaning to save him the trouble.

"Pleased to meet you," he said, coming in. "Where's your basement door?"

After searching the basement he went through the upstairs bedrooms, peeking quickly into each closet. On the ground floor Miles told him he needn't check the room with the closed door. It was his landlady's bedroom and she was sleeping.

"I've got my orders," said the trooper. He opened the door.

Miss McGee sat up in bed and pulled the covers up to her chin. The man touched the visor of his hat, got down on his knees, looked under the bed, stood up, touched his visor again, and was gone.

"Am I dreaming?" said Miss McGee.

"No, Agatha. The police are looking for Jeff Norquist and they thought he was under your bed."

"The poor man, he looked hungry. I should have thought to offer him a sandwich."

The phone rang. It was the Giant. The search was proving fruitless, and he wanted Miles to talk once again to Mrs. Norquist. He was convinced that Mrs. Norquist knew where her son was hiding.

"I can't believe you're sending your men through houses at seven thirty in the morning," said Miles. "Do you realize how awkward it is having a stranger walk in on you at dawn? Staggerford will be up in arms."

"Nobody's up in arms. It happens so fast they don't know what hit them. Now, will you go see Mrs. Norquist, or won't you?" There was an edge in the Giant's voice that Miles hadn't heard before, the sharpness of fatigue.

"What would she tell me that she hasn't told you?"

"She hasn't told me anything. She won't speak to me."

"Did you search her house?"

"Yeah, I got in there about midnight. Ho, boy, you never saw such a mess. Her and the house both."

"You searched her house at midnight and you're wondering why she won't speak to you?"

"Who said I was wondering?"

"You'll never find Jeff Norquist. You know it's hopeless, don't you?"

"We'll find him. He's somewhere in town. Now, I wish you'd go over and talk to his mother and save us all this work of searching houses."

"All right, if I must. But not for an hour or so. Give the poor woman a chance to get out of bed."

"She's been up all night. I've been watching from the street."

Miles hung up and waited an hour anyhow. He drank coffee. He took his time shaving and dressing. It was nearly nine when he put on his rubber poncho and walked out into a slanting mist thick as fog and wetter than rain. He apologized to Mrs. Norquist for making a pest of himself.

She was wearing her bathrobe and looking a mess. She said that Jeff was probably gone for good. He had stolen all the money in her purse—over three hundred dollars—and she had no idea where he might be. But she knew where *she* would be, and pretty damn soon. She was going to pack up and sell the house and she never wanted to see Staggerford again. She was going to New Jersey and live near her daughter Maureen and her son-in-law, who was a truck driver and one of the nicest men you'd ever want to meet. He was of Italian descent. She would come back to Staggerford only one more time, and that would be on her way to the grave (she pointed in the direction of Evergreen Cemetery) because she owned a plot out there where George was buried and there was no use letting it go to waste. She didn't know what arrangements her daughter and son-in-law would have to make to get her body back to Staggerford, but she wasn't going to worry about it. That was the least of her worries, she said, and she closed the door.

Miles walked down Main Street to the Hub. He stepped inside, shaking the rain off his poncho, and there was Beverly. His heart lifted--it was like the surge of excitement he had felt when he was eighteen and wearing his new double-breasted suit and in love with Carla Carpenter.

Beverly was not in uniform.

"Coffee," he said. He sat on a stool.

Beverly was shaking. Coffee spilled into the saucer as she served it. She came around and sat next to him. "Christ," she said, and lit a Marlboro. "I spent last night in Sandhill. I stayed at my dad's cousins'. They live in a shack and I slept on the floor. My life is coming apart at the seams."

"Waitress," someone called from a table.

"I went home after school to change into my uniform and there was a guy with a gun standing in the driveway, and I never even stopped. I figured they were having some kind of a shoot-out in there with my mother because of what I said in class. I never even stopped to find out. I just kept going." She looked at Miles through the part in her hair. She drew deeply on her cigarette. "I never came to work at all last night."

"That man with the gun was a soldier, Beverly. The

National Guard spent the night on your farm because of today's meeting in Pike Park."

"I know that now. They told me in Sandhill."

"The Indians know?"

"Everybody knows. God, what do you suppose my mother is doing out there all this time? She'll be wild."

"Waitress, more coffee."

"Don't worry about your mother, Beverly. We're going to step in and take care of things for you. Mrs. Workman is going to talk to Dr. Maitland first thing Monday morning. If what you said in class is true—"

"What do you mean, if it's true!" She bumped the ash tray off the counter.

"Waitress."

The cook put her head out through the serving window and said, "Get busy, girl. There's people waiting to pay."

Beverly stepped on her cigarette and went to the cash register.

A man dressed all in red rose from a table and went behind the counter to fill his cup with coffee. He looked at Miles and said, "I guess you have to serve yourself in this place." He set his cup down and spread out his hands for Miles to see.

"Blood!" he said. His hands were caked with a mixture of dirt and dried blood. "Didn't you see my deer out there? It's in the back end of my truck. The season opened at eight o'clock, and I had her wounded and tracked down and shot dead and gutted out by eight thirty. A big doe. She'll go close to two hundred pounds. You ever seen a doe that big?"

"Here's your two orders of cakes, girl," called the cook. "Hurry up before they get cold."

"You can bet I ain't washing my hands all day today," said the deer hunter. "I live for this day every year."

305

Again he spread his hands before Miles. "There's nothing like it. I'll have myself this cup of coffee, then I'll go home and hang the doe in the barn and let her cool down and dry out, and tonight I'll come back to town and go on a toot. The town will be full of deer hunters and we'll have a rip-roarin' time. And tomorrow if it clears up and gets colder like it's supposed to, I'll take her out of the barn and hang her in a tree. There's nothing like a good cold wind to dry out your meat and age it nice. Then on Monday I'll have her butchered and wrapped and froze, and by Monday night we'll be eatin' fresh deer liver." He turned his hands over once more, back, front. Miles nodded, indicating he had seen enough. The hunter took his coffee back to his table.

"What's this about Dr. Maitland," asked Beverly, back at his side. "Is he going to have her put away?"

"The commitment process is going to begin on Monday. I don't know how long it will take. We'll start with Dr. Maitland at the clinic, then she'll have to be taken somewhere for examination—"

"By force?"

"By whatever means are necessary. When people are committed to a hospital, I guess the sheriff sometimes has to be called in to pick up the person. I mean if the person doesn't want to go and can't be talked into it, there's no choice but force."

"It will be force. And it will be Monday, you think?"

"I should think some time Monday. And you'll move out of the house between now and Monday."

"Where to? I'm not sleeping on any floor on any reservation again, I tell you that." She was facing away from Miles and speaking from behind her hair.

"The Workmans have a room for you. Thana—Mrs. Workman wants you to move in with them."

306

She turned quickly to see if he was serious. "The Workmans? Live with that grouch Mr. Workman?"

"What's your alternative, Beverly? Living in the gulch alone? The Workmans' landlord is gone for the winter and they have plenty of room. It's like Miss McGee's house—big and old and well kept. Mrs. Workman and you will become great friends. You'll like it fine."

"So we leave the chickens out there to die."

"Don't worry about the chickens."

To attract Beverly's attention, a woman at the table in the front window put her hand in the air and snapped her fingers several times.

"I'll be back this afternoon," said Miles. "We'll plan your move into town."

"All right, I'm off at three." Though she wasn't eager to live with the Workmans, she *was* eager to move to town.

"I'll be back before that. I should be back from Pike Park by one."

"*You're* going to Pike Park?"

"I'm one of the Staggerford delegation. There's three of us. Mr. Workman and Jeff Norquist and I."

"There's two of you. Jeff Norquist is gone."

"Where?"

"I'm not supposed to say."

"Who told you?"

"They told me about it in Sandhill."

The woman snapped her fingers five quick times. From the kitchen the cook looked out the serving window and said, "For the last time, girl, will you get up off that stool and go to work?"

"I'll be in this afternoon." Miles put a quarter by his cup and left.

Beverly handed the woman at the table a menu and watched Miles walk down the street. She wished she could move into Miss McGee's house. At least Miss McGee had a garden. And Mr. Pruitt.

In Room 8 of the Big Chief Motel, Wayne Workman was smoking, pacing, and chewing his mustache. The Giant was bent over the dresser studying a map of Berrington County.

"Jeff Norquist has stolen three hundred dollars from his mother and run away," Miles announced.

At this, the Giant put on his holster and hat and sunglasses and went out into the rain. Wayne followed him. Miles closed the door and watched them through the window. They got into the patrol car and the Giant spoke into his radio. The heavy rain was falling at a slant and splattering the patrol car and the Mustang and the pebbles of the parking lot. Miles took off his poncho, sat down, and picked up the only reading material in the room, the *Staggerford Weekly*. He looked again at the photograph of Lee Fremling backing into Peter Gibbon's kick. Lee was unidentifiable. His face was turned away from the camera and the number on his jersey was obliterated by a careful retouching of the photograph.

The caption said, "Owls Block Stag Kick."

Miles read the want ads. He read a pound-cake recipe. He read a column of astrological prophecies. For Pisces like himself this day, Saturday, was good for "disposing, once and for all, of disquieting perturbations."

At eleven thirty Wayne Workman came back into the room and the Giant drove away in the patrol car.

"You drive," said Wayne. His car keys jingled in his shaking hand.

308

"We don't leave for twenty minutes."

"We're going over to Stevenson's house."

"What for?"

"The superintendent should be with us."

"Are you serious?"

"We need more than just the two of us."

"We've got the National Guard. What could Stevenson do that an army can't? Except maybe die on our hands?"

"Damn it, Pruitt, it's his school. He's the one who should be taking this responsibility. Now let's get going." Wayne's voice trembled.

Miles drove the Mustang to Stevenson's house, wondering if Wayne was seeking the superintendent's help or the superintendent's death. He stopped at the front gate.

"Come to the door with me," said Wayne. "You're his fair-haired boy."

Crossing the lawn in the rain, Miles thought he glimpsed Stevenson's face in the living-room window, but Mrs. Stevenson opened the front door and said, "Ansel is in St. Paul for a meeting of the Minnesota Historical Society." She spoke in the sort of steady, heavy-jowled manner that turns the boldest lie into truth. "He's on the board of directors, you know. I'll tell him you both stopped by. He'll be sorry he missed you." The two men were running back to the car before she finished. "He'll be impressed with the way you two are handling the Indian question," she called after them.

"That's the kind of leadership we work under," said Wayne. "Doesn't it gall you?"

Miles started the car.

"Swing by Doc Oppegaard's."

"It's ten to twelve," said Miles.

"Doc Oppegaard is chairman of the school board. He should be with us."

Miles drove to Doc Oppegaard's office. In the waiting room Doc was drinking wine with Stella Gibbon. "How's your tooth?" he asked Miles, who had forgotten about his tooth.

Wayne said, "We'd like you to come with us to meet the Indians. Jeff Norquist has run away, and we'd feel better if there were three of us. The superintendent isn't available and I thought you might like to speak for the school."

"Oh, how exciting," said Stella.

"Why not?" said Doc. He put on his coat.

Wayne helped him into the back seat of the Mustang, then said, "I'd feel better if there were four of us."

"It's five to twelve," said Miles.

"One more man. Think of somebody." He clamped his lower teeth on his mustache as Miles pulled away from the curb.

"Bartholomew Druppers enjoys occasions like this," said Doc Oppegaard, a bit drunk. "I'm sure he could make a little speech, being mayor and all."

"Anybody will do," said Wayne.

Miles stopped at the mayor's house. Wayne went to the door and came back alone. "He won't come."

"He'll come," said Doc. He squeezed out of the back seat, went to the front door, and came back with the mayor.

Mayor Druppers was jumpy. As soon as he was fitted into the back seat with the dentist and the car moved off, he began fretting in a loud, rhetorical voice. The more he fretted, the more Wayne bit his mustache.

"I tell you we've got ourselves a nice little community here in Staggerford, and I'd hate to see it turned into a testing ground of hate and bloodshed. Is the American Indian Movement in on this yet?"

"Oh, God," said Wayne.

"No, they aren't in on it," said Miles.

"How do you know?"

"As far as I know, they aren't."

"Relax," said Doc Oppegaard.

"That's all we need is the American Indian Movement," said the mayor. He sat on the edge of the back seat and spoke directly in Wayne's ear. Like any good speechmaker, he had sized up his audience and he knew which man was most moved by his words. "I tell you we've all seen towns in this nation of ours turned into testing grounds of hate and bloodshed. It all started years ago in Selma, Alabama. One thing I'll say in favor of this meeting, it's three miles from town and that shows good forethought, because that way at least our homes are safe."

"I hope to God," said Wayne.

"Relax," said Doc.

"Now what I say is this. When we get to Pike Park, we get out of the car and speak our piece and get right back into the car and drive back to town as soon as possible and hope it all blows over."

Wayne nodded.

"How many Chippewas do we expect?"

Wayne shook his head.

They drove a mile in silence.

Suddenly Mayor Druppers clutched Wayne's shoulder and shouted, "Where's Norquist?" looking about him as though Jeff might have been riding, unnoticed, in their midst.

Wayne shook his head. He didn't want to say the words, *he ran away.* "Tell him, Miles."

"He ran away," said Miles.

The mayor sank back, speechless.

Wayne gave Miles a bitter look. "How can you be so calm?"

"Why shouldn't I be calm?"

"Why? Because your life is at stake!"

Although Miles didn't believe it, it was a disquieting thing to hear. A disquieting perturbation.

They passed the Bingham driveway and saw a soldier standing guard beside the mailbox, a forlorn figure pelted by the rain.

Pike Park. At the entrance, the governor's Giant stood on the shoulder of the highway. He waved the Mustang into the park, and Miles, according to instructions, parked next to the pump. No other car was there. As soon as he switched off the engine, the windows steamed up.

The four men were silent for a long time. In the back seat, Doc Oppegaard drew hearts on the window with his finger. The mayor's breathing was a tense whistle through the nose. Wayne frowned. Over and over again, Miles rubbed the steam from his side window and peered out toward the highway where the Giant's patrol car was parked. Cars of sightseers passed slowly on the highway. One of them stopped.

"Here they come!" said Wayne, leaning over and looking out past Miles's ear.

"That's *my* car," said Doc Oppegaard. "And that's Nadine driving. Relax."

The Giant sent the car on its way.

"Maybe they won't show up," said Wayne.

"They'll show up," said Doc. "Indians are always late for appointments." He continued to draw hearts on the window.

312

"I don't like sitting out here without Norquist," said the mayor. "It could get mighty unpleasant."

"An Indian will listen to reason," said Doc.

"We'll promise them anything money can buy," said Wayne. "The governor says the sky's the limit."

"But only one thing at a time," Miles reminded him.

Across the river a shot was fired. "It's an attack!" said Wayne. The mayor ducked his head.

"A deer hunter," said Doc.

While they weren't looking, a car drove into the park and pulled up in front of them, bumper to bumper. They saw its dark shape through the steam on the windshield.

"Here they are!" shouted Wayne. "Don't let them into this car. Don't get into their car. Stand clear of both cars so the trooper in the hills can see us at all times."

"What trooper in the hills?" said the mayor.

"Don't let them lay a hand on you! Promise them anything!"

"Let's see who it is," said Doc.

With his sleeve, Wayne wiped the steam from his half of the windshield, but he couldn't see through the rain flowing across the glass.

"You know who it will be," said Miles, wiping his half. "It's bound to be Bigmeadow and Bird." He turned on the windshield wipers and bent forward over the steering wheel to see his adversary, and he looked into the face of Miss McGee. The car was his own, and Thanatopsis was at the wheel. Sandwiches.

Wayne and Miles got out and stood at the windows of the Plymouth, Wayne on his wife's side and Miles on Miss McGee's.

"You forgot to bring the lunch," said Miss McGee.

Wayne told his wife to get the hell out of the park.

313

He said she was throwing a monkey wrench into the governor's plan. He said any minute all hell was going to break loose. He spoke of an ambush. Meanwhile, Miss McGee was handing Miles, through her window, a pair of shoeboxes containing two dozen sandwiches. "The coffee is in the back seat," she said. "It's a shame you couldn't have had a nicer day for your meeting. Rain is so discouraging."

"Beverly is at the Hub," said Miles.

"Yes, we stopped there. We told her we were coming in this afternoon when she gets off work. To plan her future."

"That big cop out there tried to stop us," laughed Thanatopsis, leaning over to talk out Miss McGee's window. The one on her side had been rolled up against Wayne's admonitions. "But we plowed right past him."

Miles carried the sandwiches and four Thermos bottles to the Mustang and handed them to Doc Oppegaard in the back seat. He went back to his Plymouth and said, "Thanks for coming out. I'm sure we'll be back in town in a little while. I don't look for the Indians to show up."

"Take a hot bath before you come to the Hub," said Miss McGee. "It's a day for catching cold."

In the Mustang the four men unwrapped a sandwich apiece and poured themselves coffee.

"What did you get?" asked Doc.

"Bologna," said the mayor.

"Bologna," said Wayne.

"They're all bologna," said Miles.

They ate in silence. The sound of rain on the roof of the car gradually diminished. They heard two rifle shots in the distance. They heard a helicopter pass overhead. It was nearly one o'clock.

Miles took two sandwiches and a bottle of coffee out to the highway and gave them to the Giant. "How much longer shall we wait?" he asked.

"Till two thirty," said the Giant. "We're calling it off at two thirty."

"Has anybody gone out to Sandhill to see what's holding them up?"

"No, nobody's gone out there. Let sleeping dogs lie."

Returning to the car, Miles caught Wayne tattling on Superintendent Stevenson.

". . . And I know for a fact that there's no meeting of the Historical Society today. Nobody has meetings on Saturday."

Doc Oppegaard was not giving him a sympathetic ear. "Bologna always gives me gas," he said, beating his breast.

"Are you saying Ansel Stevenson is not a truthful man?" asked Mayor Druppers. "Because, my goodness, if you're saying Ansel Stevenson is not a truthful man, that's a strong statement. Ansel Stevenson has been a public servant in our community for a good many years. I was on the board when he was hired and I've been on the board ever since, and I know he sometimes doesn't take the bull by the horns the way he should, but to say he is not a truthful man is saying quite a lot. I would want to be very sure of my facts before I said *that.*" He sat back and folded his arms.

"Then let me ask you this," said Wayne. "When is the last time you heard of a meeting on Saturday?"

"I'm at one right now," said Doc, pressing his chin to his chest and working up a burp.

Miles fell asleep.

At two thirty the rain stopped altogether. The Giant radioed his trooper in the hills and his troopers in the helicopter and he radioed the army in the gulch. Across the river Miles could see the trooper in the hills leave his station and drive down through the pines. The Giant made a U-turn on the highway and returned to Staggerford, followed by several cars of disappointed sightseers. The military convoy of six jeeps and four trucks passed the park in the opposite direction, crossing the bridge, then turning north toward Berrington. They disappeared between the hills on the other side of the river.

Miles started the Mustang. Doc Oppegaard told him to wait. He had to piss. Once he mentioned it, they all felt the urge, and Miles switched off the engine.

"Who's that?" said the mayor as they were getting out of the car. He was pointing across the highway where an old white Buick was emerging from the woods and bouncing along a trail, heading in their direction.

Miles said it was Alexander Bigmeadow's car.

"God, don't tell me!" said Wayne.

"Judas Frost," said the mayor, and he got back into the car.

The Buick climbed the grade to the highway, crossed it, drove into the park, and pulled up next to the Mustang. The Buick contained three men and a boy. Alexander Bigmeadow was at the wheel, and with him in the front seat was Bennie Bird. To Miles's great relief, the carnival-hatted Indian who had found so much to laugh at on Wednesday was in the back seat. He was already grinning and raising his eyebrows expectantly, as though all that remained of the Pike Park meeting was the punch line. Sticking out of his lime-green hat today was the bent tailfeather of a grouse. Also in the back seat was little Hank Bird. He had scabs on his face and his finger was still in a splint. In his good hand he clutched an empty Pepsi bottle. He jumped out of the Buick and went to the pump to fill the bottle with water.

"How would you like a brand new motorcycle?" Wayne asked him.

Little Hank stopped pumping. This man who last week had made him stand for forty minutes on two sheets of paper was now offering him a motorcycle. Hank broke into a great gap-toothed smile.

Alexander Bigmeadow moved his great bulk out from behind the wheel and carried two six-packs of beer over to a wet picnic table under a wet pine tree. The green-hatted Indian and Bennie Bird followed him.

"Help yourself," Bigmeadow said to Doc Oppegaard.

Doc thanked him but said he never drank beer.

Green-hat chuckled.

"Beer gives me asthma," Doc explained.

Green-hat let out a deep, joyous roar.

"How about you two?" said Bigmeadow. Miles and Wayne took the beers he offered them.

"Who's that in your car there?" asked Bennie Bird. It was a civil question asked in a civil tone. Bennie appeared not to be angry today.

Doc said, "That's Bartholomew Druppers."

"Druppers the mayor?"

"Yes."

"Maybe he'd like a beer."

Wayne and Miles glanced at each other. Was this the same Bennie Bird they had met on Thursday?

Doc beckoned to the mayor, but the mayor didn't budge, except to lower himself a bit deeper into the back seat.

"How come you brought along the cops and the army?" asked Bigmeadow, looking pained at having to ask.

"We didn't," said Miles. "You might say they brought us."

"We've been sitting over there in the woods since ten thirty, waiting for the cops and the army to go home. Just drinking beer and waiting. Except Hank, he was drinking Pepsi. I'll be damned if I'll drive into a park that's surrounded by the cops and the army."

Bennie Bird nodded. So did Wayne.

Miles decided it was time they heard the bad news. "Jeff Norquist ran away," he said.

The Indians did not look surprised. Bennie nodded.

Wayne said, "How would you folks like a tar road through Sandhill?" His voice was tight and high.

"How come the mayor stays in the car?" asked Bigmeadow.

Doc Oppegaard went over to the Mustang and brought back the mayor, as well as the sandwiches and the coffee.

"Nice to see you," Mayor Druppers said to the Indians. "I'm glad to be here. Not the best of weather, but it's always fair weather when good men get together. Right? You bet." As the mayor gingerly shook hands with Bigmeadow and Bird and Green-hat, a chilly breeze sprang up and the pine tree they stood under sprinkled everyone with water.

"Have a beer," said Bigmeadow.

"Don't mind if I do. Yes, sir. You bet." The mayor was bobbing up and down nervously like a boxer and causing Green-hat to chuckle.

The Indians were hungry. Bigmeadow and Bennie Bird and Green-hat ate two sandwiches apiece. Little Hank ate three. The Indians switched to coffee. Wayne and Miles had another beer. When little Hank reached for a fourth sandwich, all seven men, like uncles, tried to top each other's funny remarks about his appetite—

until Bennie Bird said, "He must have a hollow leg," and all the others laughed and gave up. Who could be funnier than that?

To make sure they understood, Miles said once more, "Jeff Norquist ran away."

Wayne interrupted, "I've been thinking, this park ought to be called Onji Park. I mean why should we call it Pike Park when Zebulon Pike was only here for part of one day in 1806, and all this land was Chief Onji's land long before the white man showed up. If you want me to, I'll see about having the name changed. I'll call the governor."

"We've searched every house in Staggerford," said Miles. "We don't know where he went."

Wayne said, "How would you folks like a brand new Community Center in Sandhill?"

"So the Norquist kid is gone," said Bigmeadow. "That doesn't surprise us, does it, Bennie?"

Bennie Bird said no, it didn't surprise him. Green-hat was greatly amused.

"Annie Bird took off night before last with Bennie's car," said Bigmeadow. "She hasn't been seen since. We figure she and Norquist ran away together."

Green-hat exploded with laughter. This was the punch line he had been waiting for, and the joke was on all of them, red man and white.

"Are you serious about the motorcycle?" asked Bennie.

"Yes, yes," said Wayne.

"If you're serious about that motorcycle, and if you fix Hank's tooth, we'll call it square," said Bennie. He put his hand on little Hank's shoulder and his weathered face broke into a slight but satisfied smile.

Little Hank's smile was wide and full of bread.

Thus, their business ended, all that remained for

319

them to do was to follow Doc Oppegaard down the path to the riverbank, where they stood in a row under the dripping willows—all eight of them, red man and white —and the Badbattle carried their piss away to Fargo, to Winnipeg, to Hudson Bay.

At two o'clock Miss McGee and Thanatopsis arrived at the Hub and sat at the table in the front window. When Beverly served their coffee, they asked her to sit down. She joined them with a bowl of stew. The last of the lunch-hour crowd, enlarged today by deer hunters, was thinning out and it was time for her to eat. She ate with her right hand and smoked with her left and said, with her mouth full, that when she was ten her mother shot a kettle salesman. In case these two women were undecided, she must convince them how badly she needed a new home—any home, even the Workmans'.

"We've heard the story," said Miss McGee.

"We're here to plan your future," said Thanatopsis.

"My sister was engaged to Harlan Prentiss and it wasn't long after her engagement was announced in the paper that this kettle salesman turned up at the farm. He had pots and pans and knives."

"You needn't tell us," said Miss McGee, cleaning the silver with her paper napkin. "Mr. Pruitt told us all about it."

But she was determined not to spend one more night in the gulch. She told the entire story as she had told it yesterday in school: the salesman's spiel, the bride's duty to provide kitchenware, her mother's threats from the front room, the sample frying pan in the salesman's suitcase, the shot, her sister screaming and jumping off the porch, the body tipping backward down the porch steps, the sheriff—it was easier to tell today, the second time.

330

"You'll come to live in town," said Miss McGee.

"You'll come to live with Mr. Workman and me said Thanatopsis. "Would you like that?"

Beverly nodded, wiping up the last of her stew with a biscuit.

It was nearly three when the Giant and his patrolmen crowded, famished, into the Hub and announced that the dreaded clash of races had been averted. The Indians had failed to show up in Pike Park.

"Miles will be here soon," Miss McGee told Beverly. "He's taking a hot bath."

"Let's not wait for him," said Beverly. "Let's go right out to my place and get my things."

"You mean now, today?" said Thanatopsis. "What about your mother?"

"I'll make up some story. She'll be all right. The National Guard is gone and she'll be settled down."

"Well, if you think . . ."

Beverly ran to the kitchen for her tattered, buttonless jacket. The wave she had set in motion yesterday in English class was rolling high and fast. She was riding the crest.

"I'll wait here for Miles," Miss McGee told Thanatopsis. She went to the kitchen to chat with the cook, a sixth grader of 1940.

On the highway returning from Pike Park, Miles saw his Plymouth coming toward him. He saw it turn into the Bingham driveway. He turned in after it.

"What the hell are you doing?" said Wayne.

"What's the idea?" said Bartholomew Druppers.

"That's my Plymouth," said Miles, "and that's your wife driving it."

The driveway into the gulch was deeply rutted by rain and trucks and jeeps. The farmyard was a sea of mud and dead chickens. It was surrounded by rusting cars and unpainted sheds leaning downhill. The Plymouth was empty, facing the front porch. Miles parked beside it.

"What a God-forsaken dump," said Doc Oppegaard.

"In town we have laws against places like this," said the mayor.

Wayne said, "I don't know what we're doing here, Pruitt, but whatever it is, get it over with fast and get us back to town."

Miles said, "I don't understand what Thanatopsis is doing here in my car."

"Damn it, Pruitt, will you stop calling my wife that crazy name?"

Miles opened his door and got out of the car. The Bonewoman, insane with fear, and resting her rat gun on the sill of the upstairs window, took aim and fired a .22 bullet that entered his skull an inch above the left eye. She had vowed to herself as she watched the singing, chicken-killing soldiers drive away in their jeeps and trucks that she would murder the next man who set foot in her yard. Into the mud beside the yellow Mustang, Miles fell backward, dying.

"Holy Christ," shouted Wayne. He saw the Bonewoman with the rifle in the upstairs window. He saw his wife and Beverly, at the sound of the shot, come out onto the front porch. "Holy Christ!" He clambered over the gear box between the bucket seats and backed the car away from the house, skidding in a circle. He shifted into low and spun his tires up the sloping yard and up the driveway and was back on the highway before the two men in the back seat knew what happened. From where they sat, neither Doc nor the mayor had seen the upstairs window. They had assumed the shot they heard was a deer hunter's. "What is it? What happened?" they said, but Wayne didn't hear them. He tore into Stagger-ford and skidded to a stop at the Big Chief Motel where he expected to find the Giant.

The manager said the Giant was lunching at the Hub.

Wayne picked up the manager's phone, dialed the operator, and told her to get the governor on the line. It took her a minute to learn that the governor was beyond reach today. He told her to call the sheriff in Berring-ton. It took her another minute to learn that the sheriff was not in Berrington. He was in Staggerford. Wayne told her to call the Hub. She put him through to the Hub. He asked for the Giant. He told the Giant that Pruitt had been shot in the Bonewoman's barnyard. He hung up. He went back to the car and dropped off the bewildered dentist and mayor at their houses. He went home and took a pill. Two pills. Three. He phoned Superintendent Stevenson and told him what he hoped would be heart-stopping news. He put on his pajamas and got into bed and pulled the covers up to his eyes.

Beverly leaped off the porch and ran to Miles and dropped to her knees beside him in the mud. She thought there was movement in his face. She put her arms behind his head and shoulders and struggled to draw him up to a sitting position. But there was no life in him. She dropped him back into the mud. Then she stood up and gripped her hair with both hands and made a noise she herself had never heard before, a faint, high warble from the bottom of her soul, from some-where further back than her birth—the anthem of the crushed spirit, the keen of the widow.

Thanatopsis on the porch turned away. She put her forehead against a porch pillar for a moment, then she went into the house to find the Bonewoman. What she would have done had she found her she didn't know. She might have tried to reason with her. She might have tried to kill her. But the door leading upstairs was locked.

Over the gulch a sudden wind from the north blew a flock of snow geese off course, and they called out as they passed blindly through swift, ragged clouds.

Beverly, still clinging to her hair, ran into the woods behind the henhouse. Thanatopsis came outside and ran after her.

There were hiding in the woods several chickens that had not made a peep since the arrival of the National Guard—six or eight leghorns that grew curious now about the man lying in the mud, and as they approached the body they made soft, throaty sounds like the purring of cats.

Word went out from the Hub. The Giant, assuming the Indians were responsible, called the National Guard and ordered the six jeeps and four trucks to turn around. The waitress who had just come on duty called Nadine Oppegaard, then put her head through the serving window and told the cook and Miss McGee.

The National Guard, nearing Berrington, turned around and headed back to the farm. Nadine Oppegaard got into her father's Lincoln, picked up Peter Gibbon, Roxie Booth, and Lee Fremling, and drove out to the gulch.

Miss McGee called Father Finn and told him that he must go to the farm and give Miles the Last Sacraments.

"He's a Catholic?" said Father Finn, whose time in Staggerford did not go back very far.

"Of course he's a Catholic. He was born and raised a Catholic, and he was at mass last Sunday. Pick me up at the Hub Cafe. Hurry, Father."

Father Finn was slow. Miss McGee sat waiting for

him in the front window. Interlaced between the fingers of her right hand was the crystal rosary given to her by the class of 1951. She clenched her fist so tightly as she waited that she snapped the rosary into several pieces.

It was twilight when Father Finn and Miss McGee arrived at the gulch and found themselves last in a line of vehicles stretching down the Bingham driveway. Miss McGee couldn't seem to get enough oxygen. She was breathing in gulps. She got out of the car and told the priest to follow her. They walked along through the mud of the sloping driveway, passing the Oppegaard car, the sheriff's car, Dr. Maitland's car, eleven highway patrol cars, four army trucks and six jeeps. All the vehicles were empty. The troopers and the army and everyone else were hiding in the woods, puzzling how they might capture the Bonewoman.

As Miss McGee and Father Finn walked out into the wide clearing that was the yard, a voice from behind a tree said, "Psst."

They stopped.

The voice said, "Don't go no farther." An arm pointed from behind the tree toward the house. "The Bonewoman's up there in the front window with a gun."

Father Finn joined the voice behind the tree. The watery mud made sucking noises as Miss McGee walked forward into the yard. When she reached Miles's body, she knelt in the mud. The hole above his left eye was tiny. It might have been a mole. With her thumb she made the sign of the cross on his lips.

She stood and lifted her face to the upstairs window and said in a strong voice that echoed through the woods, "Corinne Kaiser, you remember me. I am Miss McGee. In 1935 you were in my classroom for two weeks when the public school didn't know what to do with you. When you left my classroom, you left school for good, do you remember, Corinne? Now I have come out here to see you. I wish to talk to you. I am coming into your house, Corinne, and I want you to come downstairs and meet me in the front room. When you were in my classroom, you always did what I asked, and you must do so now. You must come downstairs this minute and meet me in the front room."

The Bonewoman drew back from the window.

"I am coming into your house, Corinne. I am going to meet you in the front room."

Gulping for air, Miss McGee stepped up onto the porch and went into the house. It was very dark in the front room. She groped along a wall. She stumbled over a stool and she knocked over a lamp. Standing still, she heard the creak of the stairs. She heard a door open. She could not see the door but she turned in the direction of the squeaking hinges. She put her hand out in front of her and felt a tube of steel. The Bonewoman was hand-ing her the rat gun.

"My daughter did it," the Bonewoman said in a thin, dull voice.

Miss McGee stood the gun against the wall and took the Bonewoman by the hand and led her out onto the porch. The yard light, which came on automatically at dusk, was flickering to life.

The Berrington County sheriff, followed by the Giant and ten patrolmen and several dozen soldiers, rushed up and took the Bonewoman into custody. "My daughter did it," she repeated. Somewhere geese called.

Doctor Maitland came forward and knelt over the body with his stethoscope, then Father Finn with his kit of holy oils.

Headlights came on. A procession of jeeps, trucks, and

cars came down the driveway and turned in the yard, making a circle around the body and the priest and the Plymouth, then climbed with a grinding of gears up the driveway and out of the gulch.

Thanatopsis and Beverly emerged from the woods. Beverly was scarcely recognizable. Grief seemed to have altered the very bones of her face. When she saw Miss McGee she threw her arms around the old woman's neck, bearing her nearly to the ground, and Thanatopsis had to pry her loose. Thanatopsis and Miss McGee helped her into the Plymouth, then got in themselves.

"Take her to my house," said Miss McGee.

"But, Agatha, I have her room ready. You can't possibly—"

"She *must* come home with me, Anna Thea! . . . She must live in *my* house . . ." Her breath was catching in her throat. "As much for my sake . . . As much for my sake as hers."

Lillian Kite, Imogene, and Thanatopsis sat with Miss McGee through the evening. Several of her former students stopped in to tell her to be strong. "Be strong," they said as they took her hand. They knew that "Be strong" was a helpful thing to hear, having heard it themselves when they were in the sixth grade and in any of a hundred sorts of difficulty. Tonight when they took her hand in their own, however, they found it quite limp, for Dr. Maitland had talked her into swallowing a large, befuddling capsule, like the one he gave Beverly.

Father Finn came in and sat in the wing chair. Whenever he spoke of eternal verities, he had the habit of raising his eyebrows and squinting at the same time, as though he were trying to peer through smoke. He said that God allowed his children to be visited by affliction so that he could see what they were made of.

Miss McGee said, "God knows what I'm made of. He made me."

"He knows our potential, Agatha, but we must prove ourselves. Today you have been given more sorrow than other people because you are stronger than other people —you are capable of more growth. In not giving in to despair, you are growing in God's love."

"I am growing like the fern of goodness and sin." She was giddy on Dr. Maitland's capsule.

"I beg your pardon?"

"I *am* the fern of goodness and sin."

Father Finn lit a cigar and changed the subject. He had never found this woman easy to understand. Of Miles he said, "I didn't know him well. But I know he was a good man and he meant a lot to everybody."

"No one means a lot to everybody, Father. To whom, I ask you—besides to Beverly and myself—did Miles mean a lot? A deep, abiding lot?" She stood. Staggering slightly, she went to the china closet for the cut-glass ash tray.

Thanatopsis offered to stay overnight, but Miss Mc-Gee said no, she and Beverly would be all right. When everyone was gone Miss McGee went upstairs to Beverly's room. As she pushed open the door, light from the hallway fell across the bed. Beverly was shivering in her sleep. The northwest wind—the winter wind—shook the window and howled under the eaves. Miss McGee went to the closet for another blanket, and as she spread it over the bed Beverly stirred, grimacing and raising a finger, responding to something in a dream.

EPILOGUE

WHEN DALE PRUITT in Los Angeles was notified of his brother's death, he phoned the apartment where Carla and his two daughters lived. He and Carla had been divorced for three years.

Carla, hearing that Miles was dead, broke into a wail that brought her younger daughter, Charlene, running from the other room. (The older daughter, Trish, was out of town on a high school choir trip.)

"I'm flying to Staggerford tomorrow," said Dale. "The funeral is Monday. Do you want to go with me? He was once your sweetheart, don't forget."

'No," said Carla. "I'm never going back to Staggerford as long as I live." She hung up.

"What's the matter?" asked Charlene, drawing back slightly from the terrible face her mother was making. Charlene was twelve and greatly disappointed in the kind of woman she was discovering her heavy, nervous mother to be; but she was always careful to be civil to her, careful never to arouse her mother's unpredictable temper.

"What's the matter?" Charlene asked again.

Carla drew her daughter to her breast. She said, "Your Uncle Miles is dead," and she buried her wet face in her daugher's hair.

"Who's Uncle Miles?" said Charlene.

Carla's father, the bald barber, had never seen his granddaughters. He had never been invited to California, and Trish and Charlene had never been to Minnesota. Occasionally at Christmas Carla would send him a snapshot, but the fact that he had never seen them face to face was the great sorrow of his old age.

Although Mr. Carpenter was seventy and hard of hearing, he still barbered part time in his shop next to the Morgan Hotel and was sometimes called upon by the undertaker to shave dead men. In the funeral home on Sunday, as he shaved Miles and trimmed his hair, Mr. Carpenter murmured, "If Carla had married you, Miles, instead of your brother, my grandchildren would be growing up in Staggerford. From the time they were babies I would have been cutting their hair."

On Sunday evening when Miles was put on display at the Carlson-Case Funeral Home, Wayne and Thanatopsis Workman were among the first to see him. They stood at his coffin as Muzak broadcast "Around the World in Eighty Days" from a beehive speaker in a corner of the ceiling. Thanatopsis noticed that Miles's double chin was not so prominent when he lay on his back. Gravity seemed to draw it down under his ears, where it rested on the satin pillow. She shook her head. She left Wayne and walked home alone through a fine, driving snow that stung like pins.

On Monday morning school was dismissed for the funeral. It was still snowing. The senior class attended as a group, but most of the underclassmen, unacquainted with Miles, sat in their cars and smoked, or went to the pool hall and drank pop, or walked through the stores lifting merchandise. It was too cold to stand around outside.

The pallbearers were Wayne Workman, Coach Gibbon, Mayor Druppers, Historian Smith, Biologist Jennings, and Doc Oppegaard. Smith was old and Oppegaard was small, so it was hard work for the other four. As they passed into St Isidore's under the huge rose window, Coach said to Wayne, "Did I ever tell you I never understood this guy? Did I tell you he thought a tie was as good as a win?"

Sitting through the funeral mass without her knitting needles—without the purple afghan she was within forty rows of completing—made Lillian Kite feel edgy and useless. Only by knitting and purling and casting off stitches could she keep her hands and her mind properly occupied. In church her mind raced. She recalled how handsome Miles had looked in her husband's ranger uniform (though not so handsome as her husband had looked) and how it was a blessing after all that Miles had not married Imogene, for the pain in a new widow's heart was like death itself. And how would Miss McGee take it? There she was in the front pew between Mrs. Workman and Dale Pruitt. Would she go right on as if nothing had happened? Lillian wouldn't be surprised. Or would she break down for once? Just what was Miles to Miss McGee, anyhow? Certainly more than your run-of-the-mill roomer. He was a sort of half-husband, half-son. Was a half-husband, when it came to dying, the equal of a real husband? If so, Miss McGee was in for some real pain. And what would she do with her hands? When someone in your household died you were left for the rest of your life with less to do with your hands. Lillian had felt this terrible uselessness in her hands the moment she went into the bedroom and saw Lyle tangled up in the quilt and dead. There was nothing to do for him anymore. No meals. No washing and ironing. No picking up after him. What would Miss McGee, who was not a knitter, do with her hands?

Beverly Bingham did not attend the funeral. She was still in bed, and Mrs. Murphy (Father Finn's housekeeper) agreed to watch over her in Miss McGee's absence.

At Evergreen Cemetery, where the wind blew snow down everyone's neck, the six men placed the coffin over the grave and Father Finn said, "O God, by your mercy rest is given to the souls of the faithful; be pleased to bless this grave. Appoint your holy angels to guard it and set free from all chains of sin the soul of him whose body is buried here, so that with all your saints he may rejoice in you forever. Through Christ our Lord. Amen."

The snow was over everyones shoes. Thanatopsis stood with her arm around Miss McGee's waist. Dale Pruitt hugged himself and shivered. He had come from California without his overcoat.

Father Finn sprinkled holy water on the coffin, where it froze in small drops, then he swung the censer over the grave. On the wind the smoke poured level out of the censer and into the folds of his vestments. "Lord, we implore you grant mercy to your departed servant that he may not receive punishment in return for his deeds; that as the true faith united him with the body of the faithful on earth, your mercy may unite him with the company of the choirs of angels in Heaven. Through Christ our Lord. Amen." He turned to Miss McGee, whose face was veiled, and said, "God bless you, Agatha." Then all hurried to their cars.

But those were not the last words spoken over Miles's

grave. When the mourners were gone, the gravedigger and his helper came out of the tool shed, where they had been warming themselves as they waited. The grave-digger was a college student from Berrington who earned tuition money by digging graves and sewers. Today he had brought along a friend to help him fill the grave. Both young men were excited by the snow, for both of them owned snowmobiles.

"I wouldn't trade my Blue Streak for any other make in the world," said the gravedigger, driving his shovel into the snow-covered mound of loose dirt piled on top of Amy Pruitt's grave. "She starts easy as pie and she runs like a charm."

"The Blue Streak is a horseshit machine," said his friend. "I had a Blue Streak once and it was nothing but trouble."

"Not mine. Mine runs like a charm." The first shovelful of dirt drummed on the lid of the coffin.

"I say it's a horseshit machine."

From the cemetery Miss McGee went home and dis-missed Mrs. Murphy. She hung up her coat and climbed the stairs and went straight to work cleaning out Miles's room. She worked in her best black dress. During the noon hour Thanatopsis came over and told her to rest.

"I must not pause, Anna Thea. If I pause I might go mad."

She sorted through Miles's belongings. She stored in the attic whatever was worth saving, including his journal. She sent his clothes to the missions. In her snowy garden she burned a lot of junk, along with a perfectly mysterious heap of green fabric she found in a box on a neglected shelf of his closet=a suit in shreds. She turned his student papers over to Mrs. Horky, his replacement at school, and she kept the leather briefcase for her own use.

Throughout the afternoon she looked in on Beverly, who had been drugged by Dr. Maitland on Saturday night. When she looked in at five o'clock she found Beverly sitting up in bed, smoking. Beverly turned her eyes toward Miss McGee in the slow, bewildered manner of someone who has been asleep for the greater part of two days and nights.

"You must dress now, Beverly, and come down and help me with supper."

Beverly slowly nodded.

"Today will be our only absence from school, Beverly. Tomorrow you and I go back on our regular schedules."

Beverly slowly nodded again as she turned back to the contemplation of her cigarette.

Miles Pruitt's obituary was the last thing Albert Fremling composed before leaving the office on Monday evening.

> Miles Pruitt, teacher and lifelong resident of Staggerford, died Saturday at the age of 35.
>
> He was a graduate of Staggerford High School and St. Andrew's College. He was a member of the Minnesota Educators' Association and its local affiliate, the Staggerford Educators' Association, of which he was a past president.
>
> Surviving are his father, Leonard Pruitt of Duluth, and a brother, Dale, of Los Angeles.
>
> Services were held Monday at St. Isidore's Catholic Church, the Rev. Francis Finn officiating, with interment in Evergreen Cemetery.
>
> Those desiring may contribute memorials to the

Miles Pruitt Memorial Book Fund of the Staggerford Public Library.

When the editor finished this piece, though it wasn't Friday, he felt like drinking and driving. He took a long pull from the pint of brandy he kept in his desk, then he got into his red Pontiac and sped through falling snow to Berrington, running over a gray cat on the way.

At the Green Lantern in Berrington he ordered a double brandy at the bar and asked to see a menu. He ordered another double brandy and decided to have the T-bone. He ordered a third double brandy and was shown to a table in the dark dining room, where Doc Oppegaard and Stella Gibbon were having the sirloin.

Doc Oppegaard stood up and invited the editor to join them.

"No thanks," he said. "You two have your fun."

"Fun?" said Doc. "We're here on business. We're testing Stella's new teeth."

Stella threw her head back and screeched with laughter, the gold of her bridgework gleaming in the candlelight.

The Miles Pruitt Memorial Book Fund was Imogene's idea. Imogene had decided immediately upon hearing of Miles's death that she would be very strong and businesslike, as Dr. Gordon Beam advised in his latest book, *Happy Me, Happy You*. Rather than grieve, she would put her energies to some useful purpose. It helped to think that she was probably the last person Miles Pruitt had kissed. The thought that that kiss might have brought bliss to his last days made her feel warm and generous and good and positive and constructive. She phoned Mrs. Oppegaard and invited her to be the initial contributor to the Miles Pruitt Memorial Book Fund.

Mrs. Oppegaard was honored. Indeed she was flattered to tears. "Oh, thank you," she said. "Whatever I can do . . ."

"There are so many good books being written on interpersonal relationships these days," said Imogene, "and library funds simply cannot pay for them. And books on women. Women are coming on strong, and with a special memorial fund the library can increase its holdings on women."

"Oh, thank you, thank you," said Mrs. Oppegaard. "Whatever I can do. Oh, I know so little about the library's holdings. Oh, I know so little about interpersonal relationships. Oh, I know so little about women."

"Pruitt would want it this way," said Imogene. "He would be all in favor of increasing our holdings on women." She lowered her voice, then, and told Mrs. Oppegaard about the kiss.

Mrs. Oppegaard pledged a thousand dollars.

Parents' Night at the high school was canceled. Delia Fritz canceled it, and it was one of her rare mistakes. She thought that after burying Miles the staff would rather not spend the evening talking to parents. However, the staff, with Miles on their minds, spent a deeply miserable evening at home. Ray Smith, historian, was typical. After supper Ray Smith went out for a walk in the snow. Then he returned to his living room and sat with his wife before the TV, but he did not watch it. His eyes were focused on the floor. After a while he got up and went to the front window and stood there rattling the change in his pocket. He went to the kitchen for a shot of whiskey neat, and then he went to bed. Ray Smith would have preferred any distasteful chore—even talking to the parents of his students—to spending the evening at home.

* * *

On Tuesday it became clear to Wayne Workman that Miles was pestering him from beyond the grave. In order to get Mrs. Horky to take over senior English, Wayne had to promise that he would sit in on second hour every morning and station himself within earshot of study hall every afternoon.

Tuesday, on his way to second-hour English, Wayne paused at the bulletin board in his outer office and looked glumly at the list of Indians turning sixteen.

"And now to top it off," he muttered to his secretary, "I've got to find Sam LaGrange a new friend."

It was on Tuesday as well that the Bonewoman was transferred from the Berrington County Jail to the psychiatric wing of St. Luke's Hospital in Duluth. Before the day was out it was determined that she would be sent to the State Hospital for the Criminally Insane.

When Dale Pruitt arrived back in Los Angeles, he phoned Carla again. "I flew to Minneapolis and took a bus from there to Staggerford," he said. "I stayed overnight in one of Miss McGee's spare bedrooms and the next morning I accompanied her to the funeral. I was the only relative there. After the funeral I gave Miss McGee a box of assorted greeting cards and I went to Druppers's law office and assigned him to probate the estate. Then I took the bus to Duluth and visited Dad. He kept calling me Miles. I didn't tell him Miles was dead. I gave him a box of greeting cards. I flew from Duluth to Minneapolis and then nonstop to Los Angeles. Miles left a savings account of about thirteen thousand dollars, so you'd have been worse off if you'd have married Miles. Thirteen thousand wouldn't last you very long. I've already paid you that much in ali·

mony and child support and it's only been three years
since you moved out."

Carla hung up and cried again, and that was when
Trish, home from the choir trip, came into the
apartment.

"What's the matter?" Trish asked. She put down her
suitcase and followed her mother as she lumbered from
the phone into the bedroom and flopped heavily onto
her bed.

"What's the matter?" she said again.

Her mother wiped her eyes on the pillow and heaved
herself over in bed so that she faced the wall.

"Your Uncle Miles is dead," said Carla.

"Who's Uncle Miles?" said Trish.

Superintendent Stevenson's health took a miraculous
turn for the better.

When Stevenson was told so bluntly by Wayne Workman that Miles was dead, his heart leaped into his throat
the way it had when Jeff Norquist jumped out the
window. When he attended the prayer service at the
funeral home, his heart rattled and thumped the way it
had at Fred Vandergar's retirement party. When he
stood at the snowy, open grave, his heart shuddered the
way it had the previous week when the study-hall girls
screamed bloody murder. His heart performed these
three tricks on three successive days, and the superintendent was certain that each day was his last, for surely no
heart would send out such frightening signals unless it
were preparing to stop.

But it didn't stop, and that was why on the day after
the funeral the superintendent began to revise his opinion of his heart. It occurred to him as he sat at his
window watching Mrs. Horky trying to open the eyes of
first-hour English in the classroom across the courtyard

that he might have in his breast a better heart than he had thought. Any heart that jumped, rattled, thumped, and shuddered and then returned to this steady beat must be a fairly good heart, a serviceable heart.

Second hour he tested it. He stood up very straight and walked quickly to the door of his private lavatory, where he stopped and timed his pulse. He took a deep breath. He trotted back to his chair. He timed his pulse again. He touched his toes. He felt like a boy.

Third hour, he went to the outer office and told Delia Fritz to get the governor on the phone; he wanted to thank him for sending out the state troopers and the National Guard. Fourth hour, he asked Delia to call in all copies of the Faculty Handbook, for it was obsolete. Fifth hour he told Delia to inquire of the Community Fund officers whether they could use his help. Sixth hour, he told Delia to see about having his filing cabinets returned from her office to his.

After school he went home and put his arms around the heavy softness of Mrs. Stevenson's middle and lifted her, astounded, three inches off the floor.

Jon Hassler

Jon Hassler lives with his wife and three children in Brainerd, Minnesota, where he teaches English at Brainerd Community College. *Staggerford* is his first novel.